CAROLINE LEAVITT

New York Times
...ng author of
...es of You
...Cruel
...ful World

WITH OR WITHOUT YOU

A NOVEL

Praise for *With or Without You*

"*With or Without You* is a moving novel about twists of fate, the shifting terrain of love, and coming into your own. With tenderness and incisive insight, Leavitt spotlights a woman's unexpected journey towards her art."   —Madeline Miller, author of *Circe*

"Leavitt has crafted an irresistible portrait of midlife ennui and the magic of breaking free."   —*People*

"It was as if I were falling in love: flushed, fascinated, filled with hope, fear, and joy. Leavitt's exploration of the many ways in which we change over the course of a lifetime—and how we keep or lose those we love throughout these mutations—is compassionate, profound and moving. Beyond being utterly captivated, I felt like I had grown wiser and more humane after reading this beautiful novel."
          —Jean Kwok, author of *Searching for Sylvie Lee*

"Leavitt's seamless writing easily carries readers through the compelling story . . . [Packs an] emotional wallop. Leavitt's fans and readers of domestic drama will be thrilled."   —*Booklist*

"*With or Without You* is a compulsively readable novel of artistic ambition and the various betrayals lovers and friends both endure and inflict on each other. It also asks fascinating questions about the stability of the self and our capacity—perhaps even our secret desire?—to reinvent ourselves. Caroline Leavitt is a born storyteller, and this is one knockout of a story."
          —Christopher Castellani, author of *Leading Men*

"One character's coma is only the first surprise in this satisfying story of middle-aged love."   —*Kirkus Reviews* (starred review)

"A page-turner by the *New York Times* bestselling author and co-founder of 'A Mighty Blaze,' this story about a nurse who falls into a coma raises issues of loyalty, friendship, love and life, all set to music."   —*Good Morning America Online*

"After all their lives are irrevocably altered by a single tragic incident, Stella, Simon, and Libby—the major characters in Caroline Leavitt's compelling, deeply moving new novel—are forced to make complex choices between freedom and responsibility, love and loyalty. Leavitt depicts her characters without judgment, and by doing so compels readers to ask themselves what they might do in such difficult moments."   —Ron Rash, author of *The Risen*

"By the author of 2010's bestselling *Pictures of You*, among other novels, it's a moving story with characters you can't help but care for, especially Stella, who must build a new life after her brush with death."   —*AARP The Magazine*

"Caroline Leavitt's new novel, *With or Without You*, seduced me instantly and held my heart from the first page to the last. Like Elena Ferrante's raw and intimate explorations into human relationships, this novel will make you laugh, cry, yell, and possibly more. At the heart of the story is the art of a woman's life, pulsing with beauty, desire, loss, never-ending change, and the grit it takes to keep going."   —Lidia Yuknavitch, author of *The Book of Joan*

"Leavitt deftly portrays Stella's mindset both before and during her coma . . . The changing points of view give each character a chance to wrestle with questions of identity, loyalty, regret, and hope. Although no character is blameless in the sharply shifting tale of love and affection, Leavitt shows that sometimes it's enough to simply do the best you can and take responsibility for the consequences, whatever they may be."   —*San Francisco Book Review*

"A wonderful novel about life as mess and disappointment, life as catastrophe and regret, but also life as transformation and resilience. Leavitt's characters are great company, and watching them find a way forward in their suddenly altered world is a joy. Deeply engaging, tense but hopeful, and completely recommended."

—Karen Joy Fowler, author of
We Are All Completely Beside Ourselves

"What I like best about Leavitt—her signature perhaps—is her fearlessness with plot. I'll take a good coma story with a miracle recovery anytime." —*Minneapolis Star Tribune*

"In *With or Without You*, Caroline Leavitt once again explores disaster's aftermath and its effect on the lives of ordinary people tethered by love and shared history. What makes this novel so poignant, and also makes it feel so true, is that there is no going back. There is only now, the newness of their altered realities and the courage to continue."

—Helen Schulman, bestselling author of
This Beautiful Life and *Come with Me*

"A poignant, instantly compelling novel . . . This is an unflinchingly raw and honest novel, but it is also propulsive and suspenseful. The characters are so wholly realized and developed that they seem to move on their own, with Leavitt simply pulling the strings above them. She is a brave and risk-taking author, and *With or Without You* is a perfect picture of what she can do when left with a spark of inspiration and a gripping premise." —Bookreporter.com

"This fresh, engaging, intimate tale of love and identity subverts the reader's expectations again and again. Caroline Leavitt refuses to take one cliched turn. A complete original, an absolute delight."

—Janet Fitch, author of *Chimes of a Lost Cathedral* and
White Oleander

With or Without You

ALSO BY CAROLINE LEAVITT

With
or
Without
You

CAROLINE
LEAVITT

ALGONQUIN BOOKS OF CHAPEL HILL   2021

Published by
ALGONQUIN BOOKS OF CHAPEL HILL
Post Office Box 2225
Chapel Hill, North Carolina 27515-2225

a division of
WORKMAN PUBLISHING
225 Varick Street
New York, New York 10014

First paperback edition, Algonquin Books of Chapel Hill, June 2021. Originally
published in hardcover by Algonquin Books of Chapel Hill in August 2020.
Printed in the United States of America.
Published simultaneously in Canada by Thomas Allen & Son Limited.
Design by Anne Winslow.

This is a work of fiction. While, as in all fiction, the literary perceptions and
insights are based on experience, all names, characters, places, and incidents
either are products of the author's imagination or are used fictitiously.

LIBRARY OF CONGRESS CATALOGING-IN-PUBLICATION DATA
Names: Leavitt, Caroline, author.
Title: With or without you / Caroline Leavitt.
Description: First Edition. | Chapel Hill, North Carolina : Algonquin Books
of Chapel Hill, 2020. | Summary: "After almost twenty years together, Stella
and Simon are starting to run into problems. An up-and-coming rock musician
when they first met, Simon has been clinging to dreams of fame even as the
possibility of it has grown dimmer, and now that his band might finally be on
the brink again, he wants to go on the road, leaving Stella behind. But when
she falls into a coma on the eve of his departure, he has to make a choice
between stardom and his wife—and when she wakes a different person, with
an incredible artistic talent of her own, the two of them must examine what
it is that they really want"—Provided by publisher.
Identifiers: LCCN 2019059071 | ISBN 9781616207793 (hardcover) |
ISBN 9781643750590 (e-book)
Subjects: LCSH: Psychological fiction.
Classification: LCC PS3562.E2617 W58 2020 | DDC 813/.54—dc23
LC record available at https://lccn.loc.gov/2019059071

ISBN 978-1-64375-143-6 (PB)

10 9 8 7 6 5 4 3 2 1
First Paperback Edition

To Jeff and Max, for ever, ever, ever

With or Without You

1

THEY WERE ARGUING AGAIN.

Stella, her nose stuffed from a cold, her lungs clogged, wrapped her arms about herself, flopped down on the couch, and grabbed for another tissue. She blew a puff of air to get her hair out of her eyes, which were watering and itchy. Her hair felt too long, her body too clammy. She thought she had taken a Sudafed a bit before, and then another later, but if she had, they weren't working. Simon was leaning against the dining room table, still wearing his lucky traveling clothes—black T-shirt, black jeans, black boots—lucky because he was afraid of flying, and he thought that something as simple as a uniform that once got him through a transcontinental flight filled with turbulence, lightning, and oxygen masks would be a talisman to protect him. Planes terrified him, even though he'd memorized all the precautions. In the event of a crash, you were supposed to sit with your legs firmly planted apart, not in the fetal position the way everyone else was—otherwise you'd break your legs and never be able to walk or even crawl away from the burning fuselage. Bring your own food so you didn't get food poisoning or sour your stomach. And never, ever take a seat at the front or in first class because that was the part of the plane that broke off first, snapping like a hard pretzel.

Disaster. Everywhere he looked, when he thought of flying, he saw disaster.

His suitcase lay open on the table, a jumble of dark clothing. Hers was on the floor, everything in tight rolls, more than enough for the week she was taking off from her nursing job at the hospital to go with him. He was staring at her the way he would if he didn't know her, which he'd been doing more and more lately, something that unnerved her so much that she wanted to shake him, point to herself, and say, I'm right here. All you have to do is look.

She took another sip of wine, just to calm herself, maybe to add some heat to her body, to stop the queasiness rolling through her. Outside, it was another freezing February New York City winter, the snow blazing down in sheets against the windows and layering over the sidewalks. There was a blizzard advisory for an accumulation of twelve inches, complete with school closings and warnings for the elderly and the infirm to stay inside. It was the main reason they were here tonight in the apartment. The airports were closed, and their flight to California wouldn't be rescheduled until tomorrow night at the earliest. The weather was too snowy for them to drive, plus they didn't have enough time.

Simon's band was once successful, but that was twenty years ago, when she had first met him and he was just twenty-two himself and his band was riding high with Simon's megahit song, "Charlatan Eyes." Simon didn't even really sing back then; he was just harmony and played bass guitar to the lead singer Rob's aching wail. Once, Stella had even heard the song as Muzak in an elevator at Macy's, and while everyone else in the elevator seemed to ignore it, she flushed with pleasure. Over the years, the band still played for decent-sized audiences and recorded a few more albums. A few more songs got some play, and Simon began to sing more of his own songs, but the band didn't build, the audiences and the stages their manager booked became smaller, and the awards they were all so desperate for never arrived.

The band had reached a crossroads. Their manager was thinking of retiring and Simon was worried that he was about to slide into rock-and-roll obscurity and never escape. He kept reminding himself of all the older musicians he knew who still toured and played and had no intentions of ever quitting, because what else was there but the joy of this? His band had kept on, even in the face of younger and younger bands, younger dreams, too. "Dad rock," someone had once called the band, which Simon knew meant you didn't rock at all.

But now, all that could be different.

Just last month, the band had been playing at Lobster's, a dive on the New Jersey shore, all chipping gray cement walls and scuffed floors, no chairs or tables, so you had to stand. Then this guy strode in, and for a moment Simon hadn't recognized him. Not until the guy lifted his face and took off his dark glasses and Simon saw those familiar odd green eyes. He saw the gleam of oil that slicked back that famous wild mane of black hair, and there was Rick Mason, twenty-six years old with three Grammy wins to his name, settling against the wall, leaning forward, and listening to the band. Really listening. Afterward, Mason even came backstage and told them how influenced he had been by their early work, how when he heard they were playing this joint he had his driver bring him right over. He talked about how blown away he was by Rob's voice, how it soared so high that it made him feel like every glass in the place would smash. He talked about Kevin's drumming, and then he turned to Simon. "'Charlatan Eyes,' man," he said, shaking his head, awed, and Simon froze in wonder that Rick Mason actually knew he was the writer, that the two of them were actually sharing the same space. "So I got this idea," Mason said. "What would you guys think about being my opening act for a two-night gig in Los Angeles? And if that worked out, well, maybe the rest of the tour, too?"

Simon had been so shocked that he felt his tongue freeze in his mouth, but Kevin grabbed Mason's hand and pumped it. "We're in," Kevin said. "We're so in."

And suddenly, there it was right in front of them, shiny as a new dime: hope. They would be noticed, they would get a new manager, one who could break them out to the bigger labels. Maybe Simon could even sing what he wrote.

It happened so fast, with the news traveling like a river breaking through a dam. There was a small mention of them in some of the music publications in print and online, how they were opening Rick Mason's show. Simon cut out the item and kept it in his wallet, another lucky piece that eventually ended up in tatters because he kept taking it out and rereading it. Simon began coming home at four in the morning after rehearsing, so keyed up that he couldn't sleep, damp and sweaty and so exhilarated that Stella tried to be happy for him, too, although inside she felt selfish, sad, and guilty.

He saw hope, but she was on the ground. This gig was just a two-night engagement, and even if it became a tour, it didn't necessarily mean stardom. Mostly she thought of all the things that she herself wanted, and like Simon's dreams, they had an expiration date she couldn't ignore.

She loved this apartment they were in and she loved him, but she felt it was time to make some decisions. She had been hoping that the grind of his traveling might finally stop. He could still do what he loved—write songs, do some session work—and he could do it right here with her. Wasn't it time to move on, to build a bigger life? Finally get married. Have a child.

"I'm glad you're going to be there for all of it," he said.

She had told him she'd go to LA because it was so important and it was the first time she'd be traveling with him in a very long time. She agreed only because it had seemed to matter so much to him—he was so anxious that everything turn out different this time. "You're going to be my lucky star," he told her. They were going out four days before the actual concert and Simon had convinced her that they could get some vacation out of it, too. But now she wasn't so sure because she knew he'd be rehearsing all the time. It felt like he was angling for more from her, rushing toward this new life and wanting her to speed there with him when still nothing was for certain.

She had given up things for him before. After their first year together, she'd left her job as an RN because it was so exciting to travel with him. And then being on the road got old, or maybe just she did. But by the end of her second year of touring with him, she began to feel the need to be a nurse again. It was like a physical pull. She missed having a community of doctors, nurses, and staff that she saw every day.

She yearned for the feeling that she had a place to be, with a job that was important. It was such a different life from the one Simon had. She hadn't known what to expect when she first told him she wasn't touring with him anymore, that she'd call him every day, that she'd miss him like crazy, but she couldn't go. To her surprise, he nodded thoughtfully and said he got it. He said he understood her loving something the same way he did his music, needing something of her own. And maybe, too, she thought, he was even a little relieved when she went back to nursing, because then he wouldn't have to worry about her increasing restlessness on the road.

Now she felt him watching her. She knew he wanted to talk about catching the next possible flight out, about what it would be like to be Rick Mason's opening act, about what could happen, about all the crazy pot-of-gold possibilities. But she wanted to talk about her own dreams.

"What are we doing here?" she said. "Why can't we make a decision?"

They were both forty-two. She knew how everything changed when you hit your forties. Everyone took stock. She wanted to buy their apartment while they had the chance. It was that rare thing, a rent-stabilized place they had found years ago, just six months into their relationship, just by pure luck and word of mouth, and so cheap and affordable they'd snapped it up the second they saw it. A small one-bedroom with an actual alcove that would fit a daybed. It was

on Twenty-Second Street off First Avenue, and it had gleaming wood
floors and a high ceiling and all the rooms were filled with light.
They could just afford it on her nurse's salary and his money from the
band. And Simon's parents (or at least his mom) sometimes sent them
money when they least expected it, which helped out immeasurably.
But Stella knew the landlord was planning to convert the building
to co-ops. They could stay renters if they wanted, but they had an
opportunity to buy at an insider's price, which she knew would pay
off for them down the road with equity and tax breaks. And if they
got married, another thing he didn't want, they'd have more tax
breaks. They could even be solvent enough to start a family before it
was too late.

But that was another thing that Simon didn't want.

"Why this again and again and again?" Simon asked her.

"I need to talk about it."

"Stella," he said wearily. "Can't we argue about this another time?
Isn't it enough that we have the weather to worry about? If this LA
thing turns into something, if we get the whole tour, maybe then we
can consider it."

"Why can't we consider it now?" she said. "What if we take out
a loan? This place is only going to zoom up in value." She paused.
"Two other apartments were snapped up already."

"You want to be saddled with a loan?" Simon said. He poured
another glass of wine and then topped off hers.

"We could break through one of the walls. Or we could have that
alcove be a baby's room." She waited, suddenly a little scared.

"Stella, Jesus," he said. "Kids were never part of what we wanted.
It was always just you and me. You said that was enough."

It was true. When they had first met, she didn't want anyone
around her but him. A child would complicate things. She remembered her parents' relationship, how close they were, like a seam
in fabric, and though they had loved her, she always felt like she
was the hanging thread at their hemline, always terrified that any

moment they might snap her free. She wouldn't want any child of hers to ever feel like that. But then when she'd hit her late twenties, she started noticing pregnant women, babies as glossy as pearls, and her whole body had yearned more and more for them. At her last visit to her gynecologist, the doctor had paused after she was done with the exam. "Just something to chew on," the doctor said, "but your chances of conceiving are getting slimmer and slimmer. At thirty-four, they're sixty-three percent. You have a five percent chance once you're in your forties."

Stella had felt herself crumple at the doctor's words. Her mom had had her when she was forty, and Stella was only two years beyond that. And she knew women who had gotten pregnant at forty-four or even forty-six. But would she be that lucky? She felt time whizzing past her. "You could think about adopting," the doctor said. "But that's not so easy, either. And it can be very pricey. Or we can talk about donor eggs. Or surrogates."

That night, when she told Simon her concerns, he was unmoved.

"You know I don't want a kid. And that doesn't make me a villain," he said now.

"And it doesn't make me a villain for wanting it." She touched his arm. "I don't want to look back and think, Oh, my God, I should have done this."

"I like our lives the way they are now," he said. "I'm happy with us like this. Aren't you?"

Stella stared at him. The wine was tart and red, and Stella finished her glass and poured another. "I'll go back to school, be a nurse practitioner. It'll pay off for us. A big money jump."

"You're going to work, return to school, and have a child? How are you going to do all that?"

"I will. I can. And aren't you part of this, too? We'll figure it out."

She knew that Simon hated when she did this, mapping out the future she wanted and planning on how to get to it. He teased her about not being spontaneous. He kept telling her about the wonder he

found in the world, the way he felt when he got lost in playing or singing, standing in front of a crowd. Instead, she was always thinking
about equity, about how when they were old, they could sell this place
and move someplace less exorbitant than Manhattan, even though
she couldn't imagine living anywhere else. She wished she could rush
ahead into the future because if Simon could see how it would be, she
knew he would change his mind. She could see everything unfurling
like a road map and all she wanted was to get to her destination.

"There's no such thing as true security," Simon said. "It's a myth.
You just want it because you didn't have it with your parents."

"That's not true," she said, even though she knew that it was. Her
parents had been bohemians, her mom a substitute Spanish teacher
at the local school in Park Slope before the neighborhood was cool,
never knowing when she'd have work but liking it that way because
of the freedom it gave her to sew and design dresses. Her dad taught
woodworking at the same school and did a little carpentry on the side.
But it was never enough. They rented an apartment instead of owning
their place or even living in a house like all of Stella's friends did, and
sometimes they didn't have the money for the electric bill, something
that always terrified Stella as a child, even as her parents joked and
set out candles, claiming it was romantic. Stella worried that her life
might always be dark. She had never wanted to be that scared again,
which was why she went into nursing, where she always would have
steady work, she'd always be needed, no matter where she lived.

"We could be able to afford a child," she said. "And I've seen how
good you are around kids."

"I like kids and babies. I really do," Simon said. "But I'm just not
equipped for them. What if something big happens in LA? What kind
of father would I be, always on the road? How many babies did you
see when you came on tour with me?"

"A few," she said. "A lot."

"You know that's not true. And you know that kids become teenagers who hate you."

"Our kid will never hate us," she said, prickling with anger. She tried not to imagine a teenager, storming out the door, face shuttered. Goodbye. Goodbye. Goodbye.

"Why the fuck do we have to argue about this again?" He threw up his hands. "I don't want this! You do!" He gave her that look again, like he was unpeeling her, causing her to lift her hands to her face to make sure she was still all there, all in one piece. She grabbed for a tissue and sneezed into it, and her eyes began to well.

"You could want it." Her voice rose to a shout. A sting settled in her throat and her sinuses hurt. She had had colds like this before, and she knew how they liked to travel to her lungs, breeding into full-blown bronchitis, despite all the vitamin C and zinc and cold meds she'd take. If she couldn't nip it now, she'd be in bed for days, miserable and sick, something she couldn't afford. If she dared to get on a plane like this, her sinuses would probably blow right out. She had to get better. She just had to. She drank a bit more wine, hoping it would make her sleepy enough to doze it off.

Simon covered his face with his hands, as if that might make him invisible.

"Why can't we ever really talk about us?" she said, persistent in pushing him. "Everyone around us has homes they own, a family—"

"You know that's not true. And we're not everyone." He folded one black sock over the other, so it looked like a tongue, and then he hurled them to the floor. "Anyway, we are so talking about us."

"No. Not really. I'm talking and you're deflecting me." She sneezed again and hunted for more tissues. He sighed and looked around the apartment. He drained his wineglass and filled it again.

"You're making me really, really sort of pissed off," she said.

His mouth tightened.

"Spit it out," she said. "Go ahead. Say whatever it is. You know you want to."

He shook his head. "No, not now. You're too upset for this conversation," he said. "Too snuffly."

"I hate it when you tell me how I feel," Stella said. "You never used to do that. You used to listen. You used to really hear me." Her sinuses were so clogged that her eyes hurt. This argument felt different, angrier than usual. They were both fed up. She was tired of feeling so raw, like her body was filled with shards of glass. Her whole face ached.

"Do you think if we keep having this conversation the answer will eventually come up different?" Simon said.

Stella wished that she could just get up and dramatically storm out, stay away for a few hours, and then come back to find everything changed, including him.

"Why do we always have to do what you want," she said. Her anger swelled. She braced a hand along the wall.

"Hey," he said. "Hey, hey, hey."

She heard the alarm in his voice and she made a decision. "I changed my mind. I'm not going with you to LA," she said. "I'm sick. I feel crappy. I just want to stay in bed." As soon as she said it, she felt a flare of surprise, because she didn't realize until now that it really was what she wanted, that it seemed like the answer. He could go to LA and miss her, and she could be here and miss him, and then, when he got back, they could reboot.

"You're telling me this now?"

"I guess I am."

He was quiet for a moment. "Well, we're not leaving at least until tomorrow night. You can baby yourself until then, get better—"

"You don't understand. I'm not telling you not to go—I would never do that. But I can't go with you this time. I can't do it."

"I don't understand you." He touched her face. "This gig is something new, something special. And you used to love touring."

He was right. It was a long time ago, but she did at first. The excitement of new cities. All those new people to meet. Being so crazy in love that nothing else mattered. She could watch Simon shine onstage, and when he sang, she felt he was singing just to her. But then, more and more on those trips, she had huge patches of time that she had to try to fill herself. She began to get tired of it, to want something other than all those towns going by in a blur. Chicago. Santa Fe. Sedona. The coffee shops where she picked at pie and drank herself jumpy with coffee while she waited for him to finish rehearsal. She tried to find hourly work as a nurse, but there weren't always jobs.

"Traveling together's romantic," he said.

"Right, romantic. Guys and instruments, and hotels with a tiny bathroom that always smells funky. I don't want to be treated like I'm part of the entourage. I never fit in."

"Who says you have to fit in? You had fun on tour. I know you did."

But the last tour she had gone on hadn't been fun at all. The music had suddenly gotten too loud for her and she started using earplugs. She knew all that screaming noise was messing up her hearing, but she wondered also if maybe the loud music was hurting her. If it was, then she had to protect what she had. "People are going to think you're my mother, with those earplugs," Simon said at one point.

He was teasing her, but she still felt hurt. She had looked over at him and noticed a few girls nudging their way closer, laughing at her, mimicking the way she twisted her hair out of her face so she could get the earplugs in. And then the plugs hadn't even helped; her ears had rung for days afterward. And shortly after that, right before her twenty-sixth birthday, she told him she wasn't touring with him anymore.

"You're not worried about him on his own for so long? You won't miss him?" her friends asked. But Stella knew how much Simon loved her, at least at first. The early days, when they were in their twenties, when she toured with him and he had some fame, there had been plenty of girls hanging around. She had gotten used to seeing the other members of the band partying it up in hotel rooms, the door wide open, the whiskey flowing, the girls so young that they looked illegal. Rob had guys and girls both. Even Kevin, who loved

his girlfriend, would wait for her to crash into sleep and then he'd
saunter into the party room just like the cock of the walk, eyeing
every woman like they were appetizers on an endless menu. Simon
refused to participate. He spent what little free time he had with
Stella, walking around whatever city they were in, later hanging out
in their room, away from the rest of the band. She never had a reason
not to trust him. Their whole time together, there had never been a
suspicious hang-up on the phone, a note stuffed into their mailbox, a
stain of lipstick. And when she had stopped touring with him, Simon
had called her every night, sometimes talking for hours. Occasionally
she could hear the band members shouting and laughing in the background, but they were with their wives or their girlfriends or, like
Simon, on their own. She told herself it was by choice.

"I'm not going," she repeated.

Simon grew still. "You don't think it's going to pan out for the
band?" Simon said. "Is that it? You think two days and, boom, it's
over for us?"

"Did I say that?"

"Your face did. Your whole body."

Simon reached for his guitar and picked out a few notes, something he always did when he wanted to retreat into his own private
little space. She didn't understand how he could do that, trance out
of the world.

"Simon," she said, and he kept playing. "Simon," she said again,
and he plucked a string so hard it snapped. She touched him. He felt
so far away.

He looked at her from under his thick lashes, something that once
would have made her want to kiss him. Now, though, she was simply
annoyed. Grow up, she wanted to tell him. Keep pace with me. She
gulped more wine, tears crowding behind her eyes.

"We're getting older," she told him. "We're not kids here."

"Forty-two still qualifies as kids," Simon said, and Stella knew
he meant it. Simon still wore the same tight T-shirts and jeans he did

when he was in his twenties. He spent hours in the gym. His hero was Mick Jagger, prancing around the stage in his seventies, making everyone believe nothing was ridiculous, nothing is impossible. Up close, she could see the fine age lines etched on Simon's face. One day, she caught him using her expensive skin creams. She watched him brush her mascara wand over his hair, coloring the gray at the temples. When he saw her watching him, he gave her a goofy smile. "McCartney dyes his hair," Simon said. "I'll bet you anything Mick Jagger wears a wig. We're not old. Not yet."

"We're getting there," she said. "Our forties are rushing past us. Then comes fifty. And whoa, coming right at you, there's seventy."

"Now you're being silly," Simon said.

She didn't have to ask herself what she loved about him, why she had stayed for so long. She knew there were scientific explanations for love, that pheromones could make you attracted to someone, that even kissing was tasting each other's DNA and seeing if you could make good, healthy children. Love, she had read, was a chemical addiction to dopamine.

Was it something chemical that allowed her to forgive him when he forgot to meet her at the movies or a restaurant where they actually had a hard-gotten reservation, when she had to nag him to see a doctor for checkups, to keep his inside as tuned and cared for as he did his outside? She remembered every anniversary they'd ever had. The first time he saw her. The first time they made love. The first time he said I love you.

The last time.

Simon flopped onto the couch away from her. She knew they had problems, but she knew that solutions were out there. You just had to trust you would find them.

He looked at her helplessly. "This gig in LA could change everything."

"You can go do it. I'll support you like crazy from here. But it won't change what I want."

His shoulders slumped. He looked up at her and she suddenly hated herself for having this argument. She reached for him, but her fingers just missed his sleeve. She tried to catch his scent, but her nose was too stuffed. "Sit by me," she said. "We can't talk to each other this way. It just makes everything worse."

He shifted and sat beside her. His body loosened, and then hers did, too. "I'm sorry," he said.

"Me, too." She rested her head against his shoulder.

"Do we not have the same dreams anymore?" he said sadly.

She looked at him, alarmed. "What does that mean?"

"I don't know," he said. "I just feel it and it scares me."

"What?" she said. "What?"

He got up and paced, his hand pushing at his hair, the way he always did when he was upset.

"We need to calm down," she said. She took another sip of wine, then set it on a table. "This isn't helping much."

He stopped and looked at her. "Do you want to smoke some weed?"

"Are you kidding?" She hadn't smoked weed in years, and she had thought he had given it up, too. "It'll kill my throat," she said, after considering the possibility.

"What else, then?" he said. He grabbed a cigarette from the table, then dug in his pocket. "Where're the fucking matches," he said, and then, startled, he brought up two small pills. "I didn't know I even had these," he said.

She frowned. She thought that he had given up drugs years ago, in his midtwenties, the same time she had. "Why do you have them?"

Simon rolled the pills in his hands. "I don't know. I just do."

In the early days, she had been so naive that she didn't know that he did drugs at all. She didn't see that other side of him until she was truly, deeply, madly in love, which she admitted seemed to happen by week three, and by then it was too late. They were already living together when one night he came home high, his eyes red, his breathing rough, and everything in her tightened. She knew medicine. She knew what drugs did to the body because she had treated addicts and, even worse, kids who had partied a bit too hard and then gotten behind the wheel of a car. "It's nothing," he'd said, waving her away. "I'm just keyed up."

She believed him because she wanted to. But then she began to spend time with the band, at Kevin's apartment, where there were cocaine lines on bureau tops, on coffee tables, on mirrors. There were tabs of acid and peyote, mushrooms, and opium, but they weren't what Simon did. He hated needles and passed on the hallucinogens. Instead, he drank alcohol. He smoked weed, which didn't seem so bad to Stella, and once or twice, when his energy bottomed out, he took Ritalin, and when she saw him with the pill in his hand, she tried to hold his fingers, to keep that pill from going up to his mouth, but he waved her hands away. "It's medicinal for me," he told her. He said that taking that pill made lightning shoot through his brain, making him so laser focused he could practice until dawn, his stage strut growing more brash, more confident. "It's for work," he insisted.

She told herself she could understand that, she could forgive it. She never saw him in a stupor. If anything, the drugs just made him happier. He couldn't believe his good luck at being in the world, being with her. And then one day, he had told her (he told her everything) that the real reason he took the drugs was so he could go onstage and not hear his father's voice thrumming in his head, telling him over and over, *Who do you think you are? Who are you that you think you deserve this because you don't.* She had held him closer. She understood that feeling. She had felt it herself, that feeling of not being enough, of being a fraud, when she was a little girl and her parents shooed her out of the room so they could be together in private. She felt it when her friends asked her how she got to be the one to get lucky in love when their relationships were all breaking apart. Who was she to be this happy?

Simon had never pressed her to try any of the drugs, but one night, after comforting a friend whose girlfriend had left a note that said, *There's nobody else, but I stopped loving you*, Stella grew scared. What if she wasn't lucky but instead was stupid or blind? What if her own relationship was in trouble and she didn't even know it? How could you know for sure how things might go? Her mother had never doubted her father's love, but his death had been sharp and sudden. Her mother had moved to Spain with all her scrapbooks of her husband, her memories, and she still brought him into every conversation, as if that were a way of keeping him present. But her mother wasn't Stella. What if Simon grew tired of her, the way she kept asking him if he loved her, the way she sometimes trailed him from room to room, needing to know he was still there?

She didn't want to feel insecure. She wanted to feel strong, in control. Free and maybe a bit wild because that could be exciting. That night, because she couldn't stand how upset she felt, how unmoored, she asked him for a Ritalin. "Really, honey?" he said, and she saw how happy he looked. That made her feel better but not nearly as good as the Ritalin did. It was as if she had been in a dark room and someone had switched on all the lights. She felt so young, so high, as if she were filled with starlight, and everything seemed possible. They talked for hours, finishing each other's sentences, talking over each other in a kind of fugue. "Dance party!" she said, getting up and blasting music, pulling him up with her. The room vibrated. The music seemed to flash all around them and she laughed out loud because it was all so great.

How could something that brought them so close be a bad thing? They didn't do the drugs every day or even every week. They most certainly were not addicts or using any of the really hard stuff. Stella took it with Simon only when she felt insecure, when she needed to feel more in control of herself and get that shot of happy. Vitamin R, Simon called it, and she thought he was right, because like a vitamin, it seemed to change her on a molecular level, she was convinced. It quieted the doubts that bored into her mind. She could get up again and go to work, her mind sharp, her body humming. No harm done.

Then she got older. By her late twenties, she couldn't spring back as easily as she used to after doing drugs. It felt silly to depend on a drug to give you courage, to make you feel that all was right in the world, when your own experiences, your own bravery, should give you that. Each time, she took longer to recuperate, which sometimes made her fuzzy at work, and that was dangerous.

It felt ridiculous to be her age and doing drugs and drinking like a kid. It ceased to be fun waking in sheets littered with last night's food and finding the carpet stained with wine because they'd been too drunk to put the glasses in the sink. And her face. Her skin rebelled with patchy spots. Her hair limped along. Gradually, Simon stopped asking her if she wanted to smoke weed with him, if she wanted a Ritalin, because her answer was always no. And though she had no way of knowing for sure, she thought he had stopped then, too.

Now he looked up at her. "We could share this and see what happens," Simon said.

"I don't know. I don't think that's such a hot idea," she said.

"Remember how much fun we used to have? How easy it was? How amazing? We'd be up all night partying and talking. Remember the feasts we'd order in, how we'd dine in bed and talk for hours about everything—everything!—and not get up for days?" He looked longingly at her. "We were so good together."

She blinked at him, noticing the pills in his hand, smooth and red and oblong like dots of jam. "We *are* good together," she said.

"I'm just so fucking tired of arguing," Simon said.

"Me fucking too."

Simon held up the pills. "It could be like it used to be," Simon said. "I always felt like you used to really know me," and Stella was so tired that she thought maybe he was right. When they had gotten high before, he used to sit and listen to her so intently that she felt the world stop. No one had ever paid her that much attention, had wondered so much about her thoughts, her feelings, had cared so deeply. "What do you want out of life?" he used to ask her. Whatever she said, he not only responded, but he remembered her responses, too.

You know me.

Oh yes. She did know him. She had known him since they were both twenty-two years old. She was standing in front of the nursery window at NYU Medical Center, where she worked, searching for her friend's new baby boy. Simon was there, too, scanning the cribs. Then she heard him talking to the infants, his voice low and serious: "So, what's going on in the world of babies? The staff treating you right? Giving you clean towels every morning? No complaints about the milk service?" She had laughed and he turned to her and then she saw that his eyes were gray and mysterious as fog.

"Which one's yours?" she said.

"None of them," he said. "I'm visiting a friend's baby." She loved the look of wonder on his face.

"Me, too," she said. She couldn't help it. Right at that moment, she wanted to kiss the crook of his neck.

He had walked her home to her crappy little studio on Fourteenth Street where they had sat up talking until four in the morning and then fallen asleep together, fully clothed, arms around each other. In the morning, he was up before her, making her an omelet and squeezing orange juice. He had even set the table. "Who *are* you?" she said, laughing. He came over to see her the next night, and the next, and suddenly there she was, responsible Stella with both feet firmly planted, Stella who never missed a shift, who read books and adored classical music, falling heedlessly for a rocker with an impulsive lifestyle and a way with words, simply because he cared so much about her, like no one ever had before.

He was riding high on a hit song he had written for his band. "Next one will be even bigger," he said. She didn't tell him that she had never heard of him before they met, but she quickly went to a music store and found a CD. She listened, a mixture of relief and giddy delight because he was so good, because his melodies were as haunting as his lyrics. His songs were all stories she could get lost in: an old man talking about the young wife he had lost and never forgot, a woman who had killed her lover and now regretted it. Stella sat listening, holding her breath. When she saw him next, she blurted, "I love your music." And then there it was, that impossible glow to him. He leaned forward so their foreheads were touching. "Zzzzz," he said, making a buzzing sound. "We're connected." She laughed, because it was so silly. Because it was so true.

And he was good in other ways. He held her hand everywhere—at the table and in the street. He wrote little love poems that would make her blush because he rhapsodized about the curve of her breasts, the point of her hip, a particular ringlet of hair that always fell over her eyes. When she came home, tired from work, he was waiting on the stoop of her building, holding irises, her favorite flower, and take-out Chinese. A bottle of wine was in the crook of his arm. "Tell me everything about your day," he said, standing to greet her.

She sighed and rested her head against his shoulder now. "It's mild," he told her, opening his palm to show her the pills.

"What is it? Who gave it to you?" She fingered the pill in her hand. "Is this Ritalin?" she asked, but he shook his head. "It probably does the same thing," he said. Usually all she had to do was look at a pill and know what it was, but tonight she was brain fried. Did she really want to do this? All she knew was that right now she felt so far away from him that they seemed like ice floes moving in different directions, and she was desperate to have him back before it was another thing that would be too late to change, to fix. What if just one more time would unlock them, bring them back to that time when they were both young and so happy and remind her of how it was and how it could be again?

"We've been drinking," she said.

"Come on. We haven't had that much."

"What is it?" she asked again.

He frowned. "Uh, Darvon," he said.

"What? Darvon? That was banned years ago." Stella used to take Darvon for period cramps way back in college, getting an endless supply from her roommate whose father was a doctor. She stopped only when her roommate had transferred to Stanford, but she hadn't really missed it. She couldn't remember what the pill had looked like back then, but she remembered bathing in its comforting buzz. "How'd you even get it? Who gave it to you?" she asked.

"Kevin."

Of course. Kevin always had one thing or another to take him up or down. He always winked at her when he saw her, like he had some secret he wanted to share with her. He brushed past her just a bit too close sometimes. She once caught him in the bedroom, snorting coke off her hand mirror. "Stop that," she said. And he had, but that didn't make her like him any better.

Simon set both pills on the table, her choice whether to take one or not. "We'll do it together," he urged. "It'll make us both feel better. Like we used to."

"Together," Stella said. She didn't know what the right thing was to do anymore. She was tired and sad and scared, too, and maybe this might help clarify things.

"What about the Sudafed I took," she said.

"What Sudafed?" Simon said. "I didn't see you taking anything."

She frowned, trying to remember, to unloosen the knot in her mind, but she was too drunk now. She picked up the pill and studied it. It looked so innocent, and she put it on her tongue. Ready or not, here I come, she thought. Blast me back to the past when everything was so good with us. Just a taste. Just a memory. It might be all she needed, like a reboot. She swallowed, and then he leaned over and kissed her. "This will be good for us," he said. "I promise. Maybe you'll even change your mind about coming with me."

"I don't think I will."

He folded his hand over hers and she felt an old familiar jolt of desire.

They hadn't been passionate together for weeks now because he was so consumed with anxiety about the new possibilities for the band and she was so intent on the apartment and a family. She missed it, the way he'd tumble her to the kitchen floor, running his hand up her skirt. The feel of his mouth on her thighs, the heat from his body an electric current into hers. She lifted his hand up and kissed it. "It's going to take the edge off," he told her. "You watch. We'll get all nice and mellow again."

Right, she thought. She hated that word, *mellow*, and she'd never been anything even remotely resembling mellow. She wondered if Simon was just buying time, hoping that she would wake in a better mood, be more receptive to giving up the argument.

"It's a onetime thing," she said, and he nodded.

Simon turned on music, Bruno Mars. Oh, she liked that. It buoyed her, made her want to move. She began to dance. She felt him watching her, drinking her in like his wine. Then he stood and joined her. She swayed, bumping against him, but her limbs suddenly felt too heavy and she couldn't keep him in focus. She narrowed her eyes to a squint, trying to keep him in her sights. "Come on, let me twirl you," he said, and he took her hand, and she bumped her hip against the edge of the wood table, wincing.

He stopped and poured them more wine and then clinked his glass against hers. *I'm with a guy in a rock-and-roll band. How unlikely. How sort of ridiculous.* He was on the road seven months of the year, the bassist and sometimes singer with the band Mighty Chondria, and as soon as Stella had heard the name, she felt a thrill. "I know all about mitochondria!" she told him. "It's my favorite organelle."

"Mine, too," he said.

She couldn't help feeling that that band name meant something, that it was a sign, somehow, that they were connected, that they were meant to be together.

She set her wineglass aside and leaned her head against the crook of his neck. He was warm. Oh, he was so warm. She shivered and cozied closer to him. She trailed one hand through his hair, which was as thick and curly as her own. She still loved how he smelled, like bread rising, like green grass. Like Simon. He wrapped his arms around her and dipped her down low so her hair was brushing the floor, then he glided her back up.

"You're staring at me," she said.

He turned up the music and swung her to him, swaying his hips. She used to dance all night long, but now her legs ached from being on the hospital floor all day. Her ears were buzzing from the pill, and she kept missing the beat. She stopped dancing and braced a hand on the wall, which seemed to move beneath her fingers.

"Hey," he said. "What's going on?"

Her head was splitting now. The wall was spongy. She felt woozy and tense, and nothing was happening the way it should. This wasn't the Darvon that she remembered. Simon was talking to her, getting her to the sofa, sitting down beside her, his words like an undertow, pulling her down, his skin breathing. She reached for the wine and drank more. I shouldn't drink, she thought, then downed the wine.

She looked out the window. Everything outside was dark. She was suddenly afraid.

"I love you," Stella blurted. "I love us." She waited for Simon to say it back, the way he always did. He tilted back his head so his hair brushed his shirt.

She set down her wineglass, her head so foggy she couldn't see the edge of the table, and her glass tumbled to the floor. She couldn't remember ever being this tired, ever feeling this strange. She was outside her own body somehow. A song was strumming in her ear, growing louder, but she couldn't make out the lyrics, and she tried to rest her head against Simon's shoulder. "We fit," she said, but he had moved away and she toppled over.

Her skin felt clammier now. She swore she was wearing a suit of flesh. Her nerve endings felt on fire, and she took off her earrings. She couldn't bear them to touch her neck. The music felt like claws scratching into her. She tapped one arm to see if she could still feel her skin, and when she couldn't, she pinched it. And felt nothing.

She wanted to turn off the music, but she couldn't. Suddenly it was a message to her. Bruno Mars was singing directly to her, telling her how her life was going to go now. "When I was your man," he sang. Stop, she thought. Stop, stop. This is just an argument. Arguments ended. Peace was struck. Starting to feel panicky, she found she couldn't speak to Simon, couldn't move her arms or legs, couldn't go over to him and pull him back to her. It all seemed impossibly scary, like she was on the edge of something. She felt a weight on her chest. She tried to cough, desperate to dislodge something, but her muscles slept instead. The music was louder now, tiny drumbeats in her cells, but she couldn't remember anyone upping the volume.

"Stell," Simon said, weaving toward her. "Are you all right?"

Something was happening. She felt that with certainty, almost in wonder. She heard the words in her head, as if they were spoken by someone else, someone she didn't know, but she couldn't shake her head to dislodge them. Simon was repeating over and over to her, "Are you all right? Are you all right?"

But was he all right? She felt him circling her, like blips on a radar screen.

She was falling now. The world was growing darker around her. She tried to grab Simon's hand, but a roaring started in her ears and began traveling through her body into her cells, and it was so loud. She shut her eyes and then there was nothing.

2

BY THE TIME SIMON woke up, it was already noon. His head was throbbing and there was the weight of Stella against him. She was lying in his arms, her skin cool to the touch. Jesus, what happened last night? He felt dark with shame. He only occasionally did drugs with the band, when practice stalled, or they needed to just kick back, and it was always something minor and mild. But he shouldn't have done anything last night, not after their argument. Not with all that wine. Even worse, he'd told Stella the pill was Darvon when in fact he wasn't certain. He had to tell her something and that was the first name that popped into his head. Gently, he slid from under her, lowering her head against the pillow. Her hair fell across her neck. Her lashes cast shadows on her face. God, she is so beautiful, he thought.

He stood up, realizing he was totally hung over. His whole body throbbed. His mouth was sandpaper, his vision was blurred. A thick haze encased his thoughts.

Stella had been right there with him last night, but even so, he still felt as though he was missing some part of her. It used to be so different between them, and he wanted that back so badly that all he could do was keep drinking. Finding the pills had been a surprise, and all he could remember about them was that he'd taken them from Kevin and tucked them into his pocket. During his argument with Stella, Simon had felt so desperate that when he dug into his pockets for a match and felt those pills, he thought it might be a lifesaver, a way to knock them back to where they used to be. He would have done anything in that moment to make things right.

But it hadn't helped. If anything, it had made things much worse. Now, looking at Stella again, he was drained and confused. He felt like a zombie. If he could just stop the thrashing in his head, the roil in his stomach, maybe he could think straight.

He wanted her to go to Los Angeles, but he didn't want to revisit the argument, pack it along with his luggage, and continue it in California. Every time they were about to leave for someplace, she would bring up the apartment and kids, making everything he thought they had together seem smaller and smaller.

His own father, a partner of a law firm, had been a terrible parent. He was rarely home, and when he was, he wanted to sit silently reading the paper, wordlessly eating dinner, and being left the hell alone. Simon's father barely noticed Simon's mother, and he certainly didn't notice Simon. "My son's in third grade," he had said once to company, which deeply wounded Simon, who was in fifth. The one time Simon's father had come to one of Simon's school talent shows, Simon looked out into the audience to see his father asleep. And then he wanted Simon to join him at the law firm when he was older.

"I don't know," Simon had said at the time, to which his father responded, "There's nothing to know."

Why in God's name would I risk repeating anything like that kind of parenting, Simon thought.

Now he stared out the window. He didn't want to put down roots here. He was tired of Manhattan. It was too loud, too cold or too hot, too dirty, too expensive. All the cool, funky little shops and mom-and-pop places were gone now, replaced by stores so pricey that no one in the neighborhood could afford them. All that rough, dangerous excitement had vanished. Where were the surprises? The creativity? Manhattan was too familiar. He felt as if he knew every street, every club and concert hall that never paid the band enough. He probably would have left a long time ago if it hadn't been for Stella, who even after all these years still looked at everything in the city with wonder.

But he was stunned and hurt that she didn't want to go to LA with him. Did that mean she didn't want to be with him anymore? Why couldn't it all be easier?

Maybe he could make it right. Maybe he could wake Stella, bring her coffee and make her some breakfast, and then he might convince her to come with him.

Simon rubbed at the window, trying to see beyond the falling snow. LA, he thought, and his heart zoomed. A whole new world. He swallowed. He still felt like shit, like he hated everything, and all he wanted was not to feel this way.

Maybe we have different dreams now, he had told her.

Maybe he wanted out.

She had told him she wasn't coming with him to LA, and he had frozen, shocked. She couldn't mean that, he had thought, but he knew she did.

What would it be like to be in California, just him and the band? What if things were so spectacularly great that they got an LA manager and the band decided to move out there? Would it be so bad? All those sunny days, that hot blaze of weather he loved, just bathing him in gold, the women in their little sleeveless dresses, their legs long and gleaming with tan. It made his stomach tighten just to think about it. He could rent a bungalow in Venice, right by the beach. He could go rollerblading every morning, play his guitar under the stars. Maybe he could get a big, rangy dog to run with him, a conversation starter that would draw people to him.

That might draw other women.

The thought shocked him. Though he'd had opportunity through the years with the band, he never cheated on Stella, never even thought about it.

He glanced back at her. Pale as parchment, she never tanned. She was a city girl, born and bred in a Brooklyn apartment, she always said with pride. She hated the beach and said it was like frying on a skillet. The water was always too cold for her. She knew everything about ocean danger, including box jellyfish stings and shark bites. "The best protection is not to go near them," she said.

There was so much more in the world than this moment. So many new and different people. He was still young, wasn't he? He was young enough to grab opportunity, to run with it. But Stella wanted to settle down, to stay put, to be anchored with a child.

He sat down next to Stella, his head in his hands. He loved her, but what if he didn't love her enough? What if she didn't love him enough? What if they needed to be apart, even for a little while, to give them a break that might bind them closer together? His thoughts skidded in his head. Slow down, he told himself. Slow down. He didn't know what he wanted.

He bent over and lifted up a curly ribbon of hair. "Wake up," he said. "Honey," he added, his tone sweet. They'd go have breakfast. Things would be clearer. He gently shook her, but she didn't stir. Her skin felt clammy to him and he lifted up her hand and felt her pulse twittering. "Stella," he said, lifting her shoulders, shaking her a little harder, his voice rising. She fell back on the couch, one arm flopping against the floor. "Stella!" he cried. He looked at her chest, but it was barely moving with breath, and then he grabbed her up in his arms.

HE CALLED AN ambulance, and when it didn't show up right away, he wrapped Stella in a blanket and cradled her in his arms and ran outside. NYU Medical Center was a half-hour walk on a good day, maybe twenty minutes by car depending on traffic, but his car was parked blocks away and it would have to be shoveled out. He stood for a moment, confused, knowing he had to do something now. He began to run toward the hospital with Stella in his arms, dodging snowdrifts and the icy slush soaking his sneakers. In this heavy snow, every block seemed like miles. The street hadn't been plowed yet. Cabs weren't running, and there were no buses or even a car he might flag down.

"Wake up!" he shouted at her, but she stayed limp in his arms. He ran faster and almost fell. Everything looked so dizzying white.

He heard a motor and turned, frantic, sure it must be the ambulance. Instead, a plow truck was pushing against the snow, but Simon couldn't drop Stella to wave at the driver, so instead he ran into the middle of the street, trying to get right in front of the truck. He screamed, "Please!" over and over. The plow stopped. A face in a Russian cap frowned out at him and then the driver popped open the door. "What the fuck," he said. "Is she hurt?"

"We need the hospital—"

The man helped get Stella up into the cab, along with Simon, and then started the plow again.

"What were you doing, walking in the freezing cold and snow?" the driver said. "What were you thinking, doing something that stupid? Look at you. You're both soaked."

"I called an ambulance—"

"Why didn't you wait? How would they find you tromping around in all this mess?"

The driver pulled up to the hospital and got out, waiting for Simon to hit the ground so he could lower Stella into his arms. "I hope she's okay, man," the driver told him as Simon pushed through the doors of the ER.

The lobby, usually crowded, was empty. The front desk where the triage nurse sat was empty, too. "Help!" he screamed, and a nurse appeared. Brenda! He knew her! She worked with Stella.

As soon as Brenda saw Stella in his arms, her whole body seemed to lengthen. "Simon," she said, astonished. "Simon, what happened?"

Two steps and she was taking Stella from him, easing her onto a gurney.

"We fell asleep." He lifted his hands and then let them fall back down. "She won't wake up."

"Did she hit her head? Was there alcohol?" Brenda asked, frowning.

"We had wine, a few glasses at the most."

"What's a few?" Her hands circled Stella's wrists.

He tried to remember, but all he could see were the glasses in both their hands, the way they kept filling them and drinking. "Were there drugs?" Brenda asked. She didn't look at him when she asked, but he heard something steely in her voice.

"She took a pill." His tongue felt thick in his mouth, his mind foggy, and Brenda looked at him. She took out her pager. "A doctor's coming," she said. "What pill?"

Sweat prickled his back. "Red," he said. "Small, oblong. Maybe Darvon?"

Her eyes narrowed. "Darvon's pink," she said. She was waiting for him to say more, but his voice was in lockdown. Even if he could speak, no matter what he said, it would feel and sound like a lie. Something acrid and burning was in his throat, and he sucked in more air and then coughed. "I don't know what it was," he said. There. It was the truth. As much of the truth as he had. "I can find out," he said. He touched Stella's hands, flinching at how cold they were.

"You do that. Now." The way Brenda clipped her words scared him. He rubbed his hands against Stella's, trying to warm them up.

"You have to let go," she told him. He released her.

An orderly snapped into view, taking hold of the gurney, pushing it through a set of double doors that led to the examination rooms. Simon started to follow, but Brenda grabbed his arm. "No you don't," she said. "You have to stay here."

The doors swung open and Simon looked through and saw all the rows of beds, the blue curtains, the IV poles and steel tables. A woman with blood dappled along her face like spray paint was sobbing. A skinny man was sitting up, grabbing for a blanket. Doctors were moving about, talking, voices jamming into one another, and after the silent emptiness of the snow, Simon felt disoriented. And then the doors swung shut again, and Stella was gone.

HE PULLED OUT his cell phone and called Kevin, who hated talking on the phone. He answered with a snarl. "This had better be good," Kevin said.

"It's me. Stella's in the hospital." He spoke fast, before Kevin could hang up. He heard Ruby, Kevin's girlfriend, in the background, the molasses drawl of her voice asking him who it was. "What?" Kevin said. "What are you telling me?"

"She's in the hospital. She's really sick. I need to know. That little pill you gave me—the red one—to chill out. What was it?"

"She took that pill?"

"What was it, Kevin?"

"Jesus, I don't know. I always have pills. It could have been any number of things."

Simon flashed to Kevin dropping acid right before an important interview, giving answers so funny it became a classic story. He remembered Kevin snorting coke before going onstage, grinning wickedly as he did it, his energy winning over the crowd before the first lick.

"It was red," Simon said insistently.

Kevin was quiet for a moment. "Sort of longish?" he asked.

"Yeah—"

"Reds," he said. "That's my recreational stash. It's just secobarbital. It's a tranquilizer. Makes you all nice and woozy. High-school kids eat it like candy. It just takes the edge off. Ruby used to take it before she went to her classes. Safe as pie."

"Who is that? What did I take?" Ruby's voice sang out. "Kevin, babe, who is it?"

"Shush, Ruby," Kevin said. "I'm trying to talk here."

"She's not waking up," Simon said.

There was silence again. He heard Ruby. "Babe?" she said.

"Where are you?" Kevin said. "I'm coming right over."

Simon thought of Kevin talking to Brenda, telling her about the drug, how it was recreational, how he had given it to Simon. All that crazy charm and noise, slick and suspicious. "No, don't come. The streets are a nightmare."

"You change your mind, you call me. Doesn't matter what time, you hear me?"

"I hear you," Simon said.

"Everything will be fine. And we'll all be on our way to the sun tonight and this will just be a funny story we'll laugh about."

There was a roaring in Simon's head. "Did you not hear me?" he said, panic rising in his throat. "I can't leave today. I don't think I can leave tomorrow—"

Simon could hear Ruby singing something low and deep in her throat. He heard Kevin murmuring something to her. "Rick wanted you," Kevin said. "He talked about your songs. What am I supposed to do, call him up and say you can't make it?"

"My songs will still be there and Rob'll sing them and you guys will play them until I can get there," Simon said. "The concert's not for four days. A lot can happen between now and then."

"Who's going to do the bass guitar?"

"Come on, we each know at least six people who'd kill to do it."

"Fuck," Kevin said. "So you'll come later, then."

"Later," Simon said, even though he couldn't imagine spending a minute outside of the hospital.

SIMON FOUND BRENDA behind the triage desk. She glanced at him with a look that said she wished she didn't know him, and he felt a flare of guilt. "I know what it is," he said. "The pill. Secobarbital. Just one."

Her brow lifted. "Just one with alcohol," she said. "You both thought that was smart?"

"Please. Tell the doctor. Please."

She nodded and got up, handing him a sheaf of papers clipped to a board, a blue pen with bite marks along its stem, attached with a small cord. "Fill these out," she ordered. "I'll find the doctor."

He stared at the forms, the words swimming in front of him. All he wanted to do was throw down the paper and barge through the forbidden door and grab Stella and say, Come on, we're going. Come on, wake up. Everything's going to be different now. You'll see.

He didn't have her insurance card—he'd have to give it to them later. Then he noticed his jeans, wet from the knees down, and his sneakers, soaked. He also realized he was shivering so hard that he could feel his bones knocking. He finished the form and set it on the desk. He looked around the waiting room, not knowing what to do. There were a few old *Time* magazines scattered about, but they were tattered and unappealing. He glanced at the TV. A cartoon was playing and he didn't know how to change the channel. He couldn't stand it, this waiting, the way his mind skittered from terrible scenario to terrible scenario. Stella unconscious. Stella paralyzed.

Stella dying.

He started to pace. What were they doing to her? Were they pumping her stomach? He didn't know whom he hated more right now, Kevin for giving the pill to him in the first place or himself for being so reckless. Himself, he decided. He definitely hated himself. He had lied to her that the pill was Darvon. He had taken care of himself this morning first, giving in to his crankiness before he noticed her. He had even thought about starting a new life out in LA without her. What kind of person was he?

He knew the answer to that.

He could feel terror rising in his chest, and he jumped up and pushed through the ER doors. No one stopped him. He heard someone vomiting. He saw a young woman sitting on a table, dazed, her nose bleeding onto her blue hospital gown, into her hands. Then he saw Stella's red socks at the end of a gurney and he ran to them.

A doctor, her hair across her lab coat as bright red as a tomato, was threading an IV into Stella's arm, flashing a light into her eyes. Simon saw her name tag: Dr. Libby Marks. He didn't know her, didn't remember Stella's ever mentioning that name when she told him about her days at work, but still, she seemed vaguely familiar. "You can't be back here," Libby said.

"I'm her boyfriend," Simon said, and the doctor looked over at him.

"I don't care who you are." Libby shut off the light and Simon saw her smoothing Stella's hair off her face. She might be all procedure, but she cared about Stella, and that made him feel better.

"Was she drinking?" she asked.

"We both were. A little wine."

"What's a little?"

"I don't know. Two glasses. Three. Wait, maybe four. She has this ridiculously low tolerance."

"Four," Libby said, her brows rising. "She do drugs with that wine?"

"No. Not Stella. Just aspirin. Sudafed, maybe." He sucked in a breath, which tasted rusty, like the inside of a tin can. "I told the nurse. She took a secobarbital."

The doctor finished with the IV. "That's a barbiturate. Phenobarbital. It's not great with wine, but it shouldn't do this. Did she take more than one?"

Simon tried to think, and his mind fuzzed into static. Her hands were in his pocket while they danced and he had shut his eyes, moving with her. What if they'd had more than the two pills and he didn't even know it? "I don't know," he said.

The doctor wrote something on a chart. "I'm admitting her. She's unresponsive. The tests should tell us a little more." Libby seemed to dismiss him. Stella had told him once that doctors were abrupt because they had to be. Sometimes they couldn't waste valuable time being nice or kind or chatty. Not when someone was sick and they had to focus.

"Coma can be complicated," Libby said.

Simon froze. "What?" Coma. "She's still alive?" Simon said.

"Of course, she's alive."

"Does she know I'm here? Can she hear me?"

"I don't know that."

"She'll get better, won't she?"

Another orderly appeared and began wheeling Stella away.

"Where are you taking her?" Simon couldn't breathe. His heart thrashed in his chest. "Is she going to get better?"

"We're going to get her in a room and cool down her whole body," Libby said. "There'll be less brain trauma that way."

"Brain trauma . . ." All Simon could think about was how cold it was outside, how still and white, and here in this heated hospital they were going to re-create that for Stella.

"Go home," the doctor told him. "Get some rest. You won't be any good to her if you don't." It wasn't until the doctor had vanished that Simon realized that Libby hadn't answered his question: Is she going to get better?

HE DIDN'T GO home, instead returning to the waiting area. A man walked by and banged into Simon's legs, but Simon didn't say anything, didn't complain. He deserved every outrage thrown at him.

He sat on the hard plastic chair watching whatever was on TV, one show sliding into another. He grabbed his cell from his pocket and looked up *coma*. He learned that only 50 percent of coma patients survive. Only 10 percent come out completely unchanged. There was a Glasgow Coma Scale, 3 to 15. What was Stella's number? He shut off the phone and hugged his arms around himself. No. No. No.

He didn't know how much time had passed when Libby pushed

through the doors, and as soon as she saw him, she started and then composed herself. "You're still here?" Libby said coldly.

"I am," Simon said. "How is she?"

"We won't know anything for a while. If she comes out of it in the next few days, we're home free."

"Her brain . . ."

"Oh no, no. In a coma state, the brain works. We're just not sure how. She's responding to some stimuli, too, which is good."

Simon tried to swallow. "What about the Glasgow scale?"

Libby tilted her head. "Don't go on the internet," she said. "You'll make yourself crazy."

"What about it?"

"We'll know more in the next week."

"A week?" Simon's body began to shake, and Libby put a hand on his arm.

"We?" Simon said.

"I'm just part of a team of doctors. They'll do an EEG to assess her brain waves, an MRI for brain atrophy."

Simon, shocked, couldn't speak.

"You can't do any good here right now. Go home."

"I can rest here," Simon said. After years on tour, he was used to sleeping on the bus, in chairs, on the floor, and on his feet, sometimes, if he had to. He could sprawl out on this orange plastic bench and be just fine.

Simon noticed the dark rings, like bruises under the doctor's eyes, a faint stain on the lapel of her lab coat.

"Go home," she said, like she was giving him a prescription. "I'll call you if there is any change at all." Simon looked at her name tag again: Libby Marks.

SIMON WAS SURPRISED by how dark it was outside. The snow had stopped and the streets were now plowed. There were sled tracks on the road where the kids must have played. Someone had made a series of snow angels, all the figures looking as if they might take flight.

He didn't realize how cold he was until he was back in their apartment, and as soon as he saw the empty wine bottles, two of them, he flung them in the trash. He couldn't sit still, couldn't keep the image of their drinking out of his mind. And those pills.

To stay sane, he'd have to get busy. He cleaned the whole place, attacking the bathroom and then the kitchen. He did laundry, changing their sheets, trying not to think about what was happening only a few blocks away.

He was wiping down all the surfaces when he noticed the message light on his phone. He picked it up to listen. The first call was Kevin, wanting to know how Stella was. Kevin told him that they got lucky, that they'd all been bumped to an LA flight the next day, and he wanted to know if Simon and Stella could make that.

Simon shook his head. What the fuck was wrong with Kevin, asking that? How could he go now? He'd have to call Kevin. He'd have to call Stella's and his friends. And then he'd call his parents. He'd also call her mother, Bette, who lived in Spain. He hadn't been around her much. He'd talked to her on the phone every Sunday when Stella called her, but he didn't really know her. What would this news do to her? Tomorrow, he thought. I'll call her then. Tomorrow, when he was supposed to be getting on a plane with the band and going to California. Tomorrow, which was supposed to be the start of his whole new life.

ALL THAT NIGHT, despite Libby's warnings, Simon stayed on the internet. *Coma* was an ugly word. He remembered that cheesy old horror film with Michael Douglas and what was her name, the pretty French actress—Genevieve Bujold—lying on a gurney about to be put under permanently. He thought of that book, *Girlfriend in a Coma*. Like it was something funny, and the whole idea of that made him feel crushed.

He clicked on another link. A fireman had been in a coma for a decade and he woke up speaking Mandarin, then quit his job to teach the language at Stanford. Another man came out of a coma after only a week, but his memory skittered around like a ball in a pinball machine.

Simon studied articles on the brain. Neuroplasticity could make the brain reroute signals and operations, but the personality could change. A person who has gone into a coma could come out completely different.

Simon called the hospital. "Stella Davison," he said.

"Are you family?"

He couldn't risk telling them that they weren't married, so he lied. "Yes," he said.

"Stable," a voice said, but what did that even mean? He shut his eyes, but when he started to drift off, he bolted awake. If he slept, would he wake up?

It was four in the morning, but he dialed Kevin.

"What the fuck," Kevin said.

"You know I can't leave right now," Simon said. "You know that. Not for a while."

Kevin sighed deeply. "Fuck, man. We need you."

"I need *her*," Simon said sharply.

"You know what I mean—"

"Look, if we get the tour, I can be there when things calm down here," Simon said. "When they get back to normal. I'll be there as soon as I can." He picked up a pen and drew a series of *x*'s on the paper. "Did you find a bassist?" He wanted and didn't want to know.

There was a funny silence. "Yeah. We got someone. A young guy, and he's good."

"You told Rick Mason?" He squinched his eyes shut, just imagining. Was Rick mad? Or even worse, did he not care?

"He's sad about it for you, but he's also cool with it. He's a good guy. He knows things can change."

"You'll let me know how it goes?"

"We'll call you from the coast. We'll keep calling you. Write us some new songs so you stay in the loop." Kevin hung up, but Simon sat there, the phone pressed against his cheek.

HE COULDN'T SLEEP after the call. He stayed up watching whatever was on TV, unable to concentrate. When he went to visit Stella later that morning, he took her iPod, which was full of songs. The faster he could get her better, the faster normal life could resume. He found her alone in the room, attached to a ventilator, a breathing tube snaking out of her mouth. He forced himself to keep his eyes open, to make his body stop quaking. He turned on the music, and there he was, singing to her, but she stayed motionless.

Libby, her fiery red hair tamed into a braid, whisked in. She nodded at him and he felt suddenly embarrassed about the music. "I read that it helps," he said, and she waved a hand.

"It does. Sometimes." She glanced at the machines, tapping her finger on the IV. "Her numbers went down and that's what you want." Libby tilted her head for a moment at the iPod. It was playing "You First," a song he had written for Stella after their first date. He had so wanted her to like him, had wanted to impress her. He had stayed up all night writing it for her, aching for her.

"I always liked that song," Libby said. "I remember it on Pandora."

He waited, wondering if she was going to ask him about his music, but she was ignoring him. She didn't know who he was other than Stella's partner. She said nothing more and then glided out of the room.

However, when he walked out of the room, everyone at the hospital suddenly seemed to know who he was. A doctor passed by and nodded encouragingly at him. When he sat in the waiting room, staring into space, a nurse came in and handed him a cup of tea. "You need it," she told him. He was so grateful and lonely he wanted to tug her down to sit with him. Who did he really have now? His parents were old and living in a Florida retirement community. His father had a bad heart and disapproved of Simon and his life decisions. His mother had diabetes and went along with anything his father said.

He walked back into Stella's room. A new doctor was there with two metal pots, striking one against the other with a loud clang. "What are you doing?" Simon cried. The doctor moved closer to Stella and did it again, and then he placed the pots on Stella's chest. "Wake up!" he shouted. "Wake up!" The doctor's face furrowed. "Stella, wake up!"

"Who are you?" Simon said.

"Dr. Alberson. The neurologist. One of the team."

The doctor turned to Simon. "Sorry," he said, and his voice was so soft that Simon had to lean forward to hear it. "Sometimes it works to stimulate the person by assaulting their senses," he said. "We never know what might work, so it's beneficial to try everything. Strong smells. Loud sounds. Cold. Heat." Then he picked up the pots and left the room. Simon leaned over Stella. "Wake up," he said gently.

While the doctors were racing around, brusque in their actions, the nurses seemed more compassionate. Stella had always told him that the one thing she loved about being a nurse was her interaction with patients. "You get to really know people," she said. Doctors might see a patient for five minutes, but nurses were in and out of the room all day. An obstetrician would deliver the baby, but that would be the end of the doctor's impact on the baby's day-to-day life. It was the nurses who fed the infants, wheeled them in to be with the mothers. The joke was that most of the doctors could identify a child by his sonogram but not by a face.

The only one who seemed suspicious of him was the redhead, Libby. When he left that day, he decided that when this was over, when Stella was able to come home, he'd bring chocolates to the nurses' station, for them and for Stella's doctors. He'd let them all know how grateful he was for everything they'd done for Stella.

• • •

THAT NIGHT, HE called their friends, other musicians he knew, people they went out to dinner with or just hung out with sometimes. When he told them about Stella, there was always a shock of silence, and some of them cried. "Whatever you need," people told him. The next day, he found casseroles in the building lobby, offers scribbled on note cards to clean the apartment, to visit. People showed up at the hospital and found him in the waiting room, and Simon didn't have the heart to tell them that their silence just made him feel more terrified.

He finally got up his courage to call his parents that night. "Why didn't you tell us before?" his mother cried. "Why did you wait so long?"

His father got on the line, a rumbling in his throat. "What's this about?" he said, and Simon told him. "What can we do?" he said.

"How could this happen," his mother said, but it was a statement rather than a question. "Will she be all right?"

"They don't know when or if Stella will come out of the coma," Simon said.

His parents were silent while he glossed over the details, leaving out the booze, the pills, the argument.

"Oh, honey," his mom said. "We're so, so sorry. We truly are. It must be so terrible."

"Can I have some money?" Simon blurted. "To help with Stella? She's in the hospital where she works, but maybe a private nurse would help—"

Silence again, blooming around him like a thorny cactus. And then Simon could hear his father's breath in the phone. "Let me give you some . . ." his father started to say, and Simon felt a rise of hope. His father coughed. "Let me give you some advice. You don't want it to be five years from now and you're still struggling for money, still depending on other people. Use the time, for God's sake. Stella's in a class A hospital and she'll be fine, most likely. Think about taking business classes. Don't let it all be tragic."

But it all is, Simon wanted to say. "What about a loan? You can't give me a small loan?" he said. "With interest."

"Do you know how much this joint costs us?" his father said. "Twenty grand a month."

"Darling," his mother cut in. "It's fifteen."

"We invested for this. We saved—" his father said.

"Don't listen to your father. What do you need?" his mother asked. "Certainly we can help. What do you need? Help for a month? For two? Name the amount and we'll send a check." Simon could hear his father's measured breathing. What if it were more than a month? What if it were for a year? He felt a thousand small fires igniting inside him, trapping him.

"Never mind, I'll take care of it," Simon said, and he abruptly hung up the phone. Instantly he felt a rise of fear. What was wrong with him? Why didn't he take the money? Why hadn't he said twenty thousand, or four, which would be nothing to his family? He called back, but the phone just rang and rang.

Simon sat, his head in his hands. He would call Stella's mother now. Bette had always been polite to him, even though she had a habit of talking about her dead husband, as well as bringing up the names of Stella's old boyfriends, all of them successful. "Mom," Stella always said, a warning in her tone, and she rolled her eyes, but it hurt Simon a little. He wanted Bette to like him, to approve of him and Stella as a couple, and he was never sure that she did. He didn't care what she said to him or how she treated him now. All that mattered was that she come, that she help with Stella, and he knew that she would.

Her voice on the phone sounded as if it were crackling, and when he told her about the coma, she screamed into the phone. "I'm flying in," she cried. "I'll be there tomorrow."

He'd dig out his car so he could pick her up at the airport. He'd make up the bed in the alcove. At least he'd have another person here with him, and that should be a good thing, right?

• • •

BETTE ARRIVED THE next evening, and it stunned Simon to see how old she looked. Her hair was white, cut into a workaday pixie, and she was in track pants and a sweatshirt and wearing none of the jewelry she usually draped herself in. Her face was crinkled, her jawline smudged. She now walked with a cane. Bette, he realized, was nearly eighty.

"Let me hold your arm," she said, and he felt the slight pressure of her weight. "Take me right to her," she said, and he drove to the hospital, neither one of them talking. Finally Simon couldn't stand it any longer, and he began to talk, to tell her what the doctors were doing, how much he loved her daughter. "Do you want to know how it happened?" he said quietly, and she reached over and touched his hand. "I only want to know about her getting well," she said. "There's no need for anything else."

At the hospital, when Bette first saw Stella, she drew in her breath sharply. He expected her to cry, to fall apart, but instead she pulled up a chair and sat beside her daughter. She took Stella's hand. "You're getting better every second," she said quietly. "I'm not leaving until you do, and we know how much you like your privacy." She tried to laugh, but it came out more of a sigh. She began talking quietly, telling Stella family stories that Simon had never heard.

Simon sat listening to the waves of Bette's voice, as if Bette were introducing this sleeping Stella to the old lively one. Then suddenly the stories stopped, and he saw that Bette's eyes were closed. She was asleep. He took her hand and warmed it between his, but she didn't stir. He looked at Stella, who somehow seemed calmer, like she knew her mother was there. "Thank you," he whispered to Bette, even though he knew she couldn't hear him.

SIMON DROVE BETTE to the apartment and helped her settle in. She put her suitcase next to the daybed in the alcove, then sat quietly on the living room couch, knitting. Simon was glad Bette was there. Having another heart beating in the apartment, especially one connected to Stella, comforted him. It would be a reason for him to get up in the morning, to not fall apart. It would make him feel so much better to be able to do something, if not for Stella, then for her mother.

They spent the following day at the hospital, coming home so exhausted that Bette went immediately to sleep. Simon, though, couldn't. It wasn't just that he was so worried about Stella. Tonight was the LA concert. He paced the apartment. All he had to do was shut his eyes, and he was there. He felt the thump of the amps, the sweat on his forehead from the stage lights, and the intoxicating roar of the crowd, the way sometimes, when things quieted, you could hear someone shouting your name, all the outstretched hands shimmying and waving like a field of wheat. He thought of the way Kevin always sashayed toward him on the stage, bending into Simon for harmony, how Rob would wink at him when he wailed. *We're all in this together.*

He was not there with them, but at least he wasn't alone. Instead of the thumps of the amps, he could hear the staccato bursts of Bette's snoring. There weren't any spotlights, but there were streetlights outside. No roar of the crowd, just the same incessant honks of taxis, the squeal of brakes and the shouts of people going by. It was all passing him by. He put his head in his hands.

THE FOLLOWING AFTERNOON, while Bette and Simon were cleaning up after an early dinner, Kevin actually picked up his phone to tell Simon the concert had been outrageous. Kevin was so excited that his words skimmed against one another, but Simon felt numb. Kevin said Rick had introduced them as one of his greatest influences. He had even stepped up and played with them on their last song.

"What, you're not psyched?" Kevin said. There was laughter in the background, the clink of glasses.

"Who's there?"

"Everyone—Ruby, the band, some other guys—a manager, too, I think—maybe I can grab him—"

Simon couldn't concentrate. Kevin's voice seemed to echo, and he gripped his phone harder.

"I'm sorry. I'm just so exhausted," Simon said.

"Well, wake up, buddy, because this is happening and I don't want it to happen without you. When are you coming out here? Rick wants us on the whole leg of the tour!"

"What? He does? He knows I'm still here?"

"Yeah, yeah, sure he knows, and he feels bad. Whenever you can come, come."

What did that look like, he wondered, Rick feeling bad? No one other than Kevin had called him.

"Where's our songs?" he said. "You know that you can pull your weight from the East Coast."

"Kevin," Simon said. He shut his eyes. A headache pounded.

Then there was a jolt of silence. Kevin cleared his throat. "How's Stella?" he said.

"The same."

"Oh, man," Kevin said, his voice trailing, but he didn't offer any help or supply suggestions. Instead, there was just the silence, stretching out like a straight line.

"I'll do what I can," Simon said.

He hung up the phone. Bette was now settled on the couch, knitting something that looked like a blanket out of soft blue yarn. She looked at him but said nothing, and when he didn't say anything about the call, she went back to her knitting. Stella had told him that when Bette designed a dress, she paid attention to every detail, right down to the extra stitching on the hemlines, but this knitting looked uneven, and there was even a hole or two that he could see. Bette must have felt him watching her because she laughed. "Oh, I can do better than this, honey," she said to him. "If I wanted to. This is just Zen. It soothes me to knit, and when I'm done, I'll rip it out and start all over again." She slid the stitches off the needles, balling the yarn. "It calms the mind," she said.

But Simon's mind couldn't calm. He tried to imagine Kevin and the band out there in the sun, or working in the studio, Kevin bossing everyone around as usual. Or maybe that was what Rick did now. Maybe they were all bonding into pals, the age difference nothing because the music was what mattered.

Simon went to the computer and looked up the review of the concert. In the early flush days, the band had gotten reviews, and then they had petered out, but none of them had cared really. Not as long as they still could get gigs, still play in front of people.

As soon as he saw the review, he felt a pull. There was a photo of Rick, triumphant, hands waving toward a huge crowd. Simon scanned:

Opening for Rick Mason were veteran performers Mighty Chondria, whom Rick introduced as "my biggest influence." Though Mighty Chondria haven't been in the foreground of the music scene for years, they proved they can still grab an audience and hold them hostage, especially charismatic front man Rob Cross, who reminded everyone why he was once a major player—and could be again—reprising his old hit, "Charlatan Eyes."

Simon felt nauseated. "Charlatan Eyes" was his song, not Rob's. Simon wasn't mentioned in the article at all. Nor was the bass guitarist they had hired to replace him, but that didn't count. Simon wasn't missed. He shut off the computer. Kevin had told him that Simon could still be a part of the band, writing songs, feeding them material until he could get there himself. But could he?

He picked up his guitar from the corner of the room, but it felt wrong, like he had never played before. G sounded like F. E-flat was now sharp. The notes seemed to have escaped or tricked him. He picked the strings, but he couldn't even manage a simple scale. Everything he had ever written a song about—sex, music, cars, even love—seemed like lousy subjects, unworthy of anything or anyone, and instead of feeling soothed, he wanted to jump out of his skin. He put the guitar back into its case, which was covered with stickers from all the places he had been while touring, all those shiny cities, all the applause and autographs.

He snapped the case shut. Bette looked up at him. "Come on," she said quietly. "Let's you and me take a walk and clear our heads." She chose one of Stella's warmest coats and bundled it around her.

He liked walking with her. They headed down Seventh Avenue to Le Pain, where they had tea, and then back to the apartment again. She didn't comment on how stressed he was or how dire Stella's condition seemed. Instead, she told him how nice it had been to have tea with him, to hear him play his guitar. "I'm glad you have something to occupy you now," she said.

"My band doesn't seem to need me anymore."

"Oh yes they do," she said, and he started, because she had never been so kind to him before, and then he thought, Well maybe she knows that she needs me as much as I need her.

But it wasn't just kindness. Maybe he had misread her before, because she brightened in the morning when she saw him, and it was clear that she genuinely wanted to be with him. "Come on, I'll teach you rummy," she told him, and the two of them sat at the dining room table, her keeping score, playing for hours. She never let him win, and he never let her win, and he liked that. It showed that they each respected the other.

Later that day, Bette went to the hospital with him. She held Stella's hand and told family stories. The stories bolstered him. When Bette stopped talking and began to nod off in her chair, Simon texted one report to all their friends: Stella's the same.

THE FOLLOWING DAY, he was at the hospital without Bette, who was still asleep in the apartment. He walked to Stella's room, and there was Libby in purple scrubs, a red bandanna tied about her hair. She glanced at him.

"You're here again," she said evenly.

"Of course I am."

"You getting everything done that you need to get done? Are you taking care of yourself?"

She was staring at him now. He saw a glittering white stud in her left ear, poking out from the fire of her hair.

"I don't. I just come here."

He thought she was going to tell him again that he should go home, pay the bills, and go to work, that it was important to act normal, even when you didn't feel that way. Instead, her eyes narrowed. "For how long?" she said quietly, and then she walked out of the room.

As soon as she vanished, he felt irritated. How fucking dare she talk to him like that? Like she expected him to be one of those guys who run when there's trouble? Like she knew him? Well, she didn't.

He pulled out a chair and sat next to Stella. Someone had drawn her ringlets into a pineapple at the top of her head, tied with a ribbon. She'd never wear her hair like that in real life. She hated hair decorations or fuss, but the ribbon was what kept him from undoing it. Someone else besides him cared about Stella enough to give her a ribbon, and that had to matter. Her lids fluttered, but with what? Dreams? A simple neurological sensation? "Stella," he said.

A new doctor came in with a clipboard. "Simon Stein?" he asked, and Simon nodded. "Dr. Warren," he said. "I want to talk to you about coma therapy."

"Where's the other doctor? Dr. Marks?"

"Stella has many doctors." He sat down in another chair.

Simon didn't know there was such a thing as coma therapy, but at least there was the word *therapy*, and didn't that indicate getting better? "The evidence is anecdotal, but sometimes patients do come out spontaneously when they smell something familiar, or they hear something familiar. The sooner they do, the better. But there's so much we don't know. Even patients in so-called vegetative states are not vegetables. They're still alive, still communicating in some way."

He nodded encouragingly at Simon. "Would you be willing to try, or do you want to leave it to us?"

Simon felt flushed with nausea. Vegetable. But Dr. Warren hadn't said that was Stella. "No, I want to help."

"Make a lot of noise, talk to her constantly. Time is on our side here." Dr. Warren bent over and pinched Stella so hard that the skin was red when he removed his fingers. "No need to be gentle here." He held up fingers in front of Stella's face. "How many?" he shouted. "How many, Stella!" He grabbed her fingers and ordered her to squeeze them. Stella's fingers flexed and moved. Dr. Warren looked at Simon, and his whole body seemed like a beam of light. "You see that?" he said.

Dr. Warren stood up. "You do it now," he said.

"Stella!" Simon shouted. He felt strange yelling at her, like he was Brando calling for his Stella in *A Streetcar Named Desire*. That hadn't worked on the movie character Stella at the end of the film. And his Stella didn't move.

"Much louder." Dr. Warren nodded encouragingly.

"Stella!" Simon felt as if he were screaming, but Dr. Warren bent close to Stella as if listening to her breathe. He put a hand on her stomach and then he shook his head. "Not this time, but maybe next," he told Simon.

After he left, Simon began talking to Stella. He told Stella about their first date, how much he had wanted her, but he didn't want her to think that that was all he was after, so he hadn't even kissed her but instead had kept his distance. He told her how scared he was about what was going on with the band, how they were moving forward without him, and he didn't know what to do about it. He played "This Little Piggy" on her toes six times, and then he kissed each toe.

HE STAYED AT the hospital all day, taking breaks to call Bette, to grab something to eat in the cafeteria. By the time he left the hospital, it was around midnight. No one ever mentioned visiting hours to him, though he always tensed when he heard the announcements. The staff were all kind to him about that. Good night, they said to him as he left, their faces soft with compassion. *Good night. Good night. Please not goodbye.*

Outside, the air felt and smelled different, like it had been drenched with motor oil. He stretched, exhausted, and then he saw that doctor, Libby, standing outside in front of the hospital, leaning into a guy in a black leather jacket, who was perched on a motorcycle. The guy said something to her that Simon couldn't hear, but it made Libby throw back her head and laugh. The guy handed her an extra helmet and watched her put it on. He helped her onto the bike, and when she threw her arms around his waist, she held on tight, resting her head against him, her mouth curving up, her eyes closing with pleasure.

Simon watched, amazed. It now seemed impossible to Simon that people could have relationships and love, that a thing as simple as laughing and getting on a motorcycle could be anything other than a miracle he had once had and had been too stupid to cherish, too blind to consider it might ever be gone.

3

STELLA FLOATS.

She doesn't have a body, though she knows it's there, apart from her, on this bed. She can hear Simon talking to her, although she can't make out the words. The rise and fall of his voice confuses her. It's rich and almost gravelly, they way it had been when he was in his twenties, when she had first met him and he was still smoking. Allergic to smoke, she had sneezed at his kisses. But he stopped for her.

Simon now says something to her, more urgent, but she can't make out a syllable. *Grr*, it sounds like. A fake kitten growl. *Bzzt*, he says. Like the wings of a fly smashing up against a pane of glass. Even though she can't understand him, his voice soothes her. It's real and known and familiar. Simon. My Simon. She wants to tell him how sorry she is that they argued. She doesn't think he meant it, about their dreams being different. It was the storm raging outside, the wine making them both woozy. It was her cold plugging up her sinuses, and her headache throbbing. They were both so tired. So exhausted.

But how funny. She doesn't have her cold anymore. Here in this place, she isn't aware of her body and its functions. Breathing, sweating, peeing, they all seem part of another life to her, something she used to do but doesn't do any longer. Wave bye-bye, body. Sayonara. The thought of it makes her laugh, makes her glad she still has her sense of humor.

Mostly what she does is smell things. Something sharp like lemon whisks by her nose. Wait, she wants to say. Please wait. But the scent fades and vanishes before she can really lock onto it. She hears sounds, and she perks with interest. Feet pad on the floor. Voices dip and rise and grow silent. She feels an elbow bumping against something hard, but she knows it isn't her elbow, so how could she feel it. She dreams, too, but it isn't so much that she is dreaming as that she feels she is actually there in her dream, dropped down from one place to another. She doesn't bother to wonder why. She isn't certain that there are any answers.

I'm here, she wants to say to Simon. I'm right here. She feels so sorry for him when she hears him crying. She can feel where he is by the heat in the room moving closer to her, warming her. She can hear it, too, little skips in his voice, the loss of control. He's a color, too, a soft gray blue. She knows there is a scientific name for that, that there are people who can hear colors, who can see sounds. *Synesthesia.* The word appears in her head, a surprise memory.

She wants to stroke his hair and tell him it's going to be okay. Don't worry, baby, she thinks, though she's never once called him baby. Don't worry.

He's crying harder. He's not a crier. She's the one who weeps when they argue, who even tears up at the phone commercial in which that college kid calls his parents to tell them he loves them. "I live with a wuss," Simon said, kissing her.

The only other time she had known him to cry was when he invited his parents to Manhattan for a visit to hear him play. Simon had planned a monologue, to introduce his father to the crowd. He was even going to make his dad stand up so his father could be applauded. But his father never showed up, and there, on the stage, Simon's eyes were wet. Everyone but her thought that he was crying because he was feeling the song, the emotion of it.

It stung. But Simon never stopped trying with his dad, and maybe that was part of what she loved about him, his willingness to believe. Back then, Stella had thought they had lots of time. She was sure that whatever was wrong between Simon and his father might work itself out, the same way whatever was wrong between her and Simon would.

She tries to remember Simon's father's name. Michael, she thinks. Fred. Frank. Names swim around in her mind. Ricardo. Henry. None of them feel right. She tries to dig deeper, but she can't find a name.

She isn't afraid right now. That surprises her. To her, being help-less was always the absolute worst. Babies were helpless, but that's not the same. Babies responded to care and love, and helplessness was their natural state. But true helplessness, a lack of power that might go on forever—the patients with locked-in syndrome, the ones who were quadriplegic—that really scared her.

She tries to move and can't. Or maybe she's moving, but it feels totally different to her. She doesn't have limbs. She knows something has happened, although she isn't sure what. Time seems to have gone elastic, stretching like a rubber band, ready to snap at any moment. Whenever she seems to get panicked trying to remember, she falls asleep, or maybe it's not sleep. It's a kind of blankness. She's been erased for a while and then redrawn. When she comes back, she always feels a bit better, though she thinks how nice it would be if she could stretch and shower, hum and brush her hair, and go outside and feel the air on her skin.

She hears Simon playing music to her, the soft acoustic guitar she likes. Simon! She wants to shout to him, to lace her fingers with his, but nothing inside of her moves. She tries to remember the words to the song he's singing, to grab onto the melody so she can sing it to herself later. She can hear he's playing badly, but she doesn't know why except he only plays out of tune when he's upset. She hears her name: Stella. At least she knows that. Wake me up now, she thinks. I'll go on tour. I'll go anywhere. Do anything.

The music stops and she yearns for it to come back. She hears voices again, a ring of them, moving in on her, closer and closer. She wishes she could pull back.

No one knows, someone says. No one knows what, she wonders. The voices blur and then fall away.

Whenever the doctors arrive, her calm leaves her. The energy of the room changes, breaking up. They do things that scare her. They scream at her. She can't move. Her speech is so jammed she can't announce her presence. I'm here. I'm here. Hello, hello, hello.

"God," someone says. She doesn't recognize the voice. Stella stopped believing in God when she was twelve. It wasn't a difficult decision. Back then, her parents worshipped only each other. They called each other five times a day. Stella couldn't remember being taken to the zoo just by one parent, or to the beach; even when a story was read to her, it was always both of them. One night, she had heard them talking and her mother calmly said that having Stella had been a mistake, and when her father didn't jump right in and tell her she was wrong, Stella froze. "I mean, I love her," Stella's mother had said. "I'm so glad she's here, but think how much easier things might be." Stella, terrified, wondered if any moment she might just die and go to heaven, and if so, what would that be like? The next morning, she made the mistake of asking her mother where heaven was, and her mother laughed and said, "Heaven is your father."

All Stella could think was that heaven didn't include her.

God, she thought, was like the Easter Bunny, a precious dream people needed to make them feel more hopeful, but now, like any-one caught in a muddle, she prays. Dear God, get me out of this. Whatever it is. Rescue me. She prays to Simon, but what she wants from him is simple. Don't leave me.

"Stella." She hears her name again. A different voice this time. A smell: L'Air du Temps. Her mother's perfume. Mom. Mom. Mommy. She feels a rush of need. And then the scent fades. Her mother's in Spain. Or is she? Mom. Does her mom need her? Stella had gone into nursing because of all the need she saw in the world, because she could be the one to take care of it.

Sometimes she panics. Right now, for example, her mind goes numb with terror. This can't be happening. This isn't real. I have to get out of here. It's as if this crazy state was the real world and everything she had lived before was a fake world. She feels like she is in a TV show, like she is wrapped in layers of cotton. There's an audience, the rustle of arms and legs and paper, the blur of conversation. A soundtrack of beeps. She doesn't know how, but she'll get out.

What happened to her? When did it happen? She remembers only shards. She had a cold. She took a Sudafed. One. Two. Did she take two? She remembers Simon was going to tell her something important.

Something shifts. It takes a moment, but Stella realizes that she is being turned on her side, that something is being done to her and she has no idea what.

Stella wants to communicate with the people around her, but she doesn't know how. She has different senses now. Simon comes close to her and leans his forehead against her, the way he used to. Mind melding, he called it, a trick he got from *Star Trek*. She's Spock to his Kirk, or maybe it's the other way around. When he used to do it, she never really knew what he was thinking, but he always wanted her to guess. Blue, she said. Green. Sometimes, just because of the law of averages, she'd get it right. He moves away, giving her room to feel his panic, his love, his gargantuan need for her. Good, she thinks, good. Because the truth is she's afraid of being alone. She's always been afraid.

"Stella." She hears her name, but she can't respond. She doesn't know who is talking to her now, who's calling for her. She's pinwheeling away. She smells Simon's hair and she wants to touch it, but she can't lift her hand. Something is brushing against her skin, something soft.

Something is floating, and then she realizes, once again, it's her.

4

SIMON MARKED OFF EVERY day on a calendar at home until February was all Xed out. How could time be moving so slowly and at the same time so fast? Every time he had to cross out another date, he felt sick with fear.

He came to the hospital every day. Sometimes friends of Stella's would show up. Martin brought two different kinds of perfumes to swish under Stella's nose, Opium and something called Nasty Girl, but she didn't react, and Martin deflated until he realized he could give them to his girlfriend, who had suggested them in the first place. Joyce came in with a bag of makeup.

"Joyce—" Simon said, moving to stop her, but she shook her head vigorously. "She'll know she has it on. It will make her feel better," Joyce insisted. "Plus, if she looks better, the doctors will pay more attention to her." Simon had his doubts about that, but he watched Joyce carefully applying something tawny to Stella's lids, lip gloss to her mouth. "At the very least, it will keep her lips from chapping," Joyce said. Joyce took out a wide-toothed comb and carefully ran it through Stella's hair. "My beautiful friend," she said, then burst into tears. Simon held her for a moment until she stopped. Joyce stuffed everything into the end table drawer. "If they wash it off, you can always put it back on," she said, and then she left.

Libby was nearly always there when Simon arrived. Sometimes she was taking Stella's vitals, but a few tines he came in and Libby was sitting beside Stella, quietly stroking her arms, her legs, saying something he couldn't hear, and when Libby saw Simon, she frowned. Well, too bad for her, he thought. Why was she acting like this was her private conversation with Stella?

"I'm her friend as well as her doctor," Libby said, reading his mind. "Having someone who cares for you caring for you helps recovery." She narrowed her eyes at him when she said it. Friend. He didn't know that.

The other doctors were noncommittal. "It's too soon," they told him. Simon sat beside Stella and played her favorite songs over and over, degrading his fancy note work with strums, because who knew what her brain could process? It was so different from singing for an audience. She never reacted, never moved, but he told himself that maybe inside her mind she was dancing, and that made him continue.

He was tired when he left the hospital, but when he got home, he couldn't sit still. Bette was already asleep, but she had left him a note telling him that she'd made him dinner. It was in the fridge and all he had to do was heat it up. Her kindness bolstered him and made him feel hopeful. Then he saw all the bills, most of them overdue, stacked on the kitchen table. Rent. Electric. Gas. Car payment. All things that Stella, with her methodical mind, used to take care of.

This couldn't be his life. It just couldn't be.

He put on his coat to go out for a walk. He headed downtown, into SoHo. The streets were still full of people. Was it Friday? Saturday? Date night? Everyone looked younger than he did, happy and laughing. Manhattan tightened like a cage and he had no idea how to wrestle open the bars. He couldn't remember the grid of the city. He walked west when he meant to go east, and then he had to backtrack. Everyone seemed to be walking in the opposite direction from him, and he kept bumping into people, even though he tried his best not to. He couldn't focus, and every time a red light or even a person blocked his forward progress, he felt enraged because he had to keep going. He just had to. He had to do something, but what? They needed money, but he didn't know what to do about it. There was disability from Stella's job. Maybe he could put a song online. Maybe he could sell a song and his band could pay him. Maybe he'd get lucky and a national commercial would want to feature one of his tunes.

And maybe pigs could fly.

He used to be able to write a song in a half hour, and sometimes that same night the band would play it. When he picked up his guitar now, his mind slammed shut. The words that used to fill his head, the riffs of melody that made him shut his eyes and breathe deeply, now came in drips, and his singing voice didn't sound like his anymore. A happy song, a sad one—they all seemed the same, and that wasn't good. His speaking voice was different, restrained and stiff; something caught in his throat.

He walked all the way to Wall Street and then all the way back to the apartment, and he still wasn't tired. He sat at the table, putting his head in his hands. He used to write music every day. He used to practice with the band five nights a week, sometimes more, working out of a cramped little practice space in an old factory over in Hell's Kitchen.

He jumped up from the couch, searching for his favorite guitar, an acoustic steel-stringed Martin, one of the first he had bought.

He swallowed. Panic rose in his throat. Well, he was stressed. Maybe he could write about that, just to get things going. Just to start himself up. He grabbed a notebook and a pen. He sat down, pushing his hair back. He wrote Mighty Chondria's first hit in the back of a touring bus. The other band members were asleep, and Stella was there, reading by flashlight, quietly turning the pages. The words had come easily. Back then, he wrote songs in his head no matter where he was. Everywhere, anyplace, was a song.

He lifted the pen now. He felt like Jack Nicholson in *The Shining*, writing the same thing over and over: *All work and no play makes*

Jack a dull boy. He couldn't think of a thing. Concentrate. Dig deeper. Start with a line. That's all he needed. One line that he could build on. Something cryptic. Something so real that you couldn't deny it. He swallowed and something bitter rose up in his throat.

Stella lies in a white, white bed, he wrote, and then crumpled up the paper. Crap. It was crap. It made him feel sick to write it.

Maybe, baby, I killed you, he wrote, and a laugh spiraled up into his body. He put his hands over his face. Take this pill, he had said, and she did. Write what feels true. Write from the bone. *Maybe, baby, you'll die. Maybe, Simon, your father is right.* He heaved with deep, cutting sobs. He pushed the paper off the table. He put the guitar on the floor.

If he couldn't sing, if he couldn't play, then who was he? Then what would he do with his life?

He put away his guitar and rested his head in his hands. He had a BA in music, but what kind of job would that get him that would pay? Really pay? He knew musicians who had other jobs. He knew a sax player who worked in the mailroom of a company. Another waited tables and wrote advertising copy, and Simon had worked with a drummer who was a personal trainer who went to clients' houses and showed them how to flatten their stomachs, all the while pretending he cared about what he was doing. Even worse, this guy had to exercise like crazy himself, because who would hire a personal trainer who was flabby and couldn't do a sit-up or six? Everyone had extra jobs.

And he had to get something that brought in money.

Well. You could do anything for a while if you had to. And in the meantime, he had to push aside his pride.

Bette was always offering money to him, but he knew she was on a fixed income now. He couldn't take anything from her, and despite the bills, he didn't want her knowing what dire straits he was in.

He glanced at the clock. How did it get to be six in the morning? How had that happened?

• • •

A FEW DAYS later, on a bright Thursday morning, Simon stood in front of his car, waiting for his Lyft mentor session so he could be a driver. "Oh, honey," Bette had said when he told her he had to work. "You know I wish I could help."

"You are helping," he said. "More than you know."

But now his stomach roiled. This was the last thing he wanted to do, but he wasn't equipped to do anything else, and no one could say he hadn't tried. He wasn't even able to get wedding work, which everyone considered the absolute scum-of-the-earth job for musicians. He had asked all his friends for leads. He had begged, until a drummer friend recommended that he drive for Lyft, told him how you could drive whenever you wanted, make as much or as little as you felt like. Simon had the car, and though it wasn't in the greatest shape, it could still get people where they needed to go. He had the license, even the background check, and now all he had to do was an hour session with an experienced driver. "Hey, it's just temporary," the drummer told him, something Simon kept telling himself like a mantra.

A guy wearing a baseball cap walked up to him. "You Simon?" he said, holding out his hand. "Ronnie."

His eyes glided over Simon. "Listen, a word," he said. "I know this is just you and me here, but when you start driving for real, you might want to spiff up your look."

"What?" Simon said. He was dressed in a black T-shirt, his black jeans. What was spiffier than that?

"Collared shirt," Ronnie said. "No bare feet, no bare chest, nothing political or objectionable, and take a shower every once in a while."

Simon stared at him, astonished.

"Well, let's go on our mandatory Welcome Drive," Ronnie said, climbing into the car's backseat. "Go to East Ninety-Sixth."

The whole time Simon was driving, he felt Ronnie's eyes boring into his back, watching what he was doing. "Make conversation," Ronnie said. "Riders sometimes like that. If they like you, they'll tip you more. We aren't supposed to take tips, but take them anyway."

Simon cleared his throat. "So, how about those Yankees?"

"You can do better than that."

"You like music?" Simon said, clicking on the radio.

"Better," Ronnie said. He stretched out his arms in the backseat, nodding his head to the music. He began to tell Simon all the secrets. Carry paper bags, or even better, plastic ones in case a rider vomits and you can't pull over to the side of the road. "Tell Lyft and they can make the rider pay for the cleaning of your car."

"Excuse me?" Simon said.

"And no cologne. Always clean socks. And watch your dental hygiene. We've had complaints about some of the drivers. Good to keep breath mints or those breath strips around. No smoking of anything. Don't eat in the car either. I don't care how much more money you could make driving while eating, don't do it. Food smells irritate people. Take ten minutes and get yourself a sandwich, and eat it outside the car. And no cell phones for you either, except to take passenger calls. Passengers can yap on them all they want, but you concentrate on the driving."

Simon was offended, but Ronnie kept running down the rules. You couldn't turn someone down just because they were black or Hispanic or any group you personally didn't like very much. You were rated and sometimes customers were just mean, but you could rate them, too.

Ronnie looked Simon up and down. "You got any aptitude for customer service?" he asked.

"I can be nice," Simon said. *I've pleased ten thousand fans with just two notes.*

"You have to do better than just nice. Help people with their baggage if you go to the airport. If someone can't see or hear or has a cane, you get out of the car and guide him." Simon thought of all the tours he had been on where the roadies had carried his equipment and his luggage, where hotel staff couldn't wait to take his bags. He thought of all the special orders the band made. Sparkling water in a cup, not a glass. M&Ms with the blue ones picked out. A single rose in a black vase. All this just because they could.

Ronnie squinted at Simon. "You allergic to dogs? Cats?"

Simon shook his head.

"Good. Because you'll get plenty of them, especially in Manhattan. Not just seeing-eye dogs, but all kinds. People don't like to take their pets on the subway, especially if they're sick. Birds, reptiles, tarantulas, iguanas—they don't care, they'll bring them into your car and you have to deal with it, the poop, the noise. And, you know, you can make thirty-five dollars an hour, fifty-five after ten at night. Any questions?"

Simon had a million, like why was he being treated like an idiot? And how long before things went back to normal and Stella was fine again? His heart felt as if it were swimming in his chest. He swallowed. "No," he said. "No questions."

"Make a right here," Ronnie said. "No sense going all the way up to the Upper East Side. You can drop me here." He winked at Simon. "You're good to go," he said.

GOD, BUT IT was humbling being a driver. He was driving his car, but when he had passengers, somehow it transformed into being their car. They got to tell him what route to take, even when his GPS said otherwise. They got to tell him when to stop, when to go. Sometimes people didn't say a word to him or even acknowledge his presence. No, he was their self-driving car. They left the same way. They got on their cells and spoke loudly about all their personal problems, not caring that Simon was right there, listening. Even though most of his riders ignored him, he still wanted to make sure everyone knew he was something other than a Lyft driver. But none of his passengers seemed to care or even want to talk with him.

He began to love the long stretches when it was just him in the car. He loved the routine. At home, he couldn't seem to write a note, but somehow, here in this car, words struggled up, melodies sprang, so insistent that he sometimes pulled over to write them down. He wrote a song about Stella, about what she might be thinking. He wrote about how Manhattan didn't seem like such a big friendly cat anymore but had become a dog, itching to bite. When he got home, he called Kevin. "Hey, I got songs," he said. He was so excited that he didn't notice that Kevin sounded different.

"Oh, cool, well, you can send them to us," Kevin said.

Simon started to tell him that these were deeper, better songs, that he was getting that old spark again, when Kevin cleared his throat.

"Listen," Kevin said. "I have to tell you something. We've got a new manager. Rick introduced us."

"What?" Simon gripped the phone against his ear. Could this be happening? "Oh my God, I knew something good would come out of this. I knew it."

He heard Kevin swallow. "Wait, wait, who is he?" Simon asked.

"Jon Merkowski."

Simon grew still, his breath stopped. He knew that name, knew that Jon had broken out singers and bands, had changed lives with a single deal. Simon's eyes pooled, and then he started to laugh out loud. He was so giddy that he couldn't speak, couldn't get anything out except Kevin's name, like he was praying to some God.

"Kevin," he said gratefully. "Kevin. Kevin."

"He's good," Kevin said slowly. "And he hired us a new guy. Fresh blood. The bassist we hired to stand in for you didn't work out, but God, this new guy? The girls got screamy."

Simon heard Kevin swallow again. "Yeah, the guy writes songs, too. And he can play bass," Kevin said.

"Good, good, so we're covered for now—with a stand-in."

"Simon," Kevin said sharply. "You're hearing me, but you're not listening. He's hired, man. He's a part of the band now."

Simon sat down. A leak had sprung in his body, deflating him. He tried to say something, but he couldn't move.

"I stuck up for you," Kevin said. "You have to believe that. We all did. But we were damned whatever we did. If we said no, we'd lose the deal. And if we said yes, we'd lose you."

Simon pressed his fingers to his eyes. "Rick Mason know about this?"

"He knows," Kevin says. "And now you know, too."

"What's his number? Rick's number? I want to hear it from him."

"I can't give you that. You know I can't. And we're his opening act—it doesn't mean we're his band."

"I want to talk to him." Simon felt the desperation rising in his body. "He loved my songs. He said I was an influence. Maybe he has an idea for me, too. You give me his goddamn number."

The noise behind Kevin seemed to grow louder. "Look," Kevin said. "I can't just give out Rick's number. You know that. And this isn't goodbye. You can still send the songs. We'll—"

"Fuck you," Simon said, and he hung up.

ALL THAT NIGHT, he drove around, fuming, ignoring calls coming in for rides. He went out of Manhattan and kept going all the way up to New Hampshire when a bit of reality struck him. He wasn't glued to Mighty Chondria. If they didn't want him, then maybe he didn't want them either. Maybe it was time for him to really move on. Why couldn't he make up a demo of his songs, send them to some labels? He had at least that clout, didn't he, to get a listen? He had a makeshift studio at home. He could put up a website, put his own music up there. He knew labels didn't expect perfection, that whatever he recorded certainly wouldn't be release ready. He'd have to add on multitracks, other vocals, and even then, it would be raw. Just thinking about it made him feel better. He U-turned on the highway and started home.

It took Simon two weeks to make his demo. He worked on it early in the morning, before he drove the Lyft, before he went to the hospital with Bette. He was relieved that she didn't ask him what he was doing, that the only thing she said to him was "Sounds terrific in there," and for that, he was grateful.

As soon as he came home each night, he began to play. And then when he was finished, he couldn't move. It wasn't that he didn't think it was good—it was—or that he didn't think he could get someone to listen to it. It was that nagging fear, what if it wasn't good enough?

"Hey, Bette," he said. She was sitting on the couch, still knitting. He knew she had heard him playing through the bedroom door, but he wanted her to talk about it now, to tell him how the music made her feel. "Would you take a listen?" he asked.

She put the knitting down. "There's not a thing I'd rather do," she said.

He played his song for her. He watched her face because he knew people said things to make you feel better, but the body didn't lie. She nodded her head in time. She tilted her head. "Stella was right," she said when he finished. "You have such talent."

He flushed, pleased. "You make me feel like I can do this."

"You can," she said. "I know you can."

HE KEPT THE demo on his phone. Some nights, he played it for himself, just to gauge if it really was as good as he hoped it was. But hearing it, feeling that swell of pride didn't always make him feel better. What if he'd had his shot and blown it? Everyone got one shot, and maybe he had wasted his. One night when his music was playing in the car, he picked up four young girls in party dresses in Times Square. They crammed into the backseat, all perfumed and giggling, four different shades of long blonde manes. They glanced at Simon and then quickly looked away, ignoring him, flipping their hair, which made him feel weird. It used to be that he couldn't walk

down the street without being recognized, women giving him inviting looks, those lowered glances, that toss of hair. He slipped a look
at himself in the mirror. He looked like shit. He had dark circles like
bruises under his eyes, and even though he wore his hair long, the
shine was gone, and it was in bad need of a trim.

"Bill is fucking hot," one girl said. "I'd tap him in a heartbeat."

The girls talked about a party they were going to, one that Bill
would be sure to attend, and then "Beautiful Baby" came on the
demo. Jesus, it sounded good, didn't it? He sounded good. He had
written this song when he had first met Stella, when he had been so
crazy in love with her, he couldn't eat or sleep.

He glanced in his rearview mirror. The girls were listening. His
whole body seemed flooded with joy, and he debated whether he
should say something or not.

One of the girls rustled in her dress. "God, that song is so cheesy,
it needs some kind of crackers," she said, laughing.

Simon's smile faded.

"Yeah, can you shut that off?" a higher, lighter voice said to
Simon. "We just want to talk."

He did, and no one said anything to him for the rest of the ride.

IT WAS ALMOST four in the morning when Simon stopped by
the hospital. He sat by Stella's bed, watching her chest rise and fall
with her breath, and then he left to grab a few hours of sleep and
then drive again. That would be his life now, watching her, sleeping,
and driving.

He walked outside into the cold, clear light, and then he heard
someone sigh and he turned. Libby was standing by the side of the
hospital, anxiously checking her phone. Her eyes were swollen and
red. He looked at her amazed.

"Hey," he said as she swiped at her eyes. "Libby," he said, and she
startled, seeing him.

"You," she said. She reached for a tissue in her purse and daubed at her nose.

"Are you okay? What's wrong?" he said, but she shook her head. "Anything I can do?" He bet it was that boyfriend on the motorcycle, the guy who had made her laugh before and now he had probably made her cry. Still, how wonderful to be able to have that. A fight. A lover. A makeup session with brilliant sex. What he'd give for that. Hello, where have you been. I've missed you. Hello, hello. Hello.

"My cab didn't show," she said. He knew it was a lie. You mean your motorcycle, he thought.

"I'll drive you home," he said.

"You don't have to do that."

"Come on. It's no trouble."

She nodded and followed him to the car, slinking down in the front seat. "Put on your seatbelt," he said, and she sighed and buckled up, and then he saw her lower lip tremble.

"I live at 416 Gramercy Park North," she said. She stared out the window, away from him. "I know it's close enough, but I'm too exhausted to walk," she said.

"Sure you don't want to talk?"

"It won't help," she said. She stared down at her lap.

"So you've been at the hospital less," she said finally.

"I still come every day," he said. "But I've been working."

She looked at him with new interest. "Doing what?"

He nodded at the car. "This is a Lyft car now."

"Is this a joke?"

"I need to work. This lets me."

"You like it?"

"It's a job. It's money. It relaxes me."

"Good. That's responsible." She nodded at him. "Stella used to talk about you all the time, you know."

Simon turned the wheel and headed down another street. "What? She did?"

"We were friends. Good friends. I told you that before. You didn't really know that, did you? You don't remember meeting me when Stella was well?"

He heard the doubt in her voice. Other than her having seemed vaguely familiar, he couldn't recall anything about her. But why not? Why hadn't he known more about Stella's life? "Sure, I knew it," he said.

"You didn't know it, right?" Libby said. "I'm not accusing you. I'm just curious."

"What did she say about me?" Simon said.

"She said you were like a kid, that you weren't always responsible. She said you lacked balance, but it didn't matter because she was balanced enough for the two of you."

"Stella said that?" He looked at Libby. Her chin tilted up. "She said lots of things," Libby said. "She loved you."

"I love her." He felt it, a pull.

"I'm so tired," Libby said. "Today I forgot where my stethoscope was and it was around my neck." She rubbed her shoulders. He glanced at her again. The skin under her eyes was faintly purple, like a stain. Her lips were chapped, and she was biting them. "Ever forget whether you ate or not?" she said.

"All the goddamn time," he said. "But then again, I have no appetite anymore."

"Sometimes I do," she said. "Only sometimes. And sometimes I just want junk, which is even worse than not eating at all."

"Are you in a hurry?"

"What? Why?" She glanced at her watch.

He turned onto a street. "Just a moment," he said, pulling the car to the street side. "Be right back."

"Please don't take long."

He parked the car and ran into a bodega. He knew what it was like, no sleep and all that worry clouded over you. He roamed the aisles full of crappy cookies and oversalted pretzels, and then he finally came out with a cup of tea and a package of whole-wheat cheese crackers for her, which seemed like the most nutritious thing the store had. This gesture had seemed like such a good idea, but as he approached the car, he began to wonder, because she had a funny look on her face. He handed her the cup of tea. "For you," he said, and then she looked surprised.

"You seem like the Earl Grey type, so that's what I got." He gave her the crackers. "It's not that bad for you," he told her, and she laughed.

"I thought you were stopping for yourself," she said.

"Doing this is for me," he said.

"Well, this food is exactly what I want," she said quietly. He watched her sip the tea. "Why did you really do this?" she asked. "The ride. The tea?"

"Sometimes you act like you don't like me," he said. "I wanted you to know that I'm not a monster."

"I didn't say you were," she said.

"You think I don't go over there day after day? You think I don't wish I could undo everything?"

"I don't know what to think. All I know is that in all the time I've known Stella, I've never seen her drunk. Some of the nurses, the doctors, boost pills, but never Stella. She wasn't that kind."

"You think I made her that kind?"

"She would have done anything for you," Libby said quietly.

She nibbled the cracker, holding one hand underneath so she wouldn't get crumbs in his car. She offered him one, and he shook his head. "No appetite," he said.

"You have to eat," she said. "Come on. You made me, now I'm making you." She handed him a cracker and he bit into it, all salt and sweet against his tongue.

She drained her tea and they polished off the crackers. Her edges seemed to have softened. Her hands relaxed. She stretched. "Ready to go?" he said, and she nodded so he pulled out of the space.

When he dropped her off, he waited as she got out of the car and walked to the front of her apartment. She turned as she put the key in the lock, watching him for a moment as if trying to figure him out, and he didn't leave until he knew she was safely inside.

5

FRIDAY NIGHT AND LIBBY was trying to grab some sleep on a
cot in the hospital's residence room. The sheets smelled like sweat,
exhaustion, and despair; the room, like stale coffee. But she was used
to it. She was supposed to rest, but she kept thinking about Stella.
Doctors weren't supposed to treat family, and Libby considered Stella
that. There was a code of ethics, and Libby was blurring the lines, but
how could she not be one of Stella's doctors?

Stella would get well. Libby would try to do everything she could
to make sure of it. Still, she couldn't help sometimes feeling afraid,
because what if Stella didn't recover? What if she stayed in coma for
years?

Libby sat up. Stop, she told herself. Don't go there.

Libby was fierce. She knew some of the other doctors called her
Doctor No behind her back because she could be so insistent. Well,
she had studied harder than anyone to be an internist, to make sure
she was the most excellent doctor she could be. Back then, she had
always positioned herself in front during rounds, so she could make
herself noticed. So she could take in everything that she needed to
learn. And when she had finally become a doctor, when she had taken
this job, she still faced obstacles, even though you'd think that people
would be over that by now. Patients thought that because she was a

woman, she must be a nurse. "I want a real doctor," they told her, and Libby bristled. One patient actually waved her away, and even when a male doctor came in and explained that Libby was a respected physician, the patient frowned and refused Libby's help. Once, on a plane, she had seen a man crumple from an asthma attack. She unbuckled her seatbelt and rushed to his side, calling out to the flight attendants to get the inhaler she knew they kept on hand. A man jumped up. "I'm a paramedic!" he said.

"Yeah, well, I'm a doctor," Libby snapped, but the flight attendant, a lean young woman with a face like a wolf, had taken her arm and pulled her away. "Let him do his work," she said.

Him. That was always the pronoun. Always *he, his, him.* She felt tolerated by the male doctors at the hospital, double-checked when she was on call for their patients, flirted with or ignored when she wasn't, and it pissed her off and she let people know it.

She knew that all the nurses were afraid of her. She had one nurse fired for giving the wrong dose of meds to a patient, who went into cardiac arrest. Everyone had acted fast, and the patient was fine, but Libby couldn't forget it. She chewed out other nurses for not flushing an IV line quickly enough, for not checking a catheter, and even for not changing the linens quickly enough when a patient was lying in her own sick. Everyone had to be as careful, methodical, and quick as Libby was.

Years ago, Stella had been among the new crop of nurses, all of them anxious, eager to please, terrified they would make a mistake that might cost a life. But when Stella was on rounds with her, she kept asking questions. Why did Libby think that patient had diabetes? Why did she put in a line that way? Stella kept prodding her until one day Stella demanded to know why Libby gave a patient a Valium to relax instead of a Xanax, and Libby suddenly wasn't so happy. "Are you questioning my judgment?" Libby said in a steely voice. Stella gazed at her calmly, not backing down. "I want to learn," Stella said. "And I want to learn from you because you're the best."

Libby had been taken aback by the declaration. Stella walked away and instantly Libby felt guilty. Most of the nurses were so busy that it was all they could do to make their rounds, let alone learn more. That evening, she spotted Stella eating alone in the cafeteria, looking so tired that she was barely managing to hold up her fork, so Libby got a tray and approached her table and sat down. Stella looked at her, blinking. "You go ahead and keep asking questions," Libby said. "And I'll keep answering them."

Stella gave her a sleepy smile, letting her fork clatter to the table. "Deal," she said.

Libby began to depend on Stella. Stella's was the call she was glad to get in the middle of the night because Stella knew what to ask her about a patient, what to recommend. She could count on Stella to follow her orders, to know the signs of a problem. Gradually they began to eat together whenever they could. They began to talk about medicine and then, slowly, about their lives.

It was a huge relief for Libby to have a friend. Doctors didn't have much of a social life. And how could they? There was too much to do, too much to worry about. She had canceled plans on her friends so often that they knew when she accepted an invitation to some event or dinner, she might or might not show up. Dates were often a disaster because just when things were getting interesting, Libby was called back to the hospital. But Stella was at the hospital almost as much as Libby was, even though Stella had a longtime partner.

Libby liked Stella, but she couldn't understand Stella's choice of Simon. She listened to Stella talk about him, his rock-star aspirations, how tired she was of his irregular schedule, and how much she wanted a baby, a home, maybe even some time for herself. "Maybe you both need to rethink this," Libby said. She worried about Stella more and more. She didn't think it was wise when Stella took off two years to tour with him, but she was thrilled when Stella came back to work. Unfortunately, though, Stella was still with Simon, and she was besotted. Libby wanted to make her see all the reasons why she shouldn't be with Simon, but Stella's love for this guy was palpable. Stella told her that Simon was sweet and funny. He was creative and wrote songs for her. He loved her and told her so. They had marathon conversations. But why, Libby wanted to ask. Why, why, why? Why not a guy who kept regular hours and could be depended on more? Why not a guy who wasn't hung up on something as transient as fame? Libby felt protective of Stella. She didn't want her wasting her time with someone who wasn't worth her.

"You'll meet him," Stella said. "You'll see."

But the first time Libby had met Simon—a meeting he hadn't even remembered, and what did that say about him that he didn't recall being introduced to Stella's best friend—she hadn't liked him on sight. He swaggered in, a denim jacket slung open, his jeans artfully ripped at the knees. All that black, too—T-shirt, jeans, sneakers, hair—like a uniform. She didn't like that he came in eating a sandwich and didn't have an extra one for Stella. Didn't even offer her a bite. And she didn't like how he had interrupted Stella's stories to showcase his own. Rude, she thought. Just plain rude.

When Stella tried to get them all together for dinner, or invited Libby over to their apartment, Libby found excuses. It was Stella she wanted to see, alone at a coffee shop or in the hospital. She was polite to Simon only because Stella was her friend and Libby loved her.

She knew she wasn't one to talk, not with her own sorry romantic history. Her love life was pathetic when you thought about it, made up mostly of quick, unsatisfying trysts in a laundry closet or a few dates that never went anywhere because she was always on call, always thinking about her patients' well-being over her own.

Getting up from the cot, she shucked off her scrubs and pulled on her street clothes. After work, she was supposed to meet Ben, the guy she had been seeing for the past two months. And she liked him, so that made her more stressed.

Ben was an elementary-school teacher who rode a motorcycle. She had met him when he was visiting one of his former students in the hospital, a seventeen-year-old boy who had a kidney infection. She liked that he visited, that he made jokes with the kid, who was jokey back. Being in a good mood made patients get better faster. She liked his pale blue eyes, and when he last visited the teen, the day before he was discharged, Ben turned to her and said, "Come to dinner with me."

"Okay, I will," she told him.

She liked, too, that he didn't push her. He didn't ask her to come to his place right away or to go to hers. Instead, they went out to eat or sat in cafes after seeing movies. When she finally decided he could come to her apartment, he did nothing more than kiss her good night. The less he moved toward her, the more she wanted him. It was another week before they slept together, at his place, a one-bedroom on the Lower East Side. He made her dinner, salmon and green beans. He insisted on doing all the cleanup, and then he took her by the hand and led her into his bedroom. He was so gentle with her, so careful, that she found herself falling for him.

Leaving the hospital, she grabbed a cab to shoot downtown to a cafe they liked. She knew Ben would be there ahead of her because he was always early, and sure enough, there he was in the corner. She felt herself glowing with happiness.

But when she got to the table, she could tell something was off. Ben looked doped up. He was sweating, and his pupils were unnaturally large. She sat down opposite him and took his hands, startled at how clammy they were. "What's going on?" she said.

He turned his head away from her. "Nothing," he said, but she could sense he was lying.

"Are you sick?" she asked.

"No, of course not. Stop looking at me like a doctor."

"But that's what I am." She studied him. "Are you on something?" she asked.

He narrowed his eyes. "Really? You're asking me that seriously?"

She grabbed both his hands and rubbed them. "I care about you," she said.

He took his hand from her. "Look," he said, "my principal's been up my ass at work. Some parents complained that I was getting too political in class, said that wasn't my mission. I got a warning, an actual warning, in my file, too. I was so nervous about that, I went to a doctor to get something to relax."

Libby let go of his hands.

"I'm stressed, okay?"

She kept quiet, knowing that sometimes people revealed things if you gave them room. She'd seen it with patients, like diabetics who insisted they watched their diet and then would gradually admit they had eaten half of a cake the day before.

"The doctor said the pill was mild, that it would just calm me down, make me feel more like myself."

Libby didn't like the way doctors handed out tranquilizers like paper clips, something to hold you together for just a while. "What something did he give you?" she said.

"Just a little Klonopin."

"Klonopin," she said carefully. People got addicted to that. It could take months to get off it. "How little?" she said.

"Come on, Libby. A baby dose, .05 milligram. And I'm not abusing it. Believe me."

She wanted to believe him. She knew that .05 milligram wasn't a high dose, but still. She had seen patients who thought that their small doses worked pretty well, but why not just boost it up a notch, see if that worked a little better? Then they got used to that little more, and then a little more, and they got addicted. She didn't want that happening with Ben. She wouldn't let it.

She yearned for their relationship to turn into something solid and lasting, and she knew that drugs couldn't be a part of it. Maybe, she told herself, it was because of all the junkies she saw in the hospital, all the people who came in with fake stories, because they wanted drugs. Too, there were all the stories Stella had told her about Simon's drug days. "You're sure?" she said.

"Will you stop?' he snapped. "You want to call my doctor and talk to him?"

She did, but she knew he'd get angrier if she asked for the doctor's name.

"I'm tired and overworked and that's all. Don't do this," he warned. "Don't muck things up for us," and then he took her hand and kissed it, and things seemed fine again.

That night, she took him home. As soon as they got in the door, he was undoing her buttons, sliding her out of her skirt, guiding her to the bed. She kissed him, shutting her eyes, trying to be more in the moment, but she kept thinking about whether or not Ben was hooked on drugs. She would talk to him about it again, she thought, later, when they bathed in afterglow. Or maybe she'd ask one of his friends whom she'd met, friends who all seemed straight as rulers, if they thought Ben had a drug problem. She'd be so subtle. She'd make them promise not to tell Ben a thing. *I'm just trying to help. I'm just concerned. It's all done totally out of love.*

"Kiss me harder," Ben said, drawing her closer, and she did. He slammed his body closer to hers.

She did what he said. Move here. Do this. Do that. Then he made a cry and rolled over, and she lay on her back, blinking back tears, still rigid with desire.

There she was, the perfect doctor. The perfect girlfriend.

She heard his soft snore. She had to face it. She had never been good with love. Ever since she was a child, when she had learned that the heart was a lying little faucet and any minute it could shut off, and there she'd be, bereft.

6

LIBBY STOPPED BELIEVING IN love when she was fourteen, and her little brother, Richie, died. They lived in Waltham, a suburb of Boston, and Richie was clearly the golden boy, reading when he was three, skipping grades so that even though he was three years younger than Libby, he was only a year behind her in school.

Back then, Libby had no idea what she wanted to be when she grew up—a dancer, though she couldn't really dance? a movie star who would stand out because of her red hair?—but Richie had always known that he was going to be a doctor.

Libby adored him, but she couldn't ignore the helpless, gnawing jealousy she felt. Her parents were always bragging about Richie to everyone, how smart he was, how he was going to be this great doctor, and when they mentioned Libby, it was like an afterthought, like they were saying, "Oh, wait a minute, yes, Libby's good, too." They didn't look at Libby the same way that they did Richie, their whole bodies seeming to turn to him as if he were the sun.

Richie's death on a blistering hot summer day was Libby's fault. She had talked him into going with her to the Millers on Greer Street because they had a pool, and even though there was a lock on the gate, she could always hoist Richie up and over and manage, with a little more effort, to scramble over the gate herself. They got to the pool, and to Libby's delight, she saw the lock on the gate was broken, hanging on its hinges. It was a sign! As they shucked off their shorts, Richie showed her a quartz stone he had in his pocket, a talisman that he said he was going to carry with him every day when he became a doctor.

It was Libby's idea to urge Richie to dive off the board. "Go ahead, show-off," Libby said. She'd never get up there herself, but Richie climbed and bounced on the board, and the last thing she saw of him was his perfect smile focused on her even as he made a perfect slice into the water.

And then, she saw it. A scribble of red in the water, Richie floating up, crumpled like a comma on the surface of the pool, blood unspooling from him. She grabbed his arm and yanked him up to the edge of the pool, her whole body shaking. Libby laid him flat on the cement and hysterically did the CPR that Richie had insisted on teaching her last year, and when Richie didn't move, she screamed and screamed for help.

THE COPS AND Libby's parents never actually blamed Libby, not out loud, but they didn't have to. Libby knew it was her fault, that she should have been responsible. Her parents hugged her so hard that it hurt her ribs, but they couldn't bear to look at her, and their faces were creased with grief and Libby felt the world go strange and cold around her. All Libby kept hearing was *You should have known. You should have seen. You should have been someone different.* Forgive me, Libby thought. Forgive me. But all she heard was booming silence.

Her parents wouldn't talk about it. She had to go to a lawyer's office with her parents, and another lawyer was there, one she didn't know. She was asked questions about what she had done, why they had gone to the pool, what she had noticed. Her mind shut. She sweated so much her dress was pasted along her back, and she felt like throwing up. She stared down at her hands.

LIBBY DECIDED THE only thing she could do was to live Richie's life for him. If he couldn't be a doctor, then she would be. It would be a way of keeping him alive in her, and a way, too, of having her parents love her, if only for the Richie inside of her.

She buckled down, and to her surprise, she began to love science, the simple beauty of a chemical equation, the wonder in the workings of a cell. You could make people better.

Her teachers noticed her, praised her, gave her prizes. But when she came home with A's in chemistry, in biology, when she announced that she was going to be a doctor, her mother looked pained. Her father didn't look at all. "Good girl," they said, the way they might praise a dog that had learned a new trick.

Libby knew her parents didn't have money, but she told them if she studied hard, she could get a scholarship to college. If she did well enough there, there'd be money for med school. "You don't have to do that. We've saved for you," her parents told her.

"How?" Libby asked.

Her mother shrugged. "We've been saving for you since you were born."

Libby didn't see how that was possible, but they assured her it was. She ended up going to NYU, first undergrad and then med school. She had decided to be a general practitioner, to help more people, but she knew the real reason was that Richie had never said what he had wanted to focus on and she felt this would cover all the bases.

At college, Libby was so busy that she didn't have time to come home very often. When she did, she felt more like a visitor than a daughter. She kept trying to get either her mother or her father alone, to really talk to them about what had happened, but her mother said, "Can't we just have a nice visit, please?" and her father told her there was nothing to talk about. When they waved goodbye, her parents held hands tightly. Libby dug her nails into her thigh to keep herself from begging them to hold her hand, too, to ask her to stay. She tried to remind herself how proud they would be of her when she became an excellent doctor.

The month before she was to start her internship, her father fell asleep while driving, her mother beside him, and the car shot over the guardrails. Both were killed instantly, and then there was nothing to talk about ever.

7

IT WAS THE LAST day of March and Libby walked into Stella's room to see a middle-aged woman praying over her. "Oh, excuse me," Libby said, and the woman rose. "I'm done now," the woman said, calmly walking out.

Libby stood over Stella. Libby had never been religious, feeling that prayers were a balm only for the ones doing the praying. But for a moment, she shut her eyes. *Please get better. I need you.*

What could it hurt?

She touched Stella's hand. "I'll be back Monday," she said, though she had no idea if Stella could hear her.

She had to rush back to her apartment to meet Ben. They were going away for the weekend, his idea, a little bed-and-breakfast upstate. She had already decided that up there, away from all the tensions of daily life, they would get closer.

Weren't things better already? Just last night, he told her his principal had invited him to lunch and was going to remove the warning from his file.

"And no more Klonie," he said. He had just been too tense, he said, that was all it was.

"Thank God," she said, and if she felt uneasy, she told herself that she had to start trusting someone. She had to stop thinking that if someone was going to be punished, it was going to be her.

It would be okay. She was sure of it.

She got to the apartment and heard music, her favorite, Snarky Puppy, all those bright, spangling horns that always made her want to dance. It always amazed her when Ben did things like that, put on her favorite music, brought her favorite flowers. When she had told Stella, Stella laughed. "Anyone would do that for someone they loved."

Loved, Libby had thought. Stella had used the word *love*.

She opened the door. On the table was a bottle of wine and two of her best crystal glasses. "Hey!" she called. It was typical Ben, she thought. So thoughtful. So romantic. She'd tell him that and maybe he'd do it even more.

"One second—" Ben said. "Be right there."

She followed his voice, past the kitchen, into her bedroom.

He was sitting on her bed, bent over, frantically scribbling something on a pad, and as soon as she saw it, she knew what it was: her prescription pad.

He jumped up. "Libby," he said. "It's not what you think!"

She felt her body tense, cold anger filling the part of her that had stupidly hoped for love. She grabbed the pad from his hands. The top one was a prescription for Klonopin. The one below was for OxyContin. Then there were three for Percodan. All with different dates. All with her name, her directions, perfectly forged.

Ben jolted upright so that he was standing. He tried to grab the prescription pad from her, but she threw it across the room. "Did you know I could lose my license?" she shouted. "Did you know you could die?"

He started toward the prescription pad and she jumped in front of him, shoving him back. She had no more voice to scream. She could barely whisper now. "You pick that up and I'm calling the cops."

He stopped. "Babe—" he said. "I'll go to rehab. I'll do anything. I just need to get over this hump—"

"Get out," she said. "Get out and never come back."

"Libby—I love you! Libby!"

She walked closer to him and shoved him, and he stumbled.

"Get out now or I swear I'll call the cops." She reached for her cell, and he rushed out of the room, slamming the door as he left the apartment.

She sat down and counted the prescriptions on her pad. She knew how many there were supposed to be. She should have done it while he was still there, so she could search him if some were missing. She counted them carefully. They were all accounted for.

Suddenly exhausted, she sprawled on the bed. There it was. He was an addict and she should have insisted he go get help. Everyone in the hospital was afraid of her fierce demeanor. None of them knew what a facade it was, how weak she really was.

Her phone began to ring and she glanced at it. *Ben*, it said. She ignored it and shut her eyes, and five minutes later, it began to ring again. She shut off her phone and left it on the bed. In the living room, she turned on the TV and searched until she found an old movie. Bette Davis in *A Double Life*. Bette played twins, one good and one bad.

It seemed like the perfect film for her to watch.

8

SIMON WAS SITTING BY Stella, watching her, willing her to awaken, when he saw her hand twitch. He jumped up. "Nurse!" he shouted, and Debra at the desk ran in. He pointed to Stella. "She moved her hand! I swear she moved her hand!" he cried.

"I'll get the doctor," Debra said, and five minutes later there was a doctor he didn't know, bending over Stella, studying her, and then rising. "It's just a neurological response," the doctor told him. "It doesn't mean anything."

Simon looked at him askance. "How can you say that? She moved. She moved her hand!"

The doctor shook his head. "Neurological response," he said.

"What if it's not? What if you're wrong?"

The doctor arched one brow. "I could be wrong," he said. "But you should remember that you don't just wake up like that from a coma. It happens very gradually. This isn't the movies," he said. Then he gently touched Simon's shoulder.

Simon left the hospital after that. He drove aimlessly, waiting for rides. April tomorrow, and the weather would be turning warmer. He knew people were going to start walking more in the city, taking fewer Lyfts, and he'd have to adjust to that. April first, he thought. The joke was on him.

He drove up to Ninety-Sixth Street and then back down and toward the hospital, when he saw Libby standing on the curb, arguing with the motorcycle boyfriend, the guy whose name he had forgotten. She was shouting, but so was the guy, who kept grabbing for Libby's pockets, her purse, pushing her so hard she fell to the sidewalk. Simon beeped his horn furiously, hoping to scare the guy, who turned and gave Simon the finger, then ran around the corner. Libby slowly picked herself up.

He pulled the car over to the curb. Libby's face was drawn and she wouldn't look him in the eyes. She shoved a pad into her pocket, and he could see despair written on her face. He rolled down the window by the passenger's side. "Libby," he called. "Come on. Get in," he said. "I'll take you home."

She looked up at him, her face streaked with tears. He expected her to tell him no, but she pulled open the door and slid in next to him. "Could you just drive?" she said quietly. "I don't think I want to go home right now."

"Sure," he said. He didn't want to go home either.

He wove through the city streets, no destination in mind. He waited for her to say something about what had happened, but when she didn't, he said, "Was that guy your boyfriend?"

"What?" she said, startled.

"I'm sorry," he said. "It's none of my business. I saw the two of you fighting. I'm just concerned. Ignore me."

"He's not my boyfriend anymore," she said. "He's a jerk. I don't even know why he came to the hospital. We broke up." She swallowed hard.

"Okay," he said, and then he turned the wheel onto another street and she began to talk.

"I know what you're probably thinking. I know what you saw. Or what you thought you saw," Libby said.

"No judgment," Simon said.

"He made me laugh," she said. "He was kind and funny, a teacher.

That's why I was with him." Her voice was breaking. "I'm sorry," she said. "You have problems of your own. You don't need to listen to me carry on. This is all my fault, anyway."

"Yes, I do need to listen," he said. "I'm glad to be hearing someone else's woes."

She swiped at her face. "Please," he said. "You'd be doing me a favor, taking my mind off myself, letting me be useful to another person."

She dug out a tissue from her purse and wiped her eyes. "I was so furious that a drug put Stella into coma, and haha, the joke's on me, because I didn't even see that a guy I let get close to me has a drug problem himself," she said. "Isn't that great? A doctor falling in love with a drug user and not even knowing it. Or maybe I did know it, but I chose to ignore it, the way his pupils changed, the way he sometimes acted a little off. I never saw him actually using, and when I asked him, he acted so offended. He hid it so well, or maybe I just didn't want to see it. I so wanted it to work that I made myself blind."

Simon thought of the way he sat by Stella's bed, desperate for everything to be different, to go back to normal. Love always lied to you. It made you believe the impossible.

Libby rubbed her eyes. "He was writing prescriptions for himself. Oxy. Percodan. The whole works." She sat up taller in her seat. "He was using my pad. I could have lost my license. I could have gone to jail. He could have died . . ."

"Please don't see him again," Simon said.

"Yeah. Don't worry. I won't. I'm going to change the locks."

"That's smart."

"But the thing of it is, I can't help feeling scared, wondering if he's okay. And then I tell myself that's not my business anymore. And he never got violent with me before. Never."

"I'll walk you to your door," Simon said. "Make sure it's all okay."

"Don't tell anybody about this," she said. "I can't tell anyone either. Not unless I report him."

"Why not?" Simon said. "I'll bet this has happened before with other doctors. And this clearly wasn't your fault."

"Wasn't it?" she whispered. "I'm a doctor. Don't you know we're gods?"

"You're also human."

She sat up straighter. "I don't feel very much like I am."

"Want me to tell you about me?" Simon said. "You'll feel better and you can even hold it over me if you want. Maybe it will be different from what Stella told you."

For the first time she smiled. "Go on," she said. "Surprise me."

So he told her about how he'd begun as a musician, how he sent himself to Manhattan School of Music because his parents wouldn't pay for something they didn't consider a real profession. He told her about California, the band going on without him, and how sad that made him. Then he told her how terrified he was about Stella, how he didn't know what to do, and every day the terror grew.

"You're doing it. You talk to her. You visit. You play her music. I see you taking care of her mom, too. That's nice."

"I do what I can." He was quiet for a moment. "I'm not any good anymore. Not at music."

"How do you know that?"

He shrugged. "I feel it. And it's hard when you don't have anything lined up."

"You should still play," she insisted. "You haven't at all?"

"I've been fooling around a little, I guess," he admitted. "Even made a demo. I thought I'd send it around, until I realized I was being stupid, juvenile. And no one even does that anymore, really. They put their stuff up on the web, on YouTube or Spotify, but if I did that, I'd be one among zillions. How would anyone even know how to find me, to look? And what if I got no hits? I'd feel like a fool. I'd be lucky to earn a dollar. I'd be the over-the-hill idiot who wants to be one of the kids, which I don't. I really don't. I just want to play music."

"Let me hear the demo," she said.

"Come on, you're being nice. You don't want to hear it."

"Yes, I do."

"I don't have it here."

"Yes, you do," she said.

"Fine. I do."

He fumbled for a minute with his phone. There were only five songs, and he had no idea if they were any good. Sometimes he thought yes, but mostly no. As it played, she sat quietly, so he didn't know what she was thinking, but at least she seemed to be listening. When it was over, she turned to face him and he waited. He knew his music wasn't for everyone, that different people liked different things, just as with books and films.

"Well . . ." he said, embarrassed.

"That was amazing," she said. "The words. The music. I could have listened forever."

"You're kidding," he said. "You don't have to be kind to me."

"Can't you still send this to the California manager?" she asked.

"No. He signed the rest of the band, but not me. And I was replaced."

"There must be someone else. What about that guy, whatever his name is—Rob?"

"Rick," Simon said. "Rick Mason. And it wouldn't even get to him. He's too fucking famous. I don't know anyone else. Not anymore. And my being replaced isn't exactly a secret in the music world. It doesn't help my chances."

They were silent for a moment, and then she looked at him, excitement flashing in her eyes. "Oh my God. You know what?" she said. "I know someone. I do. He was my patient for three weeks, and we became friends. When he left, he brought me flowers and gave me his card. He's a CEO on one of the labels."

"He was flirting with you. They don't give anyone anything for nothing."

"No, no, he wasn't. He had a wife he loved who was there all the time. I loved her, too. He told me to contact him, but I never had a reason to because I don't know any musicians. But now I do. I could pass your demo on to him."

"Come on. Nothing's going to happen. It's crazy. He probably won't even remember you. Why would he think that his doctor knew talent? And why would he do anything for you or for me?"

"So what?" she said. "So you hear a no or you hear nothing. But at least you try, at least you never give up."

"What label?"

"A new one, I think. Cancun Records."

Simon started. He knew that label. He'd heard that they took chances. "What's this guy's name?"

"Michael. Michael Foley."

"Why would you do that for me?"

"Why wouldn't I? It's such an easy thing for me to do, and if it makes things better for you, it'll be better for Stella. And if it's better for Stella, it's better for me. As a doctor and as her friend." She took out a pen and paper from her purse, scribbling something down and handing it to him. "Send me the file. At least it will put both of us in good moods, right? We could both use some hope."

Simon stared straight ahead, trying to think. It was night now, and he glanced at the sky, knowing that there were stars up there. He could wish on every one of them, but nothing would happen. "Okay," he said finally. "You can do it. But I'm not expecting anything."

She looked at him. "Yes, you are," she said quietly. "You know you are."

9

THE NEXT MORNING, BEFORE heading to the hospital, Simon sat in the apartment, panicked. What had he done? How stupid had he been to send Libby the file? Nothing was going to happen, or if it did, it wouldn't be good. That guy wouldn't remember Libby, or he would and he'd want something sleazy from her, despite what she said. Or he'd remember Libby and he'd listen as a favor for her, and then he'd have to regretfully tell her, "Sorry. Not for us." And then Libby would have to relay the bad news to him, and he didn't know how he would face that or face her.

He felt sour with shame. He wanted to tell her to forget sending the file to that guy, but that thought mortified him, too. He'd never say anything about it to her. He'd have to see her today and pretend that nothing had happened.

But what if something did happen? He felt the sharp spark of joy, and then he shut it off. Magical thinking. That's what he had always done to keep himself centered. If I touch the door three times for luck, I'll have a good day. If I end the stairs on my left foot, all will be well. Stella used to laugh at him, but still he did it. For the longest time, music had been magic for him. His safe place, a cone of sound he could hide in.

He pulled out the bills and spread them all around him. He put his hands in his hair. How was he going to manage all this? No amount of magical thinking would do it. There was always something else he needed to pay for.

Bette sometimes came home with groceries she had paid for herself, but when he protested, she touched his shoulder. "You let me do something nice for you," she said. "Please. It makes me feel better."

He couldn't ask her for anything more.

Every once in a while, a check came from his mother in the mail, but it was always something small. Two hundred. Once five. Grocery money. He couldn't ask them for more either.

He made up lists of things he owned that he could sell or cash out. His IRA was already gone. His bank account, too, and Stella's, which he shared. One of his guitars. He combed the apartment until he found a box of press photos he had saved, some of them signed. Some of them could be worth money, maybe not a lot, maybe not unless it was from an actual superstar, but it could be something. The photos slid across one another, and he picked up a few. There he was standing with his new guitar, smiling. Fourteen years old and a total innocent, thinking he knew everything, that the world was going to be his. He wished he could go back in time and sling his arm around his younger self and tell him the truth. He wished he could live his whole life over.

Kevin had once told him that he believed the world was a computer simulation run by advanced super-smart aliens, and that was why things felt so out of whack sometimes. Simon had laughed, but Kevin was adamant. "Aliens like to fuck us up. And the way we get to stay in the game is to rise to their challenges. To be entertaining by getting in trouble now and then."

Right, Simon thought. Then the aliens must love him. They must adore Stella, because look at the life those so-called aliens had given her.

He lifted up another photo. There was Stella, laughing, her hair wet from the shower, so beautiful he wanted to weep.

He riffled through the pile, picking out another photo. His breath quickened. He stared. There was Silverwood, his parents' vacation house in Woodstock, their respite from the city. The house was originally Simon's grandfather's, a man he had never known, and it was to be Simon's, handed down like an heirloom. At first, Woodstock had been great for Simon. He loved to swim in the local pool. His mother took him for walks around the reservoir and into town to see kids' plays and movies. What did he know except it felt like a paradise that would never end?

But then he got older and his mom became busier with her social obligations. His father was tied up with accounts and clients, and he always wanted Simon to be busy, too. "Here," he would say, handing Simon a stack of envelopes. "Make yourself useful. Seal these." His mother was always joining clubs and going to meetings, or working out with her personal trainer at the gym. "Learn to amuse yourself," his father said.

Simon didn't know what to do. He read, but after he finished a book, he felt restless. He played chess with himself, but that wasn't much of a challenge because he always knew what he was going to do next. There weren't a lot of kids around either, and his parents wouldn't let him invite anyone up to visit because they didn't want the responsibility, even though Simon could care for himself and his friends, too.

The house was supposed to be handed down to him. And if it was supposed to be his, he could surely sell it, and that would bring in enough money so that he wouldn't have to worry about the bills. He hadn't even thought to ask his parents, but he could call them again now; if he could just get the courage, he could face talking about that horror house.

SIMON, AT FOURTEEN, had already given the Woodstock house that name. He hated it. He never wanted to go there, but he never had a choice. It was so lonely there, with no friends, no one to talk to.

It was music that saved Simon when he was at Woodstock. Simon glued himself to the radio with headphones, lost in the sounds. These people singing, playing guitars or horns or drums, were speaking to him and it wasn't long before he wanted to answer.

"I want to take music lessons," he told his parents.

"When you get straight A's," his mother said.

"When you're older, maybe. And you can really focus," his father said.

So Simon waited. He made a keyboard out of paper and taught himself piano, hearing the notes in his head as he pressed down on the imaginary keys. He practiced every day. Then he did the same with guitar strings, patiently working out the chords. And he sang when he was away from his parents, widening what he was listening to musically, trying it all out. While in the city, he began to frequent String Me, a local Upper East Side music store that had a beautiful steel-string Martin in the window that he yearned to own. They taught lessons there, too, and every time Simon came into the shop, one of the musicians who worked there grinned at him encouragingly, but Simon knew it was pointless.

His father was convinced Simon would go to law school and Simon knew it did no good to argue with him.

Still, that year, Simon asked for music lessons. "Music lessons?" his dad said. "You should be prepping for the SATs."

Instead of a guitar for his fifteenth birthday, his father gave him stocks, pieces of paper Simon only stared at. "They'll grow," his father said. "Here, come sit down. Let me show you." His father spread out the stock pages, and the numbers jumbled in front of Simon's face. Simon's father's voice grew stronger, more excited.

"So, this is worth money?" Simon said, holding up the paper.

"Yes. And it will be worth more money the longer you hang on to it."

"When can I cash it in?"

"Let it grow; it'll be worth more."

Simon could wait only a year, and then at sixteen, he asked again.

"Why do you want to do something so foolish?" his dad said. "Didn't I tell you? Didn't I explain how this all works?"

"I want to buy a guitar. I want to take lessons."

His father looked as if Simon had told him he wanted to fly, using his own arms as wings. "Do you understand what you're saying? What you're giving up?" his father said.

Simon thought of the beautiful light-wood Martin at String Me, how he thought he would die if he couldn't get it. He thought there would be a bigger argument, but instead, his father said, "This will be a good lesson for you, then. You wait and see. You'll discover the mistake you made."

Simon's father gave him the money from the stock. "You're sure?" he said.

"Yep."

"Well, you can always change your mind," his father said.

Simon rushed to the store and pointed to the Martin. He had enough for the guitar but not for lessons, but it didn't matter. Didn't Bob Dylan teach himself? Didn't lots of musicians? He was smart and there was nothing he loved more than music. He could teach himself, too.

He didn't know any rules about playing music, so he didn't know what you could and couldn't do. He just did it, playing for hours. He got better and better, and he even began toying around with writing songs. But every year, his father made a point to show him how his stock would have done, and every year Simon ignored him and loved his Martin all the more.

ONE NIGHT WHEN Simon was seventeen and reluctantly at Silverwood, his father was having one of his parties, fifty people all dressed up. His mother had hired caterers, and a band, too, called Zoo, five guys playing rock-and-roll oldies on a special little stage his father had built. They were good, Simon thought, though he'd rather hear something modern. Still, people were dancing. Simon could feel the rhythm throb up through his feet, talking to him. His father shoved him into the crowd. "Being able to mingle and make small talk is one of the best skills someone can learn," he said.

Simon didn't talk to anyone. Instead, he slipped off to his room to play his guitar. No one would notice in all this noise. But opening his bedroom door, he startled two guys from the band, snorting coke. No one said anything for a while, and then one of the guys nodded at Simon's guitar. "You play?" he said, and Simon nodded. "Well, come on, then, dude," he said. "Play for us."

"You don't even know if I'm any good," Simon said. He wasn't sure if they were making fun of him or not.

"Come on. What's to lose? What's your name? What do you want to play?"

So Simon took a chance. He played the one song he'd written called "SmashMe," one word because he liked the way it looked. It was about an Upper East Side kid who had his heart broken by a hard-hearted woman. He used the tricky chords he had learned, the weird open tuning he had picked up from listening to Joni Mitchell records, and he belted out the song. He couldn't look at the guys, because he didn't want to see boredom or, even worse, laughter, but when he was done, they both jumped up and clapped him on the back.

"Man oh man, where'd you learn to play and sing like that?" one of the guys said. "You are so fucking good, it's mad-crazy."

"What?" Simon said, astonished.

"Come play the next song with us," the other guy said.

"I can't do that—"

"Yeah, you can," the guy said. "Come on. It'll be a blast."

On stage, the band pushed Simon to the front. "We have to play oldies for the oldies," the bass player said to Simon. "But one new tune won't kill them."

"Once again, ZOO!" someone shouted. The guy who had urged

Simon to play took the mic. "Guess what," he said. "We're going to show you some new talent here. Playing a song he wrote himself. Not to worry, the oldies but goodies are coming back at you right after. This is Simon and he's going to sing 'SmashMe,' a song he wrote."

Simon took a deep breath. He shut his eyes and then began to play and sing. And the longer he played, the more he felt the crowd was with him. *This is what I'm meant to do.* The band began to sing harmony, and it worked perfectly. At the end, there was a crash of silence followed by a deafening wave of applause. Simon stood there, bathed in sweat, trembling. Around him, the rest of the band was bowing low, so Simon did, too. "Give it up for Simon!" the bass player screamed.

Then Simon saw his father moving toward the stage. He stepped up and took the mic. "I hope you enjoyed my son's hobby, but let's leave it to the pros for the rest of the evening." His father didn't look at Simon, didn't see him wince at the word *hobby*.

"He can play with us. He's really good," the bass player said.

"I'm paying you, not him," Simon's father said, still close to the mic, so Simon knew everyone could hear. His father turned to Simon, his eyes hard. Simon bit down on his lip so he wouldn't cry. His father leaned down next to him so that only Simon could hear. "Only idiots do that. Don't embarrass yourself."

Simon got off the stage. People were patting him on the back, grinning wildly at him, grabbing his sleeve, wanting to talk to him, but Simon kept moving. His father had toppled him as easily as he would a house of cards. People were making a path for him. Someone ruffled his hair, like he was a child. He heard the band blasting out "Tusk," an old Fleetwood Mac song, and the crowd began dancing, talking to one another again.

Simon went straight through the house and began walking out of the neighborhood, across the town and down to a small lake. As soon as he saw the water, he started to cry.

He didn't go back to the house until the sky was light again, and even then, as soon as he opened the door, he felt his father's disdain, his belief that his son was a failure.

He vowed he'd never go back to Silverwood again.

BACK AT HOME, Simon spent all his time playing his guitar. He joined bands at school and played at Sweet Sixteens and then even at weddings, and he began saving money, until he had enough to apply to Manhattan School of Music. "Well," his parents said. "It's your life. Waste it if you want."

They never came to his shows, not even when he hit it big. They rarely asked about his career, but when they did, they treated it like an obsession he eventually would outgrow. He knew they were disappointed in the choices he made, but it didn't matter to him, not anymore. In his mind, he saw crowds lining up for a ticket to one of his shows, for a chance to touch him, to know just who he really was.

BUT HE DID come back to Silverwood, one more time, and that was because of Stella. Then they were newly in love, dizzy with the excitement of it. To his own surprise, he wanted his parents to meet her. He wanted to show off and make his parents know that an extraordinary woman like Stella had chosen him. "Bring her to Silverwood," his mother said.

Stella was a city girl. He wasn't sure she'd like it there. But she agreed easily. "I'm happy to meet your folks," she said.

They went for a week in August, when the city was a steam oven. Stella packed sundresses and sneakers, and a gift for his parents, a vintage pitcher shaped like a chicken. His parents made a fuss over it and even more of a fuss over her. His mother got out the china and the real silver and made steak tartare, and when Stella shyly confessed that she was a vegetarian, his mom laughed and said, "There are plenty of other things for you to eat." His mother brought out greengage plums and Granny Smith apples, six kinds of sharp cheese and brie, a crusty bread.

"Oh, thank you, thank you," Stella said, so enthusiastically because Simon knew she was hungry, but it made his parents laugh. Simon's father grinned at him. "I like your girl," he said.

That's right. Mine, Simon thought.

All through dinner, Simon still felt like an outsider. His parents peppered Stella with questions. What, her father was no longer alive, her mother had moved to Spain? Oh, so far away. Oh, what a shame. When his mother put her arm around Stella, it felt conspiratorial to Simon. "Now, how can we do something about Simon's hair?" his mother said, and Simon bristled, but Stella laughed. "I love his hair," she said, reaching over and smoothing it over his brow, her fingers cool and steady.

His parents treated Stella like family. They showed her where they hid the spare key under the mat on the porch, so she could come and go as she pleased. His father gave her maps so she could wander into town and walk back home if she liked. They pointed out the bikes in the garage and were so friendly that Stella later said to Simon, "I don't understand. They're lovely to me. And they seem to be lovely to you. How can there be any problem here?"

He told her how they had treated him when he had played with the band. "You were a kid," she said. "And they were wrong. You've become a success. People can change, you know."

He was about to say, Yeah, right, you don't know them, but she was so happy, her face had a glow, so he just nodded.

By the third day, Simon felt like he was going out of his mind. There wasn't anything to do, and all he wanted was to get back to Manhattan. Stella, though, who was even more city centric than he was, who called anything even remotely country "outer Mongolia," seemed ridiculously content. Every morning, she had coffee on the porch with his parents, telling them stories about her life.

Later Stella walked to the little lake and then back. She shucked off her shoes and walked in the shallows, shivering with delight. Some days she took a book from his father's library (she was allowed!

Simon had never been allowed!) and curled up on the porch swing and read. When she saw Simon, she smiled. "I could get so used to this," she told him.

"I thought you were afraid that if you ever left Manhattan, you'd have to take a test to get back in. You know, name all the bridges, the best diners."

"I love it here."

"Want to go to the village green again?" Simon asked. The farther away from the house that they got, the better he felt, the less he heard the house whispering to him. Part of him kept imagining that they might run into someone famous, someone he had seen before but had been too tongue-tied to speak with. He had once seen Stephen Stills buying cucumbers at the farmers' market there. He had spotted Deborah Harry on a bike. Stella nuzzled his nose with hers. "I don't care about celebrities," she said. "You're my celebrity." She stretched out her long legs. "And it's nowhere near as hot here as Manhattan," she pointed out.

"You haven't experienced a Woodstock winter," he said.

"But I'd like to. I'll bet it's pretty."

"Wait, what? You would?" Simon shook his head. "You don't mean it," he decided.

He went with her to an outdoor concert. They packed a picnic, which they shared on a blanket, and even though it wasn't July, there were fireworks, and Stella looked up at them in wonder. "What a magical place," she told him, and he held her closer and shut his eyes.

BEFORE THEY LEFT for the city, Simon combed the house, gathering up anything that was his, including his boyhood bedspread. "You're doing our spring cleaning for us," his mother said with a laugh as Simon packed the car with bag after bag of stuff.

He waited until they were halfway home to find a trash bin, and he began dumping things out. "What are you doing?" Stella said.

"Why are you throwing this out?" She held up an old sweatshirt that said WOODSTOCK on it. "This would still fit," she said.

"Nothing fits," he told her. "Not anymore." She studied him quietly, and then she helped him throw everything away.

They never went up to Woodstock again, though Stella had asked to. Then, after a while, his parents mostly stopped going to the house, too. They were older, tired more easily, and city living was too crazy for them now, even on the Upper East Side. They moved to Florida, along with their friends. Only once in a great while did they come back to the Northeast to visit the house. But they'd never sell the house, wouldn't even consider renting it. They told themselves, You never know, you might want to come up, even if just for a weekend.

Sometimes Stella would sigh and say, "Remember Silverwood?" For her, it became a code for everything that had been perfect between her and Simon.

Now SIMON PUSHED the photos away and glanced at the clock.

It wasn't so late that his parents wouldn't be up. Silverwood was worth a fortune. His parents still told him that all the time. His mother said that she had read in *People* magazine that Jennifer Aniston was in Woodstock, buying pottery from one of the artisanal shops. Daniel Craig—James Bond, for Christ's sake—had a spread there now and could often be seen eating at one of the outdoor cafes. It was an incredible time to sell or at least to rent the house for income he desperately needed. Surely his parents might understand that.

His hands shaking, he punched in their phone number.

"Darling," said his mother when she heard his voice, and Simon gripped the edge of the counter. He felt ten years old again, completely unsure of himself. "How are you? How is Stella? Did you get our check? We put in a little extra this time."

"I did. And thank you, thank you so much." He swallowed. "Stella's the same," he said, and he heard her sharp intake of breath.

"I was wondering," Simon said. He made himself slow down and took a breath. If there was bad news coming, there was no reason to rush for it. "I know you've been so generous with money, with helping us."

"Darling, what are parents for? Your father and I know you're having a hard time. We'll send more money soon."

Simon felt a headache, small and hard as a dime, forming in his temple.

"I was wondering. The Woodstock house is mine now, right? Since you aren't going there again?" he said.

"That's right, darling."

"So, if it's mine, I'd like the papers that go along with it."

"Why? They're safe in our deposit box."

"Because I want to sell it. I need to sell it."

"Silverwood?" his mother said. "Why would you ever want to sell Silverwood?"

"No one goes there anymore. Not you and Dad. Not me," Simon said. "You guys are always in Florida. I mean, I don't have to sell it. Even if I could just rent it, the money would be so helpful, and you wouldn't have to give us money from your accounts."

"That house is for you," his mother said firmly. "For you and your wife when you get around to having one. For your children—our grandchildren. That's how it's always been done. That house was your grandfather's."

"I know that. But I don't want it, Mom. I never wanted it. You wanted it for me. I just want to sell it."

"It's out of the question," his mother said. He heard a door banging behind her, the thread of his father's voice. "Who's on the phone, honey?"

"We'll send you more money," she said, and then his father got on the phone, on the other landline, and even his voice sounded suntanned.

"What's this about?" he said, and Simon told him.

"It was my father's. I can't sell my father's house."

"Grandpa's dead," Simon said. "I never even knew him. And it's not his house anymore. It's yours, and then it's mine."

His mother cleared her throat. "Simon," his mother said. "We will float you some money, to get you through this, but we're not selling the vacation house."

"We'll send you a check this evening. Tell us what else you need and it's yours," his father said. "You know that. You're our boy."

Simon was startled. They had never offered money like that, and it confused him. Still, his father had called him a boy, not a man. His father didn't think he was responsible, either, and it made him feel dark with shame. "Whatever you think is good," he said finally. "And thank you. Thank you so much."

Simon hung up and rested his head against the cool of the table. But then, he thought, his parents were frugal. No matter what they sent, it would certainly help, but he knew it wouldn't be enough.

10

STELLA MAPS OUT TIME by noise, music, scent, and heat. The morning sun on her body, the coolness of night, sometimes the rough wash of a cloth over her body. Everything looks and feels different now. Sounds are sharper. She sees colors behind her lids, but when she tries to focus, tastes flood her mouth. Apples. Roast beef. Once, strawberry ice cream, just out of nowhere, like a kind of wonderful surprise. Her senses are all mixed up and she keeps thinking, More. Please, more, more, more. The surprise of it makes her feel more alive. It's something new, something positive, so surely it means things are changing. Someone touches her hand and she sees a flash of turquoise. Someone says something and she smells oranges, making her mouth water.

Stella shivers at a kiss on her hand. She knows it's Simon's, and though she can't see him right now, she feels like a light has been switched on. His lips seem to blend right into her skin, heat coursing through her body like a stream. "It's time for you to wake up, honey," she hears him say, but she doesn't really understand what he means, except for the word *honey*, but in his mouth, it sounds sad rather than loving, and that bothers her.

She hears people yelling at her, calling *Stella, Stella, Stella,* her name like the clang of a bell. She hears a banging noise so close to her face that she would flinch back if she could. She hears Simon, and sometimes Libby, too. Libby. Her friend Libby. She knows when Libby is there because she can smell her, like coconut, like a weird float of red and blue that has a scent all its own. She can feel her stirring the air.

She shimmers above herself. Her memories are hazy. They seem like a book she had read one too many times, but a book she had loved. Who was that Stella? What was on her next page?

"Simon," she hears, and she recognizes Libby's voice, and a flood of happiness washes over her. Libby, she tries to say. Libby, my friend!

"The drive," Libby says. "That was nice."

What drive? Stella thinks.

"I know a place that has the best pizza," Simon says. There's a funny silence and Stella rides it like a wave, coming down with a bounce. "I sometimes go there when I'm done with the hospital. You should eat, too. Something other than that awful hospital food."

Stella listens in wonder. She remembers how much Libby had disapproved of Simon, how she didn't think he was good enough for Stella. Do Simon and Libby like each other now? Stella hopes so because she loves them both, but still there's a flare of jealousy zigzagging through her stomach. They can like each other, she tells herself. It's all right.

"Stella," she hears him say now. She tries to let him know, sending out thoughts that have sound attached, but he doesn't say anything more to her, so she has to assume that he's oblivious. He cries, but there's nothing she can do about it, except think, meanly, Well, why didn't you cry before? "Come back," he says. "Please come back."

I'm trying.

Simon never gives up hope. She knows this about him. He always thought he was going to go right to the top in music and stay there. He thought he would be the next Dylan, that his band would be the next Pearl Jam, that the songs he uploads on the band's website would go viral. And at first it seemed possible. But then she saw how his audience was getting older, not younger, and that wasn't a good sign, how the concert halls weren't filling anymore, so the band had to play at fairgrounds, singing to drunks and kids who were only there to snag some weed. The band was background noise, a reason for another beer, another toke, but she didn't say anything to Simon. She had always just hoped he would find his way, and fool that she was, she had hoped that his way might be her.

Light pours into her, warm as a shower, and she feels herself contract. "Oh, that's good," Libby says, and Stella wants to scream, I'm here, I'm here, don't go away, I'm here.

The light gets brighter and she feels herself flinch again. "Come on, Stella," Libby says, and Stella thinks, Oh, shut up. I'm doing the best I can. She read once about people who saw white lights when they died, but she never believed it. That was hokum, just the brain being starved of oxygen. The body trying to keep itself from reaching the edge of panic. The light flashes again, and her mind rolls over it like water over a stone. Is she dying? Is this all there is for her? Peggy Lee sang that, she remembers. Simon played the song for her. She needs Peggy Lee singing.

Simon comes closer. His sorrow is rich and fragrant. "She doesn't know I'm here," he says.

Yes. Yes, I do.

She had had lots of men in her life when she was in college, guys who wanted to be doctors, psychologists, electricians, but she had never loved any one of them enough to settle down with. Then, degree in hand, her career under way, she met Simon.

"We don't know that," Libby says, and her voice has something new in it that Stella can't place. "Stella, wake up! Stella, wake up!" Libby says.

I would if I could.

Coma, she hears someone say, and something twists in her stomach. She had seen coma patients right here in the hospital. There was a single mother, and Stella still remembers her name: Doris Harper. Young and blonde and gorgeous, with a tiny diamond nose ring and a big smile. She came in all by herself to have her baby, and everything interested her, the labor pains that she said were like having a *T. rex* inside of her, the monitor, even the surgical gown that she fastened in the back with two glittery diaper pins. But something happened on the table. Her heart stopped. She went into a coma for two weeks, and when she came out of it, she didn't ask about her baby, a burly little boy she had wanted to name Jake. She didn't want to see him. "Why should I?" she said. "I'll be gone again. I made the wrong decision. I want to go back."

The doctors monitored Doris. The nurses put Jake in her arms, and she rocked him, sang to him, and kissed his little cheek. Everyone thought everything was going to be fine. But then Doris had gone home, with her baby, and two weeks later, roiling in postpartum depression, she killed herself and her baby went to Social Services.

You never knew how things were going to turn out.

"Coma," Stella hears again, and then Libby's soothing voice. "She'll come out of it, Simon. You told me she was a fighter." When, Stella thinks. When had Simon told Libby that?

Well, this state is nothing like coma. Not that she's ever been in one before. Not that she would know. But this feels like nothing anyone who has come out of coma has told her. It's nothing like anything she has ever studied. She can feel Libby and Simon moving about the room, and then suddenly, she is moving, too. Like a spirit.

She swirls about the hospital and sees and hears things she didn't notice before. Is she hallucinating? she wonders. She rounds a corner, and if this is a hallucination, well, the details are all so right, so specific, right down to the hand lotion on the nurse's cart, the stack of diapers on the bottom. Is this all some sort of vast cosmic joke, and is she the punch line? In her room again, Stella sees Madonna in a black lace bustier smoking a cigarette and grinning at her before she flies away.

Stella knows that there are specialists who work to bring people out of comas. But, really, who knows what works? A child's puppy licking his face. A favorite perfume. A swish of velvet.

A kiss from someone you love.

In her bed again, Stella tries to think of what she knows about herself. She is here. She can sense things. Something is wrong. She loved Simon.

The past tense bothers her.

"Baby girl," she hears, and she thinks, Mom, Mom, Mom again. She wants to reach for her, to burrow her face against her mother's warm neck.

Something feels different. There's been a seismic shift. Or a time loop, the past and present all entwined. Animals know when an earthquake is about to happen. People, too, sense things, and she feels herself floating up again, as if she is moving into the future. She can't tell what's in the future, though. All she knows is this bed, the smells of the sheets, and the senses around her.

Now she hears something crashing against her ears, and then she's floating higher, up against this raging tide, and her ears hurt, and then her skin hurts, and then there is a blink of light before she falls back again, settled more deeply into the dark. She feels different now, new somehow. She wants to laugh out loud.

"Stella!" She hears her name and something sharp is poked under her nose. Cinnamon, she thinks. Or maybe table salt. She's rising up again. Something is trying to get out of her body, and for a moment, it hurts. Pain. For a second, she feels as if her body is moving. Her hand. Just a twitch. That's what it is. When was the last time she felt pain?

There is that blink of light again, growing stronger, pressing against her eyes like a thumb, and she opens them, and everything is so bright she can't see for a minute. Her body, heavy and dense, falls back into the bed. "Glasses," she says, and it is strange to hear her voice, hoarse and hollow and filled with fluid, but she means sunglasses, not the glass of water someone is handing her because it is all so bright, so new, and then she blinks and her vision clears a little, and there, standing at the foot of her bed, beautiful and strange, his whole body shimmering, is Simon, before she's pulled back down, into the murk. "Simon," she tries to say. "Simon."

11

LIBBY CHECKED HER EMAIL in the morning before heading to the hospital. Junk. More junk. And then at the bottom, an email from the record label, from Michael Foley, the CEO who she had asked to listen to Simon's MP3.

She felt suddenly nervous. Her heart hammered as she clicked it open.

> Dear Libby,
>
> How good to hear from you! Thank you so much for giving us a chance to hear Simon Stein's music. I've shared it with colleagues, and we all agree there is something here that we would very much like to explore further. Please have Simon get in touch with us as soon as possible so we can set up a meeting and get things rolling.

Libby didn't realize her hands were shaking until she knocked over her pen-and-pencil holder on the desk, sending everything onto the floor.

The label wanted to meet Simon. Oh God. She had done it. She had taken a chance and she had actually done it for him. It wasn't a guarantee, but it was something positive, something with legs to it. She thought how excited Simon would be. So why did she feel so sick?

She didn't know much about the music business, how it worked. Maybe Simon would be on the road again. Maybe he could be a studio musician or sell songs to a music publishing and licensing company who might market and pitch for him. That meant that he wouldn't be with Stella every day, talking to her, holding her hand. If she came out of the coma, Stella was going to need someone to lean on for several months, and it should be someone she trusted. If the music thing worked out, Simon would be busier than ever. He might be gone for extended periods.

And what about me, she thought, and then she immediately chastised herself for being selfish. She liked him, but that didn't mean she had a right to consider anything with him. They were just this united front, both of them pulling for Stella. Maybe she was just pretending there was something more, masking the real fear she had for her friend with something more comforting. She felt a strange, restless thump in her head. It was just grief and loneliness. It was watching Simon trying, really trying to be better. How often did people do that?

Of course she had to tell him. Of course. At the very least, it was something to hang on to, a chance. But maybe she should wait, just a little. Just until Stella was out of danger.

She grabbed her things and headed to work.

THAT EVENING, WHEN Simon was driving her home, he kept asking her why she was so quiet. "Oh, I don't know," Libby said. "I guess I'm worrying about Stella."

"Me, too," Simon said, and then he suggested grabbing some veggie burgers at Quantum Leap before he took her home, and she found herself saying yes because anything was better than the quiet of her apartment, where her mind would start accusing her and she would have to listen.

• • •

EVERY WEEK SHE told herself she was going to tell him. April was flying by. Maybe she'd tell him now.

Or maybe she wouldn't.

She got herself ready. She even rehearsed what she would say, but something new was happening to her. Every time she saw Simon, she liked him more and more. She began to notice how beautiful he was physically, how his eyes shone, how, when she touched him, she felt something spark, and she couldn't help but wonder whether he felt that, too. She kept repeating to herself that it was Stella who counted, Stella who had to get well, that what Libby had was a crush and it shouldn't have anything to do with anything. As a doctor, her first job was her patient.

She waited, telling herself if Simon asked about the reaction to his songs, well, then, she would certainly tell him. She wouldn't keep it secret. And if the label CEO emailed again, she'd tell him for sure. But he never did. And Simon never asked. Maybe because he had to keep hoping. And that made Libby hope, too. Everything has a cost, she told herself, and you just had to weigh it and hope that you were right.

Since Simon didn't bring it up, maybe he had forgotten. Maybe she could forget too.

THAT NIGHT, SHE started watching a horror movie about a woman who finds monsters living in her basement. Oddly enough, it made her feel better. At least there were no monsters in her life.

When the phone rang, she reached for it automatically, especially when she saw the hospital number. "Yeah," she said, her eyes still focused on the screen.

"Libby," Debra said. "They need you at the hospital for Stella Davison."

12

STELLA SAT UP, HER heart pounding, her breathing labored. Everything was in black and white, like she was trapped inside an old TV program, but she blinked hard, then shut and opened her eyes again, and colors snapped on, bright and shiny, and there was Simon, only it wasn't Simon. He was different somehow, and she couldn't figure out why or how. Machines beeped beside her and she tried to lift her hand to touch him, but she couldn't. Did he always have those streaks of gray in his hair? Was that scar on the bottom of his neck new?

"Shhh, sleeping beauty," he said, and then she recognized the voice, the one she had held on to all through her long sleep. "I've been waiting and waiting for this," he said. "You can't imagine—"

His eyes were brimming with tears, and she looked at him, astounded. He wasn't a crier.

"Simon," she said. Her voice sounded funny, like scraping her nails against concrete. "My voice—" she said.

"That's from the breathing tube. It'll come back."

"What?" she said, alarmed. She tried to cough to clear her throat, twisting the sheets in her hand. The blue hospital gown rustled against her; the machine clicked and then stopped. She tried to hoist herself up, but her arms and legs were noodles. "What happened?" she said. "What am I doing here?"

Simon pulled up a chair and moved as close to the bed as he could. He grabbed her hand, and she felt a shock of cold. "Do you remember?" he said.

She shook her head. "It's foggy."

"You've been in a coma," he said.

The air grew clammy around her.

"You were in a coma," he repeated.

She felt his fingers stroking her hand. Stop, she wanted to say. Stop. Stop. Every time he touched her, she felt sparks. "Since February. It's April now," he said.

"I don't believe you," she said. He was talking to her slowly, the way he would to a child. And then she thought, Oh God, what have I missed? Could this possibly be true?

"How?" she said. Why did people go into coma? She used to know that, but now she remembered nothing.

"All that matters is that you're okay."

"Am I okay?"

"You're awake and talking and you know who I am. That's okay as far as I'm concerned."

"I want to know what happened. Please. You have to tell me."

Simon's grip tightened on her hand. "Tell me," she begged. "You have to." He shook his head. "Someone else will tell me, then. I'll ask everybody if you don't." She knew she sounded ridiculous.

Simon looked unsettled. "We were partying. Remember the way we used to when we were young?" Simon said.

Stella shut her eyes. She could remember dancing with Simon in the kitchen, but it was morning and they were in their pajamas. She had another flash, a party full of musicians, but she had stayed by herself in a corner, trying to attract Simon's attention because she wanted to go home.

"I don't . . . I can't remember."

"We were drinking wine."

Wine, she thought, and a tartness filled her mouth.

"We both took a pill."

"A pill?" An image flashed. A suitcase. No, two suitcases in their apartment, both of them open like mouths trying to tell her something, if only she could understand the language. If only the image would stay in her mind instead of fading out. Drinking. She remembered drinking, but it was someone else's memory, not hers. Someone else was gulping down wine, reaching for a pill. She wouldn't have done that. She slid down into the sheets, tugging her hand free. "That's impossible," she said. Talking to him felt like a garbled phone conversation, with echoes.

Simon leaned closer to her. She could smell his aftershave. Was that pine? Or something oceany? Had he ever worn aftershave at all? "You're alive and I'm here with you. That's what matters," he said.

An image sparked. That guitar case. Stickers all over it from every place Simon had ever been, like they were gold stars for being so good, so talented. They were supposed to go to California. She remembered that now. Had she wanted to go? Why would they be drinking? Were they celebrating? Is that the way they celebrated? His band had a chance at something, she remembered that, too. "California." The word had a metallic taste on her tongue.

"No, honey. There's no California. The band went. I stayed. I'm driving a Lyft now."

It made her impossibly sad, Simon not going to California with his band. He had dreamed so much about that, had wanted it so much. She thought about Simon driving a Lyft. Having to be somewhere, having to listen to other people and take them where they wanted to go, when he was always the driver and navigator of everything. "But who are you playing music with, then?" She couldn't imagine him without his guitar.

"Your mom's here," he told her.

"My mom? Where?" She looked around wildly, wanting to see her mom, to hold her hand. "Where is she?"

"I called her. When you first got sick. She's staying at the apartment. She'll be here later."

Stella tried to remember sensing her mom in this room, hearing her voice here in the hospital, but her mind went blank. Her mother here? And living in their apartment? Stella looked at Simon in confusion.

"Libby's here all the time. You have a whole team of doctors, too."

"Doctors? What doctors?"

He touched her toes, which was a little disconcerting. He gave them a wiggle. "It won't be forever," he said.

"What won't?" she said. Was he talking about her mom staying here or about her being in the hospital?

Simon didn't answer. He drew an extra blanket over her, and she threw it off. She didn't want to be tucked in, held in place. She wanted that warm buoyant feeling again, the touch of the colors she had seen. "I was floating," she said. "There were so many colors, Simon, it was sort of amazing—"

"What?"

"I can still see them. Right in this room. If I try really hard, I can feel them."

He shook his head. "No, no, honey. It's probably the drugs that did that—"

"No. No, it isn't."

He patted her hand awkwardly. "They'll wear off."

"And then what?"

"Then we'll wait and see and watch you get better and better until you're your old self."

Her old self. What was her old self? It was all muddied in her mind.

We can't remember the future, Stephen Hawking had once said, but she felt as if she could, because time was all mixed up. She saw her mom, so vivid and alive, but then she vanished. She saw Simon, but it was Simon when he was twenty-two and cocky and full of hope. He was skinny and bouncing up and down on his high-top sneakers.

"Is there a mirror?" she asked, and Simon shook his head. At least she could see her hands, her body. She held up her fingers, and to her surprise, her nails, which she always bit, which always shamed her, had grown long and beautiful. They were painted a dusty rose. "Oh, will you look at that," she said in wonder.

"Joyce did that. She thought you'd somehow know. She made up your whole face."

"Joyce? She was here?" She gestured. "Please can I see a mirror?"

"I'll see what I can do."

He was gone for a moment and then came back with a pocket mirror. But he kept standing there, not giving it to her. "Are you sure you want to do this?" he said, and she reached for the mirror and turned it to her face.

It was and it wasn't her. She moved her eyes and watched them move in the mirror. "I have yellow hair?" she said.

"Always."

"Really? Always? And it's curly?"

"Is it ever."

Stella was skeptical. How could this woman be her? The face in the mirror was tired. She remembered this Daphne du Maurier story she had once read, a story that had terrified her. A woman was in the hospital, and after her operation, she saw all the doctors as having the heads of insects or animals. When she told them, they said, "We'll fix it." They put her under again, and when she woke up, the doctors looked normal. It wasn't until she was handed a mirror that she saw that she had the head of a cow.

"Can I keep this mirror?" she asked.

"Sleep," he told her, pocketing the mirror. "I'll be back later."

• • •

BUT HE DIDN'T come back, or maybe he did. Maybe her mom did. Or her friends. She checked her nails: the polish was a little chipped. She looked around the room because people usually brought things to people in the hospital. She took inventory. Chair. Water pitcher. Magazine. There was nothing new, nothing special. Or was there? She felt as if she had had that one bright moment with Simon, in which she understood where she was, and she was so happy to see him. If she didn't quite get the why and how of it all, at least she didn't feel as detached as she did now. Time knotted on her and looped around. She couldn't tell if it was day or night because one second things grew darker, but in the next moment she was blinded by light.

Doctors came in and out. She remembered a cold stethoscope on her chest, questions she couldn't answer because as soon as they asked them, she forgot what they were. Once, she remembered seeing a group of med students standing in a circle around her bed, a doctor she didn't know talking to them. "I'm not here," she said.

"She's having visions," the doctor said to the med students, who all stared at Stella and then hung back, like they were afraid to catch what she had. Then they were all gone.

Night came, and she was terrified because everything seemed to be slowing down. The lights dimmed. There was less commotion in the hall. Only sometimes did she hear a patient crying, a man's voice saying the same name, like the sob of a cat. *Diane, Diane.* But then she swore she heard something, like the stamp of a boot, and then the guy stopped calling, and she didn't know if it was because Diane had appeared or the patient had fallen asleep or was just tired of crying. There was the pad of shoes on the floor. Nurses, orderlies. Only occasionally a doctor. Out in the hall, she could hear two nurses talking. "And after all that, he was a lousy lay," said one. Stella recognized the voice. Betty Rosman, a redhead single mom, who was always sneaking breaks to have another cigarette.

"You know how I tell who's going to be good in bed?" another voice said. "They have to cup my face when they kiss me. It's a little thing, but, boy, does it count for me."

She felt an electric surge. Libby! That was Libby's voice. She knew what that felt like, too, having your face cupped for a kiss. Simon used to do that, but now, since she had awakened, he just gave her gentle brushes with his lips, like he was afraid any greater pressure would make her shatter.

"Jaxon was a lousy kisser," Libby said. "That should have told me everything I needed to know about him."

Stella remembered Jaxon. A scientist, no, an architect. That was it. She felt as if she had won a prize, grabbing that memory.

The voices blurred and grew faint. *Come back. Come back.* And then they were gone. Everything seemed to be moving at warp speed, so fast, images came at her in blurs, so intense, that she wasn't sure if she had entered another world. She was skiing down a blindingly white mountain, pitched so sharply, she was nearly horizontal. It was so freezing that she felt her bones might snap off, but she liked this cold, no, she loved it. She wanted more. She had never even considered skiing, had always been too conscious of all the ways you could hurt yourself, breaking a leg, snapping an arm, or even ramming into a tree and dying just like Sonny Bono had. Organ donors—that's what the nurses called people who were daredevils, who laughed at helmets, at safety belts or harnesses, who ended up dead on a gurney with viable young hearts and lungs and corneas that would continue to lie in someone else's body. But here, in her dream, if it was a dream, she zoomed around and over moguls, she jumped high into the hard blue sky, flying, landing even faster, never stopping. Never wanting to. She zipped around a curve, she slashed through the white powder, her breath coming in pants, *huh huh huh*, and there it was, a jump ahead of her, rising up into the mountains with a thrilling loop in the middle, and she couldn't help grinning as she tore through it. *Breathe*, she heard someone say, a voice swirling around her with the snow, and she did, whirling around, upside down and then right side up again, her skis cutting into the air. She was triumphant with joy, with the wind whooshing like music about her. She was laughing and so alive that she swore she could feel every cell inside her vibrating, and then someone was shaking her and she bolted awake. Her eyes flashed open.

She was alone in this hospital bed, rigid with confusion. No one else was in the room. Or if they had been, they were gone now. The snow and ice were gone, too, the skis, the cold hard bite of the air. *No. No, no, no. Come back.* Her face felt chapped. She searched the room for snow. She didn't know which life was real, but somehow the one she had awakened to felt like the biggest disappointment. Stella, Scaredy Cat Stella, who always wore bike helmets, who wouldn't ride in a cab even on a rainy day if it didn't have a working seatbelt, who yearned for everything to be calm and still. She had almost completed the high jump, and all she wanted now was to go for it again.

The hospital felt asleep, but she couldn't be still. She felt like she almost made sense of herself now. She leaned over and looked for something to occupy her, a magazine maybe, a book. She squinted harder. There was a pad of paper on her nightstand, a pen, and she grabbed for them. Maybe she could write what she remembered, and that way she wouldn't forget it again. She knew the paper and pen were real, but she wasn't so sure about her memories.

She couldn't get her mind to work right. She wrote down *I was on a mountain*, and then, without thinking, she began drawing circles, over and over, faster and faster, as if her pen itself were skiing, and the more she drew, the better she felt, pulling into a trance. She covered one whole side of the page, then flipped it over. It reminded her of something, this frantic drawing. Who was it, what was his name, who drew like this? That nastily funny comic-book artist, the one who drew horsey-looking women with big leg-of-lamb thighs, the one with the schizophrenic brother who killed himself? R. Crumb. That was it. He had a brother, Charles, who tranced out when he drew, who made magnificent illustrations using circles, covering every bit of white space because all that blankness hurt him, and gradually his circles grew into people, into stories, into a life he could manage to live in.

She was on her fifth sheet of paper when a nurse she didn't recognize came in, all white clogs and blue scrubs.

"Well, what's this?" the nurse said, and then Stella looked down and saw the paper spread across her bed, the sheet in her lap. She put the pen down, panting. "I don't know," she said.

"That's enough, then," the nurse said. "You need to rest." But as soon as she took the pen from Stella's hand, Stella's fingers kept moving, making loop after loop in the air. "Sleep now," the nurse said, gathering up all the pages and stacking them neatly on the nightstand. Stella grabbed at her sleeve.

"Please, can you ask Simon to bring me paper and pens?" she begged.

"Sleep now," said the nurse.

"Tell him. Please tell him," Stella said.

"I will."

Stella shut her eyes. She dreamed of circles, spirals whirling faster and faster.

THE NEXT DAY, Simon brought her six notebooks in rainbow colors and colored pens in varying thicknesses, and as soon as she saw them, she felt dizzy with pleasure. She held out her arms and hugged them to her. "Thank you," she said, almost breathless with excitement. "Thank you, thank you."

"Are you writing your memoir?" he said, grinning, and she ignored him because how could she explain something she didn't understand herself?

Stella looked around. "My mom, is she really here?"

He gave her a funny look. "She was here this morning. She sat by your bed for a long time."

"No. No, she wasn't."

"The two of you talked."

Stella slumped back down into the bed, shivering.

"She'll be here later," he told her. "She wants to come again this evening. Your friends want to come, too, but I don't want to tire you out. Would that be okay?"

Her friends had been here? She couldn't remember. Libby was her friend, Stella thought. She had heard Libby talking, and she knew as a doctor, Libby would visit her every day. Debra, another nurse, used to go out for Cinnabons for both of them when a day would start to sour. Her mind shuttered. Surely she must have more friends. Maybe she'd know them when she saw them.

"Is it okay, you and my mom together in our apartment?" She couldn't remember if the two of them got along, if they liked each other.

"Really, it's fine," he said.

She opened one notebook, grabbing the first pen, a purple one, and began to draw. "Is that supposed to be me?" he asked jokingly, but she kept drawing circles and circles and circles. The more she drew, the better she felt. By the time Simon was ready to leave, she had filled half of one notebook.

"Is this weird, what I'm doing?" she asked him when she finally put the pen down. She felt exhilarated, as if she had run a marathon.

"Does it feel weird?"

"I don't know. Except I want to do it. I like to do it."

"Then it's not weird. And I'll bring you more notebooks," he said.

He leaned down to kiss her, a peck on her cheek, and then he was gone and it was just her again.

At night, Libby came in to check on her. As soon as Libby walked in the room, Stella felt the air grow warmer, safer. She looked up and there was Libby carefully scanning Stella's notebooks. Stella swore that Libby looked as if she had been crying, but when she asked her, Libby took her hand. "I'm just glad you're awake and back with us."

Libby put the notebooks down. "Well," Libby said, her voice trailing off, "you've been busy."

"Why do you think I need to do this?" she asked.

"I don't know," Libby said, and then she bent over Stella and shone a light into her eyes.

"Will I stop?"

Libby clicked off her light. "I don't know that either," Libby said. "But here's something interesting that I'll remind you about. You're a nurse. I know you know this. We're always re-creating ourselves. Every seven to ten years, most of our cells replace themselves. Some cells do it even quicker. Isn't that something amazing?"

"I don't know," Stella said. "I just feel so weird."

"I know you do."

"Did you see my mom?"

Libby's face softened. "I did. Just for a bit. I like your mom. She brought cookies for the staff. Good cookies, too, from a bakery."

A memory floated into Stella's mind, her mother bringing her elementary-school teachers elaborate holiday gifts, hoping they would make the teachers like Stella more. It always bothered Stella that her mother somehow thought her teachers didn't like her enough. Stella always wished the presents had been for her.

"Did you see Simon? Is he okay?"

Libby smoothed Stella's sheet, the blanket. "He's fine," she said.

"I know you don't like him, you don't approve, but—"

"Stella, don't be silly."

"What's going to happen to me?" Stella whispered. She felt Libby stalling. "Come on, this is me. Tell me the truth."

"There are a lot of maybes," Libby said finally. "You may get dizzy spells. You're most certainly going to feel weird. You might be nauseated." Libby sat down on the bed and took Stella's hand. "Honey," she said, then stopped.

"What?" Stella said. "Tell me. What?"

"You might experience personality changes. Learning disabilities.

You won't be the same, Stella. Maybe not for a while. Maybe not ever. Like I told you, the brain rewires itself. That's how it heals. We just have to wait and see."

"How long do we have to wait?"

"Honey, I don't know. You're going to have some tests. You have a whole team of doctors here, me, a neurologist, a physical therapist. We just don't know how things are going to play out. We have to wait and see."

Stella blinked. She tugged back her hand. *Wait and see* was what you told patients when you had no idea. *Wait and see* was when you didn't like the answer. "Why am I drawing like this?" Stella asked, and Libby shrugged.

"I don't know," Libby said. "You told me your mom was a designer. Who knows, maybe it's those genes finally expressing themselves."

"My mom made beautiful, elaborate dresses. These are just scribbles."

Libby was quiet for a moment. "I know, honey," she said finally.

"Will it go away?"

Libby shrugged.

"Can you go now?" Stella said quietly, and Libby nodded.

Libby left the room, and as soon as she was gone, Stella reached for her pen and notebook again and began to draw even more frantically than before.

SHE WAS DREAMING. Her mother was sitting beside her, beside Simon, and her mom was telling her stories about her childhood, but the language was too garbled and she only caught a few words. Sixth grade. Backyard. Your father. "Mom," she tried to say, "Mom," and then her eyes opened and her mother was there and Stella reached for her arm and there was real flesh. She started to cry. "You came!" Stella said. "You came to me!"

"You're my daughter. Of course I came. I was always here, darling. Simon and I both come every day."

"Tell me. Tell me about you," Stella said. Her mother's hair was short and white, and she was in an old T-shirt and sweatpants, something in the past Bette would never have been caught wearing in public. "You look so different—" Stella said.

"It's me, honey," Bette said.

Her mother told her about the flight from Spain, about the turbulence that made the woman next to her scream out loud. She told her how she had painted her apartment in Spain the most lovely shade of deep green, just like the sea, just like her dress. "You'll both visit me soon," her mother said, and it made Stella sad, because she didn't know yet if she could get out of the bed, let alone cross an ocean.

She couldn't recall with any certainty if Simon and her mom had liked each other, but they seemed to now. Simon stayed close to Bette. When Bette shivered, he got an extra blanket and gently wrapped it around her. And when Bette and Simon left, Bette leaned over to Stella. "You have such a good man," she whispered.

THE DOCTORS TOLD Stella that recovery would be gradual. "How gradual?" she asked, but they never really told her anything other than "We'll see."

There were more tests. More physical therapy and MRIs and CAT scans. Debra came by with a Cinnabon. "Sense memory," she said, and she was right, because Stella remembered sitting in the nurses' station, gorging on the icing, her favorite part. She took a nibble, but it didn't taste right, so she politely took another and then set it down.

Most of the friends who came to visit were nurses. Stella had spent most of her time in the hospital, and when she wasn't there she was with Simon. But as soon as she thought that, she wondered why she and Simon didn't have mutual friends anymore, why they never really went out with other couples. "We're busy people," Simon told her, and then he picked up the Cinnabon she couldn't eat and polished it off.

April turned into May and Stella was getting stronger. It took her a single week and the help of one burly physical therapist named Lou

Rodriguez before she could walk from one end of the corridor to the other, shuffling like an old woman at first, then walking slowly, and finally, moving with some grace and just a little speed, and it bothered her how amazed the nurses were, the doctors, too.

Lou was in his late twenties and funny and he always told her about his husband, Stanley, who was a first-grade teacher. Lou also talked about his mama, Estelle, who made the best tamales in the world. In between tales, he urged Stella on. He told her that she could do anything she set her mind to.

"Right," said Stella doubtfully. He showed her how to get up from the toilet by bracing her hands on her knees and leaning forward and then pushing up, how to use a special metal grip to reach for things so she didn't have to bend over and risk losing her balance. "Use them or lose them," he told her. "Make them work—that's all muscles want you to do."

She felt herself getting stronger. She liked the way that felt. She had never really paid much attention to her body before, but now she was suddenly noticing what it could do, what it wanted.

One day, she overheard Simon talking to her mother, asking her if Stella had ever drawn as a child. "She flunked art, if I remember," Bette said. "She couldn't think outside the lines." She heard Simon talking to Libby, too, asking Libby if this was normal. "She's not even trying to draw," he said. "And she gets so frantic. Should we try to stop her?"

"Her brain's rebooting, that's all," Libby said. "Just keep her in paper for now."

For now, Stella thought, her heart clutching. And then what?

SHE WAS WALKING with Lou, without the IV, all on her own. "I've never seen such an amazing recovery," he told her, and she preened, pleased. It made her want to try harder. Every time she put a hand on the wall to brace herself, he gently took it off. "No train-ing wheels," he said. "Girl, you got to fly!" Stella almost laughed because she thought of how she *had* flown, how she had swerved effortlessly between moguls, lifting off a jump into the hard, blue sky. Lou brought her some of his mama's tamales, heating them up in the nurses' microwave, and they were so delicious that she almost swooned. "Now you're fortified, right?" he said. Then he made her try to climb a flight of stairs, up and then down, but her legs were leaden and she panted as she struggled to lift them. "They're betraying me!" she said.

"When you can do this with ease, then you can go home," he told her. "But don't try it on your own." Fat chance, Stella thought, because all she had to do was try to get out of bed and a nurse would appear, warning her to be careful. "And you still will have to check in with the doctors for therapy every week, and there'll be checkups."

Two more weeks passed. She could see her mother clearly now, and it sometimes disturbed her, because now she noticed the way Bette's hands shook, the wrinkles fanning out under her eyes, the way Bette sometimes fell asleep in the chair. Simon helped Bette up from the chair. He bought her food to eat in the room. The two of them were always exchanging looks and she didn't know what they meant, and when she asked, Simon said, "We're just amazed by you." Why, she thought. Why, why, why?

She was eating anything she wanted, which was mostly Japanese noodle takeout that Simon brought her, or, when she was lucky, she had Lou's mom's tamales. She had never liked spicy food before, but now she was asking Lou to please tell his mom to add some heat. She filled four notebooks full of circles, which she refused to throw out because she liked looking at what she had drawn.

I want to go home. I want to see what home is like.

She was restless, more aware of sounds outside her room. She knew what this tense, dreamy feeling was: hospital psychosis, a strange kind of cabin fever that arose because you saw every little thing that was new, you were always held in place, stuck in a routine. There wasn't a clock in the room, so you couldn't count the minutes.

The air was stale and dry, the windows sealed shut. La la la, Stella thought. I am going insane.

ONE MORNING, A woman with dreadlocks poked her head into Stella's room. "Hey, I'm Virginia," she said. She was wearing jeans and a sweater, so Stella didn't realize she was a patient, not until she told Stella she was waiting for a transplant. She thunked her stomach. "I need a liver giver," Virginia said.

"Wait, I'm a nurse here. Transplant is ninth floor. What are you doing here?"

Virginia grinned. "They don't let us out because of infection, but we sneak and walk around the hospital anyway. Sometimes we even go outside."

"You sneak out?" Stella said. The nurse part of her was horrified, but the patient part wanted to go outside with Virginia, too.

But she didn't, of course, and a week later the doctors told her she could go home, that her memory might come back entirely, or parts of it might always be shadowed. She'd still have to check back with the doctors every week, but the rest of recovery was up to her.

"What does that mean?" Stella asked.

"It means you're ready," Lou told her, but Stella was terrified. What was it going to be like living with Simon again, after all that had happened? And would she be able to live with her mother? With herself?

WHEN SHE LEFT the hospital, it was almost June. Simon and her mom showed up with her favorite black shirt, black jeans and sneakers, and soft bright yellow socks. Simon also brought Godiva chocolates tied in gold ribbons, with fancy cards attached, for all the nurses and doctors. "I can never thank you enough," he said.

All the nurses brought gifts, too, and there was a small cake for her, which was just a big chocolate cupcake with a waxy yellow candle stuck in the middle. They clapped and toasted her with grape juice. Look at you, you're amazing, they said, while Libby took photos with her cell phone and Simon leaned against the wall, smiling. "I'll be back here at work before you know it," Stella told them. "Just not as a patient again, please." No one laughed or even cracked a smile. Instead, they grew more silent, and she saw the look Simon flashed Libby.

"I will be back," Stella insisted. "Don't you dare give my job to anyone else."

"Take your time," Libby said. "What's the rush?" She looked over at Simon. "She's going to need you more than ever," she said carefully. "It's a long process."

Stella knew everyone in this room, the other nurses, the doctors, her physical therapist, and they knew her, too. But now they all knew her in a different way. She wasn't Stella the nurse anymore. She was no longer one of them.

13

ON THE DRIVE FROM the hospital, Stella had stared out the car window, marveling that people could walk and laugh and look in store windows so casually, having no idea how lucky they were. She loved the feel of air on her face, real air and not the hospital packaged kind. How could it have turned into spring so fast? Look at all the women in those floaty sleeveless dresses, the men in their shirtsleeves, their jackets over one arm. Everyone in sunglasses. How dare you take this for granted, she wanted to shout at the people on the sidewalk. Simon kept talking to her, but it felt like a wave washing over her, and she couldn't find a word to grab onto. By the time he had parked the car, she was sweating.

"Ta-da!" Simon said as he opened the door to their apartment. She blinked at the light. What was this place? She tried to remember the velvet couch, the broad wood table by the window, the daybed in the alcove. They looked brand new to her. There were plants growing by the windows, healthy, tilting toward the sun. The wood floors were shiny and clean, the table was clear. There was a scent, an undernote, like damp moss maybe, and she didn't know if she liked it. "You hired someone?"

"I cleaned."

"I supervised," Bette said, laughing.

Something's wrong. Something's very wrong here.

Stella understood that her mom was too old to clean, but she knew also that Simon didn't do tidying. She wandered the apartment. The bright yellow kitchen seemed an affront to her, and she wanted sunglasses to temper the color, and the glass shower in the bathroom, with its potential for breakage, made her anxious. She wandered to the bedroom, Simon following her.

I live here. We live here. My name is Stella. I have my mom and Simon here to help me find what I need.

Set kitty-corner was their double bed with a green comforter on it, but she couldn't remember ever buying it or even liking the color green. Photographs lined the walls. In them, she and Simon laughed as they looked at each other, dazzled with joy. There was Simon singing, his eyes half shut, lost in the music. She couldn't remember any of it. Something was missing, something in her. It was like one of those pictures she used to show to kids in the hospital. Find the difference in the two pictures, she would say. It was always something subtle. A guy in the first photo wearing a blue shirt would be wearing a green one in the second. A vase would vanish from a shelf.

Her life felt like that. Simon touched her shoulder and she flinched. He looked different, too, here in this place, different from how he had been in the hospital. Or maybe she just hadn't noticed what she was noticing now. His jeans hung on him, and for the first time since she'd known him, he was wearing a belt. He must have stopped coloring the gray in his hair, because it was streaked, all salt and pepper, and now too short for the ponytail he sometimes wore. She used to love to stand near him because the air crackled with his energy. But now she didn't feel anything, and the way he kept looking at her was unnerving.

She picked up bills on the table. Utilities. Phone. All marked paid. "That's my job," she said. When she and Simon had first moved in together, they had divvied up the stuff that needed to get done. She'd do the laundry and take care of the money, and he'd cook and do dishes. She loved keeping order, ticking things off her list. It all made her feel capable, strong. She flapped a bill in her hand and when she looked down at it, the numbers were moving, smearing into one another, and none of it made sense. When she saw circles on the page, she put it down. "I'll gladly give this job back to you later," he said. She set the bills down. "You don't have to," she said. This whole apartment felt like a coat that no longer fit her, buttoned up too tightly against her throat, making it hard to breathe.

"Surprise!" Simon said, leading her to the refrigerator and opening it. Everything inside was healthy. Greens. Yogurt. Fresh fruit and vegetables and, in the freezer, a whole chicken. All the things Stella ate and tried to get Simon to eat. She used to live on apples and yogurt, but now they turned her stomach. "I can make you anything," Simon said, but what she wanted, to her shock, were things that in the past had always disgusted her. She yearned for french fries, a greasy burger, a chocolate shake. She could feel the rub of salt against her tongue, the slip of the burger, the shake so thick a straw would stand up in it. She hadn't eaten junk like that since she was a kid, but now she felt that if she couldn't have it soon, she might die.

When she told him what she wanted, he looked appalled. "You want that? I've never seen you even look at it," he said.

"I want it now, I guess."

"You sure about this?" her mother said. "I could make us all some soup. You used to love my white bean soup."

Stella felt her stomach churn. Never had anything sounded more unappealing to her.

He called Seamless so that they didn't have to go out, ordering Thai noodles for himself, chicken and rice for Bette. As soon as she saw the burger, caught its greasy whiff, Stella was ravenous. She ate a fry and licked the salt from her fingers. She bit deep into the burger and shivered with pleasure. Bette was eating slowly, but Simon stood watching her, not touching his noodles. "You aren't eating?" she said. "We can split this." She held up the burger, but he shook his head.

"I'll eat later," he said, his voice funny, and that was when she knew he was breathing through his mouth so he wouldn't have to smell her food. "Should I eat this in the other room?" she said.

"No, no," he told her. "You stay right here with us."

"God, this is heaven," she said with a heavy sigh. When she was finished, Simon put the oily wrappers in the trash, then washed his hands, smiling weakly at her. "I'm glad you ate," he said.

THAT NIGHT, SHE stood in front of the bathroom mirror, staring at her face. She looked at the back of her hands to see if they'd aged, but they looked the same, ropey with veins, the skin starting to crinkle a little with age. She had makeup on her dresser, but to her surprise, she had no idea how to use it anymore. Besides, she didn't want anything fake now. She had to get to the core of herself.

She put on a T-shirt and gingerly got in their bed. Her heart was pounding. Could she go to sleep beside Simon? What would it feel like to have him touch her? Did she even want that? What if she went to sleep and didn't wake up? She tried to focus on what she knew, to list those things in her head. They had been together. They had been happy. She lived with him. They had had sex. A lot, she thought, because look at him. He was like a thoroughbred with angles and sinew, those strong shoulders. She remembered that women had thrown themselves at him, but he had always come home to her. She reached out a hand and put it on his chest, and he stilled, which made her nervous. She could feel his heart beat through her fingers. "Are you sure?" he asked. "We don't have to do anything, honey. We have all the time in the world."

"No, we don't," she said. And she suddenly knew that it was true.

"Your mom. She's in the other room, in the alcove."

"She's a deep sleeper. There could be a fire drill and she wouldn't wake up."

She wanted to draw loops and loops, over and over on paper, but instead she did it across his chest, her fingers moving as if she were holding a pen. She shut her eyes, breathing more deeply, calming herself. She felt like her body was raging with fever. I love you, she wanted to say, I love you, but she couldn't find the words. She swung a leg along Simon's hip and drew him closer to her. She breathed in the smell of his back, and kissed his shoulder.

The more he took his time, slowly stroking her, the more impatient she became. It had to be fast. It had to be now, now, now. "Quick," she said, pulling him to her. But once he was inside, it felt like she was having sex with a stranger, like she was outside her own body, floating, looking down, wondering what that woman was feeling. She raised her hips and heard him coming, the cry that he made, the shudder of his body. "Oh, honey," he said, collapsing against her. She didn't want to look at him, didn't want him to know that what she felt wasn't desire or frustration. It was terror, because everything felt wrong. She waited until she heard him breathing, longer, slower, easing into sleep. One of his arms was cradling her, but she extricated herself and went into the kitchen.

She had to kill this roller-coaster feeling. She sat at the table, drumming her fingers on the surface. She took a pad of paper and a pen, and wrote her name in large letters, over and over, faster and faster, not noticing what she was doing until her name turned into circles and she suddenly blinked hard, and there in front of her were sheets and sheets of paper, all of them covered in ink. Some of the pages were ripped where she had borne down with the pen. She didn't remember drawing, but she could remember the feeling she had as she drew, the absolute joy.

She wanted it back.

She crumpled the pages and stuffed them in the trash. She didn't know why, but she knew, no matter what anyone else thought, that all this was important somehow, part of a process, that it would reveal itself to her when she was ready. And then maybe it would reveal itself to Simon, too, and they would both understand it.

WHEN SHE AND Simon were first dating, they used to talk about everything, including their future. They'd always tell each other how they were feeling. "We're in sync," Stella said. She remembered that the first month they were together she had asked him what kind of relationship he was looking for, because she wanted to be sure she wasn't wasting time on a party guy, on someone who would smash her heart. He had smiled, like he knew a secret. "I want a relationship like Bob and Carol's."

Bob had been one of his professors at Manhattan College of Music. He was older than Simon, in his late fifties. He had mentored Simon through music theory and a couple of other difficult classes. Simon later met Carol at a departmental banquet, and after graduation they all became casual friends. He told her that Bob and Carol had been together for seventeen years, that they still held hands and called each other pet names, like "love" or "darling" or "boochie," that sometimes it felt like you had been dipped in sunshine just to be near them. "When he breathes out, she breathes in," he told Stella, and that was when Stella started falling in love with Simon, because that was the kind of connection she wanted, too.

She saw it for herself when Bob and Carol invited her and Simon to dinner. The two of them were so happy that Stella had whispered to Simon, "We're as happy as they are, aren't we?"

"Sure we are, dopey," he said, kissing her nose.

Bob and Carol continued to be the template Stella measured her and Simon's relationship against. But one day, after Stella had been with Simon ten years, to her surprise, Carol called, sobbing. Bob had left her for another woman. A bodybuilder.

"What?" Stella said. "A bodybuilder?" She knew Bob as a slightly overweight good guy with shaggy hair. She couldn't imagine him wanting something so extreme.

"That's who he is now," Carol said. "That's who I'm not. He shaves his head. He oils his body. He turned our basement into a weight-lifting room. He won a competition pulling a truck with a rope in his teeth."

Carol told her that something had happened to him. Suddenly, at dinner, when they used to talk about books and movies, he began to talk about deltoids and goblet squats. Worse, he began to criticize Carol for not following his passion. "You always did before," he said.

Stella was stunned. Simon, too. He looked as if he had been punched in the heart. She and Simon talked all night about the couple, wondering how such a thing could happen and also how they didn't want to be friends anymore with someone like Bob, a man who could be so hurtful. And then Simon said, "You know, before he met Carol, he was a hunter. Big and burly and married to a big woman, too. When he met Carol, she wasn't keen on hunting, so he gave all that up. He cut his hair shorter. He changed."

Both Carol and Bob moved out of the city, and neither kept in touch. One day while looking around Facebook, Stella saw that Bob was no longer weight lifting, that he now lived in California and he was surfing. There was a picture of him and his new wife, the two of them gleaming in the sun, the ocean behind them. Stella couldn't find Carol on any social media at all.

Bob had never been in coma. He had never hit his head. He had never done drugs except for whatever would give him more stamina and muscle. And he and Carol hadn't lasted. Would she and Simon? She crept back into bed, curling her body around him. Stay, she thought. Stay.

THEY ALL SEEMED to wake around the same time. It bothered her how both Simon and Bette kept touching her, almost reassuring themselves that she was real, how she'd catch them staring. It bothered her, too, how close they seemed, how they'd sit and talk intently, like they had known each other forever. "I'm fine," Stella said over and over. "I'm fine." What was worse was when either one of them had puffy eyes from tears or worried expressions, even though she was home now, she wasn't still in the hospital.

Simon took short showers, so she went in second, turning up the hot water so high that the bathroom clouded with steam, staying in for nearly an hour. "Sauna, anyone?" Simon said when she opened the door.

She dressed the way Simon did, black T-shirt, black jeans, sneakers. "Look at us," she said.

"I hate going to work, leaving you," Simon told her, both of them wandering into the kitchen. Bette came in, already dressed, her makeup on. "I'm here," Bette told him. "We'll be just fine, the two of us."

"You could come with me," he said to Stella, but she shook her head. "I can't just sit in a car all day. And I'm fine."

Bette took it upon herself to make strawberry smoothies, and when Stella didn't want one, her mother looked so disappointed Stella forced herself to drink it. "We should have these every day," Simon said.

Once Simon left for the day, kissing her, hugging Bette, Stella began to feel her mother's presence tightening around her.

"Come sit beside me," Bette said, patting the sofa. Stella sat stiffly. "You want to play cards?" Bette said, and Stella shook her head. "How about a show on TV?" Bette said.

"I don't think I can concentrate," Stella said.

"Well, then," Bette said. "Let me tell you stories about you, my beautiful daughter. I'll entertain you." Good, Stella thought. She'd try to remember every word her mother said.

"When you were little," Bette said, "we thought it was important for you to have your own room, but you always woke up in the night and came to our bed and squeezed in right between your dad and me, spreading your arms, taking up the whole bed. When we walked, you had to be in the middle, each of your hands holding ours, just like you were afraid we'd fly away."

"I did that?" Stella tried to remember but couldn't.

"You hated being alone, and you were a screamer. You slept only if you were right beside us," Bette said. "And even as you got older, you were always afraid that we were going to leave you, though we assured you that we never would."

"I never thought I was that important to you," Stella said.

Bette started. "What? How could you say such a thing? You were everything to us. Everything."

Stella shook her head. "No, you saw only Daddy. He was your everything."

"You're wrong. You're so wrong." Bette leaned closer to Stella.

"How am I wrong?"

"Because your father was different."

"How?"

"Because I knew when we married that he was going to die young, and we didn't have much time."

Stella looked at her mother, shocked. She couldn't remember her father ever being sick with even a cold, let alone something serious. "What? How do I not know this?"

"Because we didn't want you to worry, pet. All the men in his family died young from heart attacks, and there was nothing to do about it. It was just something congenital. He kept saying that he was going to be the one who was different, that he would be with me into our nineties, but I knew the odds were against us. And I focused on him so much because I didn't know how much time we'd have and I wanted every second. But then I wanted other things, too, the chance to pass on his genes, to have a child. We argued about it for years because he didn't want to be an absent father, but then he gave in."

A memory floated into Stella's head, vivid as a shout. Her father dying of a heart attack, and she was standing with her mom in a funeral parlor, in her last year of nursing school, holding on to her mom, stunned with grief.

"But then you moved away from me," Stella said. "All the way to Spain."

"And I'm here now," Bette said.

Bette walked over to the shelf and pulled out a photo album. "Come on, you tell me stories now," she said.

Stella opened the album and suddenly she couldn't breathe. She could recognize herself in the photos, and Simon and some of her friends, but other people were unknown to her. Who was this woman with the short white hair hugging Stella as if they were the best of friends? Who was this bearded guy with her and Simon, his head thrown back, laughing?

"Oh, can we not do this now?" Stella said, and Bette shut the album and then yawned. "Goodness," she said. "Time for me to take a nap. Will you be okay?"

"Absolutely," Stella said. "I'll be fine." She sat at the table and found her paper, her pen. The circles skimmed over the surface like figure skaters. Her mother had no reason to lie, but was this the whole truth? she wondered.

WHEN SIMON GOT home, it was like a small shock, like she had almost forgotten he lived there. He was so handsome, it was exciting to see him. She loved his lashy eyes and his hair, especially now, crisscrossed with silver. There was an energy around him when he moved, but every time she tried to get closer to it, she felt something pushing her away.

As soon as Simon came in, Bette called out to him. "Yoo-hoo, I'm here," she said, coming into the room. "You are!" Simon said, kissing her on the cheek while Bette beamed.

That night, Stella came out of the bathroom to find the two of them talking quietly, stopping as soon as they saw her. "What are you saying?" she asked. "Are you talking about me?"

"Honey, no," her mother said.

"Because please don't do that to me," Stella said. "I'm right here."

"And how happy we are that you are home," Bette said.

But if her mother seemed a stranger, so did Simon. Stella felt him watching her all the time. Was he worried that she'd do something dangerous? That she'd collapse? That night she woke up to find him sitting up in bed, looking right at her. She turned over and pretended to sleep, waiting for him to fall sleep, too.

When friends came over that Thursday, crowing, "We come bearing gifts," and showering her with lipsticks and nail polishes, with body lotions and books, they crowded around her. But Stella had trouble following their conversations. She missed questions or didn't know the answers. "Hey, I get that way, too," Debra said. "Don't worry."

Libby visited the most, but even when she took Stella's hand, it felt to her like a medical action, as if Libby were taking her pulse. And when Libby looked Stella in the eye, Stella felt as if Libby were checking the dilation of her pupils.

"Let's not make this a doctor visit," Stella said, and Libby stepped back.

"Oh, how I've missed you," Libby said, and Stella hugged her.

One day, Libby showed up with a puzzle. Three hundred pieces, a photo of a family and a dog. "Ages three to eight?" Stella said, glancing at the box lid, frowning, and Libby laughed.

"It's going to help your brain, you'll see. And I'll do it with you," she said. "Come on." The two of them sat at the long wood table and Libby spilled out the pieces.

"Find the edges first," Libby said. "Then we'll separate it into colors."

Stella had never really liked puzzles, but now, every time she found a piece with an edge, she felt a thrill of satisfaction. There was the puzzle, slowly growing into something that made sense.

Another day, Libby showed up with special headphones. "What's this?" Stella said. Libby plugged them into the computer, and then clicked onto a site.

"What are you doing?"

"Binaural beats," Libby said. "Two different frequencies of sound play into each ear. The brain makes up the difference between the two frequencies and it sort of reorders how you feel by creating new brain waves." She put the headphones on Stella. "Here, try," she said. "This one's for theta waves. It'll help your memory and calm you."

"I don't know," Stella said.

"I'll stay right here with you while you listen," Libby said, which made Stella feel better.

She shut her eyes. Sound thumped in through the headphones. There had always been music in this apartment, always, but Simon liked it loud, which her oversensitive ears couldn't tolerate. She never wanted to hurt his feelings, so she told him she'd listen on the headphones, and then she could control the volume, moving it so it felt comfortable.

This was different, though. Now she felt that she'd been thrust into a strange new world.

The beats didn't have a melody and there was no tune, just a kind of pulsing, but she found herself relaxing, her eyes drifting shut. Were they really putting her to sleep? She blinked hard, and then the door opened and Simon came in, a bag of groceries in his arms, and when he saw her with headphones, he grinned.

"You listening to me?" he said, pleased.

"It's not music," Libby said.

"What is it, then?" Simon walked over to Stella and gently took the headphones off and put it on his ears. He frowned and then took the headphones off and put them back on Stella.

"Beats," Stella told him. "To reorder my brain."

Simon slowly nodded. "Whatever works, then," he said finally, but Stella couldn't help but notice that he looked a little hurt.

BY THE END of June, Stella began to wonder if it wasn't time for her to do without all this help. She saw her doctors once a week, including the neurologist Dr. Alberson, and then Libby, and they all

seemed to be happy about her progress, but if that was so, why did she
have to keep going to see them? The next time she saw Dr. Alberson,
she pressed him about the possibility of her not coming to see him
anymore. "It makes me feel worse," she said. "It reminds me."

He grew quiet. "There are no hard-and-fast rules," he told her.
"Every situation, every patient, is totally different, in my experience.
Some come see me for much longer. Some don't. You seem to be doing
great. If you feel like you want to stop coming to see me, then stop
coming to see me."

Stella felt a wash of relief. "Really?" she said, brightening.

"Really."

Libby, though, wasn't happy when she heard about it. "It's my
decision," Stella reminded her. Libby kept asking her if she wanted to
see a shrink, if she wanted medication for depression, but Stella waved
her away. "Why do you think I need that? Am I acting depressed?"

"I think anyone would be who went through what you did," Libby
said.

"Just be my friend," Stella told her, and Libby grew quiet.

But Stella had to deal with Bette, too. She liked having her mother
around, but she couldn't help but feel watched. If she even went into
the kitchen, Bette would follow her, making sure she was all right.
When she napped in the living room, Bette would read or knit just so
that she could watch over her.

Things were, of course, better, but Stella still felt trapped in the
wrong life. She wanted things to be the way they had been before, and
maybe the way to do that was to make some decisions, to pare things
back down a bit and see how she'd do.

One night, she cornered Simon. She put her hands on his chest. "I
think my mom needs to go home," she said.

"Really? But she helps us out. She's someone to be with you when
I'm at work."

Her fingers trailed down to his belly. "I just want you," she said. "I
think we need to be just us. On our own. See what that's like again."

She swallowed. "I need to see what it's like to just be me on my own, without someone always around, always taking care of me."

"Are you sure?" he said. "I'd feel better if she were here with you during the day."

"She's old," Stella blurted, because she didn't know what else to say. "She needs to go home. To her home. She'd never say it, but I know it's true. It's a stress on her." She put her hands on Simon's face. "Please," she said. "Please. Will you tell her?"

THAT NIGHT AT dinner, with all of them sitting at the table—Simon and Bette eating take-out Chinese, Stella with her hamburger—Simon gently told Bette that they couldn't take advantage of her kindness another moment, that they wanted her to be back at her home. Bette's chopsticks stopped midair. She sat up straighter. She looked from Simon to Stella, as if deciding something.

"I love you," Stella said. "I've loved having you here. But I need to get stronger on my own."

Bette carefully placed her chopsticks down. "Of course, darlings," Bette said.

"I just need to try . . ." Stella said.

"And I can always come back anytime," Bette said. "I'll find a flight right after dinner."

BUT AS SOON as Stella's mother left, and she and Simon were alone again in the apartment, Stella wanted her mom back.

She noticed new things. He didn't play his guitar very much. He didn't listen to music. Instead, he seemed to be listening to her, as if she were on a different wavelength.

She missed her mother, but now she missed Simon even more.

14

IT WAS TEN AT night and his Lyft shift was over, and Simon was rushing home. Sometimes he half hoped that Bette would be back in the apartment even though she had called him the moment she was resettled in her own place in Spain. "You know, you can always call me. Anytime, day or night," Bette said. He knew she meant it, and he loved her for it.

When Stella had awakened, Simon was stunned. He hadn't allowed himself to think into the future. He wasn't there when she came to, but Libby had called him, her voice full of tears, and the first thing he thought was that Stella had died, but Libby reassured him that Stella was alive, awake.

Of course, he had rushed to the hospital, to her. Of course, he had cried when he saw her lying there, struggling, her eyes floating open and then closing again. "It takes time," Libby told him. "You have to be patient," and then he saw Libby's own raw, red eyes, and that made him cry harder.

He had thought everything would be different now that Stella was awake, and it was. Just not the way he thought.

Stella didn't act like Stella. She didn't speak like her or move like her, or even smell like her, and it tortured Simon. He leaned into her neck, the way he always had, resting his face against her skin. An amazing thing about her had always been that though she never used perfumes, she always somehow smelled like evergreens. Now, though, all he could smell was soap.

"Let her find her way," Libby said when he'd asked her about it, but what way was that, and why couldn't he act as her guide? He had thought—no, he had prayed—that she'd wake up, and when she did, it felt like someone new was inhabiting her body. When he looked at her eyes, he didn't have a clue anymore what she was thinking or even if she was thinking about him, which made him feel strange and shy and unhappy. He kept trying to make things the same as they had been, telling her old jokes, singing old songs, but none of it worked. She didn't get the jokes, and she couldn't concentrate on the movies, instead excusing herself, leaving him alone on the couch. "I'm so sorry," she said quietly, but he couldn't make her feel guilty, so he told her it was fine. In bed at night, he felt her moving toward the edge of the bed instead of looping one leg around his, drawing him closer. When he dared to touch her, the curve of her breast, the thing she had loved, she seemed to draw into herself, even farther away. She acted as if he were wounding her. The last time they had made love, he got lost in it, in her, feeling like they were the same couple again, and he was about to tell her how much he had missed her, how happy he was she was back, how he'd never leave her side again, and then he opened his eyes and saw she was staring at the ceiling, and when he stopped moving, she didn't pull him back to her.

"Maybe we can just talk," he said, lifting himself up on an elbow.

"I don't know what to talk about," she whispered, and he saw the panic in her face, and so he just smoothed back her hair. "Maybe we should just sleep," he told her. She nodded again, which broke his heart even more.

He paid the bills. He bought the groceries, trying to remember what it was she liked to eat now. He made sure the bathroom was scrubbed, that their friends were kept in the loop about what was going on. "Look what I did," he told her once, showing off their kitchen, how every surface gleamed, how even the canned goods were orderly in the cabinet, but her face was blank, unsure. How funny, he thought. He had become the person she had wanted him to be, and suddenly it didn't matter. It was only when Libby came over to see Stella that he felt that anyone realized how he had changed, too. "The house looks great," Libby told him. She noticed the bills stacked neatly in a box, she watched Simon making tea, fielding phone calls politely. Libby was the one who put her hand on his arm, and when she did, Simon felt it like a tiny electric shock.

He knew Stella had to go out in the world, but he worried each time she left the apartment without him, making sure she had her cell phone with her, that he knew exactly where she was going.

"Don't go too far," he said.

She didn't. She took baby steps, walking from the apartment four blocks north and then coming back. She went to the bodega to buy milk or just to sit on a nearby bench by the Chelsea Cinema and people-watch for a while. She came back with her cheeks flushed, both from the summer heat and the excitement. "There's my baby," Simon said, hugging her, but inside, he worried: she's going to go out again, and what if something happens to her?

STELLA'S DRAWINGS, WHICH had begun as nothing but spirals and circles, gradually morphed into something more creative. She sat down, and without thinking about it, almost in a trance, she started to draw. First there were shapes. Real shapes. The vase on the kitchen table. Simon's guitar perched against a wall. Then parts of faces. An eye. A nose. Before, she hadn't known how to draw, but here, on the page, she was doing it like an expert.

Libby had told Simon that some people developed talents along with new personalities, but he hadn't really believed her. Libby had said that a coma could awaken the part of the mind, the temporal lobe, that had to do with visuals. Some people might become savants, able to brilliantly play the piano when before they couldn't find middle C. Simon still didn't get it. How could someone who had never done anything more with a pen than scribble a grocery list suddenly want to do this kind of drawing and be able to do it well?

One evening when it had turned to July, he came home and she was sketching her lunch, a sandwich with a bite out of it, so accurately that it might have been a photo. "Stella—" he said, and she looked up, her eyes glazed. "How are you doing this?" he said, and she shook her head, pained, and looked at the drawing, a look of surprise on her face, as if she hadn't been the one who drew it.

"I don't know," she said, and then she blinked hard. "I just do."

"What made you want to draw the sandwich?" he asked. "Do you—do you choose what to draw? Do you just draw what's there?"

She looked alarmed and pushed the paper away from her. "I don't know," she said.

"Do you see how good this is?"

Stella got up from the table. "I don't want to draw anymore today," she said.

He carefully took her drawing and put it on the shelf in case she wanted it. He left her alone, not pushing her. None of them, he, Libby, or Stella, knew why she was doing this, but at least she had something to occupy herself, though it worried him when she was alone. It worried him that she didn't have a job now, though it certainly would have worried him more if she did. Maybe he'd ask around, see if anyone had an opening at a shop or a bakery. Someplace with people. Something just to give her a start.

But instead, he let her draw, and he decided that if she could be creative, so could he. It made him sick and ashamed to think that nothing had happened or would happen with his demo. He hadn't told Bette or Stella that Libby had sent it out to a CEO she knew, and he was too demoralized to follow up on it with her, too disheartened to try to send it out again on his own. But even so, he wouldn't give up. So he tried to finish a song he had been working on, one about Stella coming home, about how his heart felt like it had tiny cracks in it and he didn't know whether it would heal itself or rupture into a thousand shards. It felt really new to him, more personal and interesting than anything he had done before.

"Want to hear my new song?" he asked her one evening when he felt it was almost finished. She sat very still while he played, her head tilted to the side. "I like when you play," she said when he was done. She got up from the table and moved close to him, resting her head on his shoulder. "You should send out that song," she said. "Call Kevin. Sing to him on the phone if you have to."

Simon hesitated, then made the call.

"What the fuck," Kevin snapped. Simon laughed. He waited for Kevin's familiar irritation to pass. Then: "Simon! How the hell are you?"

It bothered Simon that Kevin didn't ask about Stella, didn't ask about anything, but he wanted to power through this, to get it over with.

"So I have this song," Simon said. "I think it's really good, really different."

"That's great, man," Kevin said.

"Let me play it for you now, okay?" Simon said.

"Sure, sing away," Kevin said.

When he finished, Simon asked, "What did you think?" He looked at Stella, who was smiling at him, her eyes half closed.

"Not quite right for us," Kevin said.

Simon shut his eyes for a moment and then opened them, and the whole room looked different, as if every color had faded. "Why not?" he asked.

"I don't know," Kevin said. "It doesn't feel right for us. It just isn't . . . there."

Simon thought of all the hours he had worked on that song. He thought of Stella, her eyes half shutting with pleasure. He swallowed. "So, then, how can I get it 'there'?" he said.

Kevin breathed into the phone, the way he always did when he was thinking about what to say. "Maybe you can't," he said. "Maybe the song just doesn't have the right bones to build on."

"Do you want to hear something else?" Simon hated the knot of panic building in his chest. "I have other songs. Lots of other songs," he lied.

Kevin breathed heavily into the phone. "Look," he said, clearing his throat. "We're a different band now. A different sound. I'm happy you're writing songs, but they aren't for us. Not anymore. You hear our latest stuff? We have a hot new single, "Blow Over.""

"Haven't heard it," Simon said, which was the truth. He tried never to listen to the band anymore because it hurt too much; it made him think about all that he had lost.

The conversation ended. Simon put his head in his hands. "I never liked Kevin," Stella said. "And there're lots of other bands. Better bands, too."

He got online and did a search. There it was on iTunes, "Blow Over." It was on Spotify, too, and niche radio, and on YouTube it already had five thousand reviews, all of them raves. This time, this one time, he'd listen and then he'd try to never hear the band again. Simon put on his headphones and turned the volume up and listened intently. Kevin's drumming was sharper, more of an attack. They had a violinist now, which felt like an intrusion to Simon. There was the steady thrum of the bass, still the same, but now Rob was purpose-fully making discordant harmonies. As Simon listened, he realized his own fingers were moving, picking notes and trying to put the melody where he thought it belonged.

What a fool he was. Kevin was right. Even if they asked him, he couldn't fit into this band. Not anymore. And they hadn't asked. They wouldn't.

He turned off his computer. *Done. Over. Fuck you. Fuck me.*

He couldn't be here now. "I'm going to get groceries," he told

Stella, though he knew they didn't need anything. Stella, her head bent, was drawing ferociously on the page a glass half full of water. She didn't look up when he left.

WHOLE FOODS ON Fourteenth Street was always packed, but he liked feeling the swarm of people around him. He threw things into the cart that might be small pleasures: a tiny tub of cashew yogurt. Strawberries as big as his fist. He was rounding a corner, going over to the ice cream when he saw Libby in shorts and a black tank top, her hair piled on top of her head, her beautiful long legs stretched into a stance.

It was funny to watch her choose two ice creams and wonder over them, when she was so certain about everything else. And then she turned and saw him. She smiled.

"Well, hey you," she said.

They talked leaning against the freezer door. She asked him about Stella, and then they both admired the Ice Dream in the freezer. "Why doesn't anyone make marshmallow ice cream?" she said wistfully.

"You can't have that. You have to have a base, chocolate or vanilla. Marshmallow gets added on. It'd be awful by itself."

She grinned. "It'd be delicious. I may just buy marshmallows and make it myself and prove it to you."

In spite of the freezer, he felt warmed somehow just standing beside her. "You are wonderfully weird," he said, and she laughed.

"See you later, gator," she said, reaching in and choosing chocolate, then dropping it into the cart.

As soon as she left, he felt the chill again.

15

STELLA SPENT A LONG time making what she called "on the same wavelength" lists, things she could do that might tug Simon and her close again: going for a walk, picking up salmon for dinner, listening to music that they both loved. But as soon as Simon left for work, she looked at the list and knew she didn't want to do any of those things.

She sat at home, confused. What *did* she want to do now? What did she like? All she could think of was that she liked drawing—it got her out of herself, out of the confines of her mind. It made her feel more grounded. Not being compelled to draw circles was a relief. Instead, she wanted to draw chairs or fruit or whatever was in front of her. The subjects didn't matter, just the fact that she could draw them made her feel more capable.

Still, though, the drawings were all for herself. She yearned for a purpose in the world. She yearned to belong. Those were things she had before when she was a nurse. Why couldn't she go back to that life? The last time Libby had been to visit, Stella knew that she was casually testing her, asking her all these questions about what her favorite restaurant in Chelsea was, checking to see how Stella had progressed on the puzzle Libby had brought her. "You're halfway there!" Libby said, pleased.

"You know I'm better now," Stella said, countering, and then Libby changed the subject and began talking about a pair of strappy sandals she wanted to buy.

Stella picked up the phone now and called Human Resources at the hospital. She didn't really know the people there and had no idea who would answer, but she knew they could pull her file. "So, can I come back to work?" she said.

The guy on the other line sighed. "You need to take more time," he said.

"No, I don't. Not really," Stella said, but he wouldn't listen to her.

Stella hung up, but she didn't give up. She kept calling, two days later, and then another two days after that. They always had the same answers. They also told her that they were overstaffed right now, which Stella knew was a lie because what hospital ever had enough nurses?

"I want to go back to work as a nurse," she told Simon, and he brightened. "That's a good idea," he said. "I'll worry less with you around all those doctors."

When she told him Human Resources didn't think so, he told her to call Libby. "She'll help you," he said.

"I'll go see her tomorrow," Stella said.

THE NEXT DAY, as she walked to Libby's office, she couldn't help looking at people's faces as they passed her in the hospital hallway, diagnosing them on sight. This woman looked anemic, that man clearly had gout. She felt a swell of satisfaction in knowing that her nursing instincts were intact.

She found Libby in her office, and as soon as Libby saw her, she jumped up. "Well, hey, hey, hey, you," Libby said, hugging her. "Come on in and let me take a look at you."

Stella noticed the shadows under Libby's eyes, like stains, the way her shoulders hunched.

"Is everything okay? You want to talk about it?" Stella asked, suddenly concerned.

Libby shook her head. "Everything's fine. Would you humor me and just let me take your vitals without protest?"

Stella sighed heavily. "Can this please be the last time?"

Libby took Stella's blood pressure, and then shone a light in her eye. "You're doing good," Libby decided. "No memory issues? Motility issues? Any changes?"

Stella grabbed for Libby's hand. "I'm better than good. The drawings. They help. They really do. Anyway," Stella said, "this visit. It's not about the medical stuff. It's about my mental state."

"You're depressed?"

"No, no. I can't just sit in the apartment. I can't figure out what to do with myself. Please. Please give me something to do. I know the hospital won't let me do actual nursing yet, but I could volunteer, couldn't I? I could do all the jobs the other nurses don't have time for. You know I could—"

"Oh, Stella, I—"

"I want—I need—to be useful. I can do this, Libby. I really can. And you know I'm good at it. Please."

Libby was silent for a moment. "It can't really be nursing," Libby said.

"I know that. At least not yet."

"And it might be menial."

"I'll wash floors. I'll empty bedpans."

"I don't know," Libby said, shaking her head.

"Yes, you do. There're all sorts of jobs a hospital needs to be done, and you don't even need to be smart, which I am, to do them. I can be a patient courier and take them for CAT scans or MRIs. I can deliver lunch trays and then take them away. How can I possibly screw that up?"

"Let me see what I can do," Libby said. "Maybe it would work a few hours a day. Maybe it would be good for you, too."

"It will be," Stella said. "I promise."

"We'll have to see," Libby said.

TWO DAYS LATER, courtesy of Libby, Stella had a job. She'd be working in the nursery, cradling babies. Strictly volunteer work and most definitely part-time. "Will you be bored?" Libby asked her. "You can wait for something else."

"I'll take anything," Stella said. She wasn't sure how she felt about working with babies. She had wanted them so much at one time, and that time was over now.

Maybe she didn't know how she felt about being around infants, but being back in the hospital was a totally different thing.

Her first day of work, she bounced into the hospital in her scrubs. ("Well, look at you!" Simon had said when she came into the kitchen that morning. "That's the Stella I know and love!") Her scrubs were freshly washed and even ironed because today felt so special. She grinned wildly at the doctors she passed, the other nurses. These are my people, she thought. Libby had found her volunteer work for now (for now!), cuddling babies in the nursery, under the eye of another nurse. Sure, it wasn't what she usually did, and it was only for a few hours, three days a week. It wasn't even on her usual floor, but it was something. It was a start. She would show them she could do this and they'd gradually let her do more until she was back to work for real.

As she entered the maternity ward, she remembered that this was where she first met Simon. Maybe that was an omen. She walked to the nursery and there was Libby, waiting for her. But as soon as Libby saw her, she gently shook her head. "You have to wear real clothes," Libby told her. "Street clothes. You're not officially here as a nurse."

"Oh," Stella said. Libby must have seen the slump of Stella's shoulders because she touched her hand. "But for today, this is okay," Libby said. She handed Stella a stick-on badge to wear, volunteer, with her name and the date printed underneath. "You get a new one each time you come in," Libby said.

Stella looked around. There was one other nurse here, someone she didn't know, feeding a baby. The hospital liked babies to be with the moms in their rooms—"rooming in," they called it—so there were only a few infants swaddled in bassinets, which decreased her chances of screwing up. She knew she was only a volunteer cuddler, but what if she couldn't even do that? She nodded at everything Libby was telling her. Libby showed her where the burp cloths were. Vomit, she heard. Diapers. Pumped breast milk. Formula. It didn't sound hard, but it didn't sound as satisfying as the work she used to do with patients, tending their wounds, using her mind.

"Feeding and growing. That's what they do," Libby said. She pointed out the crack baby waiting for his mom to get out of rehab. "His name is Raymond. He needs kangaroo care," she said. "Skin-to-skin contact takes care of so many ills." She showed Stella another infant who was there because her mom was ill. "So you're all set," Libby said. "You have any questions, Laura is right here." She nodded at the other nurse.

"I can do more than just hold them," Stella offered.

"No, you can't," Libby said. "Really, I mean it. Listen to what I'm saying." She looked very serious, but she gave Stella a hug. "I'll be back later. Maybe we can go grab lunch," Libby said.

The first baby Stella held was a little girl named May, a blue-eyed doll, a preemie whose mother was what the nurses called a semi-crunchy mom. The crunchy moms were the ones who insisted on everything organic, on cloth diapers because they were better for the environment, on breast milk and attachment parenting. They drove some of the nurses crazy. But May's mom was only semi-crunchy, because she used formula instead of breastfeeding. May seemed to sleep through everything. She snoozed through the story Stella recited, didn't rouse when Stella sang or rubbed a bottle against her lips. Sometimes, when she needed to, Stella made circles on May's back, so if Laura looked over, she'd think Stella was comforting the baby. It calmed both of them. Stella liked the weight of May in her arms. She found herself marveling at May's tiny nose, at the sounds she made, soft growls and burbles.

The next baby she held was Raymond, and as soon as she lifted him up, he arched his back and his neck, pulling away from her. He flapped his arms at the bottle she offered. He looked pained when she sang to him, and then he cried, a noise high and shrill, like a wild bird. She tried everything, talking soothingly to him, rocking him, even whispering "please." He peed all over her and threw up his milk on her shoulder and then screamed for more of his bottle.

His brain, like hers, had also transformed, his because of the crack. And it was sadder for him because he had never had a real chance to know what a properly wired brain felt like. He never had a clue about who he really was. "I know how you feel, honey," she crooned to him. Maybe that was why he made her feel afraid.

A week later Stella came in and found that May was gone, and suddenly Stella felt all the air around her constricting. "Well, you don't expect her to live here now, do you?" Laura said. But the truth was that Stella actually did. She had gotten used to May, had begun to feel comfortable holding her. She loved the baby's scent, those sweet blue eyes. It was the perfect setup—an hour with Raymond, who never relaxed in her arms, who always seized up, followed by the soothing slumber of May. "There's still Raymond," Laura told her, pointing to Raymond's bassinet. His little face was screwed up like a clenched fist and he was angrily flapping his hands.

As difficult as he was, she couldn't help feeling for him. It was easy to love babies like May, who were no more trouble than a doll, who grabbed for your finger and liked to be tickled. But wasn't it worth more to love the troubled baby, the one who could learn to be happy if only someone would show him how? "You spoil Raymond," Laura told her. "But keep doing it."

She had new babies to tend to, which meant more monitoring from Laura. Every once in a while, Libby dipped her head in, took a quick glance, smiled at Stella, and then left. Why did Libby have to check on her? she wondered. Wasn't it enough that Stella triple-checked everything she did? She went over and over the names on the baby bassinets. She made sure she didn't feed one mother's colostrum to another's baby. She was extra careful with Raymond because she was terrified he might squirm out of her arms. Babies could do that, and a fall could fracture their skulls. She wished there were a chart monitoring her progress. She wished she could relax, that her mind would stop stumbling. She felt so restless at the end of each day, like she hadn't really done anything, like she hadn't really mattered. A trained monkey could do my job, she thought.

When she was done each day, she took off her volunteer badge and walked through the hospital corridors. She didn't feel like a nurse anymore, maybe because she had to wear her own clothes instead of the scrubs. Maybe because no one gave her that look of respect anymore. Here, now, she could be anyone. She came home without all the funny stories she usually had, because the truth was, nothing much of note happened in the nursery. Some days, she felt like she could drift into a milky sleep along with the babies. But she told Simon that she worried about whether she had done a good job. There were all sorts of mistakes that could happen. She might not notice that a baby's pulse was thready or the eyes were misaligned. How hard would it be to screw up simple cuddling? All she was doing was holding these tiny living things. Tomorrow, she'd look closer at the babies she held.

"You can do this," Simon said.

When she went to the hospital on Friday, she had some soft toys for Raymond, black-and-white rubber, the colors infants could see. She knew the hospital wouldn't reimburse her, but she didn't mind using her own money. She wanted to do this. She was hopeful he could respond, his peanut face turning sunny. But when she got to the nursery, his bed was empty. His name tag gone. She gripped the edge of his bassinet. "Where's Raymond?" she asked Laura.

"His mom got out of rehab. She took him home."

"What? But he won't thrive there . . ." Stella helplessly held up the toys. "I thought these might make a difference."

Laura took the toys. "The other babies will love them," she said. "Don't look so worried. Raymond's mom will be checked up on. And so will he. Anyway, it's not our business anymore."

Stella's stomach hurt. She loved the calm babies, the little ones who were here just so their moms could get some rest. But missing Raymond felt like a vacuum was growing inside of her. She could have helped him. She knew she could.

She tried to concentrate on the other two babies now in the nursery, the feel of them wriggling in her arms. They slept and fed and looked a little bored, but she realized, with a shock, they were no more bored than she was herself. At the end of the day, she smelled like spit-up, and when she lifted her arms to her nose, she swore she smelled like baby, which made her smile.

After work, she walked the hospital halls and looked into rooms. In one, she saw a patient, an old man with a grizzled face, throw a cup at a nurse. "You goddamn Nazi!" he shouted, and the nurse calmly picked up the cup and smiled, just the way nurses are supposed to, because agitating patients could raise their blood pressure. Stella walked around the hospital, and she was surprised to realize she didn't love it anymore, not the waves of people, not the patients peering out from their rooms, the confident strides of the doctors. Certainly not the antiseptic smell, the dizzying scents from the flowers in the rooms. She passed two doctors debating cardiac arrest treatments and swerved away from them. It used to thrill her, all that medical talk. She used to want to know more and more and more, but now she just felt numb, as if all her passion for medicine had left her.

The next day in the nursery, she had just settled a baby for a nap when Laura said her name sharply. "Stella!" She turned and Laura was picking up the baby she had just placed down. "Stomach sleeping is a SIDS risk factor," Laura snapped.

Stella froze. She knew that. Certainly she knew that, just like every nurse on the planet knew that, everyone who had ever been or wanted to be a mother, but even so, she had settled the baby on her stomach anyway, and then she had walked away. She fought back tears, crumpling onto a chair.

"Good God, don't get upset. It's fine," Laura said, coming closer to Stella. "There's no harm done. Just remember it for next time. That's all."

Stella stood up, her body shaking. She could write directions for herself on her arm, or on a piece of paper, but she could never be sure that she would remember, and she would always worry. Who was she to think she could do this job? And did she even want it anymore? She went through the motions the rest of that day. She walked back to the nursery and Laura looked up at her expectantly, and as soon as she did, Stella knew: she couldn't be a nurse anymore. The desire she had for it was gone. "I think I'd better go home," Stella said quietly.

Laura took both Stella's hands in hers. "Why? We need you here, Stella."

If she told Laura she didn't want to be a nurse anymore, Laura would try to convince her to stay. "I fucked up," Stella said. "No one needs that."

"You think I haven't screwed up myself?" Laura said.

"You're being kind."

"I'm being practical."

But Stella knew that she wasn't coming back, and as soon as she thought that, she felt some weight lifting inside of her.

By the time she got home and into the apartment, her cell phone was ringing. The first call was from Libby, assuring her that what had happened was no big deal, but all Stella could think was, How did Libby find out?

"Did Laura tell you?" Stella asked.

"Laura told me she needs you—that you were doing a good job," Libby said.

"I don't feel right coming back," Stella said. "And if it's no big deal, why did she tell you?"

"Listen," Libby said. "You were such a great nurse, the best I ever worked with. I could always count on you."

Were, Stella thought, and then hung up. The phone rang again, and there was Simon. "Oh, babe, I'm sorry," he said. How did he know what had happened? Who had told him about her, and did that mean that everyone knew? Were they all talking about her?

"Who told you?" she said.

There was a moment of silence. "I came to the hospital to pick you up," he said. "I ran into Libby."

"Right," she said, a headache sprouting over her left eye.

"Honey, I'll be home soon."

Great, she thought. She felt tense with anxiety, as if all her neurons were firing. She had to do something physical. Simon used to run, but she had always hated it. It gave her stitches in her side. It seemed pointless to her, too, covering all that ground, just to end up years later with knees so damaged that you had to get them replaced. But now, somehow, the mindlessness of it seemed like a plus to her. Simon had always told her that running cleared his head, that sometimes if he was having trouble with a song, with a particular piece of music, he'd get the answer as soon as he got into the endorphin zone.

She put on shorts and a tank top and laced up her sneakers.

She ran in the city, heading uptown, dodging people, going faster and faster, bobbing and weaving like a prizefighter. The air was soggy with heat, but she liked it. Her sneakers slapped the ground. Her breathing had a rhythm like music. She looked up and wanted to kiss the sky. She took the A train up to Seventy-Second Street and ran in Central Park, swerving onto a trail that was empty and rocky, the thorny bushes smacking against her body. No one was around. She realized that here she could be mugged or killed or raped, and that pure sharp thrill of danger felt like medicine, and she found it exhilarating. She had moved back onto the city streets when she saw

Simon's car, and she started to wave at him, jolted with happiness. But then she saw that he had two passengers in his backseat, two young girls. He looked so unhappy that Stella couldn't bear it. She turned down another street and kept running until she was back in the park again.

She was practically flying now, running so fast that when she zipped by another runner she accidentally knocked the phone from his hands. "Hey!" he shouted. She heard his steps slow, turned and saw him crouching down, picking up his phone. She kept running, alone on the path. Then she heard a different voice, like a caw. *Wait up, cupcake! Wait up!* She heard footsteps behind her and she turned, and a guy in jeans and a baseball cap pulled over his face was gaining on her. *Cupcake*, he shouted, huffing. And then: *Cunt. Pay attention to me when I'm talking to you.* She ran faster.

No one was going to hurt her. Not now. She pushed harder. *I can do this. I can do this.* The sweat fell into her eyes and she shook it off and ran faster. Her shirt was pasted to her skin. Sprinting, she veered back toward the street, among people, but suddenly she stumbled, falling hard on the sidewalk and scraping her knee. She scrambled to her feet and twisted around. There was no one coming after her. "Hey, you okay?" a man in a suit said, offering her his hand to help her up. "I'm fine," she said, but the man frowned. "You don't look fine to me," he told her, and she shook her head, thanking him, moving on, feeling him standing there, watching her. But when she turned back around, he wasn't there anymore. Had she imagined him?

She walked until she got to a drugstore. She leaned against the building wall, catching her breath, and then she felt it: the thrill. A release like a jet breaking a sound barrier, zooming higher and higher into the sky. The air on her skin felt like fingers caressing her. Her heart thrashing. When she looked around, colors seemed so vivid she thought she could almost eat them. Sounds were like fireworks. A baby's laugh rang like bells. A woman shouting made Stella feel like a knife had flashed close to her. Her mouth opened in wonder. She heard everything, everything, all at once, streaming through her.

There it was. Life! And it was amazing.

"OH MY GOD, I was so worried . . ." Simon said when she entered the apartment. She looked at her watch. Eight o'clock. How had she managed to use up so much time? Her clothes were dry by then but rumpled, and there wasn't anything she could do about her hair. Simon was pacing, the phone in his hand. "I called and you didn't answer. Then I realized you'd left your phone in the bedroom."

"I had a run," she said, triumphant. "The way you used to."

He squinted at her. "But you hate to run."

"I love it now."

"Is that okay for you to do?"

She stretched. "I feel incredible," she said. "Strong."

"Next time, feel amazing with your phone. Please. Or let me come with you."

"You'd come with me?"

"I would love to."

All that evening, through dinner, through the movie Simon put on, a comedy she couldn't really follow, about a couple who made a pact to kill themselves if they weren't married in a year, she felt this glorious ache rippling through her. Simon, laughing, touched her hand, and she looked over at him and made herself laugh, too. She thought about running again tomorrow, faster this time. Much faster. There it was. She had a goal.

AT FIRST, SHE felt thrilled that she and Simon were going to run together. When they were first dating, she used to love it when he took her hand and kissed her, not just because she loved the warmth but also because she felt like the people around her were her witness. They would look at her and think, Isn't it wonderful that that woman is loved so much? She must really be something special.

Now, though, when Simon took her hand, she felt tethered. "Can't run holding hands," she told him.

They went to Central Park, and as soon as Simon started running, Stella felt irritated. He was going so slowly. She sprinted ahead of him and then heard his steps quickening, but when she turned off the main trail, he called, "Stella!"

She turned around.

"Why don't we stay on the main trail?" he said.

"This one's more fun."

"Humor me," he said.

She continued to run, but she didn't feel that adrenaline rush anymore, and whenever she sped up and was just feeling it begin to build, Simon would shout to her, telling her to slow down, to stop, to wait for him, and the delicious moment was gone.

They had run for only a half hour when Simon stopped, panting. "I'm sorry, baby. I have to get to work," he said.

"I can finish on my own," she said.

But he looped his arm around her. "Come on home with me."

AFTER THAT, SHE did her running when he was away. When he got home and asked her if she wanted to run with him, she would shrug and lie: "I don't like it that much anymore."

Oh, but she did. She would run fast and far, for an hour at least. She ran along the emptiest paths in the park, because she felt so fueled by the danger. But more than that, she felt invincible. The worst had already happened to her, so she was safe now. She came home dripping with sweat, her hair pasted to her head. Happiness thrummed inside her.

One night, she was running and suddenly found it harder than usual to reach the peak point, to feel truly, excitedly alive. She tried running faster, but that didn't do it. She ran along a rocky path, dangerous because she could have fallen, but still she felt something was missing.

No. Don't do this to me. I need you.

She slowed down into a jog. She felt the sheen of sweat on her body, the damp drip of her hair tickling her shoulders. The lump of terror loosened, even if it wasn't replaced with joy. She'd go home. She'd try again tomorrow. Maybe this knot of disappointment would lift then, because if it didn't, she didn't know what she would do.

She got out of the park and onto the streets again, walking past a gourmet food store, and then a cafe filled with people holding up glasses to clink, throwing their heads back to laugh. She turned down another street and passed Mickey's Bar, a squat little place blaring a bad loop of eighties hits through the open door. Stella slowed and looked through the smudgy window. She knew that the only kind of people who went there were the sad drunks, the people who started drinking at two in the afternoon. Even the bouncer looked worn down. A woman with a slash of red lipstick was swirling a swizzle stick into her glass, staring at the back door. A man in an expensive-looking suit was slumped at the corner, a hat pulled down over his face, so she couldn't tell if he was young or old. Then she heard a Madonna song, and she remembered how for a moment, when she was emerging from the coma, she had seen Madonna in her hospital room. Maybe it was a sign. Madonna would go into this bar. She would own the place. Stella walked in the door. Everything smelled of alcohol and she knew she would smell of it, too, when she left, that Simon would ask her about it, but so what.

The man in the hat looked up so she could see his face. Younger than she was, but not young. There were deep grooves by his mouth, crinkles circling his eyes. He took off his hat so she could see his thick dark hair, or maybe he was just being gentlemanly. He nodded at her and sat up straighter. He patted the empty barstool next to him, red plastic with a rip on the side.

There was a raw pull in Stella's stomach. Her heart started to race. This wasn't like her, not this place, and not sitting next to a strange man, but she couldn't help it.

She eased herself onto the plastic stool. The man turned and took her in. She made her hands into fists so they wouldn't shake. She must look ridiculous, in her old shorts and tank top, her sneakers and wet hair. "Gin and tonic," she said to the bartender. Her voice sounded shaky to her and she willed it to still. The bartender slid the drink in front of her and she took a sip. The glass clicked along her teeth. The drink was sharp and she wasn't sure she liked it. She pushed the glass away to the edge of the bar.

The man beside her was drinking something dark and muddy looking. "What's that?" she said, pointing.

"You're soaking wet," he said, glancing at her sneakers, her running shorts.

She felt his gaze on her, like a hot breath. He moved closer and tilted his drink toward her.

"It's a Fireball," he said. "It takes you by surprise. A little innocent-looking thing like that, and boom—it explodes." He smelled like stale coffee, but he had Simon's gray eyes. He watched her.

"What's your name?" the man said. "I'm Tom."

"Brenda," she said. "Brenda LeFay."

"What do you do, Brenda LeFay?"

She could say anything. She could be anyone. "I'm an engineer," she said, and he laughed.

"Doesn't that beat everything," he said. "So am I." He tipped his glass into his mouth, and she felt herself hyperventilating. She didn't need to be in this bar, with this man, in this moment, but she didn't want to go home either, where Simon would look so worried that she wouldn't be able to relax. She didn't want to think about tomorrow either.

"Can I have a taste, Tom?" she said, surprising herself, and then she felt her whole body vibrating harder and harder. She couldn't help it. She had to do it. She leaned toward him and kissed his mouth, soft and sharp with alcohol. A match lit inside her. Another kiss and it would be a flame. She wanted to run out the door and never come back. She wanted to brush her breasts against his arm. What would it feel like to be with a stranger? *This isn't me. This isn't me.*

This is me.

She took his glass and drained it, felt the fire spread in her mouth. He put some bills on the table. "Let's get out of here," he said quietly.

THEY BOTH WALKED fast, neither one of them talking. There were plenty of people in the street, so she could easily pivot away from him if she had to. She could call for help or grab someone's arm, or she could simply take flight because she could easily outrun a guy like him. But when she thought about doing that, the flare inside of her dimmed and sputtered. She was sweating now, and everything in her ached toward him, and the more danger she felt, the better she liked it.

They turned down a quiet street and she couldn't help it as she pushed him gently to the wall, her face lifted to his. His hands flew up. "Not like that," he told her, grabbing her hand, taking her forward to a building, to a doorman in a uniform, all spit shine and braided epaulettes. The doorman opened the door for them. "Good evening, Mr. Cohen," he said. He looked at Stella. "Good evening, miss," he said.

She was a person now. She was Miss.

They took the elevator, six flights up, then walked down a shiny marble hallway. His apartment was right at the end, and when he opened the door, he held out his hand. "Ta-da," he said. His place was huge, with glass and steel tables, a black leather couch. Real art on the walls.

"Can I get you a drink?" he said, and she pressed her mouth against his. She let him pull her down to the floor.

There was a roaring in her ears. She kissed his mouth again and tightened her arms about him like she wanted to put her whole self inside of him and come out someone different. He started to unbutton his shirt, but she ripped it open, the buttons scattering on the floor. She grabbed his hair, grabbed his tie, and she felt herself flying outward. She rolled on the floor to the wall, taking him with her. She was invincible now. A goddess. A rush stormed through her, a kind of lightning.

AS SOON AS it was over, she felt sick. How could she have done this? What was the matter with her? All these years, she'd been faithful, but now . . . She didn't feel invincible anymore. She felt like a whore. She looked at this man, at his craggy face, the way his mouth was open. She got up and put her clothes back on, her stomach roiling.

"Let me get your number," he said. "I think we could be good together."

She was faster than he was. She got out the door and headed for the stairs, taking them two at a time until she got to the bottom. She threw the door open, and there was the friendly doorman, only this time he didn't look so friendly. He gave her a fish stare. She threw open the front door, gasping in the cold air. And as soon as she was on the street, she vomited.

SIMON WASN'T HOME when she got there, so she peeled off her clothes and saw the rip in her shorts, which made her hot with fury. She stuffed them in the trash and then put the trash in the incinerator. She took a shower so long that it pruned her skin.

She sat down on their couch, listening to her heart slow, nauseated with shame. She hadn't hurt anyone. She hadn't stolen anything. If anyone was the loser in this, it was her.

It was just adrenaline, she told herself. It was the reason that people bungee-jumped or parasailed or climbed mountains without ropes or stepped on a high wire across two towers. The reason that she had run and run and run. You could get addicted to it, she knew that, and you had to count the cost. At the hospital, patients came in with their bodies shattered from racing on motorcycles, from leaping off cliffs. It made you feel alive, and that was why she had done it.

She wouldn't do it again. Instead, she got out some paper and began to draw circles, as if she were hypnotizing herself. It didn't work to relax her. She looked up at the window and began drawing the frame, the blinds, but her breathing still felt ragged. When Simon came in, he smiled. "Don't you look lovely," he said. She tried to smile back.

She lasted a week without going out again, prowling for men. She spent mornings going through the want ads, trying to find something she could do. She looked for courses online, training for a new career, but nothing really grabbed her. She didn't want to work with computers, didn't want to learn photography, and just the idea of teaching frightened her. One morning, she decided to run again. Maybe she'd pass some stores with HELP WANTED in the window. Maybe something would happen. It sometimes did when you started small. She could manage a store, maybe. Too bad no one would pay her for drawing.

She was in Midtown when she walked past a cafe and saw a man standing there, the white lab coat jolting her, making her dizzy. She felt switched on and she started to walk toward him, but then she tripped hard on the sidewalk, banging her knee, wincing in pain. "Hey, you okay?" he said, and then he crouched down beside her, his hands on her knees.

"Just bruised," she said. "Nothing broken."

"You should let me dress it," he said. He nodded at the building. "I live just upstairs," he said. And then she knew what was going to happen next.

His apartment was all glass windows and burnished wood floor. He was younger than she was, with thick dark hair and a lean build, and she was glad that he didn't seem to want to talk, not about himself or her or anything. "Hang on," he said, shucking off his lab coat and walking into another room, coming back with antibiotic cream, a bandage, and a hand towel. He kneeled in front of her, carefully wiping her knee, dotting it with cream and then covering it with a bandage. She put one hand on the top of his head and he locked eyes with her. Then she tilted her face to his, bent down, and kissed him. He led her into a room on the far end of the apartment, a bed with a carved-wood headboard. "Let me," he said, sliding off her running shorts and pulling up her top. He lowered her to the quilt. He took his time undressing himself, and then he took his time with her, kissing the curve of her hip, her breast. But she got on top of him and pushed him inside of her. She shoved her hair from her face and then, there, in the hallway, she heard footsteps.

She looked up, astonished. There was a little girl in footed pajamas, her thumb in her mouth. He had left her here alone while he went out.

Stella froze. "What," the man said, and then he looked up and saw the girl, too, and shoved Stella off him onto the floor. Her hip hit against the wood floor and she braced herself up on one elbow.

"Daddy," the girl said, her voice rocketing. "I had a funny dream. I don't want to sleep anymore." The girl looked at Stella. "Hi," she said. "Who are you? Do you have to nap? Do you hate it, too? Do you like stories?"

The man grabbed for his pants, jerking them up. He threw on his shirt and strode to his daughter, crouching so he was at her level, smoothing her wild riot of black hair. "Come on, sweetie, I'll read you a story," he said. He looked over her head at Stella, his face blank.

She could hear him talking to his daughter as he led her back to her room. The little girl kept turning around to stare at Stella, but her father kept pulling her back. *You had a dream. That's all it was. It isn't real. Daddy was just too warm so he took his clothing off. No, no, that lady is just a visitor and she's leaving. Yes, Mommy will be home soon. Mommy will be home.*

He hadn't worn a wedding band. He didn't have a stripe of paler skin where one might have been. Stella heard a peal of childish laughter. There was a little girl who might innocently tell her mommy about her. The marriage might collapse, and it would be her fault. Stella pulled herself up and stumbled to the sink, her stomach heaving, bile rising in her throat. Her skin was glossed with sweat. In the other room, the man was singing to his daughter.

She dressed and strode to the door, and then she saw it, by the entrance, a big photo she had missed before. There he was at the beach, in a swimsuit, his arm slung around a handsome blonde woman, the little girl standing in front of them, making a silly face. There was a date on it. Two months ago. "Forgive me," she whispered.

She cried when she got outside. The sky was already darkening, and looking at her wrist, she realized her watch was missing. It must have come unhinged when she fell. Was it still on the sidewalk, or did she lose it at his apartment? Either way, she wasn't going to retrace her steps. She'd have to lie if Simon asked about it, say she lost it and didn't know where. Maybe the guy would find it and throw it out. Or maybe he'd give it to his daughter. A big-girl watch. A prize for being so good.

When she got home, Simon was cooking something that smelled like curry. He leaned in to kiss her. "Where were you?" he asked.

She laughed, like a bark. "Oh, just walking around," she said. Then, to distract him, she told him how delicious dinner smelled. "I'm starving," she said.

THAT NIGHT, SHE bolted up from sleep. Simon was snoring beside her, one hand thrown over his face, his hair ragged, needing a cut, something she used to do but wasn't sure she could do now. She kept seeing that little girl, her pajamas with the zebra pattern. The images exploded in her head. She went to the kitchen and got a piece of paper and a pen. Her hand flew across the page. She was someplace else. Not in this room and not in her head anymore. Suddenly she wasn't just drawing for herself, soothing herself, making sense of the world. She had this feeling that she was doing this for someone else, and that made it bigger, more dangerous.

She kept drawing, in a fever, and then she stopped, panting, her eyes focusing like lasers.

There, on the page, was the little girl in her pajamas, and her eyes were looking right into Stella's. Stella looked closer and gasped. She knew she had been getting better at drawing, but this was something different, something new. This was a drawing so good that it seemed alive. How could she have done this? But more than that, she felt that she could see inside that little girl now and understand what that child was feeling, because Stella was feeling it, too. The girl's eyes were haunted. This little girl was lonely, scared and shy, and the more Stella looked, the more she felt she knew what was going on in that apartment, and most of it was terrible. Everything felt clear, like a piece of cellophane wrapped around her and the girl both.

She felt her body trembling. What was she supposed to do with this? She couldn't go back to that man's apartment and accuse him because the only thing she had proof of was that he had left his daughter alone in the house. Authorities would think she was crazy.

Stella shut her eyes and put her hands over the drawing. *Be okay*, she whispered to the little girl, making it a blessing.

STELLA, DESPERATE, UNABLE to stop thinking about her drawing of the little girl, tried something new. She joined the local gym and began running there, and swimming, too, everything fast and sometimes furious. It wasn't the same as running in the city down those dark paths in the park, or picking up a man and inhaling him, using up the tension like a cigarette. But it was something.

One day in the water, she was deep under the surface, her eyes open behind her swim goggles. For a minute she felt as if time had turned a page, that she was in her old life, her old coma, trapped and terrified and haunted, swimming in an element she didn't understand, hearing noise bubbling around her, dragging her down. Her heart scuttled in her chest. She couldn't breathe. Panic stung her and she felt herself crying. *You cannot win over me. You can't make me afraid.*

She shoved herself forward, moving under the water until it started to feel familiar, like she was back in the comfort of that other world. She bolted up to the surface.

She looked around. There were only three other people in the pool, an old man wearing a red bathing cap who was slowly doing laps and two teenagers who were horsing around in the shallow end. No one noticed her.

She drew in another breath and sank to the bottom of the pool and then rose up. She did it again and again, until she wasn't scared anymore. Until she was laughing, filled with joy. *I did this. I did this. I did this.*

IN AUGUST, SHE began to regularly take her sketch pad and pens to the park. She sometimes sat in the Sheep Meadow, other times by Bethesda Fountain. It took her a while to relax, but then she felt the pull of one person, and then another, like a kind of force field urging her to take notice. She began to tentatively draw again, people this time. *Don't be frightened. Go with your gut.*

She watched a young woman with a baby, on a bench opposite her, and she began to stealthily draw, until, like always, she felt in the zone, as if her hands were moving on their own.

When she finished, she looked down at the drawing.

This woman was happy. Stella's breathing began to even. The baby was happy, too. The only negative thing she saw and felt in the woman's face was lack of sleep, a toppling exhaustion.

She looked up and saw the woman looking at her, and then the woman plucked up her baby and wandered over to Stella. "Why, that's us," she said, amazed.

"You need more sleep," Stella said, then hastily apologized. "I need to mind my own business."

"But you're right," the woman said. "I do need more sleep." She looked down at the drawing again. "It's like you got inside me, like you read my thoughts," the woman said. "Can I buy this?"

"You can have it," Stella said, handing her the drawing. "Especially if it makes you happy."

STELLA FOUND HERSELF drawing in the park more and more. People began to ask her to draw them, but she would sketch only the people whom she was drawn to, as if they had a message they needed to get out and she could be the conduit to help them see it. There had to be that feeling, that connection.

She still didn't know how and why she could do it, only that she could, and it astonished her as much as it did the people around her. They began to insist on paying her. "Whatever you want," she told them, and they began fluttering twenties at her, and then fifties.

16

SIMON KEPT PLAYING MUSIC and she kept drawing. People now. That was what interested her. At first, she had to actually see them, but now she could work from memory. She drew the guy at the bodega down the block, the young nanny with the twins who was always strolling with them past London Terrace. Every person she drew was so alive. It was like they were breathing on the page.

"What are you drawing?" Simon asked. She blinked at him. If she told him, he'd have all sorts of questions. She knew she could ask him to sit for her, that she could draw him, but was there anything about him that she didn't know already?

She put her drawing away. "Oh, nothing much," she said. "What do you say we go out for dinner? We haven't done that for a while. Would that be okay?"

They went to a new Italian place in SoHo, but the dinner Stella had imagined didn't happen. They weren't loose on a glass of red wine. They weren't laughing over their pastas. Instead, they each seemed lost in their own heads. Stella reached for Simon's hand and flinched at his fingers, chilled from the air-conditioning. "I'll warm them up," she said, but he was rubbing them himself and then he fanned his hands out. "Done," he said.

• • •

One Friday, they went to Central Park together. They found a bench and Stella began drawing. People came over to watch her. Stella acted as if she wasn't even aware of them, but Simon could feel the sharp edge of their interest, the way people leaned in, their gaze focusing on the movement of her hands. "It's always like this," she told him.

"What? It is?" He couldn't believe the people coming to her, as if she were a magnet. How had this happened so fast, so easily for her? He wanted to ask her how come it was okay for strangers to see what she was drawing but not for him when they were alone. He wanted to put his hand on her hand as she worked, because maybe then electricity might transfer to him, too. "Oh my God," people said. "So amazing. Is this for sale?" Stella looked up, dazed. "What would you want to pay?" Stella asked, and Simon bumped her elbow, amazed.

People seemed to know about her. "My friend had her drawing framed," a woman told Stella. Simon, stunned, watched the money come in.

"Draw me," a young woman with dreads said. "I'll pay you." Stella looked up at her. "Ten bucks," the woman said. "I know it's worth much more, but that's what I've got."

"Okay," Stella said. "Sit over there." She focused on the woman and her hands began to move, and after a half hour there was the woman on the page. "I love it!" she said, and dug in her purse for money, but Stella raised her hands. "I changed my mind. I can't take your money," she said.

"Oh my God, thank you, thank you," the woman said, taking the drawing holding it as gently as a fine piece of china.

"Why didn't you let her pay you?" Simon asked after the woman had left, the drawing tucked under her arm. Stella shrugged. "I think she needed the money."

"What? How do you know that?"

"I don't know how. But I did. It just all seemed to make sense as I was drawing."

By the time they left the park, she had twelve commissions. People would come back tomorrow, and someone asked if Stella could come to his place or meet somewhere neutral. Stella glowed.

SIMON CAME HOME the next night from driving and Stella, who usually carefully counted out all their money and put it away, had bills and coins splashed across the table and she was staring at all of it in wonder. "I had a good day," she said.

"What?"

"I went to the park."

He blinked at her. "By yourself?"

"I love it up there."

"There are closer parks, you know."

"I know," she said. "But you should have seen it. All these people gathered around me." She looked up at him, her eyes shining. "I'm getting better at it. It comes without even thinking."

"What comes?"

"I can tell what a person is like. I can draw them, like their deepest selves. Somehow . . . everything comes alive on the page for me."

She suddenly frightened him. How could she do that? And why would she want to? She didn't seem interested in drawing him, which relieved him a little. At least he could have some control over his own self.

"It isn't woo woo or anything like that," Stella insisted. "Libby told me the brain can change. After coma, you can pick up things you couldn't before. Including talents."

She took up her pencil again and began drawing a face with a pointed chin, wild hair, and then he realized she was drawing herself, and Simon moved in closer, curious. "Is that you?" he said. He didn't want to tell her that it didn't really look anything like her, but she must have known that because she let the pencil roll from her fingers.

"This was a stupid idea," she said. "I don't know what I'm even looking at here. It's just lines and shapes." She sighed. "I'm better with other people. That's what it's all about."

"You'll get it," he said, trying to be reassuring, but she seemed to be looking beyond him.

WHO WAS HE kidding? That force, that creativity. He was jealous of it. He went into the bedroom and onto the internet and read about a guy who became a famous artist after a coma, whose paintings now hung in galleries. "It's all I want to do," the guy said, and that scared Simon even more. There was another famous case of a guy who had awakened to believe that he was Matthew McConaughey. The mirrors were wrong, he insisted. He kept waiting for film roles and it took them months to convince him that he wasn't the actor. "How disappointing," he said.

That night, Stella went to bed early, but Simon couldn't sleep. He went to the dining room where her drawings were stacked and he looked through them, marveling at her gift but unsettled by it as well. She was right. She had gotten better. He wouldn't have been surprised to see these drawings in a gallery. Again, he felt a tightening in his stomach. When was the last time anyone had clamored for his talent?

Simon left her a note, *Be back soon*, in case she woke up, and got in his car and drove down Bleecker Street, to Le Poison Rouge, a live music club. They booked indie bands there and were willing to take a chance on unproven talents. Hell, the club had once booked Mighty Chondria, and the band had been good enough to get asked back twice. He remembered the sound of the crowd, the sweat, the crowd heaving like wild animals. Everyone in the band had been soaking wet by the time the set was over. They slapped their hands together, laughing and shouting. Simon had gone back to the dressing room to find two girls there in various states of undress, one in a glittering tube top cut off at the midriff, the other in a skirt that barely covered her upper thighs, but the only person he saw, shining like moonlight, was Stella seated in the corner. She got up when she saw him. She moved through the other girls, gliding, and then he shut her eyes with his mouth and kissed her, and there was nothing else. Not then.

He slowed the car. Maybe he'd stop in. The club might remember him. They'd surely remember Mighty Chondria.

The place was jammed and dark and filled with the sour smell of beer. He had been on that stage only a few years ago, but now he felt out of place. He pushed his way to the back. Everyone else seemed so young, and it startled him. When had this change happened? Why hadn't he noticed? The people here just moved faster, even reaching for a drink. They talked rapid-fire and their skin had a kind of sheen to it, a smoothness as if it had been ironed and polished. He bumped against a young woman with a white crew cut and a nose ring, and she looked through him. He felt as if he were trapped behind a wall so dense no one could even see him.

Stop, he told himself. Don't do this. Don't be ridiculous. Mick Jagger was in his seventies now and he was still a show pony. Maybe Simon could try out his songs here. He didn't have a manager, an agent, a presence online, but this club knew his old band. Maybe he'd catch a break.

He wove his way to the bar and asked the bartender who did the booking now. The guy shrugged and leaned across Simon to take the drink orders of two young girls. Then a roar went up and he saw people congregating by the stage area, pumping their fists into the air and whooping. There were no seats, not that he had ever minded before, but now his knees were aching. His back hurt. He pushed through the crowd to the wall, so he could lean against it. Maybe it was just stress doing this to him.

Maybe it was because he was getting old.

Beside him a girl tilted her face up to kiss a guy, who ran his hands up under her shirt. They looked sixteen, so young, so fresh, that they might as well have been airbrushed. When he and Stella were young, they'd go to clubs. They'd find a dark corner, and he wanted her so much, he'd kiss her neck, move his hands under whatever little dress she was wearing. She'd whisper to him, pressing herself closer and closer, and they both felt mad with love. She was so happy then. And so was he. When was the last time Stella had wanted him? Or he had wanted her? When was the last time any woman had even looked at him? A knot lodged in his belly, and Simon felt sorrow gathering in his throat, but he forced himself to swallow it down because he couldn't cry in this club.

A man strode onstage. "Give it up for Backyard Anarchy!" he screamed, and people began to hoot and wave their hands. Four guys slouched out to the stage, growling. "Fuck you!" one of them screamed to the audience. "Fuck you!" they yelled back. And the band began to play.

There it was, the shock of the music. It used to work as a key, turning him on. But now it was too loud. Had music always been this loud? He couldn't hear the notes or the words or even the melody, which was mush. He put his fingers to his ears and then saw two people laughing at him, mocking him, and he thought of Stella, the way he had chided her because she had embarrassed him by wearing earplugs when they played, how he had told her it was an insult to the musicians. His ears rang, a tone tightening into another octave. Even with the wall support, his back throbbed with pain. He peeled himself away, pushing through the crowd until he found the door, walked past the long line of people desperate to get inside. He stood on the street, hunched over, his hands on his knees, gulping in the cold air.

He couldn't play here. Not on his own. Not with a band. Not with his songs. He had let Libby send out his demo to the record CEO she knew, but she never spoke of it to him again, and he certainly wasn't going to ask. Anyway, he knew why she hadn't told him. She was being kind, not telling him. No, thank you. That must have been what they had said. Who was he fooling? The knot in his stomach tightened, and then he started crying. It was gone. That whole golden moment in time for him had faded away.

He got back in the car and drove, his hands shaking. He didn't know where he was going, only that it wasn't home and it wasn't to pick up any passengers. He drove from downtown all the way up to West Eighty-Sixth and then back to the Gramercy Park area. It was so late, and this was so crazy, but he was so lonely. His eyes felt heavy. He swore that every tear he had ever felt like crying was dammed up inside of him.

He stopped in front of a redbrick apartment building where a parking space waited, like a fateful sign. He got out of the car and walked to the front door to buzz, but then he heard a window open. He stepped back, looked up. There, in her nightgown, was Libby. She didn't say a word but stepped back, and then he heard the buzz of the door letting him in. He climbed up the two flights, and when he got to the top, she was standing there, waiting. As soon as he saw her, he was crying again, standing there in the doorway, and she took him into her arms and drew him inside the apartment.

He cried on her shoulder. "I'm so sorry, I'm so sorry," he sobbed. He saw the curve of her throat, felt the heat of her body. He looked into her eyes and he felt as if she knew what he was thinking, knew how he felt, and she felt it, too. He knew this was crazy, that it was wrong.

"Come on, sit down," she said gently, guiding him to her couch. She sat so close to him that he could feel her breath on his face.

"Libby," he said, and then she leaned forward and kissed him, and the two of them sprawled along the couch, their legs entwining, his mouth on hers.

AFTERWARD, HE FELT dark with shame. How could he have slept with her? He couldn't look at her, and when he finally dared to, she was looking anywhere but at him. She dressed quickly, feeling that any moment something terrible would happen, and she had to be ready for it.

He pulled on his clothes. For so many years, Stella had worried that he was cheating on her, but he never had. There were so many women around the band, sliding up against him, showing up in his room. He had always ignored them or sent them away. It didn't matter to him what the rest of the band did—that was their business. He had so many chances, but he never betrayed Stella. Not until now.

He looked at Libby. She was sitting on the couch, fully dressed, and he hated the yearning he felt toward her, the way he wanted to stroke her hair, to touch the curve of her hip. "I'm so sorry," he said.

She chewed on her lower lip, studying him.

"It can never happen again," he said.

"It won't." He couldn't tell if she was hurt or angry, or if maybe she, too, felt she had betrayed her best friend. She went to the front door and opened it. "We'll just be friends. Not lovers. That's the best thing to be," she said.

When she closed the door and he stood in the hall, he felt his stomach tighten. He put both his hands on the outside of the door as if he could feel her energy burning through the wood.

On the way home, he told himself all sorts of things. He hadn't exactly cheated on Stella because she wasn't fully Stella yet. It wasn't cheating because it was just a release of tension, something he needed in order to function in his life. He put one hand over his eyes for a moment. *Liar. Cheat.*

He went home and Stella was sleeping. He took her hands out from the covers and folded them together so she looked like she was praying.

17

STELLA USED TO TELL Libby that whatever you wanted most to avoid was the thing that always appeared, forcing you to deal with it. Stella was right, Libby thought, because more and more, she kept running into Simon, and every time she did, she felt a pull, an attraction, and she didn't want to feel it.

She hadn't liked him originally, judging just from what Stella told her. How he forgot her birthday. How vain he was, with that fake darkened hair. She had him pegged from the moment she first saw him. All the hospital staff knew guys like him: and as soon as things got difficult, those guys would walk away. But Simon had surprised her. Every time she walked into Stella's room, he was there. When Stella finally went home, which often was harder than being in a hospital, he was there for her, too.

But now, she noticed the new gray in his hair, which made her like him more. She saw how he kept the apartment humming, even as he was wearing the same T-shirt she'd seen him wearing yesterday and the day before. He had actually changed, and she found herself thinking about him. She hated how much he came into her mind, like a melody she couldn't forget. It was just being lonely, she told herself. Just being human. She'd make herself forget him.

She hadn't planned on sleeping with him. If she had been rational, she never would have. But he had been so naked in his emotions, so real somehow. She hadn't thought of Stella. She hadn't thought of herself, how much this might hurt her later, how much she'd remember how she was the one to initiate that first kiss, and somehow, that made her like him even more.

Well, it had been a mistake and it was over, and they both knew it. She wouldn't let it happen again. She'd stay away from him and she'd protect her friendship with Stella, because that was what mattered the most.

Still, she saw him everywhere. Of course she saw him when she went to visit Stella at the apartment, and it made her feel so terrible with guilt that she began to suggest that Stella just meet her at a cafe for coffee instead, where there was zero chance they'd run into Simon. She sipped at her coffee and picked at a pastry and listened to Stella talk, and when it was her turn, she found herself going into default mode, talking about her patients, the hospital. "No guys you're dating?" Stella asked.

"Nothing that's right," Libby said.

Stella tipped her spoon at Libby. "There will be," she said.

When Stella invited Libby to dinner with her and Simon, Libby had easy excuses. She had late shifts. She had other plans. This would all blow over, she told herself, and Stella would never have to know. Then time would take care of whatever wound she felt, and life would go on.

She just knew it.

Later that week, Libby was going into a drugstore as Simon was coming out, and they both froze in place, and then, after clipped hellos, she sped inside while he rushed outside.

One sultry August night, she went into a diner for a late-night coffee, and there was Simon, sitting in the back, buried in a book. Why wasn't he with Stella? She knew she had told him to let Stella find her way, but it hadn't been all that long, and she knew that Stella still needed attention.

Of course, the other part of her was happy to see him there alone.

She walked over, scrunching down to see what he was reading. *The Martian Chronicles*. Ray Bradbury. "Did you get to the one about the bees yet?" she said, and he looked up at her, smiling. "Tell me about it," he said. "Come sit down. The pie here is great. So is the coffee."

She sat opposite him and ordered both, but when she had a slice of the lemon pie in front of her, she found she couldn't touch it. Instead, she sipped at the coffee.

He finished his coffee and then had another, and so did Libby, though she knew wouldn't sleep that night, that she'd be far too jittery. But Simon was telling her about a new film series at the Film Forum. "All Hitchcock," he said. Simon gulped the rest of his coffee. Libby could imagine sitting in a theater beside him, so close she could hear his breathing, the place so dark she could reach over to take his hand. And then he reached across the table for her fingers, and she pulled her hand back.

"This isn't going to end well," Libby said quietly. "We both know that, right?"

"I'll never tell her," Simon said.

"Neither will I. But what happens next? How can we do this? It's so wrong. It's so evil." She bit down on her lower lip. "I betrayed my best friend."

"Me, too," he said.

"I wish I still hated you."

"I owe her so much," Simon said. Libby took the book from him, leafing through it until she came across the story with the bees. "Here," she said. "I found it for you." Then she got up and left, telling herself that she wasn't going to look back at him, but she did, and he was reading, and she told herself that was a good thing, because if he had been looking at her, she would have gone right back to his table.

All that night, she thought about Simon. He was a fever she couldn't shake, no matter what she did. Everything she saw reminded her of him. Did he like this color? Did he like this restaurant? Where was he now and how could she bump into him? She had whole, long conversations with him in her head.

She began for the first time to actively try to date, hoping that one man might blot out the other. She got on Match.com because she thought it was for older, more serious people than the other sites, and she had six dates in two days, and though all of them had looked okay in their profile and had professional jobs, they mostly lied. She had drinks with a guy who slid his hand up her skirt, so she had to walk out of the bar. She met a lawyer at the Central Park Zoo, and as soon as she saw him, she knew he was in his seventies. One man, who had told her he had a great sense of humor, never said anything even remotely funny. In the end, she took her profile off the website.

She loved Simon.

You asshole. You cheat. This isn't love, she told herself. But what if it was? What could she possibly do about it? She began to think about the email from Michael Foley again. What if Simon had signed with Michael Foley and gone off on tour? What if Stella had been well enough to accompany him? She sighed. If that happened, then she wouldn't have fallen for Simon the way she had. She wouldn't have to torture herself with her own feelings. If Simon had signed and went off on tour, she wouldn't have to think about any of this.

She had believed that Simon needed to be near Stella. And the horrible thing was that she needed Simon near her now, too. Maybe she could tell him now. Maybe it wasn't too late. She could find the right time. She could explain.

BY THE END of the month, he was showing up regularly at her place. "What are you doing?" she said, but she opened the door. She let him in.

One night, he came with his guitar. "I wrote a song. I want you to hear it," he said.

She sat by him on the couch and listened. The song was about a man who cheated on his wife. He sang about her bare face, the way her skin smelled like coconut, the churn of desire that never let up. And then he finished, and he looked at her.

"That song makes me so sad," she whispered.

"I know. Me, too," he said.

But then she leaned into him and rested her forehead against his.

THE NEXT DAY, Libby was back to hating herself again. She used to tell Stella everything, but how could she tell her that she had fallen in love with Simon? She hated lying to Stella. She couldn't tell her the truth, but she couldn't not tell her either. All she could do was continue to hope that it would all stop. What a fool she was. Falling in love with Simon was like an addiction, something bad for her, bad for everyone around her. How was she any different from her old boyfriend Ben, with her yearning, hungry need that would bring nothing but trouble? Oh, Ben, she thought. Now I understand you.

But she didn't forgive Ben, no more than she could forgive herself.

She picked up the phone and called Stella. "Hey, you," she said. "Come to my place for lunch."

STELLA CAME TO lunch on Wednesday, a day Libby had off. She knew Stella's taste in food had changed, so she figured she was safe ordering a pizza, keeping it hot in the oven until they were ready to eat. She put down a tablecloth and poured prosecco into glasses. She downed a glass quickly, hoping it would make her relax, that it might hide the feelings rumbling inside of her.

"Hey, hey, hello," Stella said when she came into the apartment. Stella looked different today, eyes more fierce and less opaque than they had been when Libby last saw her. And as always, Libby noticed how Stella was still too skinny, so her jeans were falling off her hips. Her chest barely showed under her black T-shirt.

"You look so great," Libby said, lying, and then she felt a pang, because she had promised herself this lunch would be about the truth. Stella hugged her, but Libby didn't feel any real warmth, which disturbed her. "Come on, sit down, talk to me," Libby said. "Let's be just us at lunch here."

Just us again. That was before so many things. Before, when she and Stella could talk nonstop, sometimes interrupting and finishing each other's thoughts. Us-against-the-world friends. But now, Libby felt as if she had been starched and ironed. She couldn't get the words out.

Libby told Stella about her patients, stopping only when she saw Stella's eyes glaze over in a way they never had before. Stella talked about going to the movies in the afternoon to see a rerelease of *Don't Look Now* and about how much more lost she got in the film the second time. How much more lost she got in everything these days. "I'm determined to be perfectly fine, even though I don't have a clue what that feels like," Stella said. Libby saw a faint tremble in Stella's hands, a wobble in her mouth.

"Nor does anyone," Libby said. She fidgeted in her seat. "How are you feeling?" she asked.

Stella raised a brow.

"I know, I know," Libby said. "I'm asking as a friend, not a doctor."

Stella sat down at the table. "Okay," she said, then paused. "One thing I know—I feel—for sure and I have to tell you," Stella said. Libby felt a fist curling inside her stomach. She knows, Libby thought. Oh God, she knows. She put down her glass. "Shoot," Libby said. "You know you can tell me anything." Liar, she thought. Liar.

"And you can tell me anything, too," Stella said.

Except that I slept with Simon. Except that I am in love with him. Except that I love you, at least the you that you were before, and I love him and I don't know what to do about it and every choice seems to be the wrong one and I would rather die than hurt anyone, especially you.

Stella cleared her throat and leaned forward to take a sip of the wine. "Okay, so here it is," she said, and Libby puffed her cheeks with air, waiting. "I know we worked so great together. I know you know

I'm never going to go back to the hospital, that I don't want to be a nurse anymore. But I know what I want to do now."

Libby reached forward and downed the rest of her wine, awash with relief that this wasn't about Simon. "You shouldn't be a nurse if you feel that way," Libby said. She tried to swallow, but her throat knotted.

"Oh, thank God," Stella said.

"I don't think less of you," Libby said. *I think less of me.*

"I feel like all I want to do is be an artist now," Stella said. "I mean, I am an artist. People say I am, so I guess it's not so strange. I feel like I've always been an artist, but I forgot all about that until now. I mean, I read that other people have come out of a coma with a talent they didn't have before. Brain change, I suppose." She looked at Libby with wonder. "The art gives me purpose. I like doing it. I don't know if I can make a living at it or even if I want to. I started drawing people, and I know this sounds crazy, but it's like I can somehow see who they really are just by drawing them and I can show that truth to them. I can help them, Libby."

"That's good. Helping people."

"I could draw you," Stella said. "If you wanted me to." Stella put down her glass. "You look unnerved, Lib. Is it me? Is it something else?"

Libby felt her body tighten. Simon had told her that Stella sometimes saw things in people, deep things. She couldn't risk that.

"I'm fine," Libby said.

"You sure you don't want me to draw you?"

"Oh, I don't know. I hate to even have my photo taken," Libby said.

"It would be painless, I promise," Stella said. "I'd love to do it for you."

"No, no, please no," Libby said. She tried to change the subject. "Your whole business is going good, right? That's sort of amazing."

Stella blushed. "It's pretty great. People are offering commissions now, asking me to come to their homes. It makes me feel weird. But it gives me something to hold on to until I figure out the rest." Stella smiled. "It's money we need." Stella threaded her fingers together. Her smile grew tight.

"What's wrong?" Libby said.

"I don't know. Simon and me." Stella looked down at the table, suddenly miserable. "We're not a fit anymore. Something's off."

"No?" Libby felt the room wavering around her.

"Maybe it's because I've been so different. Maybe because he seems different. I feel sometimes like we don't know each other anymore. It's not the way it used to be, but then again, I'm still figuring out who I am," Stella said quietly. "There's so much I used to know and now it's just a blank. I can't read him anymore. I can't draw him. I can't read myself. How can I be expected to navigate anything when everything feels so different, *is* so different? Do you know . . . do couples where one has been in coma stay together?"

Libby's appetite was gone. Coming out of coma wasn't all that common and she didn't know any couples in that situation. Kids— they did the best. "Sometimes," she said.

"Oh, fuck. I wanted a different answer."

"Then yes," Libby said. "Yes. Sure they do." She was reeling. "Let me just get the food." She went into the kitchen and brought out the pizza and more prosecco.

Libby watched Stella eating, polishing off a slice. Libby took a small bite of her own piece, so at least she'd look normal. But it was like eating wallpaper paste and she set it down on her plate. "I love you," Libby said. "I want you to be happy and healthy."

"I want that for you, too."

"I love you," Libby said again. "You know I'd do anything for you."

"Can you make me less anxious? Without meds? That would be a miracle."

"It would be weird if you weren't anxious," Libby said. "Anyone would be in your situation. You've been through so much."

"I wish I could remember that night when it happened. Remember other things, too. It's like someone ripped holes in my life," Stella said. "I feel so different. I am different." She peered at Libby. "You're different, too."

Libby seamed her mouth into a line. "I am? How?"

"I don't know, but it's not just you. Everyone is. You, me, Simon," Stella said. "I wish I could just relax." She half laughed.

It's my fault. It's all my fault. Libby wanted to place her hands on Stella and bring her back to where she was, bring their whole lives back to the Big Before. But how was she supposed to do that?

Then Libby remembered.

The stone. Her precious stone. The one Richie had carried in his pocket because he thought it had magical healing properties. White quartz. She had kept it all these years, sometimes carrying it in her lab coat pocket, as if she were carrying his memory with her. "Hang on," she said, and went into her room. There it was, on her dresser.

She had made it through all her schooling, her internships, always carrying Richie's stone in her pocket. She felt grounded with it, calmer somehow. At night, she put it by her bed stand. She picked up the quartz and ran her fingers over it, feeling soothed.

She gently plucked it up, a small weight in her hands, cool to the touch. Richie, she thought. Maybe by giving away something that mattered so much to him, so much more to her, she'd be absolved. Maybe it would be a penance or even a promise.

She came out and handed it to Stella.

"What? It's a stone," Stella said. "A pretty one." Stella ran her fingers over the surface.

"Clear quartz," Libby said. "Said to be good for healing, it's thought. Actually, you can think of it as just pretty. And tactile, which is calming."

Stella balanced it carefully.

"Feels good in your hands, right?" Libby said, and Stella nodded.

"Maybe it will help you," Libby said. "Make things seem calmer."

"You're giving this to me?"

"I want you to have it." Libby knew Stella didn't know the real power of the stone, why it mattered to Libby, but Libby knew she had to give it to her. When Stella put it in her own pocket, Libby felt a wash of relief, as if something important had been passed down.

AFTER STELLA LEFT, Libby slumped on the couch. She and Stella had eaten and talked, but she didn't feel any closer to her. She didn't feel bonded. It felt like they had glided around each other, like she was trying to be friends with a new person. Worse, she immediately missed the quartz stone, wanted it back. How had things gone so wrong? She sat up and tried to think of how this could work out. Maybe her fever for Simon could burn itself out just as quickly as it had flamed on.

She put her head in her hands. Who was she kidding?

She loved someone she wasn't supposed to love, and she'd have to stop. She had been through grief before with Richie. She knew what to expect. She could go through it again, for Stella. She could come through it alive. She would take on extra hours at work and come home so exhausted she'd fall into bed, too tired to even think of Simon.

18

AS SOON AS SHE got home, Stella sat at her table and began to draw Libby. She couldn't shake the feeling that she'd had the whole time she was with her. Something was off. Libby was really troubled and she was hiding something. Stella drew and drew, fueled by a kind of light switch that she couldn't turn on. The drawing of Libby was perfectly acceptable. There was Libby's hair, her big eyes, but it was like a shadow of Libby instead of a picture of Libby herself.

Maybe she was just too close to Libby, Stella decided. Stella was used to drawing strangers, approaching them like they were a door that she could simply open. She and Libby were just too intertwined. There were parts of Libby that would be tender, and Stella wanted to protect them rather than reveal them.

Stella studied the drawing, squinting until she could see a little bit more. In it, Libby looked torn and unhappy. Actually, she looked haunted. She looked in love and Stella bet it was that asshole Ben, still on Libby's mind. Stella wouldn't show this to Libby. It wasn't anything that Libby didn't know, anyway, and what good would it do either one of them. She ripped up the drawing and stuffed it in the trash.

She dug her hands in her pocket and drew out the stone. She felt calmer, like she had made the right decision. She'd keep this stone with her from now on. Thank you, Libby, she thought. Thank you.

To HER SURPRISE, Stella found she loved the stone. She loved being able to feel its weight in her pocket. At night, she put it on her bed table, so when she couldn't sleep, she could look at it. Oh, how she loved looking at it. The stone was supposed to be clear, but she always saw something new in it, a little vein of pink racing through it, a part that was bluer than another. It was a beautiful object. It seemed to pulse like a heart, and sometimes, she felt as though it connected her to Libby. *I am here. I'm right here*, it said. *Like a true friend.*

The stone, Stella was convinced, made her think more and more about art, because it somehow opened her up. When she felt it resting in her hand, colors around her seemed brighter.

One morning, she got up and carefully researched all the art stores in Manhattan. She read the Yelp reviews ("Staff are morons! They didn't know the difference between acrylics and oils!") and then decided on the League because everyone seemed to love it ("Artists' paradise! They know what you want before you even do!") and because it appeared that all the art students went there.

She went to the store, her heart thumping, feeling like a usurper who didn't belong there because she wasn't really an artist, not yet anyway. Her only artist tool was a pen or pencil. She'd never tried watercolor, oil, pastels, or those gorgeous shiny acrylics. Could she learn to work with them? Would she be any good with them? Or was her gift—or whatever it was—only with drawing?

The store was packed with people. She should have known that. It was September now, and all the art students were here, crowding around all the counters, but she didn't want to go home. A man stood in the back holding up three sable brushes and studying them. In the corner, a woman was trying out pens, scribbling something over and over. They all were hipper than she was. She wandered the aisles, unsure of what she wanted or needed but certain she'd know when she saw it.

"Can I help you?"

Stella turned around. A girl with a blue streak in her hair was standing there, and Stella saw her name tag: Sheila.

"I probably don't belong here—" Stella said, and to her surprise Sheila took her arm. "You do," she said. "Everybody's an artist in one way or another. We're all creative, don't you think?"

"I guess so," Stella said.

"What do you think you want to do?" Sheila said.

Stella looked around. There were rows of tubes of paint along one wall, the caps different brilliant colors. Each one called out to her, as insistent as a push. "Those," Stella decided. "I'm brave enough to try those."

She wanted to buy everything. She wanted to run the sable brushes along her skin. She wanted to eat the colors. For a moment, she remembered how it had been in the coma, when colors had a feel to them, a sound, a smell. How much she had loved that sensation and here it was again.

In the end, Stella was loaded down with acrylics, watercolors in tubes, and five different kinds of brushes. She had watercolor paper, a palette to mix paints, an easel, and four already-blocked canvases because she didn't know how to do that yet, and she was in a hurry to start.

"You can always come back, you know," Sheila said. "I'd like to see your first acrylic." She gave Stella a hug. "You're my kind of people," Sheila told her. "Come back. Be sure to come back."

When she left the store, Stella was so happy she felt she was floating. There it was. Artist. Something to be.

She got home and pushed the dining room table to the side. She spread newspaper on the floor and set up her easel and daubed color on a palette with a knife and then reached for a sable brush. Before she put it in the paint, she stroked it along her face. It was as soft as a makeup brush. Cobalt blue, she thought, and then she carefully, gently, painted a line onto the canvas, so deep and dark she could have tumbled down into it.

There it was, the jump of excitement. This was who she was. She dipped her brush again.

WHEN SIMON GOT home, the apartment had the distinct smell of paint. Stella had pushed the table to the window and she was sitting in the light, painting something on an easel, not turning when he came in. Her happiness radiated, and to Simon's astonishment, the painting was even more extraordinary than her drawings. It was a portrait of a woman he didn't know, older, with glossy white hair and blue eyes, rendered in colors so rich and vivid he swore he could taste them. There was a kind of light in her painting that jumped out at him. Stella could see things in people, and she painted those things into her works, but trying to see what she had felt in this painting only made him anxious and confused. "Stella," he said. "This is beautiful."

"Not finished yet," she said, daubing red into the white hair of the woman in the painting, something he never would have thought would work, but here it made her hair somehow whiter. Stella's hands were moving, conducting a kind of symphony. How did she know to mix colors like that?

"Stella," he said again. "You hungry? Want to order Chinese or something?" But she didn't answer, just kept painting, entranced. He could wave a hand in front of her and she wouldn't notice him.

He sat down beside her and Stella didn't even look up. Her brush flew over the canvas.

"Sorry. I can't stop," she said, but Simon didn't care. He liked being here, sitting quietly with Stella. Watching the glide of the brush was comforting until a wave of loneliness washed over him. He put his head in his hands.

"Hey," Stella said. She put her brush down and studied him.

"I'm okay . . ."

"Was it the picture?" she said. "Sometimes people get weird when they see what I do. It's like a puzzle they can't solve."

"Can you solve it?" he asked her.

"Soon," she said. "Soon I will be able to."

"What are you seeing?" he said. "What does this painting mean?" He looked at the painting again, and for a moment he felt it was whispering secrets to him. Louder, he thought. Louder so I can understand.

She went back to the painting. "I'll tell you when I'm finished," she said. "Then I'll know."

But then she finished, and when he asked her, she shook her head. "I don't know. I thought I would know, but I don't." Then she turned to him. "See what you see in it," she said.

And he tried, studying. "I don't know either," he said.

"Maybe later we'll know," she told him.

ALL THROUGH SEPTEMBER, Stella went to a new place, Washington Square Park, this time with a portable easel and paints. She sat away from the hub where people were playing music or doing magic or demonstrating for or against one thing or another. From her bench on the periphery, it felt greener and leafier, and less crazy. Soon enough, though, people started noticing her and her work, and they clustered around her easel.

A few commissions followed. People began inviting her to paint them in their homes. She obliged, in part because she loved seeing how they lived. Sometimes the places were immaculate, and she knew they had cleaned for her. There was the scent of pine cleaner. Other times, she saw dishes piled in the sink, scrambles of cat hair in the corners by the heaters. It didn't matter. She knew that homes weren't necessarily extensions of people, that a neat home could be a reaction to a tortured mind, that a messy place could belong to someone creative.

The people she met in the park told other people about her. The phone kept ringing. It unnerved her a little the way her new clients looked at her, as if she had magic inside of her. "How did you hear about me?" she always asked. "How did you know?" They all had stories. One client told her that her best friend had commissioned a portrait of her child, and the more she looked at it, the more she understood why her child was so shy. "She doesn't realize how beautiful she is," the mother said. "And that's something I can do something about. Especially with the help of this painting."

Stella came home excited, wanting to talk to Simon about her experiences, but she sometimes felt that he wasn't really listening. "Play music for me while I paint," she'd asked, but he always said no. He was happier when she was doing something else, watching a movie, baking cookies, but she felt herself becoming resentful. She had done so much for him. She remembered how much she had supported him and his music, never asking him to give it up, even when things weren't going well. And now she couldn't give this up, not even for him.

Besides, he hadn't asked her to.

ONE DAY, STELLA was in the park with her face tilted to the sun, doing nothing more exciting than enjoying the day and listening to a man who was playing a piano that he'd hauled outside, when someone tapped her. She looked up. A man in a dark raincoat, his haircut crisp against his head, smiled at her. "You're Stella Davison, right?" he said.

"Last time I looked," she said. She shaded her eyes against the sun.

"The artist," he said. The word still sounded funny to her.

"I'm not painting right now," she said. She nodded at the bench. All she had with her was her handbag.

"Oh, I don't want you to paint me," he said, and then he dug in his pocket and handed her a card. Jack Mantor, it said. *Time Out New York.* "I want to interview you," he said.

"Why?" The card fluttered in her hand.

"You're famous. And you got there in a weird way," he said. "And that's always interesting."

She wasn't sure. Did she want people to know more about her? *Time Out* was a magazine weekly. She didn't need any more clients. She sometimes felt harassed by them. Sometimes they seemed to be looking for something in her when they should have been looking at the artwork. Fame was something Simon had always chased. He had told her it was like being dipped in gold, it was like getting dark chocolate sprinkles on delicious ice cream, and she hadn't been able to imagine it.

"Okay," she said.

19

IT WAS THE LAST week of September, still hot and muggy, the city sour with humidity, when the magazine piece came out. Simon sat in the apartment, stunned, unable to open the issue of *Time Out* magazine he held in his hands. Stella had told him the interview was going to be in it, but he hadn't quite believed it, even when she had excitedly shown him the proofs. How had it happened that Stella got famous so fast? Simon knew that in the hospital she was the notorious coma woman who had awakened scribbling circles. But real artistry and fame—that was something different.

Stella no longer had time for anything other than painting. She didn't have to go to the park anymore, because she now had so many commission requests that she was forced to turn some down. She traveled all over the city, to the Upper East and West Sides, to NoHo, to Tribeca; sometimes she found work in her own neighborhood in Chelsea. A few times people came to her, and then Simon, in the other room, would hear them talking: *I heard you were the one who noticed that my best friend's little girl was depressed. She's better now, on medication.* Or: *I heard you painted my friend and then told her that she should leave her relationship. And she did and she's so much happier. How did you know?*

"I just feel what's going on in a person while I'm painting them," Stella said. "There's no magic about it."

How could Simon begrudge her this sudden success? She was so excited about art. She jumped out of bed every morning, anxious to start working. She painted people and tortoises and houses and anything someone wanted. It was a talent, as startling to Stella as it was to everybody else. "Sometimes I'm terrified it's going to go away," Stella told him, and while Simon assured her it wouldn't, a part of him hoped that it would. But he could never tell her that.

Next the *New York Times* did a full-page story on her, including a photograph of her looking beautiful and shy, dressed in black jeans and a black sweatshirt, a pad of paper in her hands, her hair a bright squiggle of gold with a big sable paintbrush stuck in her curls like a hair clip. In the photo, Stella seemed full of doubt and wonder, as if she couldn't see why a newspaper would be interested in her. "All that happened is my brain rewired," she was quoted as saying. "The temporal lobe has to do with inhibitions, with freeing up creativity. Maybe that was what happened when I was in a coma. And suddenly I could draw." The word about her spread further. She was photographed by the "Humans of New York" guy, who told her he had been looking for her, something he didn't usually do. He spoke to her for a half hour. She told him she didn't know why she did what she did, only that she had to, and she was sure there was a scientific explanation for it. "Mystery brain," she said, tapping her head. "For now, anyway." The interview made her sound sort of profound, and her entry on the Humans Facebook page had received over twenty thousand likes, and many more comments, including more than a few requests to buy her dinner or have sex with her. Stella didn't answer any of these messages but not because she was rude or overwhelmed. She simply didn't know what would be the right thing to say.

If it had happened to Simon, he would have been bursting with joy. He would have bought twenty copies of every interview, every article, and spread them all over the apartment. But Stella just seemed embarrassed by the attention. She was happy to talk about her art but not about fame. She wouldn't even say the word. Maybe he was a little jealous, too, because when was the last time anyone had clamored for his talent? He knew what fame could do. He had almost tasted it.

Simon wondered if Stella actually needed him anymore. She seemed to. She slept with one arm across his body, practically pinning him down. She lit up when she saw him, but she still seemed to be whirling in a place where he couldn't reach her, circling further and further away from him.

The song "Nowhere Man" popped into his head, but he wasn't going to feel sorry for himself. This wasn't about him. Good for Stella. He hoped she would win prizes, that she'd have what he never could, that rocket ship of fame. That was what you did when you cared about someone—you wanted the best for them.

He went out, walking against the flow of people. He wasn't planning it, but then, there he was, at Libby's building. She buzzed him in and was standing at the door with the *Times* in her hand. "I know," she said quietly. He leaned against her, feeling the heat radiating from her into him, like a transfusion.

He told himself it was just a way to cope, to be a fellow survivor of what had happened with Stella. That was why he began to see Libby more and more. And Stella simply wasn't home as much anymore. She was at other people's homes, painting them, or at the art store, fired up about a new kind of oil paint, a new shade of ochre she had found. All her clothes had bits of paint on them, her little summer dresses, her jeans, her tops. "I'm a marked woman," Stella said, laughing.

Simon and Libby didn't talk about Stella when they were together. He knew Libby and Stella had lunch every week, but Stella didn't really mention those lunches to him either. When Simon went over to Libby's, they sat curled on her couch and talked about movies they were watching or books they were both reading. They talked a little about their childhoods, about growing up, and sometimes, they talked about nothing at all but just held hands. They kissed and then got up and tumbled into bed, and when Simon left, the door quietly shutting behind him, everything felt recharged again.

Stella was in her own private world now, Simon thought, but he and Libby were, too, and it was saving all of them.

At least for now.

USUALLY STELLA WELCOMED the change of seasons, but here it was October and still so relentlessly muggy. Coming home from Chelsea Market (where she had intended only to browse, not buy), she found herself balancing two paper bags, one of them stealthily ripping on the bottom and making her wish she had brought the little red cart she sometimes used for groceries, which was both adorable to look at and a pain to maneuver. She hoisted the bag up higher, cradling it underneath with her sweaty forearm. She caught the scent of the ripe pears she'd bought, and it made her feel better.

She had taken on a new commission that morning, a woman in her seventies who said she had fallen in love for the first time. A radio show recording had followed that. And now that shopping was done, she'd go home to celebrate the day. She'd get out of this sulky heat and into the air-conditioning.

The radio show was going to air at the end of the month. The interviewer had called to tell her, his voice bright with excitement, but Stella had just shrugged. She didn't really think about fame, though no one really believed her. "Oh, come on," the radio guy had said. "You don't find this exciting? It doesn't make you feel like you've been bumped up the ladder of life or something?"

"What ladder?" Stella said. "I just love painting. People knowing about what I do helps me be able to do what I love."

The radio guy had laughed. "Sure," he said. He didn't believe her, but she knew it was the truth.

Libby and her other friends were happy for her, though most of them didn't want her to paint them. "I don't want to know anything deep about me!" Debra said. "Let me stay the happy idiot that I am!" Stella laughed. She wouldn't push, no more than she had pushed Libby or Simon. She knew that it wouldn't work if the person was resistant. They'd just hide whatever was deep inside of them. Simon didn't even like looking at the paintings she did, and at first she didn't know why. "They aren't good?" she said.

"They're brilliant," he said quietly, and then she knew what the answer was for him.

Fame. It was always fame. She knew how much he wanted—no, needed—it. But fame for Simon was something different than it was for her. For Simon, it was a way of telling his father "I matter" and showing him how everyone else thought so, too. For her, it just meant she could do more of what she loved without worrying about money. It meant she could make people happy and be happier herself.

"Does this publicity make you feel funny?" she asked Simon, because she didn't want to use the word *jealous*.

"I'm proud of you," he said.

"It's really just noise. Flavor-of-the-moment stuff. It doesn't mean anything," she told him.

"Yes, it does," he said.

She began to feel more and more lonely around him, because now there were things she couldn't talk about, things she had to shield him from. At dinner out one night, a man came up to the table, and she saw Simon's face when the man gushed about Stella and her artwork. Stella cut him off as gently as she could. "Thank you, we're eating now," she said, and the man apologized and left, but Simon stayed quiet for the rest of the meal.

Keep up with me. That's what she thought when they had their argument before she went into coma and changed. She thought it now, too. She urged him to write more songs, to drive for Lyft less, but he seemed unmoored. Sometimes she tried to hold him tightly, but she always felt him tensing up, and she let him go.

Walking home with the groceries, she thought about seeing Simon later. Tonight she would light candles. She'd put on music and the blue satin slip dress Simon loved, and this time she'd really, really try to make everything beautiful. She thought of a magazine her mom used to read, because there was a series in it, Can This Marriage Be Saved? A marriage counselor would weigh in, and 98 percent of the time the marriage could survive, with just a few minor adjustments.

I can do this. I can do this.

Stella's steps bounced as she turned the corner.

She passed the little Clement Clarke Moore Park, the whole area already dimming into twilight, and there, by a bench, she saw a couple kissing, their bodies pressed together. There it was, love, solving everything. She came closer, because they seemed like a fire she could warm herself by. But then the couple pulled gently apart, and suddenly she saw who the lovers were. It was Simon taking Libby's face in his hands. Libby leaning into him. Libby's eyes were closed, her mouth half open, and then Simon kissed her again.

They didn't see her and instead kept kissing and kissing, practically devouring each other.

Stella couldn't unlock her eyes from them. Now she knew what she had sensed in the drawing she had made of Libby, the thing she couldn't quite articulate. Libby was in love. Stella just didn't know with whom then. And now she did. And now it made sense to her why Simon had never asked her to draw him. Why she had never wanted to. Somehow, somewhere, she must have known.

Stella was suddenly sweating and dizzy, and the groceries fell from her hands, the lamb chops, the dried cranberries dotting the sidewalk like punctuation marks, the pears tumbling, and the glass of the bubble bath breaking. All sound was gone from the world except for her heavy breathing. All color was missing except the red of Libby's mouth, the gray of Simon's eyes. She pivoted and started to run.

BY THE TIME Stella got back into the apartment, she was crying. What could she do? What was even here for her now? She couldn't be a nurse anymore, even if she wanted to. And worse, she couldn't be a partner to Simon or a loving friend to Libby. All that was gone with a kiss.

Why hadn't she seen this before now? Why hadn't her drawing of Libby told her?

Because, she thought, she hadn't wanted to see.

Panting, she began to stuff clothes in a suitcase, along with her drawing pens, the oil paints, the canvas and the pads of thick-cut watercolor paper she liked to use. She would stop at the bank and take the money she had been hoarding, five grand, enough to at least buy her a month before she had to figure out what to do. She'd go to the Port Authority. She'd find a town where no one knew her, and then she'd figure it out because this—all this life with Simon—was over.

She grabbed at the pad of paper by the phone, reaching for a pen beside it. She stood writing, bearing down so hard the tip of the pen broke. She reached for another pen. A million words crowded up inside of her, but all she wrote was:

Dear Simon,
Fuck you. You liar. I know you love Libby.
Stella

She put down the pen and left the note on the table where Simon would see it. She walked to the little dish that had the good-luck stone Libby had given her. She had loved that stone, had sometimes sat at night just running it from one palm to another, stroking it because it was so soothing. She grabbed an envelope and stuffed the stone in it. The note she wrote to Libby said only *Fuck you. I know about you and Simon.* She sealed the envelope and wrote Libby's name on the outside. She would drop it off at the hospital mailroom, and then she would be done with both of them.

Suddenly she felt calm settling over her like a coat thrown over her shoulder. That rage, that sorrow—it all felt like it belonged to a woman she was never going to be again. She got her things, and she opened the door, giving her apartment one last look, and then she left, letting the door slam shut behind her.

She knew that she didn't have much time. Even when he was working, Simon never came home past 10 p.m. He would be expecting her to be there for him, and when he saw the note, he'd be frantic. He'd look for her. Maybe Libby would look for her, too, and they'd both try to explain themselves to her, or maybe they'd lie, but Stella didn't have the energy to listen.

She wasn't really sure where she was going. She just knew that she had to go, that she couldn't take any more of this feeling of being so disconnected. She needed someplace quiet, where she could regroup and think.

She flagged the first yellow cab she saw and went to Grand Central Station and looked up at the board. Boston. Washington, DC. She didn't want to go to either place. There were trains for Chicago—that might be far enough, but did she want to go there? How nuts was it to come here and have no idea where you wanted to be or how long you might stay? Well, whatever train was leaving next, that's what she'd take. But an announcer proclaimed that the train to Hartford was leaving in five minutes, and she didn't want to go there. Then she looked up at the board again and saw it, her destination, and she went to buy her ticket.

20

LATER THAT DAY, AFTER they had been kissing in the park, Simon and Libby were lying on her bed when Libby started crying. "I can't do this anymore," she said.

They both sat up and leaned against the headboard, their voices rolling over each other. "I can't do this to a friend," Libby said. "I can't do this to myself."

"I know," Simon said, his unhappiness audible. "I can't eat. I can't sleep. I hate myself."

"I want more," Libby cried. "I need more than just this sneaking around as if we were teenagers, this love on the sly."

Simon started. "You love me?"

Libby cried harder.

"We have to figure this out," he said.

They went through all the scenarios. Libby knew people who were married for years and had other relationships on the side and no one knew, so no one was hurt. She knew people who did know and they didn't care. "We didn't plan on this," Libby said. "We fought it."

"It wouldn't have happened if Stella was herself," Simon said, and then he felt suddenly sick, because he realized it might have happened anyway. Simon's mouth went dry.

"I was thinking about leaving her," he said quietly. "That day, before she went into coma." He crunched down into the bed, staring at the ceiling. "I thought we'd wake up and I'd go to California with the band, and maybe I wouldn't come back."

"Maybe," Libby repeated.

"I don't know what anything is anymore," he said, and then Libby put her hands against his face and scooted down lower in the bed so that she was lying beside him.

"Neither do I," she said. "Except you. I know you and I know me." Libby tilted her head. "She's still having doctors' appointments. When those stop, things might be different again for her. I've seen it happen."

Simon turned his face to the pillow. Memories flashed in his mind: he and Stella on their second date, sharing a hot fudge sundae, Stella eating all the ice cream and laughing. Stella now, drawing and drawing, so intently that a part of him felt a little anxious at how easily she could shut him out. How else could Stella be, and how else could he be in reaction to that? He turned to Libby. She was sleeping, her hair a storm on the sheets, her mouth faintly open.

Simon knew he had to get home to Stella, but he didn't want to just slip out while Libby was asleep. He glanced at his watch. He could be a little late, couldn't he?

He got up and dressed. Restlessly, he walked around Libby's apartment, something he often did when she was sleeping. It made him feel more connected to her. Everything here could tell him something about her, from the Walden Pond T-shirt she had framed because she grew up near the pond, to the pulpy 1950s paperback novels she collected because she thought their covers were fun.

Libby was so meticulous a doctor, but her apartment was disorganized. Once he had found silverware in her desk drawer. Another time, he had been looking for scissors to snip a thread and he had finally found them in the coat closet.

He had never intended any of this to happen. Falling in love with

Libby had been so gradual a process, he hadn't noticed it at first. She had started out as someone who made him believe things could be better. Then she made him believe that he could be better.

His whole body was humming. He wandered into the living room and saw that Libby had left her laptop on, the cord unplugged. She'd run down the battery that way. He'd told her that repeatedly. He plugged in her computer, then looked at her desktop in amazement because it was covered with icons.

What kind of crazy system was this? If it were him, he'd delete almost all of them. What did she need to keep Spotify, Skype, and Pandora open? He told himself he wasn't snooping. He certainly wasn't planning on deleting anything. He was just curious about her and this wacky system she seemed to have.

He saw folders on the bottom of the desktop, unmarked, floating. Maybe when she woke up, he could suggest ways for her to straighten things up here. One folder was labeled "Meet for Dinner?"; another, "Ideas." He shook his head in wonder. He was about to turn away when he saw his name on a document. He blinked, then saw the name of a record label, the same one that she had said she was going to send his music to. He hesitated, but then, with his pulse quickening, he clicked on it, and there it was, a copy of an email dated months ago, back when Stella was still hospitalized.

The words hit him like a punch in his heart. *There is something here that we would very much like to explore further. Please have Simon get in touch with us as soon as possible.*

He made a noise in his throat. Or maybe it was the sound of Libby's bare feet coming up behind him, her hand on his shoulder.

He whipped around, standing. There she was, beautiful and pale, a liar wearing his T-shirt. He watched her face crumpling. "Oh, babe," she said quietly.

"Why did you lie to me?"

"I . . . I was going to tell you," she said. "Eventually I was . . . when things calmed down."

"When? When I was eighty years old? Never? Is never the time you were thinking about?"

She put her hand to her mouth. "You don't understand," she said.

"Fucking right, I don't. Why would you do this if you weren't going to let me follow up?"

"We didn't know each other that well then . . ."

"You know me now."

"I did it because I wanted you to hope! I didn't know anything about music. When this email came, Stella was still so dicey. And I wanted you to be there for her. I thought if you knew you had an out, you might take it, you might leave and not come back."

"What?" He stared at her, incredulous. "What are you saying? I would leave? I could have worked here, right here. I could have gotten studio work maybe or a chance that one of my songs might get picked up by a music publisher and then go to someone big. At the very least it would have been a connection—"

"I wasn't in love with you then, Simon!"

"How did you know what I'd do? How fucking dare you assume—"

"I didn't really know you then! I just knew what Stella had told me about you! What I saw!" She started to cry, so softly it was like an undertone to the buzzing in Simon's ears. "Then I started to love you—"

"Love? You're talking about love? All of this is a mess—"

"I'm sorry! I'm sorry!" She tried to grab his arm, but he pulled away. "But you never asked me about it!" she cried. "I thought maybe it didn't matter, maybe you'd forgotten . . ."

"Are you blaming me? Do you even know me at all?" he said, astonished. "Do you even believe what you're saying to me?" He tried to move as far away from her as he could. But the air seemed to be moving, too, locking him in place. Oh Jesus. Everything could have been so different, and now it was all in the past. He could have taken that chance that guy had told Libby about, that one shining moment to be someone, to prove everyone wrong, from Mighty Chondria to his father.

He bent over, enveloped by a sense of nausea. It had been his choice to make and she wrenched it from him.

"Do it now!" Libby cried. "Contact them! If he was interested once, he'd be interested again!"

Simon stepped away from her. "That's not how it works," he said. He couldn't look at Libby. Why had he thought that he could trust her? "You don't get to decide my life," he said.

"I would do anything to take it back!" she said. "I love you, Simon, I love you—and I know you love me!"

Simon picked up his messenger bag and slung it over his shoulder.

"What are you doing?" she cried. "Where are you going? Why do you have to leave now?"

"Because I don't know who you are anymore." He opened the front door. "And because I don't know who I am anymore, either." And he walked out of her apartment.

21

SIMON TOOK THE STAIRS two at a time up to his apartment. He had agonized so much about his and Libby's relationship, and now it was over, slammed shut like a door, and on the other side was his future, bleak and yawning in front of him.

He put the key in the lock. He was late. Stella had stopped asking him where he was anymore when he came home at odd hours, which both relieved and depressed him. He'd tend to her. He'd stop thinking about his own voracious need for love and fame and instead he'd focus on her and nothing else right now. He'd see to it that she could live the life she wanted, that she had a support system in place.

"Stella?" he called. The lights were off and he flicked them on. "Stella?" he said again, and his eyes moved to the open closet, to the racks where Stella's clothes had hung. Then he saw a note on the table, and he picked it up. There it was, Stella's careful scribble: *Fuck you. You liar. I know you love Libby.* And that's when he began to be afraid.

How did she know? How had she found out? He looked down at the paper again. She had borne down on it so hard, it had ripped.

FOR ONE CRAZY moment he thought he should call Libby because Stella might have gone there, but then he lost heart. Who was he kidding? What would Libby know that he didn't? He ran out to all the places Stella might be, her favorite spots. He scanned the little park on West Twenty-Second, where he'd been with Libby, but it was empty except for one exhausted mother trying to placate a screaming toddler who was up well past his bedtime. He passed the art store, which was closed of course, and then circled back to the apartment. He didn't know where else to look.

The night was so dark now. Stella wasn't picking up her cell, so he called her friends, his voice breaking. "I don't know where she is," he said. They were all sympathetic, but none of them knew either. "Truthfully, it's not the way it used to be with us," Debra said. "It makes me sad, but it's true."

It's not the same for me either.

He thought about calling Bette, to see if Stella had reached out to her. But Bette was old and he didn't want to upset her. Or maybe the truth was that he really liked her, and he didn't want the truth of what had happened to make her stop liking him.

He went to the local police station and stammered out what had happened, but the cop was unimpressed. "She's a grown woman," he said to Simon. "And she's barely been gone a few hours. Give it some time. Wait. Save your panic for later."

"You don't understand—" Simon said, and then he thought, How could this cop, or anyone else for that matter, understand? "She was in a coma."

"But she's not now, right?" the cop said. "Look. She'll come back. They almost always do."

ONE DAY PASSED, then two, and then four, and Simon kept looking for her, kept texting and calling her. What if she was hurt? What if her brain changed again? Doctors didn't know everything that was possible with coma. They couldn't predict how she'd proceed in life. He thought he saw her when he was driving a passenger uptown and swerved the car to the curb. "Jesus!" the woman in the back said as Simon pulled the car to a stop. He put his head in his hands and cried. "You okay?" the woman said. He straightened and saw in his rearview mirror that she was checking her watch.

"I'm fine," he said. "I'm just not myself."

And then he put the car in drive and headed on.

22

LIBBY WAS STRICKEN. SHE didn't know what she expected, maybe that Simon would call her, that he'd show up. Instead, her phone had no messages, no texts. Her buzzer rang only for deliveries. She sat on her bed, unable to move, getting up only to gulp down water and then come back. She had ruined everything, the way she always did.

She had always been pragmatic, and she didn't have to be a genius to figure this one out. Simon would go back to Stella and they would work things out. Or Simon would go back to Stella and then they would separate. All she knew for sure was that he didn't want to be with Libby, he could never trust her again. What was left for her?

She couldn't sleep, so she went to the hospital, hoping work might save her the way it always had. Because she couldn't face talking to anyone any more than was necessary, she ate from vending machines rather than in the cafeteria. When she tired, she lay on a cot in her office rather than returning home to her own bed, but sleep remained elusive.

One day passed, and then another. She was going on her rounds when Eileen, the head nurse, stopped her. "Something was left for you," the nurse said. "It somehow wound up at the desk on another floor a few days ago, but here it finally is." She handed Libby an envelope.

Libby took it, curious, hearing something rattle, and then she opened it and there was her quartz stone. It warmed her hand, but why had Stella returned it? She dug deeper into the envelope and there it was: *Fuck you. I know about you and Simon.*

Libby felt herself turning to ice.

Stella knew.

But how did she know? Had Simon gone back to the apartment furious and broken and told Stella? But that wasn't like him, to be cruel. She couldn't imagine him doing such a thing.

"Are you okay?" Eileen said. "You don't look okay." Eileen came around and took Libby's wrist. "I'm getting a doctor to cover for you."

"No, no, I'm okay," she said, but she had to clutch for the edge of the counter.

"I'm calling you a Lyft," Eileen said. "You need to go home."

"No. Not a Lyft."

"I'll call a taxi, then."

ONCE AT HOME, she called Stella's cell. "Call me," she begged on voice mail. "Please call me."

She couldn't call Simon to try to speak to Stella. Not now. He hated her. He blamed her. And she blamed herself. Whatever happened now, she surely deserved it.

ON HER WAY to work the next morning, Libby walked through Washington Square Park, where Stella had liked to paint, but on Stella's usual bench, there was only an old woman knitting, a couple kissing on the bench opposite her.

She couldn't focus at work because she kept thinking of how she could possibly make things right. She checked in on her patients, starting with a middle-aged man named Frank Stepford, wolf faced and way too skinny, who had developed an infection after stomach surgery and spent most of his time staring at the wall, curled in pain.

"We'll take care of that," Libby said. Simple, she thought, and she strode into the hall and ordered an antibiotic, a good warhorse. A pharmacy robot would get it off the shelf and measure it out, a nurse would administer it, and Libby knew that Frank would feel better in a few days.

But an hour later, a new nurse she knew only vaguely tracked her down in the hallway. "What?" Libby said.

"The order . . ." the nurse began. "For Mr. Stepford. It's . . . I think it's wrong."

Nurses didn't question Libby. They knew her reputation. "He's got an allergy to this. It's in his file." Libby glanced down at the tablets in the nurse's hand, at the order, and then she felt her stomach wrench. She had never made a mistake like this. If the nurse hadn't caught it, if she had given him this antibiotic . . . Libby looked at the nurse's name tag, Amy Silver. She was new, eager to please, determined to do it all right. And then she looked at Amy's face, and it began to fade, and Libby's legs buckled underneath her, and she fell to the floor.

WHEN SHE CAME to, she was lying on a cot in the nurses' station, Amy beside her. "Thank you," Libby said, "for catching that mistake of mine." There. She said it. She admitted to an error. She struggled to sit up. "Wait, wait—" Amy said, but Libby stood. "Thank you for taking care of me," Libby said. She put one hand on Amy's shoulder. "You're a really good nurse."

Amy nodded doubtfully. "I'm going to report myself," Libby told Amy. "I'll offer to resign. I'm going to tell them how great it was that you caught this, because you should get credit."

"No, no," Amy said. "Nothing happened. I don't have to say anything." Amy swallowed. "I don't want you to get in trouble over this. It was caught and nothing happened . . ."

"But it could have happened," Libby said. "And I do have to say something. It's my job."

• • •

LIBBY WENT TO talk to Angela Martoni, the chief of staff. Libby didn't know Angela that well, but she had heard that Angela was fair, that she really cared about the hospital. The whole time Libby was speaking, Angela sat rigidly, her hands folded.

"Well," Angela finally said.

"I'll resign," Libby said. "I take total responsibility." She wanted to plead, Please don't fire me. This is all I have.

"You know how valuable you are to the hospital," Angela said quietly. "What a stellar physician you are. And you know that every single one of us makes mistakes. For every mistake that's committed, there are at least two hundred that almost happened but were caught in time. Like yours was."

"But not by me," Libby said. Libby knew how valuable top-notch doctors were to a hospital because they brought in patients, and that meant money, and in a hospital, there was never, ever enough money. Doctors could be stars, on the Best Doctors in New York list in New York magazines, the page framed and hanging in their waiting rooms. They could be personalities, speaking on the news about whatever the latest epidemic was. Nurses like Amy didn't mean as much because they actually cost the hospital money in training, and virtually none established reputations that attracted patients.

"I fucked up," Libby said.

"Almost," said Angela. "But you didn't, and so no action is necessary except more vigilance on your part. And after this, I'm confident you won't do anything like this again."

Libby thought about going back on the floor, and her mind shuttered. She couldn't. Not yet. "I need to take some time off, then," Libby said.

"And we need you here. How long a leave are we talking about?"

"Three weeks," Libby decided.

Angela was quiet for a moment. "Two," she said. "You come back November first and we're good." And then Libby nodded.

• • •

LIBBY DIDN'T ANNOUNCE her leave. She had a quiet meeting with the doctor who would take on her patients while she was away, explaining only that she was overworked. "Don't I know how that is," the other doctor said. Libby talked to Amy who looked stricken when Libby said she was taking a leave. "Oh no . . . no," Amy said, but Libby shook her head. "You did a good thing," Libby said. "The right good thing. And when I come back, I hope you'll work with me."

BACK IN HER apartment, Libby felt a restlessness she'd never known. She couldn't sit still. She paced her apartment, exhaustedly walking, but unable to stop. She couldn't sleep, couldn't concentrate enough to read or watch movies, so she finally went to see a therapist, someone unaffiliated with her hospital but with good patient reviews on Zocdoc, but the real reason she told him she came to see him was because his name made her laugh: Dr. Sheep.

DR. SHEEP'S OFFICE was in Libby's favorite New York City building, the beautiful Beaux-Arts Flatiron, on the third floor, which she took to be a good omen. Another good sign was that he was able to see her almost immediately upon her arrival at his office.

Once seated, she studied him. He was in his early forties, around Libby's age, with punk-cut yellow hair and red high-top sneakers. He leaned forward. Libby had intended just asking for something to help her sleep, but he seemed so calm, so interested, that instead she began to cry. "Oh! I didn't mean to do this!" she said. She began to talk about all the ways she had failed Simon and Stella, how she had failed herself, too. She told him how she had lied to Simon and that he didn't want to see her anymore.

"Maybe you were trying to do the best thing," Dr. Sheep said.

"Then why do I feel so anxious?"

"Anxiety is a puzzle, an enigma. It can be a beast," Dr. Sheep said. He gave Libby some yoga breathing exercises in which she had to practically hyperventilate, but practicing them, Libby felt better, or maybe it was just because she had something to do. "What do you do that's physical?" he said.

"Well, I've been racing around the hospital."

"Not then. Now."

"Nothing," she admitted.

"Figure out something you want to do, even if it's just walking around the city. You want something that could kick up endorphins. But I want it to be something you love, because otherwise you'll just get more anxious because I told you to do something you hate. And that won't be good for either of us."

"And," said Dr. Sheep, reaching for a notebook, "I want to see you again in a few days. I want you to come three times this first week."

"No meds?" Libby said. Part of her had hoped to be in a pill-induced stupor and not have to think, but the other part wanted to be in control—not that that seemed possible anymore.

"Let's try this first." He reached for his calendar. "Now what day is good for you?"

LIBBY WASN'T SURE what physical activity she wanted to attempt. It had to require no skill. She had to be able to do it any time, night or day, and she had to be able to do it by herself. That ruled out tennis and Soul Cycle. She began to run at the local Y. She was the slowest, sloppiest runner there, but no one seemed to notice her. On the first day, when she finally stopped, she was drenched with sweat. She rested her hands on her knees, panting. She felt good.

BUT AS SOON as she got home, she felt miserable again. She thought about her patients and the hospital, how she had failed them and was so ashamed, and she thought about Simon and Stella, because she had ruined things there, too. She had been such an idiot. She hoped Simon and Stella had made it up, that they were together again. She hoped that Simon had called that CEO and he had given

Simon the chance he deserved. For herself, she didn't really hope for anything at all.

Her hands shook and she sat on them to still them. You have to face what you're afraid of, Dr. Sheep had told her, and Libby couldn't help thinking, What a smug bastard, let's see you do it. Shrinks are just as screwed up as their patients, she thought, but she didn't say it to him. At the same time, though, she wondered if Dr. Sheep was right. It was easy to spend her sessions talking about the hospital mistake, worrying over Simon, over how she had betrayed Stella. But at the end of the session, when she snuck a look at the clock, she felt this story wasn't the story she really needed to tell. Instead, it felt like an offshoot of something older, a rehash of a wound that had started in childhood with her brother, Richie, a crime she had never been able to forget, and neither had her parents. She could talk about Simon and Stella and her hospital mistake all she wanted, but she kept feeling the Richie story rise up in her, taking more and more force to swallow it down. She couldn't tell Dr. Sheep about the most important thing of all.

If Richie were alive and had become a doctor, what would Libby have done for work? Certainly she wouldn't have become a doctor, too, because then she'd be measured against him all the time, and she'd never achieve the heights he could reach, and she'd always feel diminished. A researcher? A second-grade teacher? She couldn't remember what else had really interested her when she was young, what she had dreamed about for her future. She hadn't had a chance to find out because she was so intent on living the life Richie might have had. And, of course, she loved medicine so much that she had had no regrets. But did she love it because it was what Richie would have done? Or did she love it because it was the right job for her? And what if Richie had lived and had become a banker? Who would Libby have become then?

Libby got up and walked over to her computer and turned it on. She searched for Richie's name, her heart pounding. She did this all the time, and even though it never made her feel better, she always thought it might. She knew she was being a fool. His name wasn't going to pop up as some happily married father of five in Boston. Instead, she found what she always found: two columns about his death in the *Waltham Tribune*, one with a photo of Richie holding up his science fair trophies. Libby felt sick. She put one hand on the computer screen and stroked his face.

LIBBY SETTLED INTO a chair in Dr. Sheep's office. She was due to go back to work soon, but she still felt strange and uneasy.

"Therapy takes time," Dr. Sheep reassured her.

"How much time? I don't feel any different yet," Libby said.

For the first time that Libby could remember, Dr. Sheep laughed.

"Why are you laughing?" Libby asked.

"Because you used the word 'yet,'" said Dr. Sheep. "That shows hope."

He was so pleased with her. "You're starting to do good, hard work here," he said.

She shook her head. "No," she said. "I'm not."

Maybe it was because she was going back to work. Maybe it was because he thought she was something that she wasn't, but she knew she had to tell Dr. Sheep about Richie. "Listen," she said, and she let the story rise up in her throat and come out. She talked without really meeting the doctor's eyes, and he didn't interrupt her, and when she was finished, he was quiet. He shook his head, which worried Libby, because she didn't know what that meant. "I'm an asshole for telling you," Libby said. "I wasted your time."

"Why do you think that?"

"Because there's nothing to be done about this."

"You can't change the thing, but you might be able to change how you think about it."

"That sounds suspiciously like shrink speak."

"You were a child," said Dr. Sheep. "You said your parents never talked to you about it. You never brought it up with them. Did they ever tell you, 'Libby, you must make up for this by becoming your brother'?"

"No."

"And when you did become a doctor, were they proud? Did they ever compare you to Richie?"

Libby thought back. When she had gone to med school, her parents acted the same as if she had said she were going to be an accountant. When she graduated, they sat in the auditorium during the ceremony and later took her out to dinner, but they still seemed steeped in sadness, wounded.

"You never talked about it with them?"

"Maybe I didn't want to know what they would say," Libby said. "Maybe I just didn't get the chance. They both died in a car crash and there you have it. No one got a chance to say anything."

Dr. Sheep frowned. "That doesn't mean you can't still resolve this. Have you ever thought of going back to Waltham?"

Libby sat up. "Are you nuts?"

"Going there might make you remember how young you were."

"I hope the whole town has been bulldozed," Libby said. "I never want to see any of it again."

"What you're feeling is the result of something that happened years ago," Dr. Sheep said. "It isn't happening now. And I think you need to see that."

"It sure feels like it is."

"It isn't," Dr. Sheep promised. "And you're braver now. You've proved it."

"I have? How?"

Dr. Sheep smiled again. "By coming to see me."

23

LIBBY HAD NO INTENTION of going back to Waltham, though she did want to please Dr. Sheep. But what could she possibly gain by going back? She was too much of a scientist to believe in ghosts. Richie's spirit wouldn't come to her and forgive her. She wouldn't feel better. Still, the idea of going nagged at her. Would she be a coward if she didn't go?

That Thursday morning, she got in the car and drove north, the radio blasting the Kinks. When she crossed into Massachusetts, though, she didn't want anything but silence. As soon as she got on Route 128, then Trapelo Road, she started to feel sick.

She went to Warwick Avenue, feeling more and more nauseated. There was her old house, painted red now with blue shutters. She parked the car and started walking, and then she was on Greer Street, where she and Richie had gone to play in the pool.

There. There it was. The house that had the pool was painted blue now, and there were all sorts of kid accoutrements scattered in the front yard. She walked to the side of the house. No gate. No pool. A bright blue patio and some lounge chairs, a little garden with a chaos of flowers. Libby sank down to the lawn. She felt the house humming to her, as if it were alive: *I know what you did. I know who you really are and I hate you for it.*

Libby put her head in her hands. This was a mistake. She'd go home. She'd go back to work on Monday. She'd try to be a better doctor. A better person.

"Hello, are you okay?"

Libby looked up. An older woman was standing on the lawn, staring at her. The woman looked vaguely familiar and Libby tried to remember who this person was. "Do you need me to call someone?" the woman asked, and then Libby stood, too.

"I live just across the street," the woman said. "I saw you and—"

"I'm sorry. This used to be the Millers' house. I used to come here—"

"The Millers!" The woman tilted her head. "The Millers moved away years ago."

"Do you know where?"

"No," the woman said. "I'm sorry."

"Actually, I don't want to find them," Libby said. She had seen the Millers after the accident, when they came to see her parents and she was made to play in the backyard while they talked. She had encountered them again in a lawyer's office, but she'd had her head down, not daring to look up.

"Who are you?" the woman said to Libby.

Libby said her name and the woman's shoulders relaxed. "Libby. My God. Little Libby. I should have known," she said quietly. "You still have the same red hair." She shook her head. "Do you remember me? Mrs. Stanislovsky? Irma? I was friends with your mom, too."

"No."

"Really, you don't? Your mom and I used to go shopping afternoons together. We'd take you, too. One of us would make lemonade and we'd sit on the chaises and talk."

"I wish I remembered."

"Please," said Irma. "Come inside. I'll make us tea."

As soon as Libby was in Irma's kitchen, she felt something familiar, like she was little again. She remembered something else. Running into this house to get her mom and finding her and Irma at this table, smoking cigarettes, quietly talking. She tried to remember seeing Irma after the accident, but everything was a haze.

Irma made them mint tea. "I loved your mom," she said.

"She and my dad died in a car accident," Libby said.

Irma took Libby's hand. "I know, honey. And I'm so sorry. I always imagined that one day she'd just show up here, come in my kitchen, just like no time at all had passed. Your mom never knew if she had done the right thing. Your family was struggling so hard. She used to cry about it."

"What right thing?"

Irma put down her teacup. "You don't know, do you," she said. "They never told you?"

Time rustled. Libby could feel the sun burning her skin, the drip of sun lotion on her back. She could see the hard blue of the pool and hear her brother's laugh.

"Told me what?" Libby said. "That it was my fault? That I had taken him there?"

"What are you talking about? Who told you it was your fault?"

"My parents thought so."

"I was there that day," Irma said.

"I didn't see you. "

"How could you have seen anything, you were so upset? And it wasn't your fault. You were a kid. It was the Millers'."

"The Millers? But they were never blamed—"

"Of course they were. It was negligence. They were supposed to have the pool locked up with a gate."

Libby couldn't speak. She remembered the gate, the broken lock, how easy it had been for her and Richie to open it up and glide right through.

"They were rich, the Millers. They had this large liability home-owners' policy that required all sorts of things if you were going to have a pool. Numbers marking the depth. The right height of the diving board. And last but not least, a working gate with a working lock."

"I don't understand," Libby said. "What does this have to do with anything?"

Irma studied Libby. "Tell me. What do you do now for work?" she said quietly.

"I'm a doctor."

"How do you think your parents paid for your med school?"

"They told me they'd saved up for it. I don't know how they managed, but they did."

"Enough for four years? Enough for med school? Your parents didn't have money. Your mom used to tell me that she knew Richie would grab scholarships, but you—she was worried about you. She didn't know how they'd get you through school."

"They never said anything about—"

"Listen to me. They didn't have money, not a dime. But the Millers did."

Libby, stunned, leaned away from her. "What are you telling me?"

"I told you, your mom and I loved each other. Who do you think sat with her comforting her while she cried? Who do you think she could trust to listen? I never gossiped with the neighbors, and she knew that."

"What does this mean?"

"It's probably good you don't remember. It was an ugly time. There were lawsuits. Your parents had to sue the Millers, and they found a lawyer who'd do it on a contingency basis."

Libby swallowed hard, the past rising up in her throat like bile. She didn't want to go back to that time, to being that vulnerable teen sitting there in a lawyer's office, wearing a freshly ironed dress, hands clenched in her lap, too terrified to look at anyone.

Negligence. She remembered that word. She remembered some of the questions the lawyers asked her. Had she noticed the lock was broken? Had she known she should have told her parents where they were going? She didn't know what the right answers were. Whatever she said, they wrote it down.

But she remembered something else. Those terrible words: *wrongful death*. The lawyers kept repeating that phrase, over and over, and every time she heard it, she winced, as if she'd been struck. She had thought it meant that the death was wrong, which it was and that it was her fault because she hadn't been paying attention. But the more questions the lawyers asked her, the more she realized that it had another, deeper meaning. Wrongful death. The wrong child had died.

"You were so young!" Irma said. "Your mom told me the lawyers deposed you. She told me how upset you were to be asked all those questions, how all she wanted to do was take you out of that room and take you home."

"She never said that—" Libby said. "My parents never talked about that day ever."

"The case was settled out of court. The Millers' insurance policy paid out handsomely, and your parents, who could have used that money, didn't take a penny. Instead, they used that money for your education."

Libby felt a buzzing in her spine. "What?"

Irma reached over and took Libby's hand, and only then, when her fingers bumped up against Irma's, did Libby realize how hard she was shaking. "You understand me?" Irma said quietly. "Your mom sat here, right where you are, crying to me about how she could never tell you because she didn't want you feeling responsible. She didn't want you thinking about that day, and she wanted, more than anything, for you to be safe, to have options in your life. Your parents were broken after that accident. It was hard for them to show emotion or even love. For your parents, money was the only love they could give you anymore. So they sued the Millers and they took money from them."

Libby went cold with wonder. The Millers' money was in everything now, she realized: the apartment she owned, her profession. Her ability to have a life.

"Is this true?" Libby said.

"Why would I make this up?"

Irma poured her another cup of tea, but they didn't talk much after that, and eventually Libby got up to leave. She left Irma's promising to be in touch but knowing that she probably wouldn't. She thought about all those years after Richie died, how she used to leave him what she called ghost notes. *Richie, check this box with this pencil if you are here . . . Richie, are you mad at me? Check box yes or box no.* There was never any checkmark. Richie was gone. And her parents were gone now, too.

Her parents had taken the money for her. Here she had spent all this time thinking they valued her less than Richie, their golden boy, that she got less attention because she deserved less, but now she realized that that wasn't really true. If it was, then they never would have fought so hard to make sure she would be all right, to keep the legal dealings secret so that she'd never feel guilty. They had loved her and she had spent her whole life imagining they didn't and she had been wrong.

A DAY LATER, Libby sat sobbing in Dr. Sheep's office. She was embarrassed by her drippy nose, her red eyes. She kept pulling out tissues from the box in front of her until she emptied it. "Forgive me," she said, but Dr. Sheep actually seemed more interested in her than ever. He handed her more tissues.

"You think of yourself as a certain kind of person, but you aren't," Dr. Sheep said.

"What are you talking about?" Libby blew her nose, then snuffled.

"You think you have no value just in your own self, but you do. Adults are the ones who are supposed to love and protect you," Dr. Sheep said. "Your parents thought they were doing that, but they were not. They left you alone. And lucky for you, you were strong enough to survive that. By going back to Waltham, by realizing there was no faucet of love that can shut off, you can go forward."

"How? Tell me because I really have no idea. I have no idea what to do next in my life."

"You'll think about it. You'll figure it out. Just listen to yourself a little harder."

Libby cried a little more. She thanked Dr. Sheep and made another appointment. Listen harder, Dr. Sheep had said. She could do that. She could try.

24

THERE IT WAS, THE end of October, and Stella was watching the stars from the porch of the Woodstock house that she had loved. She couldn't help feeling that Silverwood loved her back.

She hadn't been here in so many years, even though she had always wanted to visit again. She hadn't expected to actually come here to this house, even after she had bought her ticket so hurriedly at Grand Central. It had seemed too impulsive, too crazy, too absolutely wrong to come here. Fueled with grief and anger, she just wanted to be as far away from New York City as she could be, but she had no business coming here. "Where to?" the clerk said, and Stella had purchased her ticket.

She knew that Simon's parents had long since stopped coming here, and Simon hated this place so much that he'd removed every trace of himself from it, and she had helped him do it. She just needed a place to regroup, to figure out what to do next. She had a feeling that it could all be okay if she could just stay here for a little while.

When she arrived, she had known where the key was hidden, right under the porch mat. EVERYBODY IS WELCOME, it said, and she figured that maybe that meant her, too.

• • •

HER FIRST FEW days there, she had worried. Every sound she heard made her jump. She knew that being there could be considered breaking and entering. The neighbors on both sides were far enough away that they wouldn't see her coming and going, but what if someone drove by and saw lights on and thought something was wrong? She had no idea if Simon's parents had arranged for a caretaker who might come by, who might call them and then force her out.

She told herself it could be okay. Hadn't Simon's parents liked her? Wouldn't they understand and maybe even forgive her? Anyway, she was just planning to stay temporarily. She rationalized that the house was safer with her in it, better than sitting empty, less likely to be broken into. She loved this house. She wouldn't let anything bad happen to it.

She knew Simon would probably be looking for her, but he'd never imagine she'd come here. He hated this house. "A burn-down," he'd called it. Or maybe he wasn't looking for her at all. Maybe he was relieved she'd left.

Maybe Libby was relieved, too. Stella felt her heart tighten into a fist. Somehow being betrayed by her best friend felt so much worse than being betrayed by Simon. Maybe because she had half expected it from him but never from Libby with whom she'd shared so many things. She'd trusted her so deeply. How could women do that to one another? Libby had been the one Stella had talked to about Simon before she got sick. Libby had been her favorite person in the hospital, the one she always wanted to work with. Well, she was on her own now.

She curled up tighter in the chair in the living room, her favorite now, and then her breath evened. She heard the house breathing around her, a kind of comfort she had almost forgotten, and then she slept.

EVERY DAY, SHE explored a bit more of the house, something she couldn't do when she had visited years ago, for fear of being a snooper. Now she ventured into all the rooms. But while she admired the wood floors and the high ceilings, she noticed spots in the floor that needed to be sanded, paint in the rooms that had dulled. Things she ached to fix but couldn't.

She made a trip into town to get a new phone; the new number she'd give only to Bette. No one knew who she was, but everyone was friendly. When she arrived back at Silverwood, she felt that the house was expecting her, delighted to see her again. "Hello to you, too," she said. She ran her hands over the walls as if she were petting a cat.

She began to go into town, taking one of the bikes from the garage. She put a watercolor pad in her basket, a set of paints, brushes, and a bottle of water. When she got to the village green, she set herself up, waiting to see what might happen. Sometimes no one came to watch her work, and she'd lose herself in her drawings and paintings. Then she'd look up, stunned, and realize the sky was growing dark, that she had been there for hours. But other times, just like in the city, people came around her to watch. They asked her to draw them. They pressed money into her hands.

In the evening, Stella hung out at the Bee diner, all chrome and black-and-white tile, with waitresses in black uniforms and red bow ties. She got to know them. One of them, Pat, who was actually the owner, had a curly head of hair and wore lipstick the same shade as her bow tie. Stella also liked Donna, a photographer who helped Pat out during the busiest hours. She was skinny with cropped boy hair dyed blue and a tiny gold ring in her nostril.

"Draw us," Donna said, so Stella did. At first, Stella didn't know if they liked the drawings; they showed things that they might want hidden, such as the fact that Donna pined for her boyfriend who didn't want to commit just yet. Donna and Pat both stared at the drawings for a while, and then Pat said, "Let's hang them up."

Customers loved the drawings. They wanted more hanging up, more to take home, and they were willing to pay for them. "You put up a sign in the diner," Pat told Stella. "Let them come to you so you don't have to sit in the park or the diner all day."

Gradually Stella began to have enough work to keep her busy all the time. She went to clients' homes, where they served her coffee and cookies. The local art store, Brush Up, gave her discounts. She began to tuck away her money in a drawer, watching in amazement as her income grew.

Stella felt herself morphing again, like there was this San Andreas fault line inside her, pulling her in two different directions, both of which felt dangerous. Some days, she woke up thinking Simon was beside her, and she hungrily reached for him only to find she was alone. Sometimes she saw a movie and thought how Libby would love it, too, and then she remembered what had happened between them. Some nights she had terrible dreams in which she was back in a coma and could hear Simon talking to her. She also heard Libby and her mom, but when she tried to speak, she no longer had a tongue.

Waking, soaked with sweat, she called her mother in Spain. She didn't want Bette to worry, so she told her she was staying upstate with a friend. She left out the part about Simon cheating, about Libby betraying her, instead telling her that Simon was working and she just needed to get away for a while.

"You can come stay with me, darling," Bette said, and Stella promised she'd think about it, though she didn't want to go to Spain, not right now anyway.

In November, Stella opened up a small savings account at the local bank, figuring she could always close it out when she had to leave. When she wrote in her address, she felt immediately guilty. She knew now that she didn't want to leave Silverwood, that this was her place, but she knew, too, that she'd soon have to find another place to stay. She combed the ads in the local paper, looked on the bulletin boards. She began looking at small one-bedrooms and places with studio space, but they were either too expensive or the light was bad.

One day, she was walking across town when she heard, "Hey, Stella!" and she turned and saw a woman waving at her, smiling. Stella wasn't sure who the person was, but she smiled and waved back, then continued on. She liked that the locals knew her. She was a part of the place.

She came home that night, and as soon as she saw the house, she felt as if it were saying hello. "Hi, you," she replied as she opened the door.

All that night, she heard the soft creaks and groans of the house as it released humidity from its beams and settled into the cooler, drier air. The stars were enormous. She sighed at them, deep with satisfaction. This felt like her life. This was her life.

25

SIMON WAS DRIVING. BUSINESS was picking up now that there was a chill in the air. For almost a month, he had gotten very little sleep, worrying. What if Stella came back and he was in too deep a sleep to hear her and she left again? The police had finally listed her as missing, but he felt their search was haphazard, so he spent a lot of time searching on his own. He scanned the streets while he was driving, and every time he saw a flash of blonde curls, he'd stop the car and get out and call her name.

Sometimes when he saw a redheaded woman, he'd stop the car, too.

Fuck you, Stella had written, and he couldn't help but think that she was right. Fuck him. It was his fault. All of it. He knew it. He should have done better, been better, loved both Stella and Libby better, but he hadn't known how, and now he did and it was too late, and both Libby and Stella were gone, and he would have to live with that.

He was covering all the bills, but he couldn't afford the apartment by himself for much longer, so he started looking for cheaper places, some of them laughably small. He scoured different neighborhoods, including Harlem, which was having a resurgence, and the suboptimal West 30s, which pretty much shut down at night. He put up a small laminated sign in the back of his car, offering free rides in exchange for news about apartments opening up.

"Better living through advertising," one woman commented, climbing into the car, but then she mentioned a small studio in her building on the Upper West Side, how it was really cheap, probably because the landlord was her father and he was amenable to renting it to anyone she suggested. She handed him a card. "Call me when you're ready," she said. "He's not even showing it yet."

The Upper West Side, he thought. More adult than Chelsea. More older people. He had heard kids in his Lyft calling it the Retirement Community and, once, the Nursing Home. All of them wanted to be in Brooklyn now, which he used to mock when he was their age. Well, everything was different now. He could at least look at it.

THE PHONE RANG in the middle of the night. Simon bolted awake and grabbed for it. Stella, he thought. Libby.

"Simon." His mother's voice was raw.

"Mom," Simon said. "Are you crying?" It startled him because his mother never cried. *Smile and people will always want to be near you. Frown and you're on your own.*

"Your father's had a stroke. Come. Please come."

SIMON TOOK THE first flight he could get to Florida and then a Lyft to the nursing facility where his mother said his father was being treated. His father! Indomitable, never sick a day in his life, not even a cold. ("Do you think a cold would dare attach itself to me?" his dad joked.)

The place where his parents had lived was a retirement community that they loved. But his mother said he was now in a nursing facility called King Gardens. Set back in the woods, with palm trees lining the walk, it looked more like a large friendly house than a facility. As soon as Simon entered, a nurse approached him and reached for his arm. "How can I help you?" she asked.

Her face was rich with sympathy when he said his father's name. "Come with me," she said, and she led him down a corridor until he saw his mother, seated by a door, her arms crossed, her shoulders slumped.

"Mom," he said, and she hugged him and he could feel how she had gotten smaller.

"He got up to pee," she whispered. "Like he always does at night. Like I always do. Sometimes several times. And then I heard a thunk. He fell. Oh my God, Simon, he had a stroke." She took Simon by his arm. "Come. Let's go see him."

HIS FATHER WAS lying in bed attached to an IV, his hands flailing, plucking at the covers. He kept trying to wrench off the blue hospital gown. But what shocked Simon the most was his dad's face. One side now drooped. He scowled and drooled, which made Simon wince. "Dad," Simon said.

His mother gently took his father's hands away from the gown. "He keeps trying to take his clothes off," his mother said. "Who knows why." She touched his father. "Darling, don't," she said. "Look who's here to see you."

Simon's father turned and blinked at Simon. For a moment, Simon wasn't sure his father knew who he was. "Simon," he said finally, waving his hand in the air.

"I came to see you," Simon said.

"Do you have your car here?" his father said. "Because there's traffic. Because you'd better go."

His mother met Simon's eyes. "Falls—strokes—they can cause a kind of dementia," she said quietly. "He doesn't know what he's saying."

"Who fell?" Simon's dad said. He squinted up at her. "Something's not right here. Something's just not right," he said. "Believe me, I know. Where are the doctors?"

"Everything is fine, darling," his mother said to him, then turned back to Simon. "All those years we've both been doing those stupid Sudoku puzzles to keep sharp. We swim. We take vitamins." Her voice trailed off. "It's age, I suppose."

"Is he going to be okay?"

"He has some dementia, the doctors say. But yes. For now, he's going to be okay."

"For now—"

"Who knows what's going to happen tomorrow?" she said.

"Could I have time with him alone?" Simon said.

"Don't upset him, darling," his mother said, which offended Simon a little, but then she left.

Alone with his dad, Simon felt helpless. The room seemed too big, the silence too large. He pulled a chair up so he was close to his father. He tried to take his dad's hand, and to his surprise, his father let him. Simon stared at the ropey blue veins, the creases in his father's nails, the way his father's hands looked like they'd been dipped into a freezer.

"Simon," his dad said. "Where'd you come from?" His father patted him on the hand. "Good boy."

His father looked so small in the bed that Simon felt tender toward him. His father had been so strong, so sure, in life.

"Listen, I have to tell you something," Simon said.

His father turned his body closer to Simon's. "Okay," he said. Simon thought of all the deathbed scenes he had seen in movies. His father wasn't dying, but he was old now and not very strong. Who knew what might happen with him? In the movies, people always got to have a finish, to say all the things that had been boiling up inside of them, the things that truly mattered. Simon wanted that, too.

"Tell me," his father said, nodding his head.

"I love you," Simon said.

As soon as Simon said that, he knew it was true, despite everything that had happened in their lives. Tears stung his eyes. He swallowed hard. He couldn't remember saying that to his father, not for a very long time. He couldn't remember his father ever saying that to him.

"Yes," his father said, nodding his head.

"I forgive you. Maybe there was something inside of you that made you act the way you did to me. Maybe you had to have outward signs of being important because you didn't feel it inside—"

"Okay." His father pinched the blanket between his fingers, studying it now with interest.

"I hope that you can forgive me, too," Simon said.

"Okay." His father pulled at his IV cord, trying to jerk it free, and then rested his hands again.

"I want to know you," Simon said. He felt himself choking on his words. "Tell me about you and me. What was I like as a little boy with you? What am I like now to you? Please. I need to know it from you."

His father looked sharply at him. "Where's your mom?" he said. And then: "Do you have a car? Traffic is terrible. You should go." His father stared at the window. "Go," he said. "Go now. Be a good boy."

When Simon stumbled out of the room, his mother was there, leaning against the wall. He walked over to her and rested his head against her shoulder, and then he cried.

SIMON'S FATHER STAYED at King Gardens for a week. He never became himself, but he regained enough strength that he could get around with a walker. He could watch TV and read a little, though most of his ability to comprehend was gone, and he kept forgetting what he had been watching. He couldn't be left alone. Simon and his mother found and hired a helper for him, a full-time nurse. They went back to their expensive retirement home, which Simon's mother equipped with all the necessary gadgets. A bathtub seat. Handles and railings everywhere.

Simon and his mom didn't talk about anything other than his dad, and that was fine because Simon couldn't burden her with his troubles about Stella, about his life. This was the moment he was in now and he would deal with it. He sat with his mother every day in her favorite cafe, drinking tea, eating too many pastries. That was what she wanted and needed.

"I actually feel that I love him more now," his mother said. "The stroke made him sweeter to me. He needs me now. And he won't be catbirding around anymore."

Simon looked at her, shocked. "What?"

"Your father had an eye for the ladies."

"You knew that?"

"Of course I knew, darling." She sipped at her tea.

"Why'd you stay, then? All these years?"

His mother looked at him, surprised. "Because *love* stays," she said. "It's easy to love someone when things are good, when you're having fun, going out with friends. But the tough times—that's the test. And believe it or not, your father and I passed it."

She took a bite of her torte. "Stop looking at me like that, please. This is the natural order of things. This is what happens when we're lucky enough to get old and decrepit."

"Don't say that," he said.

"You know it's written all over my face," she said. "See these lines here? And here?" She pointed to the crepe-paper skin around her neck, the fan of wrinkles crinkling her eyes. "You reach a point where you can't keep them hidden and all the expensive creams and potions won't stop more from coming."

"You're still beautiful," Simon said, and he meant it.

"Baloney," his mother said cheerfully. She polished off the torte and then looked at him. "Darling, now that things are settled pretty much, I have something I need to talk to you about," she said.

Simon felt a chill. He knew she had diabetes, but he thought it was managed. "Are you okay?" he said.

"Don't be silly. I'm fine," she said.

"Then what?"

"I should have listened to you before, but I didn't realize there was need. I want you to sell the Woodstock house. The upkeep is too much for me. The worry that someone might break in and then I'd have to deal with all of it. And I don't like even thinking of that house without your father in it. I'll transfer the title to you. I'll give you the deed and I'll front the money for the taxes and the upkeep until it's sold, so you won't have to. And once it's sold, take the money and do whatever you want with it."

"Dad loves that house. He'd never want to sell it—"

"He's forgotten that house already. If you said Silverwood, he'd say, 'What? Where?' All he remembers now is me."

"I can sell it?" Simon thought of how he had begged his parents last spring, how much that money would have mattered to him and Stella. Now having to ready it for sale felt like just another burden for him to deal with. But at least it would be money that might float him for a while.

"And something else," his mother said. "We have accounts for you, stocks. I used to think waiting was the best thing to do." She sighed. "But now I think you should cash them all in."

"What?" he said. "Really?"

And then she said something he had never heard her say before. "It's only money."

"Okay," he said finally. Then he took his mother's hands in his. "I love you," he said.

"I know."

SIMON STAYED FOR another week. His mother was right. His father was sweeter to her, his eyes glazing over with love, but his father never looked at Simon that way. He still squinted at Simon as if he couldn't quite place him.

One morning, Simon was riffling through the paper when he saw

With or Without You 243

Kevin's photo. The band, still the opening act for Rick Mason, was playing in Miami, one night only, which Simon knew was meant to fire up excitement. (One night only! Better move fast!) The band name was in a bigger font than Simon could ever remember seeing it. He could probably get backstage to see Kevin and Rob and meet the new bass player who had taken his place. He could talk to Rick, mention that he was still writing songs, and maybe Rick would be interested. Maybe Rick would even remember him. Maybe, if he could get to them before the show or during intermission, Kevin would even let Simon play with them for old times' sake.

Memories flooded back of how it had been in the old days, with Kevin and him onstage playing to each other even more than to the audience. The delight they had felt. The glow of the music. A kind of enchantment. Simon didn't know what it would feel like to play with the band again—would it be like that horrible night when he had gone to Le Poison Rouge, that club where everything, even the air, felt too loud? It was the kind of place that used to be a home to him, and now he didn't belong there at all. He was a guest, a visitor.

He looked over at his parents sitting in the living room, his father stroking his mother's hair. He couldn't leave them to go hear Kevin. He didn't want to. Well, at least he could say hello by phone. He called the venue and left his number. Kevin could always call him back.

They were eating dinner that night when Simon's cell rang. "Excuse me," he said, getting up from the table to take the call in the other room. "Is that for me?" he heard his father say.

"Simon."

He recognized the gravel in the voice. "Kevin," he said. "I didn't think you'd call me back."

"I guess I'm getting soft in my old age."

Simon listened to Kevin talking about the band, about their grueling schedule, about the songs they were doing now. Simon felt the words rolling over him. He studied the kitchen, the special railings they had installed for his father. The locks on the burners for safety.

"They love us so much that it's insane," Kevin said, and Simon looked into the other room where his father was reaching for his mom's face, cupping it in his hands. That was love.

"So where the hell are you?" Kevin said. "You want a ticket to our show? I can get you front row."

"Ah, I can't," Simon said. He waited for Kevin to ask him why he couldn't come to the show, to ask him what he was doing now. "Just wanted to hear your voice." He thought about Stella, how she didn't want to be a nurse anymore, and he hadn't believed her because she had loved nursing so much. But then she had gone on and found something else she loved.

Maybe Simon could do that, too. Maybe everything changes, and that was the way it was supposed to be.

"So, yo, keep in touch," Kevin said. "Ruby says hello."

"Sure," Simon said, and he hung up. He stood in the kitchen for a moment and then went back into the dining room. His parents smiled up at him and he smiled back.

In the morning, his parents needed almond milk (his father wasn't supposed to have dairy), so Simon went out to get groceries. It was quiet, and he got the milk, some whole-grain bread, and even tofu in case his mother felt like being adventurous.

He was walking back when he passed a music store, Tune Me Up. In the window were all sorts of guitars, different colors and shapes, and one that was actually a mirror. He felt a pull in his gut, the way he always did when he thought of his love of music. He couldn't help himself. He went inside.

A bald guy was reading a book behind the desk, and the only other customers were a father and his skinny kid with an unfortunate-looking whiffle haircut. They were trying out guitars, and it was clear neither one of them knew how to even hold one properly. Simon walked slowly up and down the rows, seeing which guitar called to him. They all did.

When he came back around to the front, the father and son were sitting on a bench and the kid was holding a guitar, but handling it all wrong. Simon tilted his head at them. "Can I just show you?" he offered.

"Please," the dad said. "You'd be doing us a big favor." He patted the kid's shoulder. "This is Bobby. I'm Jake."

So Simon sat down and repositioned the guitar for Bobby, who stared up at him like this was the greatest, most exciting thing ever. Simon showed him how to strum, how to do an E minor chord, which was an easy start, and he had Bobby strum it for him, over and over, until it was right. The kid couldn't stop grinning.

Simon helped them choose the right guitar, made sure Bobby liked the way it fit in his hands. Jake pumped his hand. "Thank you!" he said.

"Thank you!" Bobby echoed.

Simon used to say to everyone, "Go forth and be a rock star." He didn't say it now, because he knew that wasn't the point. Not anymore. "Find out if this place gives lessons," he advised, and Bobby lit up again, and then the guy at the counter looked up from his book with interest. "We do," he said.

"Can I, Daddy?"

"Certainly you can," Jake said. "And then maybe you can teach me, too. We can have our own band."

"Okay, but I get to name it," the boy said.

Simon walked out. For the first time in days, he felt good. Maybe he had changed Bobby's life, just through the simple business of passing on his joy in music.

That had been fun. Maybe he could get a job at a college, a job with benefits and vacations. He had a degree, maybe not a PhD, but he had been in a well-known band for many years, and that sort of recognition might make him a desirable hire. And he could still play and write songs.

He stopped at a bench and looked up the number for Cancun

Records on his phone. What could this hurt? But when Simon got someone on the line, she had no idea who he was and told him they weren't looking for new songs or artists right now. When he mentioned Michael Foley, the woman on the other end of the line snorted. "He's not here anymore."

To his surprise, Simon wasn't decimated by the news. So what, he thought. There were lots of doors in life, lots of moments. Simon could still love music and make his life around it.

He felt lighter. The air sparkled around him.

TWO DAYS LATER, when Simon left his parents, his father was holding on to his mother. A little old man, Simon thought. But a happy one. He kissed his dad, knowing that this might be the last time he would see him. Or maybe there would be other times, and because he knew what to expect now, they would be sweeter times, more loving because he wasn't asking his dad for anything. Not anymore.

"Bye!" his father said. "Have a good time! Bye!" His father opened and closed his hands in a cupping wave. "Good boy!" he called to Simon. "Good boy!"

SIMON WAS ON the plane home, watching a terrible movie about a horse trainer, a film he'd selected only because it had closed captioning, so his already-compromised hearing wouldn't have to additionally strain over the rumblings of the plane. He had to ask the flight attendant three times what the juice choices were, and he finally just nodded and stayed silent when she handed him tomato juice, which he didn't want. He wasn't even fifty yet. Did people get hearing aids in their fifties? Maybe they did if they had been around screamingly loud music for most of their lives. Maybe they did if they were just getting older.

Life, Simon thought, was short and mysterious. Or maybe it was long and mysterious. He didn't know. His father could go on living like this for years, or he could have another stroke tomorrow and die.

Maybe something came after you died, but maybe it didn't. Scientists had found pixels in space, but did that mean everyone was part of a giant computer simulation? Some scientists thought consciousness continued, that you might know that you were dead. But then what? What happened next?

Maybe all anyone had was just this one moment. And then the next moment. Or maybe every moment happened all at once at the same time. Maybe all you could do was try to make the most of it. He'd go home. He'd think about what he wanted to do with the rest of his time. He'd get in the car and drive up to Woodstock and all that had haunted him there, and he'd hire a real estate agent to sell the house because he didn't need those ghosts anymore and they didn't need him. He'd think about doing something different. Going someplace different, too. Start anew. Maybe Savannah, which he had fallen in love with when the band had played there. All that moss and friendliness, the dense air like a comforting blanket. Or maybe he'd stay in New York City, call the number that woman had given him about the studio on the Upper West Side. Maybe he could do a lot of things. But first he needed to sell the house.

BACK IN THE city, Simon retrieved his car from where he'd last parked it. He drove north, getting to Woodstock by nightfall. It was a sleepy town, something that always drove him crazy, and tourist season was over. He didn't want to run into anyone he might know, like old friends of his parents. He was just too tired for that. He had never loved the house enough to carry a key with him, even though his parents kept telling him that he should. He knew where the spare was hidden. He'd be fine.

He looked at the house from the car, suddenly hit with an array of feelings, the stench of failure, the memory of the humiliation he had always felt here.

But now he could do something about it.

He bounded up the porch stairs, feeling for the key under the mat, but it was gone. Fuck this house, he thought. Had his parents taken the key when they moved, knowing he was unlikely to ever return?

Then he heard music, faint as a sigh. He saw a light in the back of the house. He grabbed for his phone to call 9-1-1. He heard approaching footsteps from inside, and suddenly the door swung open, and then, in front of him, like a mirage, was Stella.

AT FIRST, SIMON couldn't speak.

He couldn't tell from looking at her how she felt—happy or angry or sad—but he wasn't sure how he felt either.

"What are you doing here?" he said.

"Let's go inside."

He followed her into the house, into the living room. He looked around the house. From the corner of his eye, he could see an easel. "Why did you come here? This isn't your house."

"I had nowhere else to go."

"You could have asked me before you came here."

"Why should I ask you? You cheated." She rubbed her eyes, and when she took away her hand, he saw that her eyes were clear. "I lost you and then I lost Libby. I needed a place where I didn't feel lost." She looked toward the window. "If Libby's in the car, you had better tell her to stay there."

"You didn't lose me," he said. "And I'm not with Libby anymore."

Stella tilted her head. "Really," she said. "No, don't tell me the details. I don't want to know." She wrapped her arms around herself like a corset.

He nodded and then looked around the house again. "Is this your 'fuck you' to me, coming here to my house? It's fucking haunted, Stella. It still is. I hate this house. Even coming here right now—"

"It's haunted for *you*," she said. "Not for *me*. You set me up not to like it, Simon, but I did. I loved this house. I felt safe here." She dug her hands in her pockets. "Does everything have to be about you?" she said. "Maybe I shouldn't have come here, but I had to. I didn't think you'd ever show up here again, not for me, and certainly not for the house. But fine, I'll pack and get out." She sat down on the couch, defeated. "Why *did* you come here? Did you know I'd be here? Do you think you have to take care of me still? You don't. I don't want you to. Not anymore."

Simon sat down opposite her, slumping in one of the chairs.

"Why are you here?" she repeated.

"My dad had a stroke."

Stella's hand flew to her mouth. "Oh, Simon, I'm so sorry."

"He's alive, but he lost some mobility. His mouth droops and his mind is fuzzy."

"I'm so sorry. I liked him."

"He liked you. More than he liked me, I think. My folks are never coming back here. They told me to sell it, so here I am. I just want to get it over with." He was so tired. If he shut his eyes, he'd fall into sleep. He didn't know what to do now.

He thought of all the things he had wanted to say to her. "I'm sorry," he said.

"Yeah. You and Libby," she said. "I didn't have to draw it to see it. Because I saw both of you in the park."

He thought of her note to him, the pain and fury in the letters, the blame. She must have sent something to Libby, too. He felt awash with sorrow. "We never wanted to hurt you."

"You were my *person*. She was my best friend. What you both did is hard to forgive."

"I can't believe you came here," he said.

"Yes, you can, if you think about it. It wasn't all bad when we came up here," Stella said. "Remember we went to an outdoor concert and there were all those stars and even fireworks?"

"Puny ones. Not like New York City," he said, but he felt himself softening because he did remember it, the two of them curled together on a blanket, sharing a picnic. They had come home and kissed through the halls of the house while his parents slept. And when they slept, he had held her so close he could feel her heart bumping up against his.

"You being here back then," Simon said, swallowing hard. "It made it easier. You made everything easier."

She studied him, the same intense way she did with people she was about to draw, but then she averted her eyes. "So did you," she said quietly. "Every time you came into a room where I was, I felt electric sparks. I always had so much I wanted to say to you."

"Fuck," he said. "What happened to us, Stell? Where did it all go so wrong?"

She was still for a moment, deciding something.

"It's not like before," she said. "We're not like before. We can talk about it."

"I loved you," Simon blurted. The words hung in the air.

"I know," Stella said. "I loved you, too. But things weren't perfect even before I was hospitalized."

"I know that, too. But we could have fixed it, couldn't we?"

"Maybe. If I hadn't changed so much," she said. "And you were so different to me, too, you know."

"There're still pieces of you that are the same."

"You, too."

Simon remembered how deeply he had believed that his life would change with the LA gig. And his life had changed, but not in the way he had wanted, not in any way he could have ever imagined. He hadn't left her. He had stayed. He had believed that she'd come back to him the way she had been, but then she hadn't. "That morning, I thought we were going to talk," he said.

He got up from the chair and moved close to her on the couch. Her head rested against his shoulder, and he could smell the ginger in her shampoo. "I remember talking," she said. "I remember thinking we were going to grow old together, one of those couples who hold hands, not just to keep from falling, but because they love each other so much that they can't be without contact."

"I thought that, too."

She leaned away and looked at him. "Why Libby? Why her?"

"You weren't there, Stell. You were in the hospital. And then when you came home, you were so different, and your being different made me different."

"But why Libby?"

"She was the one who understood what I was going through."

"That wasn't my fault," Stella said. "What else?"

"Because she pushed me to be a better person."

"I wanted you to be a better person, too," Stella said. "I didn't push because you didn't like it." She bit down on her lip. "Everyone has to love you, don't they," she said bitterly.

"I don't want everyone to love me anymore," Simon said.

Stella straightened. "Good, because they don't," she snapped. "You were a big baby some of the time, and I had to do so much of everything. And now, thanks to Libby, you're a grown man, only I don't get those benefits, those things I kept hoping you might be."

She was now clearly angry, and it scared him. She looked so different, and an old feeling shot through him. Need and love and desire. He used to be so excited to see her, like she was some miracle that had come into his life. Imagine that, someone so smart and beautiful loving someone like him. He had missed her when she wasn't with him, a real physical pain. "All my friends are going to be strangers," he said, borrowing the title of a Larry McMurtry book he had loved, about a young novelist who goes on tour hoping for fame but finds instead that he's lonelier than he ever was. Simon thought that could have been written about him.

"You got famous, not me," he said. "And that's okay."

Color flashed in Stella's face. "I didn't intend that. I just want to do my art. It makes me feel good."

"You're handling it better than I ever did. Than I ever would."

"I don't want fame, Simon. I never did. That was you."

"You never drew a picture of me," he said.

"That's right," she said quietly.

Stella got up, pacing, then strode into the kitchen. He followed her, watching her bang the teakettle onto the burner and light the flame.

"Stella," he began.

She turned and gave him a shove. "Who do you think you are?" she said. "Who did you think you were?"

"I loved you," he said.

"Loved," she scoffed. "I don't even know how I feel about you now." She shoved him again, and then he reached for her arm to stop her, and for a moment their stares locked. He felt her heat. She touched her fingers to his lips, and then he wasn't thinking at all. He was so tired, so confused. His father was dying and would never know him again. Simon's music career was dead. Libby had betrayed him and he had shouted at her, and now she was gone, too. Everything he had ever cared about or wanted was gone.

"We loved each other," Stella said. "For a really long time. Not everybody gets to have something like that. Not their whole lives. Not even for the time we had. We were lucky." Her voice dropped with sorrow.

Simon didn't know what he felt about anything anymore. He didn't understand Stella now. She spoke to him in a low voice, and it soothed him as much as it confused him. She walked over to the table and sat on it, studying him. He felt something roaring toward him like a tsunami.

"Stell—" He thought of how beautiful she had been the first day he met her at the hospital, the two of them standing in front of the babies. In his mind, he saw her at the lip of the stage, dancing. He saw her making him soup when he had the flu, staying up late talking to him, making him laugh. There was that night when neither one of them could sleep, and it was Stella's idea to do a Manhattan Midnight Marathon—they hit three different all-night diners and went from late dinner to breakfast. He had been so happy. So madly in love. He came closer to her and touched her mouth. He felt all their memories swarming around them, all the love and need and anger and more, and then he was kissing her, pulling off their clothes, lowering her back onto the tabletop, and then both of them were diving back down into their past.

IT WAS MORNING and Simon was in the guest room, dreaming. He was in Times Square, in a huge crowd of tourists and people dressed in yellow Minion costumes, and then he saw her, a flash of red hair. Libby, he thought, and his whole body grew buoyant. Libby. Everything in him ached for her. Libby. There was so much he wanted to tell her, so much he had to say. She wasn't angry with him. She was smiling. He pushed through the crowd, reaching for her. "I thought you were gone!" he yelled, but the tourists' shouts grew louder, drowning him out. The people in Minion costumes jostled toward him. "Five dollars! Take a picture with us!" they screamed. He couldn't see her anymore. "Libby!" he shouted, and the Minions descended upon him.

He woke up with a start. There was someone's hair on his shoulder, but it wasn't smooth like Libby's. There wasn't the familiar coconut scent, but instead something strange and different. His eyes opened and he saw Stella, still asleep. He bolted up, confused, his head pounding. And then he remembered. The kitchen table. Their moving to the bedroom. The whole night.

Everything felt totally wrong. What had he done? What had he been thinking? Did he really believe that you could shuffle the past and the present like a deck of cards, and everything would be okay again?

Simon got up and pulled on his pants.

He was tying his sneakers when Stella awakened. She immediately looked sad and uncomfortable. She turned away from him and pulled on a long T-shirt.

"I'll make breakfast," she said awkwardly as she left the room.

He remembered they used to make pancakes. They'd try to make them into different shapes: elephants, dogs. Mickey Mouse was the easiest. They'd sit at the breakfast table and tell each other stories about what the unrecognizable pancakes were supposed to be.

He joined her in the kitchen, and there was the pancake mix, like an omen. He leaned against the sunny counter watching her mix it up. "Here goes nothing," she said, and again he thought how beautiful she was.

But the pancakes burned at the edges, and she frowned. Then, trying to flip them, they broke in the pan. "Oh fuck, I didn't mean for that to happen," she said. "Oh no."

He quickly shut off the heat. "They'll still be delicious," Simon said.

They sat at the table. "You first," he said, and she looked at her pancakes. "This one looks like . . ." she said, and then she put her fork down. "I don't know," she said finally. "I don't know what it looks like."

"My turn, then," he said, and he studied one of his pancakes. He used to be able to make her laugh with his descriptions, but she wasn't even smiling. All he saw were burnt pancakes and he looked at her, helpless. He took a bite. The pancakes were doughy inside. He put down his fork, pancake still attached.

"Well," she said, and he heard the resignation in her voice. She leaned toward him and rested her hand on his face as if waiting for something. The heat he had felt last night was gone, and she must have felt it, too, because she took her hand away.

"I'm so sorry," he said.

"I'm so sorry, too," she said.

She started dumping out the pancakes, cleaning the dishes. He could hear her voice above the rush of water. "I'll pack up today," she said. "And you don't have to worry about the mess. I'll hire a cleaning service." The sound of the water got louder. "I like it here, this town. I want to stay. I'm sure I can find another place, get a bike so I can get around." She turned off the faucet. "I can keep watch over the house for you, if you want. Stop by and make sure it's okay."

"I'll contact the caretaker and let him know that he doesn't have to come anymore. Odd that he hasn't been here already," Simon said with a frown. But then he brightened. "Oh, and there are bikes in the garage. Take whichever one you want."

"Really?"

"It's not enough," he said, waving his hand. He watched her leaning against the sink. The first time he had met her, before he had even seen her face, he felt a charge in the air, a vibration. His memory was nudging him, reminding him: *I know you. I've been searching for you all this time, and where have you been? And what does it matter because we're both here now.* Everything had fallen into place after that. He looked at her now, seeing her solemn, open face, the blaze of her eyes, but the vibration was gone and all he kept thinking was how much he wanted forgiveness for its leaving. He knew then that he wanted her to be happy, even if it had to be without him.

"I want you to have the house," he said suddenly.

She scoffed. "Right," she said.

"No, I'm serious."

"Then you're crazy, because you know I can't do that," she said. "I have some money now, but not what this house would go for."

"You'll have it soon enough," he said. "You're getting more and more clients. You've got this crazy kind of talent. And yes, I can do this. My parents signed the deed over to me. It's completely paid off. The house is willed to me. I'm paying the taxes on it. And I can let anyone I want rent it or live in it or throw a party in it—"

"Simon—"

"You have to let me do this for you."

"Simon, what about you? You need the money. You could live on it and keep writing songs."

"Maybe I want to do something for you."

"Simon—"

"My mother's fronting me the money for this place until it's sold. She loves you. I can't imagine she won't be thrilled that you're here. We can do a lease purchase—you can rent this house and then the rent will go toward the purchase price. When you're ready, you can get a mortgage from the bank. Then the bank will pay me and I'll have the money and you—you can *own* this house, Stella. And in the meantime, you live here."

He felt lighter, as if he might float away.

She stared at him. "Are you sure?" she whispered.

"I won't change my mind," he said, nodding.

"I won't do it unless you promise me it's okay."

"Okay," Simon said. "We'll get a lawyer to draw up the papers. So you'll feel safe."

She shook her head, clearing it. "Yes, draw up the papers, but what's so weird is that I feel that I don't even need them." She looked at him, amazed. "I trust you," she said. "Isn't that strange? I totally trust you now. I didn't before. Not really. But I do now."

"Too bad that's not who we were then," Simon said.

"At least we are now," she said.

SIMON LEFT SOON after that. There was no point staying. He could see how excited Stella was, how her gaze kept flying about the house. She was in the future now, seeing how the rooms would change, how she'd make them hers. No one loved this house the way Stella would, and that was what counted, because houses, like people, craved connection.

He drove onto the highway and started to cry, but in amazement, not sadness. For once, he had done something right. But then he realized that he had given himself something, too. He had cried when he left his father because he knew now that no matter how much he had wanted to, there was no way left to make things right between them, that whoever the person his father had been was gone and he'd have to make peace with that. And maybe he had.

He and Stella would still be in contact. Every month, he'd see her scribble when she sent him a rent check. He'd get to hear her voice if she needed to know something about the house. But then she'd have a mortgage with the bank, and he'd be out of the picture. It wouldn't be the same. He knew that, and already it felt like a great loss to him.

Simon drove, the radio blasting a station that was all rhythm and blues, all voices calling for salvation. I hear you, he thought.

He thought about Michael Foley again, the record label guy Libby had contacted. What if Libby *had* told him right away that Foley was interested and Simon hadn't had to find out for himself, when it was too late? Simon had been so desperate.

I would have told myself Stella was being cared for, that nothing was changing, that I could leave then. I would have left Stella in her coma.

He would have gone to see this guy, charmed him into taking him on. He would have done whatever was necessary to get out some music, to get his name out there, put together a band, be on tour, away from the problems, away from Stella. He'd be back in the lime-light. That's where his head was at the time.

Now he felt dark with shame. Libby had been right. She had known him, even back then, had known that he was insecure and self-centered, that he was used to having Stella take care of everything adult in his life. Libby hadn't let him get away with anything, even when it meant denying him the thing he had most wanted. He had needed to be there for Stella, even when Stella became someone other than the Stella he knew.

Stella had loved him, had given him a reason to grow up, but he had refused to see it. Libby had wanted him to be a better person, but he had shouted at her when he should have been shouting at him-self. He needed to tell Libby that. He needed to see her and ask her forgiveness.

26

LIBBY WAS AT WORK, striding the halls. She spent both the morning and afternoon with her patients, but today, instead of just asking about symptoms, focusing on the facts and numbers, she really talked to them. She took their hands. She asked about their families, their pets. She listened. "I know you're busy, Doctor," one patient said to her, but Libby waved her hand and pulled up a chair and sat down. "Tell me how you feel today," Libby said. She listened to the patient talk about his symptoms, his life in general, even about his dog, and though nothing this patient said gave her any more medical information, he looked like he felt better when she left.

Libby had a new batch of nurses, and she saw how they hung back, how frightened of her many of them were. She looked for the one who seemed most intimidated, a slight blonde who stood at the edge of the group, her eyes to the floor. Libby singled her out and put her arm around her. "We're all partners here," she told her.

It wasn't just the staff for whom she showed new care and concern. When one patient, a postpartum woman who had contracted a rare blood disease, told Libby she didn't want to take the chemo Libby had prescribed, that in fact she had called the head of hematology at the Mayo Clinic, who had told her not to take it, Libby didn't cut her short, the way she would have in the past. Instead, she sat by the patient's bed and said, "Good. It's good that you're thinking about the care for your body."

Libby usually allotted no more than ten minutes with a patient, but ever since she came back to work, the clock was forgotten. When a patient told Libby she didn't want to go on blood thinners, not yet, Libby paused to reconsider. "Maybe we can compromise on this," Libby said. She had other patients to attend to, but she sat, holding this patient's hand, watching the beginning of a Lifetime movie with her.

"You're a good doctor," the woman said, and Libby felt herself blush. For the first time, she allowed herself to believe it might be true.

She still saw Dr. Sheep, once every two weeks. "You're doing good," he told her.

"Ah, the Dr. Sheep seal of approval," she said, laughing. But she felt it, that goodness, coursing through her. She had changed and he had helped her do it.

She was friendlier to the other doctors, to the nurses, too, and one night Hank Fray, one of the cardiologists, actually asked her to come to dinner with a bunch of them, something that had never happened in the past.

Libby hesitated. She had planned to go home and take a bath, have some wine, and read a book. But this was a chance to change the perception others had of her and she didn't want to blow it.

"I'd love it," she said, so she and four others went to a pizza joint on Second Avenue and ordered three mini pizzas and wine. She learned new things about her colleagues, like the fact that Ed Harper, a cardiologist, was adopting a baby girl from China. She discovered that Emma Ronson, an obstetrician, used to raise and show St. Bernards. One by one, their pagers went off, and eventually Libby was the last one at the table. She thought she could still hear all the laughter. Why hadn't she ever done this before? Smiling to herself, she thought how happy this was going to make Dr. Sheep, how he'd cheer

her on so she'd do this again. Taking her time, she polished off the
last slice and paid the whole bill. We have to do this again, someone
had said. Yes, she thought. We do.

Libby also began to notice men in the hospital. She used to think
she was attracted to only one type, the bad boys, the ones who would
smash her heart into smithereens, but now she found herself attracted
to men who were gentler, less brash, more attentive to the needs of
those around them.

Gradually, Libby began to realize that Richie was growing smaller
and smaller inside of her, that she was no longer living her life for
him, constantly wondering what her brother would have done in the
many cases she worked on. His life had been his and no one else's,
and it had ended. He was a kid when he died. She'd always carry him
with her, but it was time now to let him go, time to live her life for
herself.

That evening she went home and looked through her family's
photo albums. There they were, as kids, the two of them laughing,
goofy, dressed as cowboys, Richie with an empty holster slung around
his hips because their parents didn't like guns. There they were with
their parents, posed for holiday photos. Libby could still remember
that awful red velvet dress, how starchy it felt. She had even saved
their report cards. *Libby needs to try harder and not socialize so
much. Richie is a joy in the class.*

What had happened had not been her fault. She knew that now.
Just like she knew she would always love her brother and miss him.
She took the photo albums and put them away. They would be there
when she needed them.

AFTER WORK THE next day, Libby strolled out of the hospital,
thinking she might actually take herself to a movie or call a friend.
And suddenly, there was Simon, standing on the sidewalk.

His face was drawn. He had lost weight, too much now, and he
looked older. The last time she had seen him, he was shouting at her,

and she had deserved his anger. She had been sure she'd never see him again.

She slowly walked over to him. The ground shifted under her feet.

"You were right," he said.

"About what?"

"I know you can't forgive me, the way I yelled at you and blamed you. But you were right about not telling me that the record label reached out. I know that now. You were just getting to know me. How would you know what I might do?"

"It wasn't my business to stop you from getting something you wanted so much," Libby said, but Simon shook his head.

"I was an asshole and I needed to be an adult, to be here with Stella. You did what you thought was right. And I'm so sorry."

He looked like he was pleading with her, and she thought about how much she had loved him. How maybe she still loved him.

"I wasn't all about being right," she said. "I wanted you to stay for me as well as for Stella. I was a terrible friend to her and I didn't mean to be."

"I've had a lot of time to think," Simon said. "I'm going to try to get a job teaching music. Do something for others instead of just myself. I can still write songs if I want. Maybe they'll sell, maybe they won't. That's not important anymore. And I'm moving to a studio on the Upper West Side."

"What?" Libby said. He was confusing her, throwing a lot of information at her at once, but the more he talked, the more she felt pulled toward him, and that made her afraid, because she knew that he was someone who was no longer hers.

"I don't care anymore about being onstage or about having fame," he said. "I don't want a big life anymore. A small, happy life sounds wonderful. Just being with someone you care about. Just creating something." He touched her hand, and she felt a flare of heat. "I don't care about anything," he said. "Except you."

Libby started. "Simon," she said, "what are you saying?"

"Do you think—you and me—maybe we can at least be friends again? See what happens?"

She grew quiet for a moment. She wanted to touch his face, to sit down with him and tell him everything that had happened to her since they had split apart, and she wanted to hear what had happened to him, learn about who he was now.

She put one hand against the side of his face, and then slowly she smiled. "Who knows?" she said.

27

ONE NIGHT AFTER SIMON left, Stella decided to go out to a bar called Oh Yes. She sat on a stool and listened to the band, Charlie's Rooster, perform acoustic versions of golden oldies hits. The music felt comforting, like a blanket, warming her.

"Beer," she said to the bartender, a young blonde woman with a tiny blue star tattooed on her shoulder. Well, well, Stella thought, here I am on my own. This feels good.

She was on her third beer, feeling a little woozy, when the bartender nudged her and pointed to a table on the side. "That guy's scoping you out," she said, and Stella looked over.

He was younger than she was, with shaggy hair and eyes that were big and deep and blue. He smiled at her, and Stella looked away. "He's a baby," Stella said.

"That's Nick Headgrow," the bartender said. "A budding novelist." She looked at Stella encouragingly. "He's cute for a cis white guy."

"He's way too young."

"He never goes out with anyone less than ten years older than he is," the bartender said. "Really. His last girlfriend was fifty and she was the one who ended it, not him, and he was heartbroken about it."

"Do you mean he's forty?" Stella said. "That's not so awful."

The bartender laughed. "He's twenty-six."

She looked up again and there was the guy in question, rising from his chair, coming over to them, waving. "May I join you?" he said.

There was an empty stool next to Stella and he settled in, leaning into her as if they were the only ones in the bar.

"So, you're a writer," she said. He told her he was, that he had won prizes for his short stories, that he had completed a novel and had sent it out, and surprise, surprise, he had actually gotten an agent—a big agent on his first try.

"What's the novel about?" Stella asked.

He looked embarrassed and then smiled. "It's about this lost guy, a writer, and his love for this older woman."

Stella nodded. Of course. He was writing what he knew, the old dictum. "Sounds great," she lied.

Stella had known writers before. She'd treated them in the hospital, talked with them at their bedsides, and she knew how hard it was, that you had to sometimes try for forty agents before you got one, and even then, there were even more rejections from publishers and sometimes you never knew why. But this guy was so sure of how things were going to turn out that she found herself turning toward him, like he was a light and she had been living in darkness. He was burning with a desire for fame. He told her that when he went into bookstores he immediately headed for the new fiction shelf. He took down one book and then another, considering the cover and studying the blurbs. "Some writers get a million dollars right out of the gate," he told Stella. "And I know one guy who was a failure until his ninth book, and now he's famous."

I can be a success, too—Stella knew that was the message emanating from him in waves, just the way it had for Simon. "I like your shirt," Stella said, nodding at the black silk he was wearing.

"I don't know if black is good on TV," he said, and then he tapped her hand. "What about you?" he said, and she told him the same story she had told her friends, that she was an artist, that she was going to stay in Woodstock, that she had a house she loved and it loved her back. That part always made people laugh, but they didn't realize how important it was, how it could honestly be true.

Suddenly it was late and people were going home. The bartender winked at Stella, which confused her. Nick took Stella's hand. "I could talk to you forever," he said. "Can we go to your place?"

She thought about it. Her head was buzzing from the beer and the music. A flash came into her mind—Simon kissing her hip—and she shook her head to dislodge the image.

"No?" he said.

Stella put on her coat, wound her scarf around her neck, and slung her bag over it. She still could remember Simon's kiss on her hip, vibrating, but less so, she thought. Less and less. She knew it was hotter not to jump into things, to wait, but he was a baby, twenty-six, and how long would this last anyway?

You need to get laid, she told herself. That would erase Simon altogether. "Let's go," she said.

NICK WAS A sloppy lover, and Stella found herself directing him to do what she really wanted, how she wanted him to kiss her, how she wanted to be on top. She gave a small cry and then he did as well, and they both fell back on the bed, grinning at each other. He tapped her nose. "I like you," he said.

"You don't really know me," she said.

"Yet."

She didn't know why, but she began to tell him her story. He listened without interrupting, once sucking in his breath, and when she was finished, he shook his head. "That's some tale," he said. He drew one finger along her arm. "Could I write about it?"

"I don't know. It's sort of my story, you know, and even I don't know how it's going to end."

He kissed her shoulder. "It's such a great story."

"Well, it's a story, anyway."

"So, would you live in Manhattan again?"

"No. I love it here. Why?"

"What if it was with me?"

"Earth to you. We just met. So, no."

"But picture it. I'd be writing and you could be painting. We could get a loft maybe."

"You know how much lofts cost in Manhattan?" Stella said. "We're talking millions."

"An apartment, then. Space for your studio, space for my office. I'm getting a book deal. My agent is sure of it. I'll be able to afford it."

She laughed and ruffled his hair. "Go to sleep, beautiful dreamer," she said. "We're way too new for such plans."

They saw each other every day all that week. They took long walks, and sometimes they just talked for hours. Stella found it odd to be in a relationship again, one that seemed to be everything for Nick but just an interlude for her, like getting her feet in the broil of surf before plunging into the waves. He slept over most nights, and he began talking more and more about his plans for them. How they'd live together in New York. How maybe she could design his book cover. She told herself she was just exercising her heart, rebuilding its strength, the same way you would do with any muscle.

She was aware of their age difference all the time. In the morning light, her face was creased from sleep, but his was smooth. Sometimes he lifted up the covers and studied her body, and she felt embarrassed, wanting to cover her belly, the sag of her breasts. "So beautiful," he said.

THEY HAD BEEN together only a little over a week, and though he kept promising to give her his novel to read, he never did, and when she pressed, he said, "Well, what if you hate it?"

One day, he burst into her house, a package under his arm. "I got the call! I sold my novel!" he cried, and she looked up at him, stunned.

"That was so fast—"

He rattled off this story that his agent had sent it out to an editor he respected, and the editor had sat up all night reading. "And that was that," he said.

He leaned against her, as if he had to keep it secret. "Two hundred thousand," he whispered, and Stella started. "What?" she said, because it seemed like so much money, especially for a guy whose sneakers had holes in them, who never managed to pay for his share of dinner when they went out. And also, it disturbed her a little the way he mentioned money like that, as if he were showing her his dirty socks. Then he put the package in her hands. "That's it. That's my novel. I want you to read it now that I know it's good." She studied it. "I wrapped it up like a present for you," he said, watching her, eager as a puppy. "But you can't show it to anyone. You have to promise that when you're finished, you'll destroy it. I don't want anyone reading it until it's in galleys."

She felt the weight of the pages in her hands. "Sure," she said.

His whole face was filled with wonder and he jittered on his legs, pacing back and forth. "I added some stuff to it. It's even better now. I'm going to be a Young Writer to Watch!" he said. He took her hands. "So, you'll come with me to New York, right?"

"You know I can't do that," she said.

"I love you. I have money. We can live it up."

"Shhh," she said. "Now you're being silly." He looked so young to her now. "It hasn't been enough time."

"What's time? There's no time. Every quantum physicist knows that. I'm going to keep asking you to be with me. Even from New York. I'll show you photos of my apartment. I'll keep writing you. I'll make you admit you love me back."

She kissed him. "I've loved being with you," she said, but inside she knew that she probably wouldn't miss him.

HE LEFT TWO days later, still asking her to pack a bag and come with him. "Not so fast," she said, laughing.

To her surprise, she did miss him. She expected to see him when she woke up or when she remembered something she wanted to tell him, books she had loved that he might like, people they both knew. However, the impulse grew weaker every day.

But he had left part of him for her, what he thought was the most important part, his novel, and Stella sat and read a little every night. It was about a writer like him and an older woman like her, and it wasn't bad, though it did feel glossily polished and overtly commercial. But when she got to the end, there was a chapter tacked on that was printed on a different kind of paper. The new material, she thought. She read, and there it was: the protagonist took a pill and drank wine, then went into a coma and emerged from it with a different personality.

Stella put the book down, unsettled. He had taken her story even though she had asked him not to, and he'd used it in his novel, giving it a new ending. And she didn't know how she felt about it.

She could call him and ask him why he'd done it. But what good would that do now? All she wanted was to move on.

She remembered he had told her to destroy his novel when she was done with it, so she stood over the wastebasket and began tearing the pages, turning them into confetti.

NICK DIDN'T WRITE her. He didn't email or text, and she felt relief growing inside of her. Good. That meant he was okay, and so was she. One day a month later, the December air so chilly it had a bite in it, she was at the local market when she picked up *New York* magazine. New York City felt like a foreign country to her now, but still she leafed through the pages to her favorite parts, scanning the interviews, the hot list, the photos of parties, and then, there he was.

He was wearing a black T-shirt and blue jeans and had a beautiful older woman slung around his shoulders like a cashmere sweater. They had their heads thrown back in laughter and people were crowded all around him.

She felt happy for him. He had been sweet and loving and really good for her at a time when she had needed someone like him. He knew what he wanted, and that was a good thing, too. He was okay. And so was she.

MOST DAYS, STELLA still biked into town. She knew more people now, some of whom became friends. She hung out with a woman named Amy, an actress-slash-waitress, and with Pat, the owner of the diner, who was a painter, too. She didn't tell them much about herself, never mentioning the coma, the whole Simon-and-Libby thing. She didn't tell them that she sometimes felt like she was still straddling two different worlds. She knew if she told them all that, she'd get pity or maybe odd looks. She didn't want her story to be the center of their conversation.

One day after lunch with Amy, she went to see a client who wanted to be painted with her pet Bengal cat. The woman's name was Edith ("Like Edith Wharton," Edith said to her, which made Stella like her even more.) Edith's home was choked with plants and cat toys, and Stella started when she saw the cat, which looked like a tiny leopard.

"That's Rivington," Edith said. "Very smart animal."

Stella covered the floor with a tarp and then set up her portable easel and paints. "Come here, darling," Edith said, and to Stella's surprise, Rivington leaped to her shoulder, kneading with his paws, delirious with pleasure.

Stella studied the two of them. Edith was in her midsixties, dressed in a teal velvet gown and sparkly earrings. Her hair was white and she wore it in a long braid down her back.

Stella was just sketching in the outlines when she suddenly felt queasy. At first she thought it was because of what she was seeing. Edith had told her that she just wanted a portrait for fun, but Stella felt something more, something deeper. Edith was mourning her lover, a younger woman who had left her and taken up with a man. Oh, terrible, Stella thought. How sad and cruel.

Stella's stomach bucked. "Excuse me," Stella said, and dashed into the bathroom, vomiting. She threw water on her face and then dried it.

It must have been the clam chowder she had for lunch, she decided.

But the queasiness continued for days, and then a week, and she thought she'd picked up a stomach virus that was going around. She began to lose her taste for meat—she couldn't even look at it anymore. The only things she wanted now were greens and carrots. But then when her period didn't come, and *still* didn't come, she went to the drugstore to get a pregnancy kit. She felt too old for pregnancy to be a possibility, unsettled. Time couldn't mix her up like this, not when her old life was falling away, peeling like an old skin, making room for something new. She knew she once had wanted a baby, but that had been what felt like lifetimes ago.

Stella bought two different kits, one with a picture depicting a happy woman laughing, triumphant. The other was plainer; it had clinical type and seemed more official. She biked back to Silverwood, into a headwind and the thickening clouds that promised snow. "Here goes nothing," she said to the house once she was inside. She went to the top floor bathroom, the same one in which she and Simon had once gloriously had sex while his parents slept. She peed on both sticks at the same time, then she held them out in front of her, watching the blue line on one turn into two and the line on the other one shout out the verdict: pregnant.

She shut her eyes for a moment. Then she went to her computer to find a doctor.

A WEEK LATER, right before Christmas, Stella lay on the doctor's table, the paper gown crinkling about her. She didn't know this doctor but had pulled her name out of Zocdoc, choosing her because of all the reviews. *Dr. Rice doesn't pry. She doesn't give unwanted advice.* One person wrote, *If you want or need to talk about sex, Dr.*

Rice is the one to go to! It made Stella laugh, which she thought was a good sign. And then she saw this: *Dr. Rice is totally nonjudgmental. She never made me feel I had decided wrong. I still go to her.*

That decided it for Stella. She was already second-guessing and judging herself. She didn't need anyone else doing it for her.

Dr. Rice was younger than Stella, with thick black hair that was cut into a shag. She wore rose-colored lipstick and a Moody Blues T-shirt under her lab coat. "So," she said, looking at Stella's file, "you think you're pregnant?"

"I took two tests, but they're junky; you can't count on them."

"Actually, you can," said Dr. Rice. "They're pretty reliable now."

Stella swallowed. "I'm on my own. I don't know who the father is."

Dr. Rice didn't flinch or narrow her eyes.

"It's not like there are more than two," Stella said.

Dr. Rice nodded. "Well, we've got you here, so let's take a look."

The gel on her belly made Stella shiver. She didn't want to look at the sonogram screen, so she shut her eyes. It had to be a false reading.

Dr. Rice put the wand down and looked over at Stella. For a moment, Stella felt that she wasn't pregnant, and relief flooded through her because she wouldn't have to decide, and from now on, every time she slept with anyone, she'd insist they wear a condom. Maybe two, one on top of the other. She'd go back on the pill, too, and soon, with age, she wouldn't have to worry about pregnancy at all.

She sat up, swinging her legs over the table, reaching for her clothes. The nausea was probably just nerves. The bloat was because she wasn't exercising enough. Well, she'd treat herself to a long walk now.

"You're pregnant," Dr. Rice said.

Stella blinked hard. The air clamped down around her.

"Get dressed. Then come to my office and we'll talk."

• • •

DR. RICE'S OFFICE was filled with framed photographs of exotic places. There were giraffes loping across the plains in Africa. A mountain range was dusted with snow. *Beautiful. Wish I were there.* She sat across from Dr. Rice, her fingers threaded together.

"So, you have a choice to make," said Dr. Rice. "Do you want to have this baby?"

"I don't know," Stella whispered. *Dr. Rice doesn't judge,* the reviews had said. Stella felt something unwinding inside of her. She tried to breathe. Her hands cupped her stomach.

"I don't know what to do," Stella said.

"Okay, let's talk about it," said Dr. Rice. "What do you think you want?"

The air felt like a live wire crackling against her.

"Were you considering ending this pregnancy?" Dr. Rice prompted. "Or do you want to have the baby?"

Stella felt her heart hammering. Was she considering having it? Nothing was going the way it should, the way she had carefully planned out her life. She wasn't with Simon. She wasn't a nurse, a job she had loved. She was an artist now. And she was pregnant and she had no idea if Simon or Nick was the father. Women didn't have to have babies to be fulfilled. They didn't have to be married. They didn't have to be mothers at all.

Dr. Rice touched her hand, making Stella start. "Go home, think about it," she said. "You have some time."

AT HOME, STELLA paced. The next morning, she showered and threw on clothes, then sat in front of her easel. She had an appointment later that day to meet with a woman who was getting married and wanted to give her husband her portrait because she hoped he would hang it in his office. Stella picked up her brush to make the outlines, and then suddenly the face changed shape, the chin began to take on a subtle point.

Like her own chin.

Stella had never successfully painted or drawn her own portrait. She'd never really tried. Maybe because she had been so afraid of what she might see. Maybe she had somehow known.

Daubing her brush in paint, she made another stroke, her heart thumping.

She worked without thinking about the brushstrokes, the way she always did when she painted, her hands flying.

When she was done, she was panting. She stepped back to look at the picture, to get out of herself and see what was really there.

The woman in the portrait wasn't sad or confused the way that Stella had thought she might be. Usually Stella's subjects were looking right at her, telling her everything she needed to know, but this one was looking off, into the future, into a world Stella couldn't see.

She put the brushes down and wiped her hands. She wrapped her arms about herself. All that painting was telling her was that she herself had to make the decision, not her art. But how was she supposed to do that?

She wanted someone to talk to, someone who knew her, who loved her. She reached for her phone and called her mother.

Bette was quiet the whole time Stella was talking, telling her the whole story of how she was living at the Woodstock house now, how Simon had practically given it to her, and how she had gotten pregnant. "I don't know what to do," Stella said. "I don't even know who the father is." And then, to her surprise, as if that made everything so much worse, she started to cry. "What if I decide the wrong thing?" She swallowed hard. "What if I make a mistake?"

She could hear her mother breathing. "Honey," Bette said finally. "Maybe there's no wrong thing. What's important is making a decision."

"What do you mean there's no wrong thing? Yes, there is. You knew it was right to love Daddy from the second you met him. You told me."

Bette sighed. "I did, and sometimes that happens. I don't regret a second of it, but honey, there's a cost for everything. You know why I left for Spain?"

"You left me," Stella said bitterly.

"No, that's wrong," Bette said. "You were a grown-up. I knew you were going to be all right. And I knew all I had to do was hop a plane or pick up a phone and I could be there with you." Her voice warmed. "I left because everything reminded me of your father. I picked a country your father and I had never visited together, and once I was here, I felt different. I was different. Grief changes you, honey. It turns you into a whole other person. And so, really, does living your life."

Stella thought of her mom in her T-shirts, her gray hair that looked as if she cut it herself. "You never found anyone else . . ." Stella said.

"Because I didn't want to. Because I kept looking for your dad in everyone else, and when I finally realized he wasn't there, I stopped looking."

"I don't want to have a baby and have it be a mistake." Stella felt her throat closing. "The way I was."

"What?"

"I heard you talking to Dad once. You said you wondered if I were a mistake."

"You heard wrong, then."

"You said it would have been easier without me. You said—"

"Baby," Bette interrupted. "Easier doesn't mean better. I loved you. We loved you. I couldn't imagine my life without you. I want you to know that there are no right answers. I want you to know that we're all on loan to one another, and whatever we get, we should be grateful for, because any minute we can lose another person. We should try to remember every experience. Maybe you'll have this baby, and if you do, I'll come and help if you want me to. I'll shower that child with love, and you, too. Maybe you won't need my help, but I'll still come and see you. I'll still shower you with love."

Stella kept crying. She bowed her head. She had no idea what the future might hold. She had no clarity about anything.

And then suddenly she knew what to do.

TWO DAYS LATER, she sat in front of Dr. Rice. "I'm going to have the baby," she said.

"Well, then," she said. "There are plans we need to make."

After talking with Dr. Rice, Stella walked out into the waiting room. She would have an amnio. She had a prescription for prenatal vitamins. "I'll monitor you carefully," the doctor said.

Everyone in the waiting room was so much younger than she was. Some of the women had their moms with them, or partners holding their hands. But so what, she thought. Who knew how good those relationships were or what anyone's situation might be?

Stella walked outside onto the street, dizzy for a moment. She rested one hand against the building. She wanted her mom, ached for her. Growing up, whenever she got sick, her mother would stay home from work and bring her rock candy and ginger ale. Stella would call her again, have her support. Maybe Bette could come and be with her when the baby was born. They'd be three generations.

Dr. Rice had given her lots of information and Stella did everything she was instructed to do. She took the vitamins. She ate better.

IN APRIL, WHEN it was time to have the amnio, her friend Pat from the Bee diner went with her to the doctor's office and held her hand. Stella squeezed her friend's fingers tightly, twisting her head so she could see the images flickering on the screen.

Dr. Rice smiled warmly at her. "You want to know the sex," she asked, "or you want to be surprised?"

Stella knew now that everything was a surprise, so she held Pat's hands tighter and said, "Tell me."

Dr. Rice grinned. "Boy," she said. "A fantastic little boy."

• • •

STELLA GREW, CHANGING shape with the child growing inside of her. She began wearing dresses and drawstring pants, and while she painted, she tried out names. Tom. Jack. Names that were simple and strong. A boy! She was going to have a boy in September, a new life to add to her new life! Her son might look like her or he might have Simon's strong nose or Nick's bright green eyes. He might just look like himself, and no one else.

A DNA test was the only way to tell who the father was. She could call Simon, and though she didn't know what his reaction would be, she knew that he would agree to take the test, and as long as he did, then she wouldn't have to ask Nick. She'd know who the father was just by process of elimination.

But then what? Did she really want to know? Did she need to do this? She had Bette and Pat and loving friends who all wanted to help her, who she knew would love her son as much as they loved her.

And did it matter who the father was? What good would it do to tell Nick or Simon, to foist a responsibility on them that they didn't really want? Did she want either of them in her life again? Nick was already in Manhattan, forging literary friendships. His story was still being written, and while Stella had enjoyed and liked him well enough, she was happy to watch him from a distance, and he clearly had already forgotten her. She and Simon no longer fit, but she had seen how he had grown up. He had just about given her this house, and if he didn't want to be involved as a father, that was fine by her, but shouldn't she at least offer him the opportunity?

Maybe it wasn't really for her or Nick or Simon to decide at all. All that mattered was what her son would want, when he was old enough to want it, and then she'd tell him the truth. The important thing was that he knew that she loved him unconditionally and she'd never leave him. But she'd tell him things about both men, good things, like how she had really loved Simon and how, in a way, he had saved her life, and his own, too. She'd tell her son that Nick was a writer, that he was younger than she was, and talented. If her son wanted to meet either man, Stella would do her best to find them, making sure that both Nick and Simon knew she wasn't asking for anything they weren't prepared to give, that it was for her son, that he wanted connection, or answers, or just to meet them this once. They would all have to figure out how it all might work.

She was forty-three now, and when this baby was born, maybe, in a way, she'd be newly born, too. She'd become someone and something different. Yes, she'd have this child, and she would love him, and already she was looking forward to the journey they'd have together, both of them growing and changing with time. *Listen*, she would whisper to him. *Nothing and no one stays still or stays the same. Everything and everyone changes. We all have multitudes inside of us, each of them young with hope.*

Listen, she'd repeat. *Any moment, something amazing can happen.*

Acknowledgments

I CANNOT BELIEVE MY good luck in having the incredible, warm, hilarious, and smart Gail Hochman as my agent, first editor, friend, and style icon. (And undying thanks to the whole agency, Brandt & Hochman.)

As always, to the best, most revolutionary publisher on the planet, Algonquin Books. Huge thanks to the gods and goddesses: Elisabeth Scharlatt, Craig Popelars, Brunson Hoole, Michael McKenzie, Carol Schneider, Katie Ford, Betsy Gleick, Randall Lotowycz, Lauren Moseley, Ina Stern, Debra Linn, and everyone else there. And huge thanks to Jude Grant, who fixed up my wonky timeline and just about everything else.

I am dazzled to say that my editor is Chuck Adams. He unlocked this book at the synopsis level and never stopped burnishing it, all the while being amazingly kind and patient and downright brilliant. Chuck, thank you.

I couldn't know half as much as I do about neurology and the brain without the help of the fascinating Joseph Clark, to whom I am eternally grateful. Thanks, too, to Kate Maloy, Anne Murphy, Ruthie Marlenee, Lea Kenworthy, Therese Murphy, Nicole Bokat, and Rebecca and Tim Dowling.

I received music help from (of course) expert Jeff Tamarkin. But great thanks are also owed to Mick Martin and to two of my musical heroes—Marshall Crenshaw (yeah!) and Dennis Diken of the Smithereens (yeah!).

Thanks, too, to Michelle Petrazzoulo Bokette, Bruce Cohen, and Tova Mirvis.

For a legal issue that had me in a conundrum, I need to thank the amazing attorney William D. Kickham, who not only spoke to me for hours but had me in stitches, and to Gregg Rosen. Greg Brodsky helped me with great Woodstock details, and David Rahall and Alex George talked me through real estate conundrums.

For reads and rereads and hand holding through draft after draft after draft, huge loving thanks to Hillary Strong, who shares DNA and so much more with me and who took time out of her own incredible debut to help me with my novel. Thanks, too, for her amazing family, Cotie and Owen and Charlotte and Fletcher. We love you. I am totally indebted to fellow novelist and screenwriting partner, Gina Sorell, and also to novelist and partner-in-crime, Leora Skolkin-Smith. I shower huge love and thanks for the smart suggestions and for making me laugh when I needed it most to Andrea Robinson, Mary Morris, Jessica Keener, Susan Henderson, Jeff Lyons, Christina Baker Kline, Victoria Zackheim, Dawn Tripp, Jonathan Evison, B. A. Shapiro, Jeff Tamarkin, and the amazing Jean Kwok.

And for help and support, my beloved tribe of writers and friends: Thrity Umrigar, Linda Corcoran, Ron Block, Thelma Adams, Lidia Yuknavitch, Jennifer Pastiloff, Stephanie Gangi, Sheila Weller, Tish Cohen, Mary Laura Philpott, Gina Frangello, Clea Simon, Barb Goren Gale, Jo Fisher, Amy Ferris, Suzanne Finnamore Luckenbach, Meg Waite Clayton, Jenna Blum, Robin Kall Homonoff, Sarah McCoy, Kathy L. Murphy and the fabulous Pulpwood Queens, Anne Lamott, Jane Praeger, Michael Taeckens, Yvonne Prinz, Peter Salzano, Ilvi Dulack and Michael Medeiros, Carolyn Zeytoonian,

Patricia Klinger-Horn, Suzanne Simonetti, Tracey Becker, Christopher Castellani, Rochelle Jewel Shapiro, and to everyone on Facebook, Twitter, and Instagram for making me feel better every day.

This book is in memory of my mom, Helen Leavitt, whom I miss every single day. I'm always writing about you, Mom.

Thanks also to Stanford and UCLA Extension Writers Programs and to every single indie bookstore on the planet.

And of course, to the two beloved men in my life: my son, Max, and my husband, Jeff, who both amaze me, make me laugh, and inspire me. I am so lucky and I love you guys forever.

With or Without You

Where Did the Old You Go?
An Essay by Caroline Leavitt

Questions for Discussion

Where Did the Old You Go?

An Essay by Caroline Leavitt

I FELL IN LOVE with my husband, Jeff, on our second date, after he told me about his favorite unchangeably-in-love couple, Jake and Abby. They'd been dazzlingly happy together for seventeen years. They didn't crumple under life's blows, but seemed to grow stronger, starting an antiques business when their editorial work dried up, raising kids and dogs and cats and vegetables, weathering illness and celebrating joys. When I finally met them, just on the cusp of Jeff and me marrying, I fell in love with them, too, making their relationship a model for ours.

Until Jake became someone else, in a way that can only be called cataclysmic, something that eventually haunted me into writing *With or Without You.*

Jake, who had always been amiable and low key, potbellied with a mop of hair, came home one day with twenty-pound weights. Abby thought nothing of it, until the weights multiplied and Jake began working out downstairs until three in the morning. His body changed dramatically: tightly muscled, he shaved his head, oiled his skin, and traded khaki for spandex. But his personality changed, too. He stopped reading anything except for bodybuilding magazines. He didn't want to go to movies anymore or even take walks. Worse, his unconditional love acquired conditions. Why didn't Abby work out? Why wasn't she more social? Why did she always have to hang on him? "Talk to me," she begged, "tell me what's happened," but instead, his silence grew stonier. When his greatest achievement became training for, entering, and winning a contest pulling an eighteen-wheeler by a rope held in his teeth, she no longer recognized him, and neither did anyone else. Abruptly, he left his marriage, his job, our friendship, and moved away without explanation. And none of us ever knew why.

Desperate to understand, I began to think more and more about the ways and whys that people in long relationships change. I popped "personality change" into Google and there, like a shock, was something personal: coma, a state I'd been in for over three weeks after the birth of my son. But while I hadn't really changed, my research showed me how others coming out of coma often did, and in mind-blowing ways. A shy eighty-one-year-old man became a predatory sex maniac. People woke with brilliant new skills, taking to the stage as a concert pianist when before they couldn't play "Chopsticks," speaking perfect Mandarin, or showcasing an obsessive talent for painting. What would that be like, I wondered. How would you know who you really were? I knew I had to write about this kind of transformation and what it might do to a couple.

That's when I saw the first scene of *With or Without You*: Stella and Simon, in their forties, arguing in their NYC apartment during a blizzard. Stella, a very practical nurse, wants to buy their apartment and have a child before it's too late. Simon yearns for his one last chance at recapturing his rock-and-roll fame. There's drinking and drugs and passing out. But in the morning, Simon wakes, and Stella is in a coma, and Simon's last chance seems to have vanished. Plus, when Stella wakes, she has a new, unrestrained personality—and a new talent that eventually puts her in the spotlight that eludes Simon. The more I wrote, the more involved I became in their lives, which seemed so different from my own.

Until they weren't. Until I had an identity change as startling as Stella's.

SINCE I WAS five years old, part of my identity has been that I'm sick with asthma. My world was ERs, hospitals, inhalers, steroids, and nebulizers. Bullied in school for being sickly, I grew shy, shamed. Cold weather could decimate my lungs, but so could humid air, so I was a victim of weather. My clothes always had to have pockets for my arsenal of meds. I never talked about my asthma, but I did write about it in *Pictures of You*, which helped me come to terms with being a person with a chronic illness.

But then five years ago, I developed terrible new breathing problems no doctor seemed able to diagnose, let alone treat. I bounced from specialist to specialist for over a year, near hysterical with panic, until I was able to get an appointment at a renowned respiratory clinic. The doctor spent over two hours taking my history and giving me tests, and then announced, "You absolutely don't have asthma. You *never* had asthma. It's your meds and your anxiety that are giving you breathing issues. And you need to stop them immediately."

I sat there, stunned, furious, and terrified. How had so many doctors been so wrong? What was it going to feel like being healthy? Going off my meds made me feel untethered, even more so when I discovered I didn't need them. I started meditating and seeing a cognitive therapist to feel better. But who *was* I if I wasn't sick, if I never had been? I gave that disconnected feeling, that exploration of self, to both Simon and Stella.

The more I wrote, the more I found I was writing myself into the story. Hey, it always happens. Like Simon, I had my own issues with identifying myself as a success, which could define or destroy you. I had had sudden fame in my twenties with my first novel, *Meeting Rozzy Halfway*, catapulting me into a limelight I loved. I was finally somebody, a star! But like Simon, my glow didn't last. I bounced from publisher to publisher and none of my books did well. No one knew who I was anymore—including me. My ninth novel was rejected on contract as "not special enough" and I knew I could no longer call myself an author. But then, unexpectedly, I became a success again with Algonquin—a two-time *New York Times* bestseller!—but what did that mean? Success didn't feel like the this-is-why-I-matter identity of my twenties anymore, but something very different. Success was now simply a river I traveled on, with twists, dams, broken places, and sometimes gorgeous islands to rest upon. It was a thing, but it wasn't *me*.

Writing *With or Without You* made me think about personality change with a new kind of wonder. Does transformation ever stop? Can we control it? Every seven years or so, our bodies replace our cells. Could it be the same with who we are? I realize that the only thing any of us—including my characters—can know is that everything you thought you knew about yourself or others can derail. But unexpected transformation can also revive, burnishing new possibilities you never expected, and that new person you might become can actually turn out to be your truest self of all.

Questions for Discussion

1. Caroline Leavitt's novel is really about how no one and nothing stays the same, and that these changes can happen in a heartbeat. Even if Stella had not fallen into coma, she would have changed. Even if Simon had not had to give up his gig, things would have changed. Since changes in relationships are almost inevitable, how do you think the dynamics between Stella and Simon would have altered even if she had not ended up in coma and emerged as a different person? Do you think the relationship would have endured? Why or why not?

2. Leavitt, who was once in a coma, did a great deal of research on personality change of people after coma. She learned that, like her, many coma survivors do not suffer brain damage or a regular personality change, but in some cases, brains really do rewire and people come out of coma with incredible new talents. Some survivors can speak fluent languages they never knew before; some can paint or are violinist virtuosos. Others, like Stella, come out of coma with not only an altered personality but also with a remarkable new talent and an ability to draw on heretofore unknown inner strength. How does knowing this science change your own views about the human brain and how much of it we don't really understand? How does this scientific knowledge affect what you think of as your own limitations?

3. The idea of home plays a big part in *With or Without You*. Simon hates his parents' Woodstock summer home because it was the scene

of his humiliation and failure as a kid trying to be a musician, but to his dismay, Stella loves it. Do you think that place really matters, that a home can really have energy and personality, or do you think a house is just a house and what we make of it?

4. Leavitt has always said she likes novels that have "never-ending stories"—where the novel ends but you still have questions about what is going to happen to the characters. Those unfinished endings involve Stella, Simon, and Libby. What do you personally imagine might happen to each of them? What do you hope will happen?

5. There are two sections of the novel in which we hear from Stella while she is in coma. Obviously, Leavitt is drawing on personal experience and attempting to give the reader a sense of what that experience was like. Do you find these trips into the mind of a coma victim to be realistic? Do you feel that they give the novel—and Stella as a character—greater depth? Why or why not?

6. For Simon, success as a musician and recognition of his ability seems to be a major driving force, while Stella seems to have no interests beyond her work, the possibility of having a child, and stability in her relationship. Why do you think the relationship has lasted as long as it has? Is it a case of "opposites attract," or do you think it was doomed? Why?

7. For Leavitt, the past is often the prologue, containing wounds that have to be healed for people to become whole. Libby blames herself for someone's death; Simon struggles under his father's disapproval; Stella feels her parents loved each other more than they ever loved her. How do you think these "wounds" influence their actions, both with each other as well as in the directions their lives have taken?

8. A great deal of *With or Without You* is about what we are willing to do for the ones we love, and the ones who love us—and what the cost might be. Would there ever be a limit for you, when giving becomes too much?

9. Leavitt ends the book with these sentences: *Listen. Any moment something amazing can happen.* Some readers might find this strange, considering the catastrophes that occur in the book. What do you think Leavitt is really trying to say about life in the light of tragedy?

10. How do you feel about the decisions Stella made at the end of the story? Do you think she used the young writer, or was it a matter of their using each other? Likewise, did she use Simon? How does the answer you feel strongest about affect how you feel about Stella as a character?

JEFF TAMARKIN

CAROLINE LEAVITT is the award-winning author of twelve novels, including the *New York Times* bestsellers *Pictures of You* and *Is This Tomorrow*. Her essays and stories have been included in *New York* magazine, *Psychology Today*, *More*, *Parenting*, *Redbook*, and *Salon*. In addition, she is a book critic for *People* and the *San Francisco Chronicle*, and she teaches writing online at Stanford and UCLA.